PENGUIN BOOKS

THE BUTTERFLY PLAGUE

Timothy Findley was born in Toronto and now lives in the country nearby. His novel, *The Wars*, was a winner of the Governor General's Award and established him as one of Canada's leading writers. He is also the author of *Famous Last Words*, a best-selling novel of gripping international intrigue, as well as *Not Wanted on the Voyage*, *The Butterfly Plague* and *The Telling of Lies*, which won an Edgar award. His two story collections, *Dinner Along the Amazon* and *Stones*, were published to immediate critical acclaim, *Stones* winning the Trillium Book Award. His most recent work is the novel, *The Piano Man's Daughter*. Findley was made an Officer of the Order of Canada in 1986.

TiMOTHY FiNDLEY

THE BUTTERFLY PLAGUE

Penguin Books

PENGUIN BOOKS
Published by the Penguin Group
Penguin Books Canada Ltd, 10 Alcorn Avenue, Toronto,
Ontario, Canada M4V 3B2
Penguin Books Ltd, 27 Wrights Lane, W8 5TZ, England
Penguin Books USA Inc., 375 Hudson Street, New York,
New York 10014, U.S.A.
Penguin Books Australia Ltd, Ringwood, Victoria, Australia
Penguin Books (NZ) Ltd, 182-190 Wairau Road, Auckland 10,
New Zealand

Penguin Books Ltd, Registered Offices:
Harmondsworth, Middlesex, England

First published in 1969 By The Viking Press, Inc., New York
Simultaneously published in Canada in 1969 by The Macmillan
Company of Canada Limited
First published by Penguin Books Canada Limited, 1986

Published in this edition, 1996

1 3 5 7 9 10 8 6 4 2

Manufactured in Canada

Canadian Cataloguing in Publication Data

Findley, Timothy, 1930-
The butterfly plague

Rev.
ISBN 0-14-024120-5 (trade format)

1. Title

PS8511.I38B8 1990 C813'.54 C90-013058-X
PR9199.3.F55B8 1990

ACKNOWLEDGEMENTS

Poem from *O The Chimneys* by Nelly Sachs reprinted by permission of Farrar, Straus and Giroux, Inc. Copyright© 1967 by Farrar, Straus & Giroux Inc. Also from *Selected Poems* by Nelly Sachs, translated by Ruth and Matthew Mead, reprinted by permission of Jonathan Cape Ltd.

Lyrics from "The Way You Look Tonight," used by permission of T.B. Harms Company. Copyright© 1936 by T.B. Harms Company. Copyright renewed.

The chapter "Chronicle of the Nightmare" appeared in *Esquire*.

For: Sheila Keddy Arnold
Janet Baldwin
Grace Bechtold
Beverley Roberts

THE BUTTERFLY PLAGUE

Ear of mankind
overgrown with nettles
would you hear?
If the voice of the prophets blew
on flutes made of murdered children's bones —
and exhaled airs burnt with
martyrs' cries —
if they built a bridge of old men's dying
groans —

Ear of mankind
occupied with small sounds
would you hear?

—NELLY SACHS,
poem published in *O the Chimneys*

Preface

This book may well be unique: that is to say, as books go, its experience of getting written may well be unique. Consider when it was begun. 1968. It then ran through a couple of drafts — maybe three, all told — and it was published in 1969. I wrote a good deal faster then. I was younger (I guess) — less experienced (definitely) — and less afraid of what I put on the page (absolutely).

So now we come to draft four: seventeen years later, if you start counting from the moment the pencil first hit the page — sixteen years, if you start counting from the moment the book had covers. That is a long time between drafts and, because it was such a long time between drafts, I had to think very seriously whether I really wanted this final draft at all. Some of my friends said: "Findley — you're a fool. A book is a book — and what is done is done. Leave it alone and go on to something else." Others of my friends said: "Here is a golden opportunity: one that will never come again. All those dreadful mistakes you made the first time around can now be rectified!" (You will note that the first group of friends did not employ exclamation points. You will also note they had the good grace not to use phrases such as "all those dreadful mistakes you made.") Lastly, there was that other — perhaps inevitable — group of friends, whose opinion of the whole affair was: *frankly, my dear, I don't give a damn.*

As for my own opinion, I tend to think that if you're going to leave a book on the shelf, you had better do all you can to leave it there in the best rendition of which you are capable. In a nutshell, that is why I have undertaken this new edition. The first edition simply wasn't good enough. And, I must add, it isn't every publisher who will afford a writer the chance and the privilege of trying again.

The subject of whether or not to re-write a book after such a long time is not exactly a moot point. In fact, it is anything but a moot point because, if there is any doubt about whether or not you will do your best — or at least attempt to do your best — then you haven't any right to call yourself a craftsman. Not to make a thing "right," when you can, is to renege on what you're about: it is to turn your back on what you do — and furthermore, to say *to hell with it* as you walk away.

Some things are done by instinct. This is how we know an actor is an actor — that a dancer is a dancer — and a violinist a violinist. From the very moment these people step onto a stage, or take their place at the barre, or pick up a violin, their instincts are right. It simply cannot be denied. Years and years ago (at the age of twelve), I had the exhilarating — not to say awesome — experience of walking onto a stage and realizing I had found, for the first time, where I could live: where I could function: where something profoundly different than anything else that had ever happened to me before could happen. And not only that, I could *make it happen*. I hadn't any fear. I wasn't alarmed when the curtain went up — and, when it came down, I only wanted it to rise again. Lord, what a wonderful feeling that was!

And then it all came crashing down around my ears. This didn't happen right away. That first experience had been at school and "the crash" didn't come until I was out in the real world walking on a real stage playing a real part in a real play. It was my first professional job — in stock — and, as with all stock companies, we were playing a new play every week. The "crash" occurred about half-way through the season when, one night, I was right in the middle of a scene and, all at once, I was completely overcome with stage-fright. My voice died. I couldn't move. I didn't know who or where or what I was supposed to be. I didn't know which play it was — and the costumes didn't help, because the costumes in stock are always the same. One week you wear your blue suit — the next week, your grey suit. And the sets never change: you are always standing in someone's living room. All the other actors on the stage were strangers — some in blue suits, some in grey. And every woman (except the maid) was in evening dress. Every gesture — all the drinks being passed on trays — all the teacups rattling in their saucers — every word being said was utterly meaningless. I was hopelessly, totally lost.

The point of this story is simple — and it does have to do with writing — and, specifically, it has to do with the writing of this book and with why, after sixteen — seventeen years, I have finally come to write its final draft.

All the "natural" talent in the world wasn't going to save me in my dilemma on that stage. The only thing that would save me would be craft, technique. And I had none. But from that moment on, I made it my business to learn my business because I realized that without the craft to carry me past panic and without the technique to help me repeat each performance as if it were the first, then I was not an actor. Certainly, I was no *pro*.

Imagine, now, the neophyte writer who sat down to make *The Butterfly Plague*. He had ten thousand ideas and a million theories and he kind of wrote like that, too, in tens of thousands and millions. Every paragraph was twice as long as it needed to be. The characters, not unlike the butterflies, arrived on the pages in droves. The events were about as large as events could get: there were murders, flaming forests, movie making, the Olympic Games and — not to be outdone by a number of other writers writing then — I threw in World War II.

I wouldn't re-write every book. In fact, I expect *The Butterfly Plague* will be the only book I tackle more than once. But it suffered, you see, from that same dreadful moment — in the earlier version — of being written by a man who was suddenly overcome with stagefright. (Or should I say *pagefright*?) It was a good idea, but its time had not come. Or rather, its writer had not made sure of his craft. He simply wrote it too soon.

In its first incarnation, this book was dedicated to four good friends, whose names are on the dedication page. But to their names I must now add another, for very special reasons. Re-doing this book — so long out of print — was initially the idea of a man for whom my admiration and gratitude are unbounded. Consequently, this edition of *The Butterfly Plague* is dedicated with affectionate greetings to Dr. W.H. Clarke.

T.F., 1986

Book One

The First Chronicle

Sunday, August 28th, 1938:
Culver City Railroad Station
2:05 p.m.

"Mickey Balloon! Mickey Balloon, come down!"

A little boy, aged four, stood screaming on the verge of the platform.

"He got away!"

The child-owner of Mickey Balloon stamped his pretty feet, encased in patent-leather shoes, and jumped up and down.

Mickey Balloon's string hung tantalizingly close, but just as soon as the child leaped near it, up it bobbled and away it jiggled.

"Oh, Mickey Balloon — Oh — Mickey Balloon! Come back!"

But Mickey Balloon was going his merry way.

Up, up he soared, further and further into the blue, blue sky. Mickey Balloon had places to go and things to see.

The crowd on the platform cheered and waved.

Mickey Balloon made a tack to the right. He passed so close to the telephone poles that it seemed, for one crowd-gasping moment, he might be going to prick himself on the little brass wires that were fraying there and then he would burst into a hundred thousand pieces, splattering himself and all his rubber features — his black-and-white painted eyes, his grinning Mickey-mouth and his great big sticking-out ears far and wide; so far and wide that all the members of the Hollywood Extras' World War Band and all the Boy Scouts of America and all the assembled members of the Norma Jean Norman Fan Club, Glendale Division, and all the hawkers and drummers, the flag wavers, the peanut vendors and all the sellers of balloons who had gathered there to meet the train, could never put Mickey together again. But they didn't have to.

Mickey Ballooned even higher now — higher and wider, floating and jerking, mingling with the birds and the soot and all the things that float and jerk and spend their lives in the air — the moths and the flies, the bees and the hornets, the dragonflies, the pieces of wood ash — and the butterflies.

Far down below him half the whole world had dressed itself up in stripes and polka dots, blazers and Panama hats. The other half had put on pink pajamas and orange scarves and dyed its hair a deep golden red. And once everybody in the whole world had dressed up in this fashion, one way or the other, they had all said, "Let's go down to the Culver City Railroad Station and cheer in the Santa Fe Super Chief. That will be exciting. Swell! We will see that new movie star, Norma Jean Norman, and we will see each other. Whee!" So there they all were, jammed on the tiny wharves of platform, pushing-and-yelling, screaming-and-jumping and losing their balloons.

Mickey Balloon just adored it. He diddled and bobbled, careened and pharoomed and smiled.

There was the parking lot. There were all the cars. Big black cars. Little blue cars. Red roadsters. Green coupés — and one purple Franklin with a rumble seat. It was just too delightful, and Mickey Balloon gave a great wide swoop and came down close to the purple rumble-seated car and spied on its occupants. There was a lady in the front seat, and she wore a tangerine-and-pink patterned dress with great big puff-up sleeves, an orange garden hat and a cigarette and sunglasses shaped like little twin hearts. And there was another person, too, supported on many white pillows, dressed in blue, and sitting very high up in the rumble seat, and these two people were surrounded by a crowd.

But for Mickey Balloon there was no time to stand around in the middle of the air, looking at such things. He had to make his journey and see what else there was to see. So, up he went. Up, up, and then something terrible happened.

Mickey Balloon was assassinated.

By, of all people, a child with a BB gun.

Standing in the window across the way, the child took perfect aim and fired.

Down came Mickey Balloon in flames and little pieces: little pieces so very small that no one ever found them.

2:10 p.m.

"Myra!"

"What, Dolly? What?"

"Get down! Someone is shooting at us."

"Don't be ridiculous, Dolly."

"Shooting at us, I tell you."

"No, Dolly. No. It was only some kid's balloon."

"What kid's balloon? Where?"

"That Mickey Mouse balloon. It exploded."

"Someone fired a gun!"

"Nonsense."

Myra Jacobs, she of the pink-and-tangerine dress, the garden hat, and the heart-shaped glasses, beamed at the group assembled before the car. Dolly sat tensely crouched in the rumble seat amidst his pillows.

"Can't you make them go away, Myra?"

"How can I make them go away! They're *fans*."

"They're revolting. Pimply-faced, dirty little boys."

"Fiddlesticks. They're lovely."

"Hah! It's easy to see where your taste lies."

"Don't get smart, Dolly."

"They'll attack us. And then what?"

"Nonsense."

"Well, they're staring at you with some kind of intent, and it's odious."

"They're just interested, that's all. They love me."

"Phooey — they're preadolescent."

"Oh, come on! Leave them alone. Smile. Go on," said Myra.

"I will not smile!"

"O.K., then. Have it your own way, Dolly."

Myra waved and blew kisses. The children waved and blew kisses and whistled.

Dolly cringed. "Dear me, I wish the train would come."

"It'll come. It'll come. Hi, there! Hi!"

"Don't solicit, Myra. Really! Twelve-year-olds. It's shameless."

"Oh, for Pete's sake! You're gonna drive me crazy. It's all your fault anyway, getting us here so early."

"That's right. Blame it on me."

"And making me *drive* like that. Fifteen miles an hour. Do you realize how long it took us to get here?"

"One hour and forty-five minutes. Exactly."

"Right. But driving so slowly they must've thought we were a funeral procession of one."

"What do you mean by that?"

"Well, who else but a corpse would drive down Sunset Boulevard at fifteen miles an hour? I ask you."

There was a pause.

"Are you implying that *I* am a corpse?" Dolly asked.

"Oh, for heaven's sake."

"Are you imply. . . ing that I am a. . . *corpse*, Myra?"

"No, Dolly."

"Sitting back here dead. Is that it?"

"Oh, come on."

"A stiff in the rumble seat! I know."

"Dolly — *please*."

"You wish I was dead."

"I do not."

"Calling me a corpse."

"Everyone's staring."

"Let them. You love it, anyway. You thrive on it. It's your damned bread and butter."

"Oh, Dolly. Please!"

Myra waved and smiled. She lit another cigarette.

"Here we are," Dolly went on, "in broad daylight in an open car, surrounded by pubescent hooligans, being fired on from all sides, and you sit there calmly insulting me and waving at brats like a tart."

"I did not insult you calmly," said Myra.

"We have to meet this train. I am terrified of speed and you know it. So we left a little early. I can't help that. I bleed."

"Now, Dolly dear..."

"*Bleed!* Will you never understand?"

"Yes, Dolly."

"Bleed at the drop of a hat."

"Yes, Dolly."

"Inside...outside..."

"...All around the town."

"It's no joking matter."

"I'm sorry, Dolly."

"How would you like to bleed when a person so much as shakes hands with you?"

"I wouldn't."

"Or when it rains." Dolly went right on.

"You do not bleed when it rains."

"I bled in a hailstorm once."

"Phooey!"

"Phooey, nothing. I did. But a lot you care. You're just like all the rest. I could lie down right here and die..."

"Everyone carries a cross, Dolly."

"You're damn well right I carry a cross. Bang! Bang! Bang! Crucified."

The fans pressed forward, fascinated by this tale of blood and horror.

"Everybody wants to crucify poor old Dolly. They can't wait. They go around with hammers and nails. Hammers and nails! Look at them."

"Those are my people," Myra said. She tried very bravely to wave and smile.

"That's right. You wave and smile. Go ahead. I'll just sit here and die."

"You are not going to die."

The crowd took in its breath.

"Yes I am. Dead."

"Really, Dolly."

"Wait and see. Dead! And then what?"

"God knows, Dolly. God knows."

"God doesn't know anything. He's just a wretched, sadistic old tyrant sitting up there inflicting diseases on innocent people!"

"Now, now, Dolly."

"We are born to be driven mad at the whim of fate!"

"Oh, for heaven's sake, have a piece of gum and shut up."

"No, thank you. And I will not sit here in this parking lot while you chew gum in public."

"Where the hell else am I supposed to chew it?"

"In the privacy of your bedroom."

"Oh, for Pete's sake!"

"Gumchewing, Myra — for your information — is a manifestation of the lower classes' taking over our culture and society. I forbid you to do it. And if you can't think of me, at least think of your image."

"They're all chewing it," said Myra, indicating with a wave of her hand the amassed cudding faces of her fans.

"Yes, and look at them," said Dolly.

"They're my public," said Myra. "If they're gonna chew, I'm gonna."

"No, my dear. If *you're* 'gonna' chew, *they're* 'gonna.' Look what it's done to your mouth."

"My mouth happens to be my best-known feature, I'll have you know. I'm famous for my mouth."

"My dear, I hate to disillusion you, but if you really think you're famous for your *mouth*..."

"I am. I *am*. Pretty mouth. Pretty mouth. Pretty-mouth Myra!"

Myra bounced in the seat as she chanted this, and the whole crowd took it up. "Pretty mouth! Pretty mouth! Pretty-mouth Myra!"

"There! See?" said Myra triumphantly.

"If you'd stop bouncing up and down like a pair of rubber balls, *you'd* see."

Myra burst into immediate tears.

"Oh, God! Now what's the matter?" said Dolly.

"You called them rubber balls!" Myra wailed, clutching herself with both hands.

The teen-age boys giggled. Dolly silenced them with a look.

"Now, now, Myra."

"Don't you now-now me, you...homo-feely—"

Dolly blushed and stammered. "Myra. Please. *He*mo. *He*mo. *Hee*-mo-philiac!"

Myra turned and gave Dolly one of her dazzling pouts.

"I gotcha!" she said. "I got Dolly!"

And she burst into marvelous, resounding, and infectious laughter.

Dolly's pale-blue suit was impeccable in cut and condition. His Panama hat had been dyed the same shade. Underneath these garments his stockings and underclothes — even the handkerchief in his pocket — were all pale-blue. He had chosen the color himself. It showed up blood.

Adolphus Damarosch was a hemophiliac.

He was also a film director employed by Niles Studios and his current film was *Hell's Babies*, still before the cameras. Its star, Myra Jacobs, now sat in the front seat of Dolly's purple Franklin. Dolly did not drive. No hemophiliac does. They are accident-prone and die all too easily. So

Myra had done the driving and that is why she had so much to complain of. Fifteen miles an hour.

They had come to Culver City Railroad Station to meet Ruth Damarosch, Dolly's sister, who was returning from Europe after a lengthy absence.

Dolly was understandably nervous.

"How long has it been, did you say?" said Myra.

"Nineteen hundred and thirty-six."

"Yeah?"

"Yes, Myra. 'Yes.' Please say 'yes,' not 'yeah.' "

"Yes, Dolly."

"She went away to swim in the Berlin Olympics. Don't you remember that?"

"Of course I remember that. Jeepers. It was only two years ago."

"Well, I wonder sometimes. Anyway, she went over there in 1936 and hasn't been home since."

"Goodness."

"Yes. My older, older, older, older sister." Dolly sighed.

"Is she *that* old?" said Myra.

"How old?"

"Older, older, older, older."

"Four years older, to be exact. She was born in nineteen hundred and seven."

"Is that all?"

"Yes. That's all. And she was a bully to boot," he reflected.

"She *kicked* you?"

Dolly closed his eyes. Really. Sometimes Myra was too much to bear, for all her loveliness.

"A bully of the mind, Myra. An in-tel-lect-ual bully."

"Oh," said Myra, dumbfounded. She turned away to think about it.

Dolly desperately wanted the washroom and wondered if he dared to excuse himself. The washrooms were so far away, and all those dangerous people lingered between. He decided against it. He thought about the fate of Mickey

Balloon. It was sad the way some things turn out. Now Ruth was coming home.

Sunday, August 28th, 1938:
Aboard the Santa Fe Super Chief
1:30 p.m.

Ruth Damarosch Haddon finished her lunch, set aside her utensils, and looked out of the windows. She was seated all alone at a table in the dining car. She had been seated alone for every meal since leaving New York but she did not know why.

She was nervous.

Ruth was a tall woman. Her figure was attenuated and spare; strong. It befitted an athlete. Her hair, cut extremely short, was pure white — a prematurity, for Ruth was now but thirty-one years of age. Her face was flat and wide and her eyes blue-gray, protruding slightly like the eyes of someone suffering from a thyroid condition. Her expression in repose mirrored the fact that she would not let go of innocence. She held onto it like a renegade child. Innocence was sanity. Just as silence was sanity.

Ruth believed that she was living in a nightmare. Childlike, she insisted there was darkness when all around her the adults were proclaiming light. She moved and sat like one who expects attack. And she had good reason.

Now he sat directly behind her, occupying a small table for one, at which he ate every day. He had followed her all the way from Hamburg. He had never for an instant not been close at hand. Yet he had never menaced her, touched her, or spoken. He was merely constant. At her back.

He was blond from top to toe, probably German, and he smelled of leather. He was extraordinary to look at. He could have been an advertisement for racial perfection. His eyes were blue; his hair was golden; his teeth were white and even. Every bone was perfection itself. He radiated strength, health, and stamina. Yet, he never seemed to sleep.

Then there was the woman.

Ruth knew her, or was certain that if she could *see* her she would recognize her, perhaps even as someone close and well known. But this woman, who had been on board only since Chicago, never presented her face. Over it she wore a wide, dark — perhaps a widow's — veil. Her clothing was expensive and beautifully tailored, and the coloring of the fabrics was autumnal — browns, golds, and indescribable reds. She inevitably wore gloves — long gloves, kid, calf, or pigskin, which were worn to the elbow and occasionally above. Her hats were small and seemed designed merely to hold the veiling in place. She was small herself, very finely made, and she moved efficiently, as though given to command an immediate respect. Her gestures were significantly brief.

It was the unswerving set of this woman's head that told Ruth she was being stared at. The gaze was leveled through the veiling, pronounced and definite as a pair of lights. In fact, this was a quality that pervaded the whole figure — the quality of light — of something metallic that shone. Insect-like, the woman's brilliantly clouded head would turn to follow Ruth's every move. Or it would lock, like the head of a mantis, into one poised and trance-like position. Ruth wondered if there were lids on the eyes or if they ever closed.

The woman was accompanied by a large, uniformed servant, who followed her everywhere, sat her down with quiet ceremonious gestures into chairs, opened doors for her, lifted baggage from her path, and shaded her by placing his bulk between her and bright light. He was a Negro. They never spoke. He did these things with inbred reactionary calm. It was his life, it seemed, to make a path for her wherever she went and to close it behind them after their passage. At mealtimes the Negro stood near the doorway of the dining car, watching the trays pass by shoulder-high beneath his nose. Ruth was certain that he was fed with the dogs in the baggage car. He had an eye for food not natural to human beings.

Ruth lit a cigarette. She practiced poise. She placed her free hand on her presentation copy of *Mein Kampf*, which rested on the table beside her half-emptied dishes. She gave the woman a stare of her own. She began to make up her mind — using a recipe of one part courage, two parts reason, and seven parts desperation — that she would accost this woman, pleasantly, and ask for her name. Perhaps the woman could not for some reason make the advance herself. Perhaps she was shy — or ill. Perhaps the Negro was her guardian. She might even be a prisoner. . . .

It had crossed Ruth's mind a day after Chicago there might be some connection between the blond man and the staring woman. But since they never met and seemed not even to see each other, Ruth had decided they were, after all, separate watchers, nothing at all to do with one another.

Ruth poured a second cup of coffee, staining the whiteness of the tablecloth. Her composure, born of years of training as an athlete, gave way, and instead of righting the pot and redirecting its flow, she experienced a small, ridiculous moment of indecision and just went on pouring, watching the large brown mark grow larger and larger. A waiter approached, his mouth open, certain he was beholding an act of vandalism or of blindness. Ruth settled for blindness.

"I — am — so — sorry. . . ." she forced. "The sun. The sun, you see." She wiped her eyes, as though removing the sun itself, and smiled.

The waiter, satisfied and relieved, retreated with a sigh.

Now was the moment to do it. Before thought. Before confusion could be blamed. Before regret. She rose, using the pretext of the spilt coffee. She took up *Mein Kampf*. She took up her purse. She paid her bill. She strode eight steps in the right direction, and the train lurched. Ruth set her gaze on the distant stare of the seated figure. Swimming in its direction against the current of the disturbed gravity beneath her feet, she arrived at the woman's table.

"Hello."

The head rose.

Its veiling billowed slightly.

There was no vocal response.

Ruth went right on. "I must introduce myself. I'm Ruth Haddon. I was Ruth Damarosch. Perhaps we've met. I couldn't avoid the fact that you were looking at me. I thought perhaps you wondered who I was. I. . ."

"No."

"No?"

"No. And please leave at once."

"But. . ."

"Leave me immediately, Mrs. Haddon. Or I shall have you removed."

The Negro.

Ruth looked down, frozen with panic, into the depths of the veiling.

"Who are you?" she said.

The eyes lifted. Ruth could just perceive them. They glistened. Dragonfly's eyes. On the tablecloth the little gloved hands took delicate hold of one another.

"I am no one," said the voice (vaguely recognizable — deadly), "I am — *no one*. Go away."

Ruth shivered. All at once, she knew who it was.

2:05 p.m.

Ruth hurried along the corridor toward her compartment, impelled by the knowledge of her discovery.

The blond man followed in leather-scented pursuit.

Ruth got to her door. She opened it and went inside. She turned then and hissed at the man, speaking to him for the very first time. Her words ridiculously echoed the words of the woman in veils: "Go away," she whispered. "Go away and leave me alone. I am no one." Then she slammed the door and burst into tears.

2:10 p.m.

Finished with her crying, Ruth sat back and counted: One, two, three and four. Five and six and seven. Eight. Nine and ten. Eleven.

The suspense was unbearable for her. To be losing one's mind. To be followed. To be stared at. To see, after so many years, that woman, and to look again into that gaze, too well remembered.

Something was going to happen. Something more terrible than anything that had happened before. It would happen to Ruth first, but she sensed that it would also happen to someone else. Perhaps to everyone. It was in the air of her mind: in the air around her. Did she carry it? She wondered.

She refocused her gaze.

The train whizzed on through an intersection, and Ruth saw carloads of waving people stopped at the crossing. She waved back and then she thought, Why do I wave? I hate you.

The Santa Fe Super Chief went on by, its brown and yellow cars going clickety-click.

The people went on waving, unaware of being hated.

2:17 p.m.

"There goes Bully Moxon."

"Where? Where?"

"Right there. Going into the station. Oh, Dolly — Bully Moxon!"

"Calm yourself, Myra."

"I can't. It's too exciting. He's marvelous."

"I thought he was dead," said Dolly.

"Well, there he is," said Myra, standing up in the front seat of the car. "Just as alive as you and me or anybody."

"Pickled to the gills, no doubt."

"No. Not at all. Looking wonderful."

Dolly stroked his beard, which was red. He did not mind shaving his cheeks — they were pretty straightforward and safe — but his chin was doubtful territory and he did not dare to lay a razor to it. So he wore a chin beard — handsome and short.

"I don't see him," he said.

"Stand up, then," said Myra.

"In the rumble seat?" Dolly whined.

"Of course, in the rumble seat."

Dolly carefully hoisted himself until he stood on the cushions with which he perpetually surrounded himself to ward off his death.

Spying Bully, he observed, "He looks nine hundred."

"No. No. He looks sweet. He looks lovely. Lovely. Bully Moxon. Oh Dolly, look! He's going to dance."

"By God!"

"Yes. Yes. There he goes. Dancing."

They watched.

Bully Moxon, in patent-leather shoes, in brass-buttoned blazer, in white flannels, in boater, and carrying a cane, did his famous "Waiting for My Favorite Dream" routine. His features, adored across the land for their pronounced and swollen redness, reflected a kind of wistful wickedness. He hated dogs, cats, children, and Sunday afternoons. But he loved to dance.

Now he danced without benefit of music — or certainly without benefit of the right music, for in the distance, nearer the tracks, the Hollywood Extras' World War Band was still playing. Bully did not seem to mind what music played. He lifted his cane; he flashed his famous feet; he did his high-stepping cakewalk — straight along the white lines leading off through the gate.

The crowd gave way. They clapped and cheered. They loved forgotten Bully Moxon, who hadn't been capable of making a film for six or seven years. The remarkable thing about Bully had always been that he had been a dancer during the silent era. Not for Bully the orchestrated tangos of Valentino, played by the local theaters' hired musicians. Not for Bully the gramophone record scratchily blared. Bully had danced to silence. The way he did now. His audiences had always hummed, and now they began to hum again.

"See," said Myra just before the humming reached them, "he has the white carnation in his lapel. Just the way he always did in all his pictures. Good old Bully Moxon."

Myra waved.

Dolly remembered. "Bully Moxon stole a carnation from my father's garden once."

Another time. Long ago, it seemed, but not so long ago at all. Only 1922. Ruth's fifteenth birthday party.

"I was just a child, more or less," Dolly said, but mostly to himself, for Myra, misty-eyed, was caught up in humming and swaying to Bully's tune. "When I was a child and you were a child, Annabelle Bully Moxon. Hah! Dancing on our lawn."

"He's heading for the gates," said Myra. "Oh, please, please, Dolly. Can't we go, too?"

Dolly knew he would regret it, but he had to say yes. Where Bully led, others had always followed. And so, clambering down with care from his pillows and cushions, Dolly held onto Myra's waist with both hands and, like two conga dancers, they made their perilous way toward the platform with Bully in the lead.

In moments, the Santa Fe Super Chief would arrive.

The festival was about to explode, like Mickey Balloon.

2:18 p.m.

Ruth splashed cold water on her face and studied her gray-blue eyes for a long moment in the mirror of her tortoise-shell compact. A gift from Hermann Goering.

"What's happening?" she said aloud to the image and then snapped shut the lid. A little puff of powder exploded into the air as she did this. She brushed her lapels and sat down.

In a few moments they would reach Culver City and she would be met by Adolphus and Myra and driven home to the house on the beach. To her mother.

People she had not seen for two years would crowd around her and she would have to be brave and lie and tell the story of her life as though it were a true story. She would hate every minute of it and hate all the people. Hate. Oh, why? She did not know why. She was forgetting how to be strong. How to be faithful and loyal: how to be kind and how to remember the dead. Or to brush her teeth twice a day. Or to brush her clothes in the morning. Or to wear clean underwear. To forgive and forget. To pay attention. To cultivate friendship. To be alive. To love. She wept again. She had not forgotten tears. She closed her eyes.

2:20 p.m.

Dolly allowed Myra to help him through the crowd and finally up onto a bench where he would be safe from the hands and feet that always menaced him wherever he went. Myra climbed up beside him.

"You O.K. here?" she asked, setting aside her chewing gum.

"Yes, thank you — and don't put it *there*," said Dolly.

"Everybody puts it there," said Myra.

"Well, for once," said Dolly, "behave as though you weren't everybody."

"What'll I do? Put it in my purse?"

"Don't shilly-shally, Myra. Just wrap it in a piece of paper, and later you can drop it in an ash can."

Dolly was watching Bully Moxon, dancing still at the edge of the platform.

"I haven't got a piece of paper," said Myra.

"Then swallow it."

Myra obliged.

"I can see smoke," she said, gulping her gum. "Here it comes!"

Everybody began to wave. Bully went right on dancing.

"Oh! Isn't it lovely to be at Culver City Railroad Station like this when the train comes in!" said Myra.

"Yes," said Dolly apprehensively. "Lovely."

Bully Moxon had now made his way very close to the spot where the Super Chief's engine would screech to a halt not fifteen seconds later. His Bully-bous, ginny nose was displaying a light of warning, but he paid no attention. His little eyes did not seem to focus on the present. His mouth twisted down and sideways with concentration. "How did it go?" he seemed to be saying. "Like this? Like that? One-two? Or one-two-three?"

He danced on.

"Lovely Bully. Dear, darling, wonderful sweet old lovely Bully," said Myra. "Dancing..."

The tune appeared to be a song so long forgotten that even Bully himself was having trouble recalling it.

"He wants to hear the music," said Myra, not knowing how right she was but only sensing something sad about the dancer.

"He's going down onto the track," she said.

The crowd leaned forward, swaying in toward him. It was all very matter-of-fact.

"Look at that," said Myra. "He's waving to us. Smiling."

"Wave back."

They did.

The rhythm began to uncloud. The crowd gave a sigh. How wonderful he was.

"He's got his cane up. Lovely Bully."

On came the Santa Fe Super Chief.

"Bully."

Dancing.

"Listen. The train..."

Wailing.

"Bully."

"Bully! Dance this way..."

"That way..."

"Back."

"Dance up."

"Here! Hold up the dancing. Stop."

"Bully."

Smiling.

"Bully."

Waving.

"*Bully.*"

Dancing.

"The train. The train, Bully. TRAIN!"

The train.

"*Bully!!*"

Bully in the cinders. Down. Decapitated. His last step upward...

Dead.

The crowd gave a kind of roar.

The band was playing and the cheering had started farther down the platform and the loved ones were arriving and there wasn't much you could do except imagine nothing had happened. Particularly if you hadn't really seen it happen. As Dolly hadn't, for at that very instant he had fallen carefully to the floor. Myra couldn't see it because *she* was crying. In the crowd, there were few who could have realized what had happened — because they cheered. And there were some who had been blinded, who — being blinded — had laughed, thinking someone had played them a trick-death until they wiped their eyes and saw the blood on their fingers and until the engine lurched and all the brown and yellow cars rattled against each other and the wheels screeched and women screamed "God help us all!" and there began to be panic because all at once the accident was everywhere and it seemed for one incredible instant they would all be down beneath the wheels with Bully and, like him, suddenly severed from life forever.

2:21 p.m.

Ruth's bags came down on top of her head.

Everything exploded and ceased. Was still.

She came to, lying on the floor. It was barely long enough to contain her.

Several people gave off screams.

The engine bellowed like a killer.

Bully Moxon's head rolled down the track.

Ruth struggled upward through her own arms and legs.

In the corridors the passengers ran in every conceivable direction, seeking immediate and personal escape.

Ruth dragged open a window and seized the strings of a passing balloon. At the other end of the string a child roared disapproval and rage.

"What has happened?" said Ruth. "For God's sake, tell me what has happened to us all?"

The child wailed. It wanted to see the body. It tugged at its balloon and ran away.

Ruth went out into the corridor. Bedlam.

"What is it? What has happened?" she asked. But no one paid the least attention.

"Get off the train!" a conductor yelled. "Get off before she fires!"

"Fires?"

"*Fire!*"

Fire. Fire. Fire.

"Get off the train!" cried all the mothers of children on board.

"Get off the train!" cried all the children themselves.

"Get the hell out of my way!" cried several other people, childless and alone.

"But what is happening?" said Ruth.

She approached the conductor. "Are we really on fire?"

"Of course not," said the conductor. "But I've got to clear this train. We have a schedule to meet."

Ruth got back to her compartment somehow and managed to struggle out with her bags.

Slowly — more slowly, it seemed, than anyone else — Ruth was moved along the corridor.

"Please! Please move faster," Ruth said and was alarmed to find she had not even said it aloud. The blond man was close behind her.

"It will happen now," Ruth thought.

"What will, lady?" said the man in front of her, who was covered inexplicably with talcum powder.

"Nothing," said Ruth. "Nothing. Excuse me."

At last they had reached the exits, and Ruth was helped down by a Brazilian Boy Scout.

She thanked him and started along the platform. Adolphus was nowhere in sight, nor Myra (whom Ruth could only hope to recognize from her films). All around her, bodies collided.

As she arrived near the head of the train Ruth became part of a crowd that had managed to get near the pieces of Bully's corpse. These were being tenderly gathered and arranged by station attendants and Red Cross volunteers. There was nothing to see except a grisly array of bloody blankets and sheets. But the crowd leaned forward — then it fell back.

Someone was coming.

"Who's that?" they whispered.

It was the woman in veils.

She approached, drawn up to her full tiny height, followed by the immense bulk of her servant. She had been joined by two men of indiscriminate age and appearance, both dressed exactly alike in leather overcoats. She was escorted by these men to the edge of the platform.

Silently and without lifting her veils, the mysterious lady stared down with remarkable poise into the cinders where still lay the head of Bullford Moxon. She seemed to view it as some gigantic and momentous ruin — and in her stance and quiet stare could be felt the power and intensity of a conqueror. She had put him there. Ruth knew it. But she didn't know how or why.

Now, amidst the murmurs and mutters of the crowd, the veiled and queenlike figure, at once revered and feared, strode away toward a waiting automobile. No one voiced it. No one dared. They too, like Ruth, remembered that walk. They remembered its portent.

They were shaken.

If Bullford "Bully" Moxon was dead by his own intent, then why had the Little Virgin willed it?

And why was she back, America?

2:45 p.m.

Dolly lay on the floor of the station. He was extremely angry because no one seemed to realize he was lying there in danger of death. But there was nothing he could do about it.

At first he lay absolutely still, paralyzed with the fear of being stepped on. He yelled, "Look out, you damn fool!" several times at people who ran too close. But no one heard him. And no one got him.

Eventually, when it became clear to Dolly he was not the central attraction, his curiosity got the better of him and he rolled to safety under the bench upon which Myra still stood crying "No, no, no," as she had when Bully first danced under the train. Dolly pulled his feet up toward his bottom and lay there very still and watching.

Myra, having begun to weep, was unable to cease.

Ruth, for her part, had now begun to sense the error of standing around like a principal mourner and turned back into the crowd in order to escape. Hoping to avoid recognition, she hoisted one of her suitcases high, obscuring her face from view, and she pushed toward safety.

"Hold it, Mrs. Haddon. Not so fast there!"

(Was it the blond man? Had he spoken?)

The voice was directly in front of her and startled her into releasing her hold on her suitcase. It fell, splashing underwear over the ground. The photograph appeared in the *Examiner* the next day.

"Thank you," said the cameraman and waved to her as he moved away.

Ruth wanted to cry. Where was Dolly? Where was this Myra who was supposed to be with him? Why was she alone like this? She wanted help.

"Help!" she cried aloud.

Dolly saw her.

He reached up and grabbed Myra by the dress.

"There she is," he yelled.

"Get the police!" screamed Myra. "I'm being raped!"

"It's only me," said Dolly. "For God's sake, Myra! It's only me!"

"*Rape!* Rape! RAPE!!" screamed Myra, immediately assuming the physical proportions of an actress playing in close-up.

Dolly, emerging from under the bench, somehow got his head pornographically involved with Myra's skirts.

Myra launched several octaves of invective into the sky.

At this point, Ruth, trailing underwear and knotted lingerie from her suitcase, lurched into Dolly's behind as he crouched in front of Myra. All three ended up in a heap on the ground.

Those who were near enough heard the following dialogue:

"Get the police!"

"It's only me!"

"*Rape!*"

"I'm sorry. My underwear's dragging!"

"Pervert!"

"I'm your sister!"

"*Help!*"

"I'm bleeding."

"*Dolly!*"

"Ruth!"

"Let's get out of here."

At which point the confused bystanders saw the apparent rapist assisted to his feet by his victims and dusted from head to toe by one of them while the other kissed him on the face and said, "I thought you'd never come!"

Beyond them, nearer the tracks, the crowd had begun again to hum some sort of tune. Shortly thereafter the band struck up and no one seemed to notice the ambulance arrive.

Four stretcher-bearers forced their way into the choiring chaos of humanity, all shoving and regrouping in order to view the remains of their late idol. "Bully Moxon is dead," they lamented, holding hands and swaying. "Had his head cut off by the Santa Fe Super Chief."

This was the end of a legend as old as Hollywood, but also the beginning of a new legend — one that most people would remember as the Butterfly Plague.

Sunday, August 28th, 1938:
The Beach at Topanga
12:30 p.m.

She looked up.

A sea gull rose upon heated air and hovered, dazed, above her head.

It might even be asleep up there, she thought, with its closed eyes and its painless breathing. Mrs. Damarosch, on the beach in a sun dress, oblivious and ankle-deep in the outgoing tide which filled the canvas shoes that hid her feet, could hardly take a painless breath. These were the weeks of her death.

Her name was Naomi, and she gazed away from the gull toward the horizon. The sunwhite sky had shed the sea like a winter skin below it. Just once, Naomi took a breath so deep that, while it pained her diaphragm and abdomen, it filled her also with a sense of serenity.

She would live, she knew, for a little while. And where there was life, she remembered, there was. . . something or other.

She began very slowly to walk toward the far end of the beach.

The house she had lived in ever since the divorce was at the southern extremity. Between this end and the north there were four more houses of varying size and pretension. One was barely a cottage. Two of the others were houses on stilts, and the one farthest away was surrounded by a high board fence through the cracks of which you could see an endless gleam of glass. This house was very modern, built three years before.

The sky above was cloudless, blank and seared. It was populated with molecules of haze and, seemingly, by fire itself. Mrs. Damarosch had traveled the world with George, her husband, sometimes watching him film in foreign studios, but never had she experienced such a heat as this. So dry a heat, it seemed quite capable of evaporating the whole Pacific Ocean. Almost a prehistoric heat, she thought — biblical — plaguelike. "Vengeance is mine, saith the Lord," and He dried up the oceans like *that*.

As George had.

As George would again, if he could.

Pictures!

Mrs. Damarosch — Naomi Nola, the silent-screen star — smiled. "Of course he won't," she said to herself.

"Science would not allow it."

She moved on.

Looking to the west, she watched the sea of peace and its gleaming surface. Placid and free, innumerable birds rode upon it, unaware of tide and sea drift. Not even bothering to feed, they were so docile surely someone must have drugged them.

The quiet prevailed in all directions. Silence was broken only by the lapping of shore water, the whirring of insect wings.

Mrs. Damarosch walked. Her gray canvas shoes squelched and belched with tidewater. She looked at them. She would find a place to sit down, take them off, and let them dry.

Unfortunately, in looking at her feet she could not avoid her ankles, shins, and knees.

"Oh, dear," she sighed. "Oh, dear."

It was still such a shock to see herself so thin and formless. Once she had weighed one hundred and twenty pounds. Now, only ninety-five.

"Oh, my," she said. "Oh, well."

And walked on.

Presently she opened an orange-colored parasol.

"Ruth hates the color orange, but I don't care. Ruth will have to put up with it."

In her mind's eye Mrs. Damarosch imagined the effect the orange parasol created, resting against the green shoulder of her sun dress. She was lately inordinately fond of a brightness in things and had recast her wardrobe to appease this taste. "Money, money, money..." Mrs. Damarosch heard George saying. To hell with it.

Changing the subject, she thought back to that first day in the blue-eyed doctor's office.

"But I don't feel anything," she had said to him.

"I understand that," the doctor had said. "But you shall," and his eyes had frozen over. Two blue marbles.

"When?" Mrs. Damarosch had said, expecting to feel the tremors of pain at once.

"All in good time," the doctor had said.

Now Mrs. Damarosch repeated his promise. *All in good time.* As though he had promised her a mink... "But I cannot," she had said in his office, "I cannot endure pain."

"We can arrange that when the time comes."

(Now.)

Mrs. Damarosch had sat very still on the hard wooden chair. Not even a cushion for comfort. She had felt the cold on her buttocks (which then had been heavier) and the silk of her underclothes had been moist.

Hating the doctor, knowing he pitied her, hating his withholding of mercy, Mrs. Damarosch had said, "Is there really nothing one can do?"

He had smiled.

"Nothing."

She had smiled back.

Well.

She walked through the sand.

She thought about the cancer inside her and about abortion. She wondered why you cannot abort a disease from the womb the way you can a child. She had aborted once herself. And considered it one other time. Well, twice. But she had finally allowed two children life. Dolly had paid the consequences. But didn't we all?

Now Ruth, husbandless, childless, was coming home. Another tragedy.

Let me live. Let me die. *Let* me — don't make me.

She stopped walking.

"Here," she said. "This is the place. The very place. Perfect."

She had selected a slight rise in the sand, just above the tide mark. Noting with her shoe that it was firm and dry, she sat down on the sand in an approximation of the lotus position, with her parasol tilted against the sun.

She sighed and removed her damp shoes.

"I really do like it here," she said, laying them neatly to dry beside her. "And I particularly like this view."

Beyond her in the shallows of the bay some rocks gave chameleon shelter to a few sleeping seals.

"I cannot waste my time with sleep," she thought. "Like you can."

Then as if to spite her words, on cue, one of the seals rose from its place, nosed the air for danger, and slipped like a dancer, graceful and awkward at once, into the water.

"Oh," said Mrs. Damarosch. "Oh! How lovely."

The seal swam directly toward her.

It's tame, she thought. It's actually going to come in.

But it wasn't tame and it didn't come in. It swam fairly close, however, and stopped to look at her, possibly expecting her to respond in some way.

Mrs. Damarosch looked back. She went on smiling.

The seal, its eyes bright with water, opened its mouth and appeared to smile back.

Suddenly, unaccountably, Mrs. Damarosch found herself waving at it excitedly, raising and lowering the parasol and gesturing with her free hand.

"Hello," she said. "Hello! Hello!"

The seal, with a final thrust of its head, slid beneath the water and was gone.

"Oh," said Mrs. Damarosch. "Damn."

She waited.

Overhead the gulls still sat on private updrafts, insolent and supreme, apparently not even remotely interested in the spectacle of the Buddha below them on the sand, vibrant with color and splendid in the patience of her posture.

While waiting for the seal to reappear Mrs. Damarosch thought about the number of fish it must take to feed one seal. She counted the number of seals on the rocks and then again thought about the fish in the waters before her.

"Infinity isn't a question of space at all," she announced to herself, as though replying to an older and touchy point of argument. "It's just the uncountable quantity of things that were and are and will be. That's what it is: the immortality of numbers."

She watched again for the seal and was in pain.

She thought about drowning: different ways to die.

About infinite death, as unlimited as life itself — the infinity of life its only limitation.

"Different ways to die."

Infinity.

The infinite heat of the sun, she thought.

The infinite movement of the waters.

The infinite seal and the infinite fish.

The infinite gull and his infinite victim, the crab.

The infinite fisherman; infinite pole.

Infinite line and tackle — infinite hook and infinite worm.

Here, too, the infinite sand, created by infinite wind and water — infinite corrosion — infinite corruption. . . .

Infinite bodies, parasites and feeders. . . .

Infinite corpse of man in infinite sunlight, giving off his coruscations, the infinite winking of his delicate lights of life and death and pain and joy. His flashes of. . .

Flash in the pan.

Mrs. Damarosch saw herself flash on and off in the eye of God.

"Well," she said. "Well."

She settled her thin buttocks, brittle with bones where the protective flesh had once sat, deeper into the sand.

George.

Sometimes she wished fervently she had been given a talent for religious belief. It would be comforting to be able to imagine that she really was going to go somewhere and wait for George to repent and die. Oh, he'll leave that Peggy, all right. Hadn't he left them all? Corrine, Eudora, Belle, Marie, and Norma —

She loved him. Had loved him, always. Would again. Did.

It lingers. How can you lose it?

Still, he was gone.

But not dead.

Death is the only total absence.

"I'm going away, George," she laughed. The memory of his having forced her out of his life seemed like a joke now.

She tried to remember being young. But nothing consummate would come back.

She could not assemble her youth in her mind because that was not where her youth had been.

"I suppose it really was a gyp," she thought, "not to tell George I was a carrier. I, this woman sitting here, old, on this sand."

Oh, but the weight of him would move just so upon my rib cage and over my thighs, right there, the delicate brushing aside of bones. (She smiled.) I held him by the hair at the back of his rumpled neck to keep him from toppling over into the pillows. I was afraid he'd suffocate. Both of us. It was like a battle for survival. And finally, because I made it happen so quickly, he would fall back thinking he'd done it and I would think, No, George, *I've* done it. . . and he never knew the real victory was my victory. Or so I thought then. Mine.

Consummation is death. She thought of her hemophiliac son and her carrier daughter.

"Dolly should have died long ago. So — he still has to die and Ruth and me and all of us. It just so happens I am first in line. . ."

At last the seal broke the water's surface and Mrs. Damarosch sighed with relief.

Her arms were wet and gleaming with perspiration. She took out a handkerchief and dried them carefully. She considered her arms, like her legs (like all of her), as thin and ugly. They were covered with liver spots.

I must really buy a dress with sleeves, she thought.

Adjusting the parasol to the angle of the sun, she resettled herself and commenced her eye exercises.

First of all she looked to the left, keeping her head and neck quite still. That was the Science of it. The point was to try and see over each shoulder in turn, moving only the eyes themselves.

Faraway in the distance to the south she could see her own beach house, built halfway up the bluff. She also saw a child (probably one of those Trelford children) with a dog and a beach umbrella.

They were like figures and objects in an old silent film — noisy, you were certain, but their voices were somehow censored. The dog barked in pantomime and the child called its name with a mute bawl. Mrs. Damarosch regarded the child unsentimentally. Childhood was a misery as she had known it — made up of unaccountable frustrations. Perhaps she was not sentimental about children for the simple reason that she did not envy them, as most people did. Besides which, this child seemed to be entirely satisfied with its existence since it was watering the sand in a wide, male arc.

Children.

Her children. Ruth. Adolphus.

And soon, my death, before I know their fate.

Oh, beach and seals and little boy peeing in the sand, forgive me for bringing my death to your life.

7:30 p.m.

Fragile, delicate, built like a woman with long slender legs, a slimness of bone and a round, firm breast that would have been the envy of a twenties flapper, Octavius Rivi lived in the house behind the boards at the end of the beach.

Naomi Damarosch did not know his identity. To her he was just a figure glimpsed occasionally in a garden through a space between the boards. The one point of interest in these occasional glimpses was that the figure Naomi saw was always nude. At least, she suspected so. She saw the glisten of an arm — a length of leg viewed sideways, and once, she was certain, the gentle curve and whiteness of buttocks, stooping.

Octavius Rivi lived alone and people did not come to visit him. He rarely went out and when he did, it was always at night to the movies.

In his bedroom there were twenty bottles of cologne, and in the bathroom large boxes of imported dusting and talcum powder, scent for his hair and various perfumes, oils, and other aromatic concoctions with which he seasoned his bath water. He even set perfume in the toilet bowl after it was flushed and he sprinkled cologne all over his towels, his linen, and his clothing. He also burned incense and set out glass decanters filled with flowers of any kind that give off a heady aroma — freesia, narcissus, orange blossoms.

His house was made entirely of different kinds of wood and glass and paper: modeled after Japanese designs. In the garden there were porous rocks and sandstone figures surrounded by miniature trees and shrubs. This, too, tended to give the enclosure an Oriental flavor.

On the evening of August 28th, Octavius Rivi was dressing to go out. It is of no consequence which film he was going to see because he did not get there.

He stood — bathed and scented, still naked — in front of the mirror. He put on one of his favorite records and poured himself a drink. Tequila. He was not of age, but that did not matter. No one watched over him. He did as he pleased.

He put on his pink cotton underwear, his black wool hose, a pink shirt with black buttons, a black silk tie, black cuff links, and, at last, black trousers and pink shoes. He brushed his hair forward and touched his slim, long eyebrows. Black. He put astringent scent on his handkerchief and placed it in his cuff. When he was about to don his black tight jacket a bell rang in the garden.

Octavius froze.

The bell rang again.

He did not know what to do. Whether to run or stand there, to call out or slam his hand over his mouth.

The bell rang one last time.

Octavius went to the door. He crossed through the garden, past the yew trees and under the bamboo harps, and at last he reached the gate.

Through the slats he could see that someone in uniform was standing there. The mailman? A telegram boy? A policeman? No. It was none of these. It was someone entirely black, with a shiny cap.

Intrigued, Octavius hoarsely advanced the words, "Who are you?" out through the grille.

A Negro voice responded, "I belongs to your mother."

Octavius was stunned.

He stood extremely straight and his hands shot out like arrows toward the bolts.

"Yes," he said. "Yes. One moment."

His fingers fluttered like stupid bugs, skittering ineffectually over the private parts of the lock. Bolts, keys, chains — my God, why had he put so many restrictions in the way of haste?

At last the gate was ready to open. He swung it wide.

"Where is she?" he cried, and the words were so loud the Negro in the uniform fell back.

Then the dark hulk shuffled gracefully forward on its toes. Somewhere under the brim of its cap, it smiled. At last Octavius could see the eyes. They were hungry.

"Hello."

"Where is she? Tell me."

Like a pilgrim, the Negro doffed his cap and stooped in through the gate to the garden. He said, with a seemingly natural inclination to lower his voice as well as his person, "You are Mr. Octavius." He nodded as he said it, looking at the slight figure in front of him.

"Yes."

"My name is Herald and I comes directly from your mother with a message."

"Where is she? What does she want?"

"I dunno. I dunno. Honest, I don't. I didn't look, Mr. Octavius. Why should I look at a private message? I'm a good servant and I don't disturb no letters." He trembled and still did not tell Octavius where his mother was. The atmosphere of hunger persisted.

Herald handed over a neat blue envelope. Octavius had

seen such envelopes before. In them came his allowance and the receipts of his bills marked PAID . He scrutinized it closely in the green light of the sunset. Yes. It was the right handwriting, too. It was indeed a message from his mother. But he shook as he tore it open. No such message, borne by a human hand directly from her own presence, had ever arrived before. Always before they had come in the mail.

Inside there was the usual stationery, blue and harsh and heavy.

On it the script was applied in thick black strokes of India ink.

The message read:

> My dear Octavius,
>
> This, as you will know by now, is to be delivered by my personal Negro whose name is Harold Herald. He is a good man and you can trust him. Tell me through him when I may come to see you. I want to come and see you. I am coming. Tell him "yes." Tell him "soon."
>
> I remain, as ever,
>
> your Mother.

Octavius turned the letter over to see what was on the other side. There was nothing.

He looked at Harold Herald and the Negro looked back and smiled. His teeth were enormous.

"Why must you smile all the time?" Octavius asked him, irritated by the jumble of thoughts in his mind and a little put off by the size of the teeth.

Harold Herald considered. He had never been asked this before.

"Well," he said, "I haven't done nothing. So why shouldn't I smile?"

That was all. Octavius turned away.

He stepped further into the garden and looked, not seeing, at the shrubs and miniature trees, the Shinto shrine and the statue of Hermes and Pan himself, crouching in stone by the pond. Then he turned and said, "You aren't allowed to tell me where she is?"

"No, sir," said Harold.

"Then wait," said Octavius.

He ran inside, found a pencil, and drew a few words on the back of the letter, which he then replaced in the envelope.

On the cover of the envelope he wrote, having crossed out his own name, the words "To My Mother." Then he ran back and handed the envelope to Harold, who accepted it with the graceful and tactful misunderstanding that the letter was being returned unanswered.

"I have written my message inside," Octavius said.

"Very well," said Harold. "Then I will take it to her to look at."

He stumbled, huge and misplaced, out of the tiny tranquil world and went away without saying any more; without even turning around and without remembering to smile. His hunger went with him.

Octavius shut the gate and, one by one, closed over all the locks.

He stood very still, remembering first what he had read and then what he had written. In the twilight, somber and green, peaceful but forever shattered, the words that he thought of were these: "My dear Octavius, This is Harold Herald. He is a good man and you can trust him. Tell me through him when I may come to see you. I want to come and see you. I am coming. I remain as ever your mother."

And then on the back of the paper in his own clumsy letters, drawn, not written, the words that made him shut his eyes with a sense of purpose and a memory of pride — huge black penciled letters spelling:

TELL ME WHO YOU ARE
with love,
your son,
OCTAVIUS

Monday, August 29th, 1938:
The Beach at Topanga
6:30 a.m.

Ruth awoke.

The nightmare had been the same and just as real as always. In it she swam and swam and swam and Bruno sat in the boat and screamed at her, "*Eins! Zwei! Drei!*" Ruth had learned to turn this cry of numbers into a cue for waking and she came to life with a start. She was sweating.

She turned toward the curtained windows and gazed at the filtered light. Morning. So early, the sun had only just begun to rise. She waited for someone to come and knock. But no one came, and it was only then that she realized she'd made it all the way home. Safe. At least — alive.

All the way home to California, to Naomi and Dolly. All the way home from Bruno, pain, and Germany.

She put her arms behind her head to ease its aching, feeling her breasts pull gently at her nightie as she did so. She sighed. My body. How I hate my body.

From beyond the open windows the breeze gave her ears the sea.

Her mother was ill. So ill there was even a nurse in one of the distant rooms. The nurse's name was Bonkers. Nurse Bonkers. With a face like Mussolini — all pudge and pout and no place for the eyes. Ruth said, "Hello" to Miss Bonkers, Miss Bonkers said "Hello" to Ruth, and that was that. Miss Bonkers was a professional death-watcher. Or so it seemed. She never signed on unless the patient was in the final stages of demise. This way she was able to read several novels and knit several pairs of golf gloves. This way she sometimes inherited money.

Ruth thought, I've seen too many faces like that — always near the dead and dying. She tried to put it out of her mind.

Someone died yesterday, she thought. Who was that? Bully Moxon. Yes. Bully Moxon died under the train. They say he did it on purpose. Suicide. Why? Old Bully, gay and charming? Never. It did not make sense.

She wouldn't think about it. She couldn't afford to think about that, or anything like it. She had come home to live. That was to be the only reason for everything she did. She was going to lie in the sun, swim in the ocean, walk on the sand. No one would touch her. No one: no circumstances.

I should pretend to be deaf and dumb and just stare at people, smiling, she thought. Everyone would say, "Poor Ruth — she can't hear us, she can't tell us what it's all about," and I could sit there and smile and very soon, perhaps, not having to tell, not having to listen, I could forget.

All the way home... She rose.

Across the room the curtains beckoned and she padded over and drew them apart.

There was the ocean.

A dog barked out on the sand.

Ruth retreated, rummaged in one of her still packed suitcases and found a bathing suit. She put it on. Custom tailored. Her size precluded anything else. Everything she wore, even her brassieres, had to be made somewhere by hand.

She looked in the mirror. White and going to pot. Oh well, a few sunny weeks would clear that up.

She left the room and went out into the hall, praying Miss Bonkers was not an early riser.

Her prayer was answered by a stillness pervading the entire house. No one, it seemed, was awake anywhere.

She made her way along the hallway and onto the balcony, which winged out, second-story high, all around three sides of the house. There were stairs, and she went down onto the sand. It was already warm, although the sun had been up for barely half an hour.

The beach was entirely vacant except for the dog who stood barking at the water's edge. Ruth walked down toward it.

It seemed a friendly dog and soon stopped barking when Ruth appeared. Then it wagged its tail — a yellow dog, some kind of retriever.

"Pretty dog," she said. "Pretty dog."

She gave it a scratch behind the ears and then began to stroll, walking in the water, toward the far end of the beach.

She did not remember that house being there. When she went away there had only been the bluff. Curious, she strolled on.

It might be nice to meet a stranger, she thought. But then it's probably just some picture star, or a hideaway for someone's lover, or something inane and private like that. I won't even think about it.

She stopped. The tide was still out. There was hardly any motion to the water. The dog lay down at her feet with its paws in the sea. It looked up at her and began to pant. Ruth looked back at the sun behind her. She felt its early, pleasant warmth on her shoulders. She remembered being sunburnt, being California brown, being salt all over and dry and tight and muscled for winning. She wanted to go back. Not to have married Bruno. Not to have cared about Olympic medals and championships. Just to swim and love it as she had back then, not really so long ago, only seven, eight years ago — ten (was it?), ten, eleven, twelve years ago — an incredibly long-boned girl standing on the beach. "I'm going to be a swimmer, Mama" — 1922. Sixteen years ago. Theirs was then the only house on the beach. Go back. Come back. Stay.

The dog stood up and waded further into the water. On the rocks the seals cavorted and mewed. Ruth sighed again. She started walking.

Keeping track of your past is pointless, she thought. All you ever do is forget it or get it mixed up or wish it had been different. Dogs were lucky. Dogs didn't even know where they came from, who or what they were — or where they were going. She slid, beside the dog, into the water.

9:30 a.m.

A parade of bathers had begun below them on the beach.

Ruth, covered now with olive oil and wearing a bandanna over her hair and dark-green glasses over her eyes, was stretched out partly in a deck chair and partly (her legs and feet) along the railings of the porch.

Naomi, in a bright-red wrapper and a huge coolie's hat, with socks pulled up to her knees, was seated in the shade of her parasol on the far side of a table which was laden with coffee cups, orange-juice tumblers, and newspapers. Miss Bonkers sat beyond the screen door inside the living room.

"Does anyone know why he did it?" said Naomi.

"No," said Ruth.

"Danced right down in front of the train. Heavens! Did you see it happen, dear?"

"Of course not, Mother. I was in my compartment."

"Oh. Yes. But afterward. Did you see it then?"

"You mean Bully?"

"Yes."

"Yes," said Ruth. "I saw it."

She watched the parade. "It." That's all we are. While there, down there on the sand, all those vibrant bodies are glowing in the sun, "it" is lying in the gutter somewhere, or in a hospital bed, or, like Bully, in the cinders.

"There seem to be more people," she said, "than there used to be." She looked at the bathers.

"Yes," Naomi drawled. She was still reading the paper.

"Where in the name of God do they all come from?" Ruth asked testily.

"Oh, from the city, dear — different places. They do that every weekend, now. And the weekends all drag on till

Monday. There's always a parade like that. Up and down the beach, up and down, showing each other what they've got and what they haven't." Naomi laughed. "They'll do it for an hour or so, then stop — exhausted, I suppose — and then begin again. We're in for it now till lunch, then they disappear somewhere and come back about four. This is only Monday, don't forget. Midweek isn't so bad."

"I was hoping it would still be private," said Ruth.

"Nothing is private any more," said Naomi, giving her daughter a look of secret worry. "You must give up that idea. Times have changed."

Ruth ruminated. The people below weren't really even attractive. Just fleshy and flashy. Lots of brown skin and bathing suits that were either too large or too small. And everyone chewed gum and yelled at each other and laughed far too much — dreary, mirthless laughter — and they threw things on the sand. American weekends, Ruth thought bitterly. It's not like Germany.

The sun buzzed.

Naomi, not intending to (intending only to ponder her daughter's mind and what might be wrong with it), drowsed beneath her parasol and hat. Miss Bonkers knitted and looked at her watch, thinking of Naomi's shots. Ruth lapsed catatonically into a stare at the beach. Her mother was dying.

A girl with red hair giggled and screeched on the sand below. Two men — they must have been in their forties or fifties — were pursuing her with blankets. The girl ran into the water and the two men stood, disconsolate and panting, on the shore. They made hopeless gestures at each other and then, clutching their blankets, strolled away arm in arm. The girl glowered after them.

Now a man riding a horse came by. The horse was a palomino and so apparently was the man. They seemed to be all one color, and for a moment Ruth thought of Chiron and the centaurs, but there was nothing noble in this horseman's bearing. He was slouched toward his horse's neck. He rode the animal forward into the sea near the girl with the red hair and gave the horse and then himself a bath.

A game of volleyball appeared next — without nets and without court. It moved all the way along the beach (the ball was bright yellow), and when it reached one end it moved noisily back to the other, trampling children and sunbathers indiscriminately in its way.

A butterfly settled on the railing near Ruth's feet. It was a vivid green and looked out of place. It came from Mexico, she decided. When she looked again it was gone. *Sic transit gloria mundi.* As usual.

Then there he was.

Ruth's heart made a noise. Her veins became speedways.

She stared down at him, knowing that all the sunglasses and bandannas in the world could not disguise her now or ever if the man had been able to follow her this far without once mistaking her destination. His mask, unmoved, looked up, and Ruth wished somehow that he would smile. He never did. In fact there was never any sign at all of emotion in his face. He just stared and drifted close by and stared again and was gone. . . . Now he was wearing a bathing suit and Ruth could see for the first time the fully muscled body she had guessed was probably under all that tweed and twill and corduroy. The bathing suit was no less ghastly than anything else he ever wore, but at least his skin was a good color. He was one of those brown Germans who always had a tan. His blond head seemed to have shed a sprinkle of loose hairs over his arms and legs and stomach and glints of blondness shimmered all over him. Beautifully, Ruth thought. How beautiful you are, and awful. As though the two must go together.

He stood loosely but with enough sense of poise not to stoop or bend or do anything that would appear ungainly. His muscles were long, not gathered into knots, and his stomach was broad and flat. His shoulders shone with some kind of oil.

"Go away," Ruth whispered. "Go away!"

An enlarging group of multisexed admirers had gathered in his immediate vicinity, staring at him from all sides. Surely he *was* someone. So they gossiped and stared and speculated, waiting for him to move. But he paid no attention. He just stood there looking up at Ruth as much as to say, "I am here now." And then, having made this mute announcement, he strode away, trailing admirers after him in such a long string they left Ruth's end of the beach quite vacant except for the man and his horse, still quietly bathing in the sea. The girl with the red hair brought up the end of the blond man's parade. She was laughing.

2:55 p.m.

In the early afternoon that day it seemed that everyone slept. The beach was exceptionally quiet; even the yellow dog lay under a porch and rested, eyes closed but with its ears pointed forward in the direction of the water. The sea was making ridiculously doglike lapping noises at the verge of the sand. Perhaps the dog found this amusing, for he did not entirely sleep and at intervals his tail wagged slowly back and forth, knocking, as it did, against a painted green watering can on its left wag and a Babe Ruth baseball bat on its right wag.

This noise in turn filtered through slats, beams, and openwork metal grilling until its off-rhythms occurred just often enough to intrude into the nap of B.J. Trelford, who owned the dog, had mothered eight children, and was married to Noah Trelford, a sculptor who slept beside her right now with a child's smile on his face and an everlasting erection battering for release against the buttons of his jeans.

B.J. awoke fully, glancing around for the time, and smiled. Noah. Noah. She gave the erection a motherly pat and slipped off the bed, knowing that soon the children would start their afternoon interruptions.

Noah did not wake up.

3:00 p.m.

B.J. went into the kitchen. The dog's tail wigwagged below: green can...Babe Ruth, green can...Babe Ruth. B.J. walked to the water cooler, noticed that it was nearly empty, and drew herself a short drink. The kids in the other rooms, some on floors, some on beds, lay stretched like so many sentimental corpses for her mind's eye to encompass. Three o'clock.

She listened to the dog, got a dish towel, wiped her breasts free of perspiration, and folded them back inside their envelope of bra. She swished her hair from her forehead. Gosh, it was hot. She nibbled at the water. Noah would have to switch the jars as soon as he woke up. The kids would want orange juice and she would have to dilute it because she had only six oranges. Might as well squeeze them right now.

She smelled smoke.

Smoke was a villain. It could mean the canyons were on fire.

B.J. allowed herself the normal moment of panic and adjusted patiently to the added adrenalin before she moved carefully (never wake anyone unless you absolutely have to) out through the door onto the porch.

Once outside she could smell the smoke more strongly, but at first she could not see where it came from. She shaded her eyes from the sun and made a crablike march around the whole square-circle of her porch, ending where she had begun.

There it was. North end of the beach, top of the bluff. A haze. Blue-gray. Not a grass fire (that would be yellow) — probably just some sap, burning paper.

Over it, there was a flight of birds, circling higher and higher; curious, staying on the updraft, watching down. Not a paper fire. The smell was wrong. Disturbing. Cloth or something. Perhaps just something wet that didn't want to burn. Rags, B.J. thought. A rag-burner. Junk.

Back she went inside, passing through the bedroom,

where Noah had his erection out now in his hand (sculptor's thumb hard up against the tip — Treats it like a chisel, she thought, me his piece of marble) but still babysleeping, kid-smiling, no fooling around, just holding it tight like a handle, "like he'd fall off the bed if he let go. . . ."

B.J. threw a white sheet over him just in case the kids came in, saw him turn for her and find only bed and pillow, gave him a dazzling love smile, and left him. One thing at a time, she thought. The kids come first.

3:10 p.m.

Octavius Rivi walked from his garden into his mirrored dressing room, set down his glass of tequila, opened one of his cupboards, stared inside at the mirrors and began to dry his hair with a large blue towel.

As the towel skimmered down around his head, and as his nose emerged from its fluff, he began to smell the fire. Danger. He stopped toweling and put on clothes.

3:15 p.m.

Miss Bonkers finished boiling her hypodermic equipment, set the needles in a pan of alcohol, wrapped the syringes in cotton and toweling, closed the little boxes, threw away bits of cardboard, dabbled her fingers, dried them, turned out the lights (the drapes were drawn against the heat), closed doors, sighed, and crossed the balcony. Going into her room, she said to herself, "Someone is barbecuing hot dogs at the far end." She selected *Gone With the Wind*, opened it, and fell at once into a deep untroubled sleep.

3:25 p.m.

Ruth whispered out of the house onto the balcony and down the stairs.

She noticed the smoke at once and thought, I'll go and see what it is.

The yellow dog joined her just under halfway up the beach. He growled for the password and, having given her a good wet sniff around the ankles, turned the growl into a wag of recognition. Ruth looked up at his house, but B.J. was inside squeezing oranges by then and Ruth concluded there was no one there and the dog might as well come with her.

"Let's go," she said, and they set off.

Passing the seal rock, Ruth looked out and for a moment thought she saw one of the seals swimming in toward the beach. It wasn't. She marched on.

Nearing Octavius's fence, she could not resist a casual glance through the slats and noticed a woman in a green dress standing in a garden. She walked on by and came to a patch that led up the bluff to the salt-grass meadows and beyond that to a low hacienda-like bar that was called, for some reason, the Spanish Maine.

The birds, seen earlier by B.J., made an ever-widening circle, higher and higher, and their numbers grew until there were twenty or thirty of them. Gulls.

Some crows scuffled off the rocks at the top of the path just as Ruth came in sight and the dog gave them a loud, officious bark.

"Shut up!" said Ruth. "Be quiet."

Her heart raced.

Why was she afraid?

No good reason. There were plenty of people within calling distance. She had a dog with her. It was broad daylight and she'd always been a good runner. The Spanish Maine was only five hundred yards away and she could even hear the sound of its juke box. Below her there was the roof of Octavius's house, his fences and his visitor in the green dress, who was sitting on a bench.

Ruth felt in her pocket. There were her cigarettes and her change purse. Her matches.

"I'll go to the Maine and buy a beer," she decided. "No one can object to that."

She wondered vaguely if the blond man would be there sitting at the bar. Better to keep in contact, to let him see her; to know where he was. Better than not to know and to be afraid like this, walking through a perfectly ordinary meadow full of perfectly ordinary salt grass, hovered over by perfectly ordinary gulls and terns and crows.

There was the fire.

It was only embers now, giving off steamy smoke.

Ruth approached it.

A dune hollow had been cleared and the grass lay uprooted and trampled in a sort of flung-out circle of anger and haste. Ruth sensed that someone had done this in a state of panic. A state of violence.

All around the hollow there were footprints, large and apparently male. They seemed to have been made by an extremely heavy person, because the impressions were deep and very clear. The fire, or what was left of it, was right in the center of the hollow and seemed to have consisted mostly of wastepaper and a few small pieces of wood.

Ruth stirred the ashes with a stick. She removed her sunglasses in order to see better. There was nothing sinister in the fire at all.

She looked up.

Why the birds? Fire does not attract birds. It repels them.

She looked down again.

No sign of food. No crusts. No wrappers or peelings. There was, however, a small blue piece of material. Ruth fished it out. It sizzled. It was still damp. Instinctively she smelled it. Nothing. Just wet fire. And vaguely, a little perfume. Part of a woman's dress? No. Too heavy.

She put it in her pocket. *Memento mori*.

The dog gave all the footprints a hefty once-over, lifted its leg on the ashes, and nosed off. He seemed to want to go back, not forward. So Ruth followed.

At 7:30 that night she heard one of B.J.'s children yelling and she went out onto the balcony, where she was witness to the discovery of a nude female corpse that had been washed up on shore. It was the body of the girl with the red hair, the one Ruth had seen that morning. "Oh," she said. "God..."

Ruth went inside and locked herself in her room. She took off her clothes and stood with her back hard up against the wall.

"Not like that..." she whispered. "I don't want to die like that...."

Her gaze shifted — watching the window as she listened to the commotion on the beach. Not really knowing she was doing it, she began to "swim." Her arms made motions — forcing her shoulders against the wall — one arm and then the other reaching up and out and in and up and out and in — the rhythm gaining in momentum — locking — as she whispered, over and over, "*eins, zwei, drei. Eins, zwei, drei...*"

In the pocket of her beach pajamas, flung upon the bed, was a small garish piece of bathing suit: scorched. Ruth knew it had belonged to the red-headed girl, now dead on the beach. Its smell was everywhere. Her nostrils and the room were filled with it.

The Chronicle of the Mysterious Lady

Friday, September 2nd, 1938:
Bel Air
10:00 a.m.

The Little Virgin was in bed.

The bed was hung on all sides with curtains. Inside, a light shone down on the occupant, casting a warm and peachy glow over face and figure, sheets and pillowcases. The effect from outside the bed was one of many-coloured shadows; no features were visible: only the delicate profile.

A maid came and went with various Implements of Beauty, while another busied herself with flowers, setting them into bowls and Oriental vases.

The Implements of Beauty, lying on little trays, were passed through the curtains, used or disregarded, and then passed back to the waiting lackey. The atmosphere was surgical and silent, while a certain aura of imminent rebuke permeated the air.

Back and forth: back and forth: silvered trays, lacquered trays, inlaid trays, and trays with ormolu handles; small white towels fluttered in the breeze as back and forth through the netted portals loads of Kleenex were passed, loads of facial cream, bottles and syringes, loads of cotton; combs, curlers, brushes, and hair ribbons; hair tonics, hair nets, rats, falls, pins, buns; loads of jellies, jars, and Jergens; trays of pencils, rouge, lipstick, kohl, and mascara; toilet water, ice water, hot water, drinking water; mirrors, mirrors, mirrors; files, scissors, and emery boards; patience and paper bags.

"That will be all," said the voice. "Bring me my lace shawl, Maureen."

"Yes, madam."

It was done.

"The visiting gentlemen," said the voice, preoccupied in tone, "will start arriving at eleven."

"Yes, ma'am."

"Coffee, biscuits. . . and sherry. Nothing more."

"Yes, ma'am."

"Do you remember what I told you about the napkins?"

"Yes, ma'am."

"For God's sake, nothing paper."

"No, ma'am. Never."

"Tell Fiona her flowers look sweet and she's not to forget to set out the potpourri."

"Yes'm."

"Now, I want that copy of *Vogue* someone brought in yesterday. And *Vanity Fair*. And the papers the minute they arrive."

"Yes'm."

"Did you listen to Louella?"

"Yes'm."

"Well?"

"Nothing, ma'am. Not a word."

"Very well, then."

Maureen wavered doorward, her stack of trays loaded onto a sort of tea wagon specially designed for madam's boudoir. There was much to do before eleven.

The eyes behind the bed's veiling shifted back to immediate matters.

"Maureen?"

"Yes'm?"

"Pour a bottle of cologne into that blue bowl."

"Yes'm."

"*Bois des Isles.*"

"Yes, ma'am."

"And Maureen..."

"Yes, madam?"

"If you spill any on yourself..."

"Yes, madam..."

"Change your costume at once."

"Yes'm."

"Maureen?"

"Yes'm."

"You look lovely, my dear."

"Thank you, madam."

"Don't forget to polish your shoes."

"No, ma'am."

"Now. Get me the *Vogue* and the *Vanity Fair*."

"Yes'm."

At last Maureen managed her escape and trundled off with her wagon down the hall.

Inside the bed there was a Virginal silence, and then a long, long sigh.

11:00 a.m.

"Mr. Maynard, madam."

"Roscoe!"

"My dear."

"Come and sit over here. . . ."

"Thank you."

"You look so elegant. Tell me your news."

"I have spoken to Warner Niles."

"And?"

"Intrigued, but at the moment, no response."

"I see."

"He was..."

"No explanation, Roscoe. Only news. Tell me who else."

"Alistair Boyar."

"And?"

"Intrigued...but no response...at the moment."

"I see."

"He was..."

"I tell you, Roscoe, no explanations. On."

"Peter Trotsky."

"And?"

"Intrigued — but no response."

"Who else?"

"Ivan Dorfmann."

"And?"

"Intrigued."

"But no response?"

"He was...No."

"I see."

"Harold Houghton."

"Yes?"

"Intrigued — but no response."

Pause.

"Madam?"

"Yes, Maureen?"

"I've brought the coffee...."

"Take it away, Maureen."

"But ma'am. You said..."

"Take it away. Mr. Maynard will not be staying."

"Yes'm."

"Well, Roscoe. Anyone else?"

"No."

"I see."

"I'd love a cup of coffee."

"I'm sorry, Roscoe, but I'm really rather tired."

"Very well."

"Good-bye. And thank you, Roscoe."

"Any time, my dear. I'm always at your service. I'm sorry things didn't work out."

"No explanations, Roscoe. That is all."

"Very well. Good-bye."
"Good-bye."
Walking.
"And Roscoe...?"
Turning in the doorway. "Yes?"
"Don't come back. You're fired."
The sound of footsteps lagging down the hall.

11:20 a.m.

"Mr. Carter Cooper to see you, madam."
"Cooper Carter."
"Sorry madam. Mr. Cooper Carter."
"That will be all, Maureen."
"Yes'm."
"Well, Cooper. Sit by the window. Show me your profile. Yes. I always love that profile."
"I can't even see you, sitting way over here like this and you behind all those curtains. Does Letitia Virden hide from *every*one?"
"Never mind, you haven't come here to look at me. You've come to tell me your news. What about Bully?"
"Before Bully — I want to know what happened with your emissary. Had he any success?"
Letitia rattled her bracelets impatiently. "Of course not," she said. "Did we really expect it?"
"No."
"It doesn't worry you, Cooper?"
"Not in the least. We don't need them. Remember, you have me and everything I am and everything I own at your disposal."
Letitia beamed. "Cooper, your faith in me is wonderful."
Cooper Carter coughed.
"And now, about Bully. It is true — was it suicide?"
"Unfortunately, yes," said Cooper.
"Unfortunately nothing. It's a miracle of timing. I was thrilled."

"You always had a cruel streak, my love."

"No. I was always practical, Cooper. And I still am."

"So."

"Go on, then. Come to the cause."

"No one is certain. There are only rumours."

"And what are they?"

"They're all predictable in my estimation. Some say it was debts, others say it was drink, some even say it had to be an accident. His daughter thinks he was murdered."

"Nonsense. He danced right under my train."

"That's what they say. And she says it was murder."

"She's an hysteric."

"Yes."

"What else?"

"Well, they're looking at the will today. Didn't want to do that till after the funeral — and that, as you know, was yesterday."

"Yes. I was there."

"A little dangerous, don't you think?"

"Not at all. I never got out of my car."

"So — I'm afraid I have nothing extraordinary to tell you. Except that everyone was very sorry and most people think poor old Bully just got too deep in debt and couldn't face the fact he was too old for a comeback."

A silent, unseen reaction. Tension.

"Has my name been mentioned at all?"

"Not a word," said Cooper Carter.

"Very well."

"I'll check out the will situation this afternoon."

"By the way, you should know that George is coming."

"Oh? Can you handle him?"

"Of course."

"In spite of what he knows? Shouldn't I buy him off?"

"No, my dear. Thank you, but no. There's no need to waste your money, no matter how much there is. I can take care of George."

They smiled.

"But I'm grateful, Cooper. You're very loyal."

"You pay me well, my dear."

"As if I paid you with money! Or needed to!"

Cooper laughed.

"Don't be so cynical," said Letitia. "Come and say good-bye."

A hand and forearm emerged, so entwined in silk that hardly any flesh was evident. Cooper Carter walked across the room. He lifted the hand; he kissed its fingers; the voice begged one last look at his richly masculine profile; he gave it. . . .

And left.

12:00 noon

"Mr. Damarosch."

"George."

"Hullo."

"You may go, Maureen. This time, definitely coffee and sherry."

"Yes'm."

Pause.

"Well, George. We meet again."

"Where the hell are you? I can't even see you. What in the name of God are you pulling now, Letitia?"

"Now. . . George."

"Don't you 'now George' me. I want to see you. Get the hell out of that bed."

"No."

"I'll drag you out, Letitia."

"No you won't."

"Yes I will."

"No."

"Yes."

Children.

"If you take one more step, George, I'll shoot you."

A gleam of metal made an announcement through the gauze. George retreated.

"Bitch."

"No, George. No language."

"Language be damned, it's what you are." He sat down.

In the bed beyond the curtains there was a sigh and the sigh sent a tingle through George Damarosch, sitting there paunchy and spruced over with the odors of male toiletry. He blinked. His eyes watered. He stared with a slightly thyroid pop, leaning forward, feet together, fingers balanced on his knees, his lips working out the patterns of possible words, but silent.

Suddenly, the voice from the bed said, "How's Naomi?"

"Letitia, you know we're divorced. For years. Years. Why must you say her name?"

"She's part of you. I can't avoid her name any more than you can avoid your own."

"I never loved her."

"That's a lie. A hopeless, stupid lie."

"I never loved her. . . ."

"You adored her. Worshipped her. Built her a temple. That's why you hate her so."

"Never."

"Always."

"You. You. It was always you, Letitia."

"Nonsense. When you married Naomi Nola I didn't even exist. Tell me how she is."

"I don't know. I never ask."

"Shall I tell you, then?" said Letitia.

"I'm not interested. I don't want to know," said George.

"She's dying."

Maureen came in with the tray. She set it down. Poured the coffee and sherry, passed these, passed the biscuits, and left.

"Dying?"

"Of cancer."

Silence.

"Who told you this? How do you know everything? You've been away for years. Now, you suddenly come back and you know everything. Everything. How?"

"That doesn't matter, George. I know. That's all."

"It does matter. It matters. Who have you seen?"

"No one."

"*Who have you seen?*"

"Your temper hasn't changed one bit, has it?"

"Who!!"

"I swear to you — no one. I merely heard that she was dying of cancer. I just — heard it. That's all. Really, George. You're so possessive."

"God damn you! You come back to me after sixteen years just to tell me my wife is dying."

"I haven't come back to you, George."

"You've come back. . . ."

"Yes. But not to you."

"I love you, Titty."

"Don't call me Titty. You love everyone."

"Love everyone. That's nonsense."

"Shall I read the list?"

"List? List? What list?"

"This list. . . ." Rattlings of paper are heard. "Corrine, Eudora, Belle, Marie, Norma. . ."

"Oh, for God's sake."

"And Peggy. You love everyone."

"Lonely old man. . ."

"What?"

"I say, I'm just a lonely old man."

"Where are your children?"

"What damn children?"

"Ruth and Adolphus. 'What damn children,' indeed. Don't you ever see them? Talk to them? Write to them?"

"Hah! What about *your* children?"

The bed froze.

"I don't have any children. You know that."

"Fairy tales!"

"How may a Virgin have children, George?"

Silence.

"How, George? Answer me, how?"

"I know your secret, Letitia. I know the lie. Don't forget, I was there the day it began. In the garden. . ."

"There? Where? What garden?"

"At Falconridge."

The gun went off. The ceiling shook. George climbed over the back of his chair.

"Sit down, George."

George sat down.

A little smoke made its way through the bed curtains and curled up through some peonies toward the ornately plastered ceiling. George watched it die.

"I understand that Ruth has come back from Germany," said Letitia.

"I — I — I. . ."

"Have you seen her?"

"I — I. . ."

"How is Dolly?"

"I. . ."

"George?"

"Oh."

"It's all right, Maureen. Go away."

"Yes'm."

"Help yourself to sherry, George."

"My God. I. . ."

"Go on. Help yourself to sherry. Have you got a heart condition? I didn't know that. What's the matter? By God, George, if you die here, I'll. . ."

"Oh. Oh. Oh, my God. You shot at me."

"Come on. Pull yourself together. That's right. Here." A hand appeared through the curtain, holding out an emptied sherry glass — silk and rings and red-lacquered nails. "I'll have some, too."

"My dear, I. . ."

"Sit down, George. Sit down. Relax. Drink your sherry."

The figure in the chair was ludicrous. Its crumpled blue suit with the ash on the lapels — its dusty black shoes — its frayed collar and its twice-turned cuffs — its badly tied cravat and its lustreless stick-pin were all the signs and symbols of a fallen Titan. But the man inside the clothes behaved as if there had been no fall; as if, like Cooper Carter, he still trailed clouds of lackeys to do his bidding and bank accounts to pay them with. He behaved as if a Rolls-Royce waited at the door and a dozen appointments were being ignored as he railed at Letitia. He behaved, in short, as if he was still the same George Damarosch who once had a right to enter this room unannounced — who could come here just because he wanted to: because he *was* George Damarosch. But now, as he began to speak again, it was the new George who spoke: the one in the crumpled suit and the dusty shoes.

"I have loved you since I first set eyes on those hands, Titty. How well — how easily I remember. That hand that lifted back your hair on a summer's day. You were the Little Virgin then, in earnest. How we all loved you, Titty. Every one of us. The whole of America sat at your feet, those lovely little Virginal feet. That day at Falconridge, and you, dressed in blue — always in blue — dancing across the lawn with Bully. Damn! Damn Bully Moxon! Laughing. Laughing. Oh — such laughter. You were every dream I ever dreamed come true."

"Yes. I remember. It was so."

"Carving your name on the steps..."

"One down from Wally Reid, one up from Marie Dressler."

"Not a fitting place, between those two, but how was I to know? Oh, Titty, how was I to know? Nobody knew how great and powerful you would become."

"George?"

"Yes?"

"The Little Virgin needs your help."

"Anything. Anything."

"I need a million dollars."

George dropped his sherry glass on the floor. It was empty.

"I haven't got a million dollars," he said. "I haven't got any. You know that. I'm broke — forgotten."

"Will you get it for me?"

"No."

"Then, good-bye."

"Good-bye? You're mad."

"Good-bye, George."

"No!"

"Yes. Good-bye."

George went to the center of the room. The window behind him, cruel, showed his roundness and the shortness of his stature.

"May I have — one — last look?"

"No, George. No more looking."

"Oh, please. Just one. . .last look, Letitia."

"No."

"Your hand. Not even your hand? Your foot?"

"Good-bye."

George went to the door. "Why do you want a million dollars, Titty?"

There was a pause. She would dissemble, just a little.

He didn't know it, but she smiled.

"To save America, George," she said. "That is my mission."

To save America?

"I hope you get it, then."

"I will."

"Yes. I suppose you will, being you."

"So?"

"Good-bye, Little Bitch."

"Good-bye, George."

He was gone. The door clicked.

From the bed, a sigh. Longer than before. Quite final.

The Little Virgin's appointments were over.

The Chronicle of the First Butterfly

August 8th to September 16th, 1938: Western North America

The journey covered a distance of roughly fifteen hundred miles. It began on an island off the coast of British Columbia and ended just south of Santa Monica, California.

The traveler was a butterfly — a monarch (*Danaûs plexippus*), a male. It had spent the past few months on the edges of a pine forest near a quiet inlet on the southeast coast of its island. The prevailing winds blew from the northwest.

On the eighth day of August, a Monday, it was sufficiently cool (sixty-five degrees Fahrenheit) and there was enough of the scent of flowers lying to the south to prompt the butterfly to commence its journey.

Part of this journey would be over water, but the monarch would avoid this whenever possible.

For a week it moved steadily southward, roosting between twilight and dawn — more because of the cooling air than the darkness. Its roosting sites were near water if possible, and the trees it chose were maples and pines. Occasionally it found a willow tree, but these were rare.

It fed on its way from the abundant fields of nectar-filled flowers that were scattered in its path. Prize feasts were provided by late-blooming milkweed. It had first spread its wings earlier that summer on the leaf of a milkweed plant.

This butterfly was a lonely traveler. It journeyed without companions. Others would follow after (some had gone before it) and perhaps it sensed this. Every night, having selected its sleeping place, it would spread its wings out wide as a signal that it was there. Clutching a leaf with sickle-shaped claws, it would wait in this display until darkness fell and the dropping temperature prompted it to fold its wings again. But it remained alone.

From time to time the butterfly encountered cities and towers in its flight. Whenever this happened it rose to a great height above them, riding the gentle breezes and allowing itself to be taken by them on its way.

On five occasions there was rain. Once there was thunder and lightning and the wind rose to such a great force that it seemed the butterfly would be torn apart. During the rain squalls it clambered far away from the piercing drops into crevices on the faces of rocks. But when this wind rose and the rain was driven from the sky like so many pellets of lead, and when there seemed to be darkness everywhere and the temperature dropped and it could barely move across the ground because of the cold, it seemed that the butterfly must perish.

At last it found a leaf-thatched burrow at the foot of a giant fir tree and it waited. It became numb. Its muscles would not respond. But it could see, and it lay inertly watching a mouse, itself searching for a hiding place. The mouse approached, nosing its way nearer and nearer, creeping noisily through weeds and grass. The mouse's eyes were very large and its whiskers were long.

Perhaps the fact of the terrible rain saved the butterfly; the mouse seemed more concerned with shelter than with food. It rested only inches from the butterfly's hiding place and apparently did not even catch its scent.

There was rain all night, and by 4:00 a.m. the temperature had dropped to thirty-eight degrees Fahrenheit on the ground. The butterfuly was immobilized. It lost awareness.

At 5:35 a.m. there was light.

At 6:00 the sun appeared. At 7:00 it broke through the trees and the air began to steam. By 8:00 it was warm. By 9:00, hot.

The butterfly responded.

It crept from its place beneath the leaves.

The mouse was gone. But there were other enemies, equally dangerous. On the ground, unable to fly, the butterfly was totally defenseless against such creatures as common ants, ground beetles, moles, and shrews. It must find the sun. It must spread and dry its wings. Flight was imperative.

At last it achieved a measure of safety on the static fronds of a fern. It lay there, groggy and hardly alive, until 11:30 a.m., when the sun struck straight down through the trees and found it.

Testing its wings, the butterfly discovered by trial and error that the rain had done some damage: a few of its scales were missing; there was a shredded irregular serration at the outer rim of its left front wing. But it could fly.

Now there were the mountains.

The butterfly selected southward-leading valleys and surmounted in dazzling arcs of flight the lower and lesser peaks. It rose on September 9th to a height of eleven thousand two hundred and fifty-one feet.

It encountered little of importance. A bird attacked it, but the bird was blind in one eye and soon gave up its attempts. (This occurred during flight.) One day, the monarch passed over such a highly populated area it found no food and midday on the 13th of September, having achieved a distance approximately one hundred and eighty-two miles north of the city of Los Angeles, it was blown out to sea.

This proved, however, somewhat providential, for the butterfly discovered, low over the water, a sea-breeze of twenty miles per hour. Riding this with easy grace, it soon found itself over land again, at a point much farther south than would have been achieved on the previous course. It traveled farther that day than on any other.

On the night of the 13th, somewhat exhausted by this excursion, it rested longer than was normal. Now the butterfly was in the area of a town called Pacific Grove, and in midmorning of the 14th, one Edwina Shackleton, a zealous amateur biologist and professional spinster, discovered it on the leaf of a milkweed plant in her garden.

Miss Shackleton ran up to the screen door of her house.

Inside, lying on a day bed and listening to the radio, Edwina's mother, Mrs. C. Clarke Shackleton, heard her daughter's urgent footsteps and turned down the volume of "Pepper Young's Family."

"Mother! Mother!" Edwina called. "You'll never believe what's happened!!"

"What is it, dear? What is it?" cried Mrs. Shackleton, torn between the adventures of Pepper Young and those of her daughter.

"They're here! They're here!" Edwina cried.

"Who's here?" said Mrs. Shackleton. "Calm down, Edwina. Is it the Japanese?"

"No, no, Mother," said Edwina, huffing and puffing and already lifting her mother from her pillows. "The monarchs! The monarchs!"

"Oh," said Mrs. Shackleton.

She went through this every year.

"Come and look," said Edwina. "He really is lovely. He's large. He must have come a long, long way, Mama. There's a hole in his wing. But he's beautiful."

Mrs. Shackleton, a self-proclaimed invalid (asthma and diabetes, a heart condition and stones), wobbled to her feet and shook her head.

"Are you going to kill it?" she said.

"Oh, no, Mama. No. You know they're always being killed around here. I hate it."

"Kill 'em all," said Mrs. Shackleton. "They give me hay fever."

"Now, Mother. You know that's a lie. Come and see him, please. It's the very first one. An occasion."

Mrs. Shackleton grumbled and swayed. "Then I don't have to look at any more?" she said.

"No, Mama. No. Just this one. The first."

"All right, then. Very well."

They got down into the garden. They approached Edwina's cultivated milkweed plot. (She grew these plants especially for the arrival of the butterflies every year.)

"He's so big, Mama. You won't believe him."

"Where is he?" said Mrs. Shackleton.

"Oh, dear," said Edwina. "He's gone."

"Maybe someone else will kill him," said her mother, wheezing dramatically and shedding nose tears. "He's left wing dust everywhere."

"Oh, Mama. Butterflies don't have wing dust. That's scales."

"And I've missed the end of 'Pepper Young's Family,'" said Mrs. Shackleton, making her way alone toward the house. She banged the door and turned up the volume of the radio until it was deafening.

Edwina stared off into the sky.

"Good-bye," she said. "*Vaya con Dios.*"

She stood quite still for a long time, with her hand up to her forehead. Then she went back to the cultivation of the milkweed.

On the afternoon of the 15th of September the butterfly was flying southward twenty-three miles northeast of Los Angeles. In the distance there rose a mighty pillar of smoke.

The butterfly broke to the west, seaward, driven away by the smell of fire.

At dusk it made for land.

On the 16th of September, noon, it reached its destination — a grove of pine trees south of Santa Monica, where the other butterflies would soon begin to join it by ones, twos, and finally by hundreds in the following days and weeks.

For the time being it rested alone.

Et in Arcadia ego.

With everyone.

The Chronicle of the Nightmare

It is always night.
I am always alone.
And so are they.

They.
They live in their own world.
It is not like any other world. No other world is real. They knew once another world but that has been forgotten. They think they remember. But it's forgotten. They remember that it was joyful and it wasn't. They remember that there were feast days and there weren't. They remember babies and there were no babies; children and there were none; mothers and fathers and there were only men and women. They remember houses and there were only hiding places; street greetings but no one spoke. Carelessness but there was always care; freedom to come and go but where you came from you hurried back to and that was the only place to go. They thought of words but the words were silence. And they thought of the One Who would come Who never came. It was the Others who came. Always the Others.
They dreamed in long rows. Lined up dreaming.
I saw them.
The world was lovely if you closed your eyes.

And there was always a band playing somewhere.

The sun shone.

The flags were up.

The streets rang in chorus.

There were geraniums on the balconies.

People wore their hearts on their sleeves. Stars and crosses. One or the other.

This was the world to belong to. The one they had never lived in, but thought they had.

This was the world they wanted to remember. It belongs to someone else. It always did.

The Nightmare is always present and timeless. It is formless. I have gathered it all the while I've been away.

America is not the Nightmare. It will be.

The Nightmare is Europe. I went there in 1936. I can tell you that all parts and portions of this Nightmare belong, fit or can be wrenched away from the period between 1936 and 1938. That is, between going and coming back; then and now. Today it is sometime in August or September. I honestly don't remember. August or September 1938. I know that I came home the other day and it was August and a dear old friend of mine whose shoes I remember and whose eyes are close to my heart threw himself down on the cinders under the very train I rode in. I was arriving and he died. It was voluntary, or so I understand. His death is important to everyone. It holds the beginnings of a new Nightmare.

This is how a new Nightmare begins. With an act. Sometimes an act of absolution. Sometimes an act of atonement. The act will inevitably involve your integrity. You will believe in what you are saying and doing and perhaps you will even have bothered to make a chart of consequences, all of them hypothetical by necessity, but all of them bound up in the parings of intellect. Lovely long sweet parings. You throw them away. You are left alone with the washed body, skinned and peeled and pure, and this is the act. Inside the body, however skinned and peeled, however washed, however scoured and pure, there are seeds. These are the seeds of everything and there are worms.

It is the worms I think of.

It is the worms.

He threw himself under the train. His lovely feet were severed and broken. I have arrived on many trains. I have never been aware of these deaths, although now I see them very clearly. Someone throws part of himself under every train, coming or going. I've just never been aware of it before.

I am never going to know why Bully killed himself. But I am certain that somewhere in someone he has started a Nightmare and perhaps I will know the consequences of that. Perhaps that Nightmare will touch me. But this is not important. What I am thinking is: just as with Bully, every Nightmare begins with integrity and action. They do not all end in death. Think of Bully's feet and what he did with them, for himself, for us. Think of Bully's feet. They led and were led. They were both guides and followers. Dancer and walker. Think of Bully's feet. In shoes they tell a story. Naked? No one ever saw them naked. They were silent. Think of Bully's feet.

Think of the dreamers.

Dreaming in long rows.

I saw them first in midsummer 1936.

I was in a taxicab and Bruno was holding my hand and we had got off the boat in Southampton and I wanted him to ask me to marry him. We were going to the hotel. As I was sitting there with my thigh against his thigh and my hand in his hand I looked out the window, waiting, thinking, He will ask me now, we will register at the hotel as man and wife and tomorrow he will marry me. We were still near the sheds. And out of one of these sheds, having come through customs, having got off a boat from France, having traveled on trains from Switzerland and Italy, having left Munich and Hamburg, Bonn and Dresden, Stuttgart and Mannheim, having left Vienna (only the very wise left Vienna in 1936), there they were in England walking in a line, the queue that had become second nature, the row they dreamed in, standing still or moving, there they were in England on their way wherever next they would be told to go and the taxicab stopped for them and they walked across in front of us, me watching, Bruno not watching and there were forty of them. Forty or fifty.

This was the first row I saw and the first time I saw that all the faces were the same so that the next time I saw them in a row I knew already that all the faces would be the same and much later when the rows fell down, disintegrated, and became uneven, and later still when I began to see rows of one, the faces were still the same and the dream had not changed but had intensified, become desperate, was held to with fists, like the fist I had to break open to find its star, and I was seeing, sitting in the taxicab, waiting to be asked "Will you marry me?" when I saw this first row of dreamers and I knew that it was the first of something but not the first of a Nightmare.

I don't know why but it seems to me a dream may be more dangerous than a Nightmare. In a Nightmare you are pursued upright. In dreams you are helpless and float. However you die only in Nightmares. In dreams you live forever. And that is marvelous and horrible.

Bruno did not ask me to marry him then. We went to the hotel and he still didn't ask me. We did, however, share a room. I thought about the row of dreamers.

"Who are they?" I asked Bruno.

Bruno had kinder eyes then. You could see all the way into them. They were brown. American brown. He wanted blue-eyed children. He didn't know that then. He wanted to be German and he didn't know that either. But he did know that a brown-eyed man isn't likely to have a blue-eyed child. He knew about genetics.

"Who?" he said, unpacking.

"Those people who walked in front of our cab."

"What people?" Shirts and socks; dirty and clean.

"All those people, Bruno. At the harbor. Coming out of the sheds. They carried bundles of children; they were all very tired and they seemed to be going somewhere together."

"They were probably people on some sort of excursion, Ruth. Put out that cigarette."

"Didn't you see them, Bruno?"

"No. I didn't see them. Stand with your back to the wall."

"They were sad."

"Throw your arms out."

"And yet they were happy."

"Swim."

"One-and-two-and-one-and-two. . ."

"Make your behind flatter. Keep it against the wall."

"What sort of excursions?"

"Ruth, I don't know. Swim."

"I hate this. It makes me ache in the ankles."

"Relax them. Keep your ankles loose."

"Am I going to win, Bruno? Do you really think I'm going to win?"

He hit me. He was my trainer.

That was his answer. He did not speak.

"Bruno."

"What?"

"They had no leader. There was no one leading them."

"Then they were lost. That's all."

"They knew where they were going."

"Then you stop worrying about them, can't you?"

"Yes."

No.
"Swim."

We crossed over into France. We were not with the team. The team would meet us there.

We went to Paris. I was sure that in Paris Bruno would ask me to marry him. We stayed in a hotel. Again we shared a room and Bruno would sit on the bed in his American trainer's uniform: sweat shirt, sweat socks, and blue jeans, and I'd put my back against the wall and swim.

Sometimes I would lie on the bed or between two chairs and swim and Bruno would stand against the wall. His ankles did not hurt.

In the evenings we would go to the cafés and I was allowed to drink a little wine. Bruno drank beer and he was always going off to the bathroom.

I had a hat I loved that summer, a large hat. The brim turned down over one side of my face and it made my profile show to good advantage. I have large eyes and a long nose and what Bruno used to call a Russian mouth — "strong and wide." My lower lip has a pleasing shape. I like to touch it with my finger. This hat was also lovely because I wore my hair in the Russian manner with a big braid and when I wore this hat, which was nearly every day, I wound the braid into a flat plait above my ear and a number of people remarked that I surely must be a famous ballerina with my hair like that on one side and the hat pulled down on the other, and because of my long figure and long legs. I remember my dresses all had cowls to show off my shoulders and back. I have those dresses still. I never wear them.

We sat in cafés. We were waiting in Paris for the others to arrive from America. Then we would all go to Germany together, where we would finish our training in the weeks prior to the opening of the Games.

We sat in cafés. I waited for Bruno to propose. He did not propose.

One night it was really late in the evening and there was still a little daylight we were sitting on the sidewalk in what had become our favorite café and Bruno had drunk too much, much too much beer and had to excuse himself endlessly.

I sat alone at the table, waiting. A number of people thought I was a ballerina and said so. Eyes looked at me and people smiled, and I smiled back. I enjoyed it. I knew how to behave inside the fame they gave me because I grew up with famous people and had been stared at all my life as though *I* was someone. All I really was was Naomi Nola's daughter. Daughter of George Damarosch. Wally Taylor was my godfather. As a swimmer I was famous, but not in Europe. I didn't swim the Channel (I swam Catalina instead), so I wasn't like Alice, who did, or my teammate Katherine, whom everyone adored because she was so much like a movie star. No. I was just me and they thought I was someone else. This had a consequence. I was approached.

It was twilight, an hour of great significance for it is the one hour of the day when the shadows play the most earnest games with your appearance. There is no comparable hour in the morning. It only happens just before the sun sets. It is also the hour when certain people make their first appearance abroad in the streets. People who pretend to be someone else by daylight. I am not speaking here of criminals and prostitutes. But of a class of people who might be called martyrs. The early Christians must have enjoyed this hour of the day. Fugitives unjustly accused come out at this hour. Real fugitives (the justly accused) have no desire to join the human race, and no desire to do ordinary things, so they stay away until it's dark, lying in rooms reading magazines and listening to radios. But these people I speak of go about in the daylight not speaking and not looking like themselves and when the evening comes they have a moment's respite and they drop their masks.

The man who approached me wore a hat. Or rather he carried a hat. He also carried a walking stick. His clothes were stylish and well cut, a simple blazer and flannel trousers. He had a clubfoot, and consequently wore laced boots, one of which had an outsize heel. The hat was a snap-brim straw. White. Like one of Dolly's. In some ways he was rather like Dolly — that height, and the same slimness. But his knees weren't knocked. Poor Dolly! How I love the way he walks.

This man stood just at the entrance to the café, where the tables separated and the tile proclaimed its inlaid name. He was just beyond the awning so that some of the twilight fell on him and although he was facing me I could not tell exactly what his features were like. Then he half-turned and his profile showed a clear impression of a nose that was positively Arabic, cheekbones very high and sloped. His chin receded at one end of his face and his hair at the other. The effect was Egyptian, like the mummified face of Tut.

He tried to appear to be waiting for an acquaintance. I have often done this myself so I know the feeling. I recognized it. If you are the least unusual to look at (my height, his profile) it is best to look concentrated when alone in public. This diverts people's attention and when they stare at you their rudeness is not so rigorous. I hid behind my ballerina pose and he behind the absence of his "friend."

Gradually he insinuated himself beyond the entrance, right in among the tables that sat close to the pedestrians on the sidewalk, but close, too, to the patrons and their conversations. He was listening. In the course of his listening it was apparent that he heard two or three people speaking of me, for his glance advanced in my direction, at first haltingly and then with attack. I noticed that at some of the tables he was recognized and turned away from. This made me feel guarded. I did not like being stared at by someone other people evidently did not wish to associate with.

Slowly he brought his body into action and he followed the line of his gaze to my table. Bruno had left his hat on his chair and I tried to lift it up onto the table to show him that I had an escort, but I dropped it clumsily, and throughout our interview it sat there underneath the chair near my feet.

"Madame," he said.

I nodded.

"*Permettez-moi de vous présenter...*"

"I'm American," I said. "I speak English."

I also speak French, but I could not bear the thought of having a conversation in a foreign language with a man whose motives I already suspected. His manners, however, were impeccable. He had addressed me as "madame." He had also allowed me the compliment of a small and tasteful bow. No flamboyance. No coyness. He was European to his fingernails.

"Then may I introduce myself? I am Jakob Seuss."

"How do you do, Mr. Seuss."

I didn't know whether to maintain my own pose in the face of his, or to give in and be myself. I wanted Bruno to come back. I was suddenly uncomfortable. Something was going to happen.

"Permit me to sit down," said Mr. Seuss.

He did so. I could not prevent this.

I waited.

He stared off over the heads of the others as though waiting for me to take him in. I watched him carefully. He was very quiet. His voice, when he spoke, was wet with sibilance. This was because he wore cheap teeth. His hands rested, one on top of the other, on his cane. He seemed tired and sad. He swung his head around and looked at me. I recognized the look at once. He was one of them, out of his row and wandering alone.

I knew then that I should learn something of the mystery of my dreamers and I began to like him. I didn't know what he was going to say, but from the weariness of his approach, from the expression in his eyes, and from the breath he took before he began, I knew that he had delivered his speech a hundred times before he delivered it to me. I knew that he had spoken it in French, Italian, German, and Dutch. Now he must speak it in English.

"Madame," he began, "I will not waste your time and interest with preamble."

He laid his hat at the edge of the table, where Bruno's should have been. He sighed. I knew that he was translating his message into my language and I waited. I looked at the others. Some of them were looking at me curiously and one or two frowned and a very large woman wearing a toque with a silver tassel shook her head with vehement reproach. She mouthed something in German which I did not understand, but I understood enough of her facial vocabulary to know that she was warning me against him. I turned back to Mr. Seuss, more intrigued than before.

"You are, madame, I understand, a famous ballerina," he said. I said nothing. I let him believe it. I needed something to hide behind in the event that the interview became unpleasant. "And thus it is that I bring my appeal to you," he continued. "I do not bring it to everyone. I am not in the habit of stopping people in the street with my hat. I cannot hope that everyone will help me. No. I must depend on people like you. Persons of quality. . ." And here he paused. His Egyptianesque eyes slid their glance down to his hands, resting on his cane. ". . . Persons of wealth."

I was stunned. He was asking me for money. A common beggar. I could not believe my ears.

"Do not," he said, "misunderstand me. I am not a common beggar." (A mind reader to boot!) "My request is for a special assistance, and only the wealthy can give it. I need," he said, "the help of someone who believes."

I stared. His knuckles turned white. He began to enunciate each word meticulously. He seemed to be holding his voice in check. The words emanated from him in wrenchings and withheld shouts, but the tone of his voice was low and it remained sibilant like menacing steam. Listening to him, I became agitated, disturbed. . . afraid, and then appalled. He went on.

"You are an American ballerina. You are *persona grata. Someone.*"

Each time he said this word it took on new and stronger meanings.

"I need the assistance of Someone like yourself. I have come a great distance. I have come — alone. I am not married, madame. I have no wife. I have, alas, but praise God, no children. I have. . . " He paused, "all I have is my father and my mother. And all they have is me. I have my father and I have my mother." He paused again. He removed his handkerchief from his pocket and wiped the backs of his hands, one by one. "I have come a great distance but not from far away. The road to Paris is short. My road is long. I have come alone." He looked right into my eyes. I was riveted. He looked away and put his handkerchief back in his pocket, replacing his dried hands carefully, one on top of the other, on the head of his cane.

"I have come alone," he repeated. "Do you understand me?"

I did not understand.

"Only I was able to come because there was foreign capital of only four thousand Swiss francs. That is one thousand American dollars. Three of us could not come. It was decided to be me. My father and my mother. . ." Pause. "I have been now in Switzerland a year. So I have come to Paris. I have been now in Paris one month, two weeks, and one day. I am living in the men's lavatory of the Gare du Nord. I have my suitcase there. I eat with the pigeons in the park, there at Saint-Germain-des-Prés. Do you see it there across the road?" I nodded. Yes. "I have tried. But I am not able to make a living. I am, alas, able only to be alive. It is my foot. People are superstitious of a foot."

I tried not to look at it, stretched before him where he sat. But I saw it and it was badly twisted and the false heel was much taller and more sloped than it had appeared to be when he approached. People are afraid of deformity. I am afraid.

"Do you know what I am saying?"

I did not know.

"Lives can be bought and sold," he said, "but life is not cheap. I had to come alone. I have been paid for. Four thousand Swiss francs."

I began to understand. To fathom it. To guess.

"I have still my father and I have still my mother. Eight thousand Swiss francs."

I understood.

"I shall not bore you to tell you that I have been to the banks. That I have been to Swiss industrialists and to French auto makers. That I have been to the Baroness de Friedlander, a great lady and a great philanthropist, to Emmanuel Koch, the artist, to the Duc de Chartres, the Duchess of Trent, Mr. and Mrs. Arnold Vandergelder of New York City, to Prince Lopakhim of the Imperial Family. That I have been to moneylenders, wealthy prostitutes, and criminals. I shall not bother to say that I have been to the Bishop of Provence and to Rabbi Guszt. Others had been before me; others were early; others will come after; others will be late. But my father and my mother. . . *my* father and *my* mother! . . ."

He could go no further. The message pushed at him urgently. He spoke it loudly and with defiance.

"Give me two thousand American dollars!"

"Mr. Seuss, I cannot. I am not a ballerina. I have no money."

Mr. Seuss gave me a look that I shall never forget. I had wasted him. Wasted his precious story, his fears, and his apprehension. Wasted his short supply of time. He hated me.

He rose.

"Oh, Mr. Seuss. Please," I said. "I would help you if I could."

"Your watch," he said. "Your watch and your rings."

"Take them," I said. "Take them, please."

"They are worthless," he said, regaining his composure. "They want foreign capital. They want it for munitions and guns. They will pay in good people. They want it so badly."

"Who wants it?" I said.

He looked at me with scorn.

"Who wants it?" he said. He stared around the café at the other patrons and then back at me. His look by now was kinder.

"Who are you?" he asked.

I did not see the relevance of this. I did not answer.

"Well, you have certainly come from America," he said, and I did not like the tone of his voice now. It was disrespectful and full of irony. "You do not know who you are. You do not look around you."

He took a step away. I was afraid. I thought he was going to denounce me in some way simply because I was an American. But then he lowered his voice.

He said, "I will give you something."

He reached into his pocket.

"I will not need it any more," he said. "I will give it to you. Free."

He fished around, unable to find what he wanted. Then he found it and kept it folded in his fist.

"You may look at it," he said, "but do not show it. Do not wear it. In Germany it is worth one thousand American dollars. Here, it is worthless. But keep it. Keep it. It will remind you of where you are and of what you do not know. Take it and do not look at it until I have gone."

He placed something softly pointed in my hand and closed my fingers over it.

"Forgive me my anger, Madame Ballerina," he said. He genuinely tried to smile but failed and he saw that I had noted this failure.

"I cannot smile," he said. "My teeth were made of gold and I have sold them."

I closed my eyes. His anguish closed them. When I opened them he had gone.

I waited until no one was watching and then I unfolded my fingers to look at his gift.

Many things have been placed in my hands. Surprises, medals, money (worms when I was a child and Dolly teased me). I have held a multitude of gifts. But never one like this.

It was a yellow star.

Made of felt.

I wanted Bruno to marry me. I had wanted it since the day I first saw him at the beach. But he wouldn't ask me. It seemed to take forever for it to occur to him. His mind was elsewhere, on other things. Riding trains and motorcars, in cafés and restaurants, in the water and out of it, by night and by day, I watched his contemplation but could not discover its subject.

"What are you thinking about?" I asked. I asked it a million times and a million times he turned his gaze on me, lost, and moved his lips and didn't speak. He read books and newspapers I did not read and corresponded with people I did not know.

I held his hand; I stroked his thighs. I laid my hands in his pockets to get as near to him as possible. I let my head fall to his shoulder whenever I could, and after training, while he lectured me in the privacy of cubicles, I would put my cheek against his square, barreled chest (he was no swimmer himself) and I would listen to his insides churning over the thoughts he was really having. Irregular heart beats and stomach rumblings; disturbances deep inside him but none of them voiced. There were no words.

I worked very hard for him. I wanted to be what he wanted. I wanted every muscle to be obedient to his will, not my own. When he did the counting my body became his machine, beyond my control. I don't know where the stamina and the rhythm came from. They didn't come from me. Perhaps from inside him. I was his instrument. I wanted to be. I wanted to obey. I wanted to be obedient. I wanted to function without thought, to respond to his voice like a dog.

I would watch his face.

Bruno was a small, hard man. His legs were like squares, a series of cubes, and they could support the whole world if they had to. All of him seemed squared off and cubed. He was not a round man. His teeth were square. His hands were square. His mouth was square and his nose was square. Every muscle had four sides. Square.

I would watch his face.

Bruno's parents were dead. He had wanted an education but there was no one to provide him with clothes and food, let alone schooling. So he taught himself. He read a lot. He had forceful, book-inspired ideas. Some of it was science. A lot of it had to do with some sort of biochemistry — food and things which Bruno translated into certain phases of my training. He was inclined to theories.

I would watch his face.

The cubes of his eyes would float on the secret inside of him. Possibly it was something he had read in the paper, in a book, in one of his letters. He seemed to be looking at something, definitely watching something, but when I turned to look, to see what it was (it always seemed to be very close, on my shoulder, or just beyond it), there would be nothing, and I would turn quickly back to see if it was gone from his face but it wouldn't be. It would still be there.

I was his object. But I did not know that then.

One day he said to me, "Take off your hat, Ruth."

So I took off my hat.

We were riding on the train, going at last to Berlin. As Bruno himself had said, "We're on our way."

"How long is your braid?" he asked.

"I don't know."

I didn't know. I knew that it reached the middle of my back, but this was a measurement I never thought of.

"Cut it off."

I stared at him.

I waited for him to smile.

He did not smile.

We were seated in a compartment with two sleeping members of our team. Boys. I looked at them, hoping they would not wake up. I was embarrassed for Bruno's sake, not my own. He was making a small fool of himself.

"Cut it off."

I put my hat back on protectively. "Don't be ridiculous, Bruno. It's my hair. I can't cut it off."

"I want you to cut it off."

I looked at him. He was serious. Dangerously serious.

"I have nothing to cut it off with," I said, hoping that

would be the end of it.

But, "Get down my bag," he said.

I stood up and got down his bag. Remember, I was dutiful.

For a moment he sat with it resting on his lap. Then he took out his key chain and opened the bag.

I put my hands on my head.

"Why do you want my hair?" I asked him while he was fishing in the bag.

"Never mind," he said. "Cut it off."

He handed me his razor. It was just like one of Father's. It had a bone handle.

"Open it."

"But why, Bruno? Why?"

I didn't want to cut my hair. I liked my hair. It was one of the few feminine things I had left, aside from my clothes.

He shouted. It was not in English.

The boys woke up. The shouting woke them.

Bruno grabbed at the razor. He seized and opened it. One of the boys gave a gasp.

And Bruno said, "You talk too much. You ask too many questions," and I said, "Bruno! Bruno! Please don't do this. What are you doing this for?"

The boys shrank back into their corners pretending they were not awake. And Bruno crossed over and threw my beautiful hat on the floor and the razor glinted and threatened and I said, "Bruno, please!" and he placed one of his knees on the seat beside me and his other foot on my hat on the floor and he held me by the braid with one hand and with the other he drew the razor through the braid at the nape of my neck, like an executioner, and I laid my head protectively down onto my knees with my hands on it and I thought, He's crazy, he's crazy. Why is he suddenly crazy? Something had possessed him. And the two boys lay in their corners silently, certain they were watching a murder, and then Bruno held my braid up and he waved it over his head and threw it down and took my face in both his square hands and turned it this way and that way until I was sure he was trying to break my neck and he looked at me and looked at me and looked and finally he let me go and sat back in his corner like an animal, exhausted, and he said, "I will sleep now," and he did.

When he awoke he asked me to marry him. In Berlin.

I said, "Yes."

And I was afraid.

I wore a white dress. I carried lilies of the valley. They did not play Mendelssohn. It was not allowed. I had to glue the veiling to my head. There was not enough hair to attach it with pins.

There were men at the wedding, men I had never seen before. New friends of Bruno's, I assumed. We were not introduced. But they clustered around him and they looked at me like inspectors.

Mr. Seuss's star was in my handbag.

Something old.

"Stand against the wall."

"Yes, Bruno."

"Stand still."

"Yes, Bruno."

"Put your arms out."

"Yes, Bruno."

"Svim."

"I beg your pardon."

"Svim."

"You said 'svim.' What's wrong with 'swim'?"

"Nothing is wrong mit it. Svim."

"Yes, Bruno."

"One."

"*Count!*"

"And-one-and..."

"COUNT!"

". . . and-two-and. . ."

"Now."

"Yes, Bruno."

"Count."

". . . And. . ."

"Listen to me. Go on counting. And listen. I am going to shave your head."

"One-and-two-and-one-and-two. . ."

"I am going to have your head altogether bald and I am going to. . . Count, God damn you. . . . I am going to buy you some new clothes."

"And-one-and-two-and-one-and-two."

"I have plans for you."

"Yes, Bruno."

"Count."

"And-two-and. . ."

"We have come a long distance. Traveled a long way."

"One."

"And we are here, now."

"Yes, Bruno."

"Count."

I began not to sleep at nights.

The fact that Bruno had used Mr. Seuss's words frightened me. "We have come a long distance. Traveled a long way." But the journey was in reverse. It was wrong, somehow. I did not understand, but I felt, This is wrong.

I tried to read the books that were at hand, literature locked in Bruno's bureau drawers. I broke the locks, but the books were unfathomable. Biochemistry meant nothing to me. Nor did *The Theory of Races*. Nor did *The Birthplace of Power*. I had the locks fixed and did not break them again.

I ceased to visit the places of interest. The streets were alien. I felt afraid.

My swimming improved.

The clothes that Bruno bought for me were uniforms — white shirtwaists, green shirts, brown dresses with buttons down the side, long-sleeved, without style and harsh to the touch. I was told to wear them for all occasions.

Bruno spent many days away. I was left alone. I worked out with the team and traveled in darkened cars. I gathered I was some sort of secret. Sometimes I worked at night in the pool, alone, with Bruno screaming at me to *svim*, and I felt as though I never saw anyone else, even when the others were there.

But my swimming improved. Not so much my style but my stamina. My control.

I was bald. This, too, was some kind of beginning.

I was given a wig for appearances in public. In order that I might not wander too far away, Bruno kept this wig hidden from me in a secret place. It would appear mysteriously when duty demanded that I be presented to any official. I had to give it back when the presentation was over and we were home.

I received a telephone call. I don't remember when this was. It came from a mysterious Countess von Buëll. She begged me to meet her at a certain hour for luncheon. I was to stand outside my billet at 11:30 and wait, holding a yellow rosebud in my hand. A car driven by a chauffeur would come and pick me up. I was not to be alarmed by the driver's silence.

I did as I was told. Perhaps this was part of the pattern laid down by Bruno. I had wanted so much to be obedient; now obedience had become a habit — something automatic.

I looked forward to being out of doors.

Fear or no fear, I longed to see the sky.

The Countess had instructed me to come alone. I was not to inform my husband of this assignation. Naturally, I did not want to do anything behind Bruno's back — but there was always the possibility that he might be responsible for this approach. Besides, the Countess's voice was vaguely familiar and my instinct said obey her and I did.

I wore an ingenious combination of interwoven chiffon to cover my baldness. I chose one of my own dresses.

At 11:30 I stood outside our billet on the sidewalk. The sun shone. The street was fairly empty. I carried my rosebud which had arrived anonymously by messenger. I had taken a liking to Mr. Seuss's star and so I had that as well in my handbag. It made me feel comfortable and it reminded me, as he had said it would, of where I was. I was on a comfortable residential street glittering with crystal air. And there were trees. The fear receded, held at bay by sky and sunshine.

We had been billeted with Herr Doktor and Frau Doktor Mittelstadt, a pleasant middle-class couple in their fifties. Their son was a lovely, quiet boy in a black uniform. Sigmund.

Frau Doktor Mittelstadt had placed geraniums on her balcony and window ledges. Everyone had. It was decreed. They were in bloom. No pinks and no whites. Just red. They were splendid.

The sun shone.

The trees were jungle-green and lush.

It was absolutely lovely.

Countess von Buëll.

I knew her voice.

Frau Doktor Mittelstadt came out on her balcony and waved at me and watered her geraniums. I hoped that she was discreet. Bruno held conversational evenings with her and the Doktor. They discussed the new philosophy.

This reminded me to look for my identification card. We had been told never to be without it. I looked in my purse. There it was. It had the Olympic insignia on it, my name, and my nationality: American. This gave me, I remember, a slight shock. The word. American. There, too, was Mr. Seuss's star. I smiled and closed my purse.

A large dark motorcar appeared at the far end of the street. Tremendous and official, its polished surfaces mirrored the sun. It was ablaze with blackness and light. At the front, near the headlights, on either side, there were fluttering standards. The insignia was plain on both. One was the usual red, white, and black. The other bore a coat of arms, silver eagles rampant on a black field.

Frau Doktor Mittelstadt stepped back out of sight. The expression on her face was extraordinary. She shaded her eyes. Her mouth twisted. She was more, much more, than afraid. She was terror-struck. But I was not. I looked at the sky.

The car stopped. A youth of remarkable proportions, dressed all in black with boots shining to his knees and fiery hair showing at his temples, beneath his cap, came round to open the door. He was like a fallen angel; Lucifer could not have been more golden.

As I stepped forward his arm shot sideways in that strange salute of theirs.

I ducked under this and got inside. The seats were covered with leather and a beaver-pelt throw rested on a silver bar before me. I sat back.

What was going to happen? Where was I going?

I was doing what I was told.

The voice had been familiar.

Obey obedience.

I was convinced that I must not show fear. Or feel it. I must look as natural and unconcerned as possible.

I waved.

Up on her balcony, Frau Doktor Mittelstadt raised her smelling salts to her nose and stumbled back inside her house.

We drove away. It was either a dream or a fairy tale or a nightmare.

But that did not matter.

It was happening.

The streets of Berlin were alive with visitors that summer. Uniforms and flags abounded. Never had there been such perfect weather as there was that August and September. The air was positively crystalline and the sun never ceased to shine. We drove for a great while and there was total silence. The car must have been soundproofed and armored. I noticed that pedestrians behaved with deference as we passed. Their expressions were anagrams of fear. The glass of the motorcar's side windows was slightly smoked and you could probably not see who rode within, although the rider could see the exterior world with perfect clarity.

At several intersections the populace gave us the salute. I felt imperial. It was marvelous. And awful.

We drove to the Wansee. The lakes shimmered and appeared warm. There were bathers and acrobats. Again, as everywhere, the flags were flying and the trees in their unbelievable foliage were like paper cutouts exquisitely painted by hand. Balloons of blue and white proclaimed the Olympiad. Other balloons were black.

We arrived at a gate.

I was not afraid.

A youth very like the driver, wearing an identical uniform and of identical stature, opened the gate and saluted as we passed through.

At the far end of the drive I saw the façade of our destination — a palace from the period of Frederick the Great. Coldly impressive, multiwindowed. Sad.

We came to the entrance. More angels in black.

The car was opened for me. I was saluted. I was led up steps and told to go through doors. I was not afraid.

I came into a high wide hall.

I stood on marble.

I waited for the Countess von Buëll.

Before me a grand staircase seemed to have abided the centuries, only waiting for the Emperor's return.

"Ruth!" said a voice, and without the distance and distortion of the telephone I knew at last who it was. I knew why my instinct had told me I was safe. That I could be myself.

It was Lisa.

I was "finished" in Italy at the Pension of the Signorina della Ponte. There were fifteen of us that year. Mother waited out the season in the mountains, near Florence. She had Adolphus with her and she paid little attention to me. She took Dolly every day to the famous Dr. Renaldo. I seemed forgotten. She had placed me in the hands of the Signorina and she entrusted me to her graces. It was our first separation.

Although I do not make friends with ease, I stood in need of a friend that year, and I chose Lisa. Lisa chose me. We were very much alike, an unlikely reason for girls and women to become close. But we never had to speak of our alikeness. We shared it the way other girls shared clothes. Our alikeness was our mutual sense of awkwardness. We were both handicapped, myself by height and lack of grace and Lisa by poverty and loss of nobility. Her mother was Italian. Highborn. Her father, killed in the war, had been German. Lowborn. It was a marriage frowned upon. Not only had the Germans been enemies, and thus Signora Goss had betrayed her country, but she had also betrayed her class. She was disowned and stripped of her rank. However, she was courageous and determined. Silently, alone, she plotted a course for her daughter's life. It was to be full of twists and patterned on revenge, but it would place Lisa higher than her mother herself had been. Her daughter, Signora Goss decreed, would become a great German lady. Thus, though her mother virtually enfeebled herself doing it, the year at Signorina della Ponte's was financed and Lissl was finished in the proper style. I remembered her as a willfully smiling, lovely girl with the best of both races in her features (dark skin and hair, blue eyes). Her expression in those days was haunted. She did not grasp her situation beyond her mother's instructions. She knew, materially, what she was working for, but she did not know why. She did what could be called "the right things." She developed grace and style. She read books. She had a natural flair for music and, secretly, she wanted to write poetry, although she only talked about this. She never wrote the poetry down. Or thought of it. We did think a lot about boys, but our thoughts were purely romantic. For our generation, all the best and all the handsomest and all the most romantic young men were dead. In the war. Boys died. And girls were virgins. Letitia taught us that. Yes. Her shadow even fell on Europe. The Little Virgin was everyone's ideal. Until you discovered men. Locked in the arms of the mountains, high above the world, at the Signorina's, men and boys played a role only in the books we read. The conclusion that both Lissl and I would marry older men, when it came to reality, was simply not a part of our lives. We were really just worldly nuns, brought up to marry not gods but mortals.

"Ruth!"

She stood at the top of the staircase. Surely it was she, and yet it seemed...

"Lissl..."

A young man sprang to leathered attention, interrupting what I had begun to say.

I fell silent.

The Countess Lisabeta von Buëll came down.

She wore blue.

She was not the same. She was impeccable. Impeccably coiffured. Impeccably manicured. Impeccably made up, impeccably gowned, and impeccable of speech. Her face was flawless. But I did not recognize this until I was able to see her eyes when she reached the bottom of the stairs. They were blind with fear.

She offered her hand, wrist first. A beautiful gesture of the kind I can never hope to master. I took her fingers lightly in my own and curtsied over them as best I could remember, sensing that I was playing a role, hoping we would both laugh about it later. Soon.

I stood up straight. I gave her my gaze. She did not return it.

"Wolf."

"Countess." The youth stepped forward. He bashed his leather heels together and bowed.

"Frau Haddon and I will walk in the garden."

(All this in impeccable High German.)

"Yes, Countess."

Lissl took my arm and began to guide me along a gallery that led, I could see, to terraces and gardens at the rear of the palace. Wolf followed.

"Wolf."

"Yes, Countess."

"Frau Haddon and I wish to be alone."

There was a stubborn pause.

Wolf said, "Frau Haddon's papers, your Grace?"

Lissl remained cool. Her expression did not alter one iota. She turned to me.

"Your papers," she said.

"I don't understand," I said.

"Identification. Have you anything at all?"

"But Lissl," I lowered my voice. "In your *home*. It's ridiculous. . ."

Her eyes stopped me. She might just as well have drawn a knife and held it between us. I opened my purse.

I was nervous, I suppose. I had thought I was merely indignant and amazed, but I suppose I really was nervous. I dropped my papers and my cards and Mr. Seuss's star on the floor.

Wolf stepped forward to retrieve them.

I bent to retrieve them myself.

Lissl stepped on them and nearly crushed my fingers.

"Frau Haddon is a great athlete, Wolf. She enjoys this exercise."

I looked up. She was smiling. She was not only cool. She was cold.

Wolf retreated three steps. I picked up my things, returning them to my purse, and handed my Olympic registration card, American, to Lissl.

She in her turn, without looking at it, handed it over to young Wolf.

He scrutinized it carefully. He took so long that I was certain he was memorizing it. Then he handed it back.

"Very good," he said.

He bowed toward me and I nodded.

I replaced the card in my bag.

Lissl again took my arm.

We stepped away.

Wolf remained absolutely static until we had gone.

When we reached the terrace I felt Lissl's whole body sigh and relax. Her shoulders fell.

"What *is* the matter?" I said.

She gripped my hand. Her expression implored me to understand.

"I thought that since you are here so short a time, my dear, you should see the gardens now while they are in such lovely bloom."

Her tone was forced and she projected her words as an actress does from a stage. I gave a long look down the terrace where there were many French doors, some standing open, and I saw the folded arms and the knees and toes of two uniformed men. Beyond us in the formal gardens where we were going there were others. They were everywhere. I looked back up onto the roof as we descended the steps and they were there as well.

My voice froze in my throat. My hands began to sweat. I adjusted my veils in an attempt to dry my fingers.

"You look well," said Lissl. Her tone remained unbearably formal. I longed to put my arms around her and to hear her laugh. Her laughter was once so marvelous.

"I am well," I said.

We looked at beds of blue delphiniums and pink tea roses. Day lilies and late poppies. She pointed out nightblooming nicotiana and snapdragons and beautifully formalized rows and ranks of shrubs and trees, japonica, magnolia, camellia. Some in bloom, some not. Yew trees and sculptured firs. At intervals, scissored and razored cedars formed archways and arbors underneath which we walked. All the while her hand held mine and her fingers stroked my wrist and palm. I sensed that this was her true conversation with me, that the words would have to remain formal and stilted, meaningless and polite, even unspoken, and that somehow her real messages were reaching me through her touches and signs. They were not in code. At least I hoped that they were not. If they were, I never deciphered them, never discovered what it was she wanted to say, but I imagined that I did decode it emotionally. It was a plain, stark monologue, messages of fear and loneliness, regret and sadness. Touching me as though I alone was reality.

None of this was evident to the watchers, with that everlasting physical pose that seemed to go with their uniforms: hands behind the back, pelvis forward, knees out, strolling in ways of menace. They were everywhere in that garden, everywhere in the shadows, everywhere in the inner passageways of the palace, behind every tree and door, at the extension of every telephone, even behind the distant eyes of binoculars. But none of this prevented my sensing what was being said.

We stopped by a bed of yellow roses. She showed me the bush from which my bud had been cut. I had pinned it to my dress.

"Yellow roses," she said, "are a sign."

A phrase that could mean anything or nothing. She had said it in the same tone as everything else. But her hand gripped mine tighter as she spoke.

On the way back inside she asked me how I thought she looked. She had waited to do this until we were abreast of one of the listeners.

I answered almost in a shout that I had never seen her look so well, that she was positively radiant, and this answer seemed to please her. She smiled.

Indeed, her beauty had increased. But it was a lacquered beauty now. Every hair was in place and I could sense in the makeup and the beautifully shaped nails the presence in the house of cosmeticians and manicurists. She seemed cared for and turned out like a film star. It was a look I recognized and knew all too well. It hid the real beauty but it had a beauty all its own. Cold layered.

"The Count will dine with us," she said.

We made a progress, nodding and being saluted, all the way down a six-hundred-foot corridor. At the far end doors were thrown open by invisible servants and we came into a room of massive distances — unseeable ceilings and such ruthlessly carved and heavily adorned furniture that it seemed to have been torn in chunks from the timbers it was made from.

We stood in the recess of tall windows, looking out at the terrace where we had been, and we drank sherry — a light, light gold in color. The glasses were crystal, with eagles cut so sharply that their claws were capable of piercing your fingers.

Lissl said, "We will wait."

We waited.

Presently, along the corridors we heard the echoes of iron steps and the battering of heels as someone approached, heralded by shouts of "Heil!" and by tones of subservience and deference.

"Put down your glass," said Lissl. "Do not look at him until he speaks."

I lowered my head. From the corner of my eye I saw that even she, not only a Countess and of equal rank but his wife and companion, bowed her head and dipped her body before him.

I smelled him first. Black leather and silver polish. Cigarettes and a curious, extremely Germanic cologne. Also the male smell of warmth. His hand, as he raised me up from my curtsy, was strong and clean. I felt womanly — a rare experience, living with Bruno.

"So you are my wife's American friend," he said.

"Yes," I replied.

I looked.

His bearing was Caesarean.

His head was enormous and his hair, silver-blond, was brushed forward.

The veins stood out at his temples.

His mouth was wide and shaped for sexual appetites and it looked as though he had come directly from a feast.

His gaze was brilliant. It hinted of miraculous kindness.

But I knew better than to believe this. Character is in mouths, not in eyes, and I had seen his mouth first.

We sat down.

Lissl was silent.

She watched him dutifully, like his dog. But I could tell that she loved him. Was trapped in this love.

I thought, She and I have walked into the same Nightmare.

Count von Buëll gave us a little of his attention. This consisted of polite remarks about my hopes of winning in the events and classes I was entered in. He had heard of me. He was interested in Bruno. He understood that Bruno had many original theories about the human body and its performance under duress. He said that the Führer himself had expressed a desire to know these theories better and he informed me that Bruno was considered with high regard in certain circles.

All this was news to me. I remained silent. During this conversation Lissl's eyes rested on her food. She did not eat.

Finally the Count rose.

We rose with him.

He had dined voraciously and well.

He was totally masculine. Self-immersed.

He wished me good fortune. He kissed the Countess's wrist. He departed. Heat followed after him and the room shadowed and became cool.

"Well!!!" I said. I whispered it.

Lissl looked at me.

"You understand?" she said.

I told her that I understood.

We walked arm in arm to the bathrooms. They were marble and spacious. There was a large table spread with linens, cosmetics, and brushes. Lissl seated herself and I stood behind her. I wrote, with lipstick on a piece of tissue, *Are we alone?* and she wrote back, *No*. She pointed to a ventilator over our heads.

We stayed there a long time in silence, she sitting, me standing behind her, both of us facing into the mirror. She carefully brushed and combed and powdered her hair (yes, she powdered it, very lightly — blue). I did not show her that I was bald. She brushed some sort of lacquer on her lips so that they gleamed for a moment and then froze. I put on lipstick. She offered me perfume, but I declined to wear it for fear Bruno should ask me where I'd been. However, I put some on my handkerchief.

She took my hand, which rested on her shoulder, and held it. She looked longingly at our reflections in the mirror. We were not as we had been. We closed our eyes, hoping together to open them on other images and other days, but we faltered in that dream and the world remained real.

She wrote, *Where did you get that star?* and I wrote *From Mr. Seuss in France*, and she wrote, *We do not carry stars*, and I looked at her and then I wrote, *We should.*

She looked at this and looked at me and nodded. Then she wrote, *We cannot meet again.* I nodded violently, meaning that we must, but she shook her head. Her eyes were sad.

I could not take the time to write. I said it. "Why?"

She thought for a moment and then stood up. She went into the lavatory and flushed our writings down the toilet.

She came back. She had not answered me. She did not speak. She took me gently by the arm and led me out into the great hall.

I realized that she had not answered me because one of her "followers" had been standing outside the bathroom. The door was ajar, and apart from being overheard through the ventilator, we had probably been watched from the hall.

We got to the steps outside. The giant motorcar with its flags and drivers was waiting.

She said, "*Auf wiedersehen.*"

I smiled. I said it too. I knew she did not mean it. Could not, for some reason. I wanted to weep with frustration, leaving her there, not knowing what was going to become of her.

She laughed. It was the last time.

"You know," she said, "your German is terrible, Ruth. You must work on your verbs. Begin again. . ." and then she stressed the next part oddly. "*At the beginning.*"

I looked at her.

The sun was in my eyes.

She was dazzling.

We kissed.

I went down the steps.

I did not look back just yet.

I got into the car.

I was driven away.

At the end of the driveway, I looked back.

She had gone inside.

Begin at the beginning.

On the way home I thought about this. The beginning. What is the beginning? I thought of her face, of her tone of voice. Of her hands. Of her husband. She had said, "Your German is terrible. Work at your verbs."

My verbs.

The beginning.

I thought of it.

The Dark Angel driving the car turned to look at me. I was weeping. It did not matter what he thought of me. I had understood. This was her answer.

The beginning of learning German.

Sein.

Ich bin.

Du bist.

Er ist.

Wir sind.

Ihr seid.

Sie sind.

This was her message.

To be.

I am.

You are.

He is.

We are.

You are.

They are.

And to this I added the word "good-bye."

I do not need to explain the history.

At the Olympics I won three gold medals. I do not have them any more. Bruno has them. After all, they were his.

I dressed always in the uniforms now. When I swam, my baldness startled people, but the more I won the more they got used to it.

But I could not.

I also had to endure another of Bruno's innovations above and beyond the baldness. This was my breast truss.

It was like a belt made of elastic and cotton. It pulled my breasts to either side as far toward the armpits as I could stand. I wore it under my suit. I had to slightly readapt my reach to accommodate it, but it flattened me and it worked. It was agony.

These things did not matter. I was a guinea pig. I was alive and I could perform. Later, this became my career.

Bruno's face changed. His mouth stiffened. His nostrils flared more often. It became impossible to see into his eyes. He shaved his own head. He gained weight. He began to carry a riding crop. He donned boots. He wore leather. He bought a cap. Slowly he changed his language. He became German.

On the last Olympic day of all, August 16th, 1936, Hitler was to speak to us. Each team was to parade before him. We all had to learn the salute.

A drill master came. In uniform.

We lined up in the underground tunnels. I was just a member of the team. Bruno was absent. Above ground there was a tumult of bands and singers. I knew that all the flags would be flying. I knew the sky was blue. I felt old. I was sad.

The drill master educated us in the art of saluting.

As each captain of each team came abreast of the Führer's box, he was to "eyes-right." At this moment, still looking ahead of us, we were to commence the count.

One: Arm out to the side.

Two: Eyes right.

Three: Raise the arm, sighting along it on a slight diagonal.

Heil!

One. Two. Three. Heil!

It was simple.

Yes. The bands played, the flags flew, and we marched up onto that resplendent field, some of us with our medals, all of us in our Olympic blazers, all the nations of the world, obedient and shouting. This was the Master Leader. This was the Master Leader's Fatherland. These were his people. We were there. We did it.

As we passed the place where he stood and as we shouted our approval, my heart leaped into my throat. I thought I was stricken. There beside him, saluting too and smiling down, was Bruno. Standing with those others. Now, I was destined to know them.

It had happened.

Up there, also, was the Count von Buëll.

And the Countess.

And no one else I recognized.

Hitler spoke.

He spoke for two hours.

He was faraway, partially hidden and small. But we heard him.

And it grew dark as we stood there.

For a time thereafter, Bruno forced me to travel with him, here and there, riding in official motorcars. We visited the doctors and scientists at Tubingen; ministers of physical education in various state capitals; teachers, physiologists, gymnasts. We visited sports centers, where I gave demonstrations of strength through joy. We called on Goering, Hess, Himmler, and Streicher. They voiced their approval. We were much in the company of Dr. Goebbels. Hanover, Leipzig, Bayreuth, Nuremburg, Regensburg, Augsburg, Munich, Saltzburg, Freiburg, Stuttgart, Heidelberg, Mannheim, Darmstadt, Frankfurt, Cologne, and always, always — home to Berlin.

Home to Berlin.

Nightmares begin with acts. Sometimes an act of Absolution. Sometimes an act of Atonement. The act will inevitably involve your integrity.

I wanted to go home — really home — truly home, to America. But no. I was married. I was a wife. I stayed with my husband.

I was his guinea pig.

I was bald. Once a week he shaved my head.

I wore his uniform. My picture was published.

He designed swimming paraphernalia, breathing devices, eye goggles, webbed feet. I even wore strange fins on my forearms and rubber things strapped to my legs. My breasts became deformed. I got ill. I was sick. I had headaches, nausea, rashes, and torn muscles. I stood in the cold, I swam in ice, I stood against walls. It was all part of a plan. I was placed in snowbanks, nude. I was told to run, walk, lie down, stand up, sit, crouch, stoop, stop and start. I had orders constantly in my ears.

Ointments and oils were spread on various parts of my anatomy. Greased with these, I was told to enter different sorts of water — distilled, salt, lake, and river. Temperatures were varied. I developed piles and chilblains.

I swam by day and by night.

I wanted to obey. I wanted to be obedient. I wanted to love and be loved. I wanted my husband. I did not know what had become of him. He seemed to be living in another world, and I tried with all my heart and all my mind and all my soul to join him there. I tried with all my body. I loved him.

Acts of Absolution and Atonement.

My ankles swelled. As though nails had been driven far up through my feet.

And wherever we went there were my rows of dreamers. Only now they did not walk. Now they sat on benches, or they stood by walls. They were always in the shadows. Always silent.

I received gifts. A gold watch from Himmler — a box at the opera from the Führer — kid gloves and a leather bag from Julius Streicher — a compact from Goering — and a pill box. And flowers from Dr. Goebbels (he called them messages of admiration). Their wives and mistresses ignored me. I was denied the company of women. I began to hoard more and more the memories of home. My real home. America.

Last spring — 1938, either in May or very early in June (I don't remember) — I was taken to give a demonstration. It was to be my last demonstration.

We traveled at first by train and then by car. We were accompanied by several officers and by three men from the Ministry of Enlightenment and Information. On the train they all read books (one, I remember, was reading *Vom Winde Verweht*) and no one spoke. Bruno looked out of the window, and as I watched his profile, I tried to reconcile this man with the man I had wanted so badly to marry two years before.

I'm not telling you everything, of course. A lot of it was private. But I can say that we had our moments of bliss and our moments of hell. That is, inside the private part of our marriage. There was the usual state of war which everyone has. But Bruno, for all his outward demeanor of leadership and strength, still had his "boy" moments. And during them, life was marvelous. He liked to be touched and to have the back of his head scratched and he could be an inventive, wonderful lover when he thought of me and himself and forgot what else was on his mind. In other words, what I am saying is that he remained human to me, as my husband. But as someone I lived with and knew and had once gone so far as to worship blindly, I could not see that I any longer recognized him.

Our journey seemed to be a long one, but it took only from after breakfast to after lunch. At the station, wherever we were, a motorcade was waiting for us, and as we got into the cars, I heard several times the word "*Kamp*." Also the word, "*Kamp-Kommandant*." Also the phrase, "*Es gibt keine Kamp-Krankenhaus*."

I was almost amused by this. Any form of fetish amuses me, and I remember thinking, "*Kamp*" is their new word. Their fetish. Just as, for a long while, the word had been "*Freude*." There had been Joy Houses and Joy Festivals and Joy Organizations. There had been Joy Commanders. Now it was camp. I wondered what they meant when they said there was no hospital. However, it did not occur to me for one minute it had anything to do with me.

We drove along pleasant roads. We passed through villages and towns, and in them people waved. A troop of Jungenvolk halted to let us pass and they waved and shouted and heiled at the autocade. They loved our flags and they loved our uniforms and they loved the shape and size of our motorcars. They loved the fact that we had imposed upon them, disturbed their marching and their labors.

We arrived.

I was not really watching. I was tired. We passed through a woods. I was aware of that. It got dark. When we broke from the other side I was aware only of the cleared terrain and of young men singing as they cut down more trees.

There was a sort of stockade. And there was wire fencing. Very high. And my first thought was: animals. All of this had something to do with animals. We had made this journey, come all this way, to see a zoo.

And then I thought, It must be a strangely special zoo, and I wondered if they were secretly training some sort of animals for some sort of warfare. And I thought, That's why they particularly mentioned the fact that there was no hospital, because of course, there should be a hospital wherever a large number of people are working with a large number of animals. With big animals, especially. Horses. Or perhaps elephants. I could not resist the thought of Hannibal and the Alps.

I wondered what I had to do with all this — my demonstrations — and I thought, Well, I swim and they are probably working with whales, and got the giggles about this and as we passed through the gates I was laughing my head off and one of the officers turned to me and smiled and said, "You have a very sensible attitude, Frau Haddon," and someone else laughed as well.

And I saw them. Then.

The rows.

This is why they had disappeared.

This is where they had gone.

This is why there were gaps in the rows outside in Berlin, in Mannheim, and in Stuttgart.

This is what had happened.

Kamps.

The motorcade stopped.

We got out.

We stared.

Yes, even they stared.

And Bruno stared.

"Splendid," he said.

Splendid.

There were several specimens to be looked at. Winter had passed. Experiments in cold air had been conducted.

Now they wanted to try experiments in water temperatures. I was to show them how. It had something to do with how long one could endure the cold before one died.

I looked at the specimens.

The frost had devoured their toes and fingers. The officials, the scientists, and Bruno conferred about prevention. My own endurance was mentioned. Their heads shook and then they nodded.

The specimens waited.

I waited with them.

I realized that I was one of them. I was their extension to the outside.

But worse, I realized that whatever I could not endure, they would have to. I saw that when I had been pulled from my snowdrift and given blankets, they were left in theirs to freeze and die or to lose their extremities. They were left there because I had failed. And my failures frustrated the researchers. If I had only been able to go on — to freeze, perhaps — they would not have had to.

It came to be time for my demonstration.

I was to be placed in sea water. At its lowest temperature.

I tried to smile.

I was allowed a bathing suit.

I climbed up to the top of the tank.

The scientists, the officers, and the men from the Ministry of Enlightenment and Information watched me and prepared to take notes.

The dreamers — the specimens — watched me.

Frau Haddon was famous. They were told they were privileged to watch me.

I became determined that they should watch me die.

That last is not crazy. That is exactly what it was like.

I got down into the water.

They could all see me through the glass sides of the tank.

At first it was cold.

Then it was not cold.

I moved as little as possible, treading water.

Bruno would not allow this.

The point of the demonstration was survival.

He got up on the edge of the tank.

"*Schwimmen!*" he yelled.

I swam.

I swam the side stroke, feminine and graceful. I felt like a professional again. I was almost happy.

"*Schwimmen!*" Bruno cried, his voice already hoarse.

But I didn't care if he shouted.

It was only flesh. That was all I had. If I had been a sailor in the North Sea, or a fisherman adrift in the Atlantic in midwinter, that would still be all I had. My flesh. And my vulnerability. My weakness. I switched to the breast stroke. Lazy and slow. Feminine.

"*Schwimmen!!*"

I smiled.

I even waved.

He wouldn't dare come in himself. I knew that.

I swam to the far side of the tank. I went under. I thought about drowning, but then I thought, No. I'll let the cold do this.

I surfaced.

I blew water, like a whale.

I thought of my first impression of the camp.
Again, I laughed.
I was achieving a measure of freedom.
I was swimming back into myself.
Nightmares begin with an Act.
Atonement.
Absolution.
I became numb.
My fingers went first.
Then my feet.
"My ankles hurt," I said to Bruno, swimming past him.
The others were watching.
Death is fascinating.
A slow death is mesmerizing.
"*Schwimmen!*"
"I am."
"Crawl!" he screamed. "Crawl!"
I fluttered my feet.
I could not feel them.
Nor my shins.
Nor my knees.
I began to kick.
I didn't want to kick.
I wanted to die with grace.
Atonement.
Absolution.
The dreamers were watching me. Praying. I knew their prayers. It involved my life.
I began to sink.
Numbness is a weight.
"*Schwimmen!*"
The cry was blurred.
I was going to die, I thought.
"*Schwimmen.*"
It became very faint and was not a word at all. Not even German.
Let me do this for them, I prayed.
Then they need not do it for me.

The dreamers in their rows began to sway.

We became One.

If I could endure more cold than anyone ever had, then they would never have to endure the cold again.

I was dying.

Rows of stars and crosses.

I was going down.

Absolution for integrity.

Drowning.

It was the Light in the Darkness that ruined it.

In the Darkness, this Light — which seemed to be Death — and was — frightened me. It panicked me. I didn't want the Light. I was afraid of it.

I shot up to the surface.

Bruno was there.

Schwimmen!

I thrashed.

I went down again.

Twice.

There was the Light again.

Terror.

The dreamers swayed. They held their breath. Their hair got tangled in my arms and legs. Their faces stared at me with prayers.

I grabbed for the surface.

I saw it.

I struggled for it.

I prayed for it.

Longed for it.

Begged for it.

I strove into its presence.

"God help me. . . ." I cried.

And Bruno saved me.

He would not speak to me after that. Not properly.

I was retired from demonstrations.

I became merely his wife again.

He stared at me a lot.

He was figuring something out. Something statistical. I had almost made it. That was the first part. I had performed magnificently. That was the second part. He had theories — that was the third part. There could be a combination of these things that would be perfect. That was the fourth part. It was genetic statistics. But he had not recognized, or was just not reconciled to, the fact that I had performed magnificently only when I wanted to die. Not live. The genetics of that is different.

And he thought he knew about genetics.

So, in silence and with scientific precision, he set about creating his babies.

But I would not have them.

I have tainted blood. I carry hemophilia. He did not forgive me.

The conclusion of this is that I survived. Unwittingly. Unwillingly.

I go back to the counting.

One-and-two-and.

One-and-two.

The Nightmare, you see, will involve your integrity.

Or do I mean. . .intelligence.

He divorced me. I was being sent home.

I went on my final motorcar ride, driven by my own Dark Angel now, to Hamburg.

There was one last thing.

I had boarded the ship and, because it was not to weigh anchor for another four hours, I got off again. I wanted to have one last look at Germany. I don't know why I wanted this, when it had all turned out so badly for me there, but I did. I sensed that there was something else for me to see.

I went down to the harbor.

It is a lovely harbor there, with old streets and ancient houses. And the ships stand up over everything. And everyone is involved in the river and in the sea. And there is something marvelously incongruous about these ocean-going ships standing inland, where there are fields and trees and houses and bridges. The sun shone that day, too.

I walked about. I went nowhere. I just walked.

And then it was that this last thing happened.

I was standing in a narrow street where the houses were extremely old. I could see ship masts and spars over the rooftops. There was little commerce in the street. A few cyclists passed and that was all.

A man came all at once, stumbling as though blind, from between the houses.

I stopped on the curb, watching him, wondering what assistance he might need.

But he was not blind, merely blinded. He had been in the dark.

Gradually he was able to see, and he looked about him.

There was only me. And the houses. And, faraway, the sky.

He looked at it. He looked at me.

He approached.

His clothes were damp. He smelled. It was a stale smell. Wet. Part of it was human excrement.

He was old. Or he appeared to be. He was bearded. His walk was crazy — this way and that — and I wondered if he was drunk.

He wasn't.

He stared at me. His eyes were clouded. He raised his hand like a word: some sort of greeting. I waited.

This was the first dreamer I had met, face to face, hand to hand, since Mr. Seuss, long, long ago in Paris.

I said, in German, "Yes?"

He said, in German, "Will you help me?"

I said, "Yes."

He said, "I must die."

I nodded. I tried to understand.

"I have hidden," he went on, "hoping for a ship, hoping for some way out. But there is none. My wife and children have not come. They were to meet me here. We were to go away. What month is this?"

I told him. "August."

"August?"

"August, nineteen thirty-eight," I said. I took his hand.

"Excuse my hands," he said. "I have waited a long time."

"Are you hungry?" I asked.

"No. I am not hungry."

He wavered. He looked along the street.

I steadied him with my arm around his shoulder.

He stood against me like a child.

He stared into the sky.

He rocked a little, back and forth. He had not stood upright in weeks. He felt like so many bones in a bag.

He said, "Walk with me."

I said, "You cannot walk."

And he said, "Make me walk. A few steps. Please."

We stepped out like strollers.

(They knew once another world but that has been forgotten.)

"I cannot walk," he said. "You are right."

"Shall we sit down?" I asked.

"No. There is not time. I shall lie down. Please. It must happen here."

I helped him down until he was crouched on the curb. The back of his head rose like a skull above his clothes. He reached up with one of his hands and scratched it. Right at the crown. I shall never forget that.

Then he said again, "Here. It will be here."

I knelt on the pavement beside him and helped him all the way down onto his back. He lay out flat.

His eyes reached into heaven.

It was unmistakably heaven.

That much was true.

I said, "Quickly. Tell me your name."

He muttered words.

I laid my ear against his mouth.

He whispered his name.

It is private to me. I will never tell it.

Then he whispered something else.

Pocket.

His hands did a dance over his damp, decaying clothes. This was the rush to death.

I followed them as rapidly as they flew. I followed after, searching.

"Quickly," he said.

Then he found it.

His star.

I had a pin in my lapel.

He thanked me. I placed his star, neatly, over his heart.

He took a short time dying.

No one came.

I stayed with him.

His eyes never left the sky.

I was sorry. I had to leave him there. I think that's what he wanted.

A sign.

When I boarded the ship I saw the blond man.

It was the first time. He is still with me.

I went to my cabin. I had thought I wanted to see the last of Germany from the deck of my ship, the city, then the green fields in the twilight. But now I did not want that.

I am not a thief under normal circumstances, but I had stolen one thing from Bruno. It was to help me understand. At least I hoped it was. A book, autographed by the author, precious to Bruno. He would miss it, but then, God help us, he could surely secure another.

The ship moved.

People yelled.

I had heard, already, too much yelling. I closed my porthole.

I walked around for a moment checking idiotically (now that the ship was actually moving) to see that I had not forgotten anything.

I hadn't.

So.

I opened my purse. I took out the star of Mr. Seuss and pinned it to my lapel and then I sat down on my bunk and began to read *Mein Kampf*.

It was a mirror for Bruno.

In my own mirror, when I finally looked, my hair, growing unhampered at last, came back to me white. As you see it now.

The Chronicle of Alvarez Canyon

September 15th, 1938:
The Road to Alvarez Canyon
10:00 a.m.

The beauty of Alvarez Canyon was known around the globe. Nominally it was a state park, but the visiting public had proclaimed it "Paradise." Birds, reptiles, fishes, and mammals roamed its precincts unharmed and free. The park was a sanctuary, and thus Paradise was governed and protected by the State of California. The laws concerning visitors were very strict.

No one was allowed past the gates unaccompanied by a warden. All visits were, of course, arranged in advance. Parties were restricted in number. No smoking was allowed. At the barrier all guns were confiscated; in fact, no weapon of any kind could be carried except by the attendant wardens, who all possessed knives which they were to use in the event of snake bite.

Alvarez Canyon Paradise lay due north of Santa Monica, in the mountains that squatted there by the sea. They were called mountains, which they were not; they were merely hills. But "mountains" sounds superb and indicates the proper respect for Paradise. So, "mountains" it was.

If seen from the air, the canyon which contained Alvarez was not very large. It was an area of approximately forty acres. The sides of the canyon were exceptionally steep and presented a formidable barrier to anything or anyone wishing to climb out. In 1928 a family of climbers had fallen to its death attempting to do just that — to climb out — and ever since, the rules about climbing had been strictly enforced.

In order to preserve the atmosphere of Paradise in all weathers, some portions of Alvarez were quite unreal. The plants in these places were made of specially treated fabrics and of rubber. Thus when elsewhere the acacia leaves were falling they did not fall down in Alvarez. On close scrutiny, too, one out of every ten animals was dead and taxidermed. A glass stare can be disconcerting, but the thrill of coming face to face with an oryx, apparently tame, made up for it.

So it was that on this Thursday, when work had temporarily come to a halt on the film *Hell's Babies*, Dolly persuaded Myra, Ruth, and his mother to venture to Alvarez. "A little Paradise," he had said, "will do us good."

Naomi concurred with pleasant surprise, Myra did a small dance and had to be quieted, Ruth (greatly upset by the death of the red-haired nude) merely said, "Very well," and fell silent — and Miss Bonkers, who had not been invited, insisted on accompanying her patient and efficiently packed a bag of drugs and got out her motorcycle. Because of the fifteen-mile-an-hour speed limit set by Adolphus, it was Miss Bonkers on her motorcycle who arrived first.

Ruth drove while Naomi sat silently beside her. Dolly and Myra, like toys, were wrapped in a tissue of pillows, veils, and sun hats. They sat in the rumble seat. Boxed.

They languished along the highway, going north. Soon Miss Bonkers, approaching ninety miles an hour, whizzed by with a wave of both hands. On a motorcycle the death-nurse was transformed. She was dressed in her uniform, of course, but over it she now wore an aviator's leather jacket and helmet, goggles, gauntleted gloves, and high black boots. She had a passion for World War flying films and doubtless, had it been practical, an airplane would have replaced the motorcycle. But as Miss Bonkers herself admitted, "At Topanga Canyon Beach there was no damn place to park a car let alone a biplane." So the motorcycle became her substitute.

As the journey progressed, the company fell increasingly silent. Even Myra.

Naomi fell asleep.

Myra calculated how many days it would be before she would eat a decent meal. Her pretty, round face could not be seen, so deeply had she swathed herself in protection from the sun. All that was visible in a sort of mold of gauze and stoles was her pursed but ever-sensuous curlicue of a mouth and her heart-shaped celluloid glasses. The rest was all hat and blond curls and round, plump arms hidden in pink-and-green beach pajamas and swaddle. She secretly pinched her breasts, one by one. They were delicious to touch. The mouth unpursed. She smiled. She'd show them a thing or two. Fat! My hat! I'm gorgeous! She recited this to herself, pinching and patting away. Then she went so far as to smirk, which was a mistake, because Dolly turned and saw her.

"What *are* you smirking at?" he said somewhat testily, because he could not endure so much quiet.

"Smirking?" said Myra, wide-eyed behind the hearts of celluloid. "Smirking? I don't even know what smirking is, so how can I be it?" She drew closer to Dolly. She whispered, "Do you wanna put your fingers inside my veils?" and leered delightfully as she spoke.

"Myra! Please!" said Dolly. "For heaven's sake remember that my mother is sitting in the front seat."

11:55 a.m.

Arriving at the barrier, they discovered that they had been preceded not only by Miss Bonkers's motorcycle but also by a large Rolls-Royce, beside which a Negro chauffeur languished in a drooping stance. His mouth was open and he snored, but very gently, adding his voice to the distant cacophony of sanctuaried birds and insects.

Ruth said, "I thought only one party was allowed in at a time."

"Maybe," said Naomi, "it's someone just about to leave."

"Or a High Mucky-Muck," said Dolly.

Myra stared and giggled.

They clambered down, Naomi handing Dolly down by the arm to Myra, and then stepping down herself.

Ruth said, "I'm going to have one last cigarette before we go in," and lit up.

Dolly, on his long, knock-kneed legs, pigeon-toed his way to the gatehouse.

"Damarosch," he said, poking his head through the little window.

"You're sure as hell right," said a sleepy voice.

"I beg your pardon?" said Dolly.

"I said you're sure as hell right. It's damn hot."

"Oh," said Dolly. "Yes, of course."

He withdrew in confusion.

"What do y'want?" asked the guard, pursuing Dolly's head with his own, sticking it out the window.

"We're arrived," said Dolly.

"I can see that," said the guard, who had been asleep. "But what do you want?"

"Entrance," said Dolly, quite annoyed. He hated any sort of personal foul-up in front of his mother and Ruth. He enjoyed, rather, the immediate response of respect that his name and person usually drew in public places. This sort of shilly-shallying simply flustered him.

"Entrance to what?" said the man, who was one of those basically cantankerous persons so often employed as custodians and gatekeepers.

"Alvarez Canyon!" Dolly raised his voice and grew red.

The head withdrew and presently reappeared at the top of a giant uniformed body whose baggy gut pendulated dangerously over a slackened belt.

"Someone's in there," said this parade of swarth and swagger, and jammed its thumbs into its pockets, letting its hairy hands hang down.

"Our visit has been arranged since yesterday," said Dolly precisely, hiding behind his cane. "If you're able to read, you'll doubtless find us in your book. The name is Damarosch."

The opposing eyes squinted between the hairs of massive eyebrows and searched over Dolly's figure and the figures of Naomi, Ruth, Miss Bonkers, and Myra. It had to be admitted that the view was somewhat odd, for it contained this man dressed entirely in blue, caved in on the support of a rapier-thin cane — plus a madwoman with a flat, youthful face and pure white hair, and a frail, reedy woman in a blue dress, green hat, and purple shoes, who was carrying an orange parasol. Next there was a simpering of veils, sunglasses, nail varnish, bosom, and bright lipstick that the guard could hardly help but guess was someone in pictures, since she rather mechanically responded to his stare with a nod and a smile and a heaving of breasts. Finally, concluding the group, there was a short stocky man in an aviation leather helmet, goggles, gauntlets, riding boots to the knee, and what appeared to be a nurse's uniform.

Beyond these, of course, lounged that dozing black of gigantic proportions, sensuously rubbing his buttocks against the metal sides of the parked Rolls-Royce. But he belonged to the "others."

From inside the canyon came the distant echo of laughter.

The Negro stirred and looked around him hungrily.

Dolly could not resist giving him a smile.

"Here I go again," he thought. He was enchanted with Negroes. One of his fantasies...

"Dam-rosch, eh?" snarled the gatekeeper.

"With an *a*," said Dolly. "With two *a*'s. Yes."

The gatekeeper retired to his cave.

They could hear things being rearranged on a table top to the steady accompaniment of a low monologue filled with sexual references.

Dolly gave the chauffeur a sly glance. He did a few elegant things with his cane, moving it about near his feet in the dust, then leaning on it casually with one hand. He had learned his cane vocabulary from Mr. Chaplin and it was a good imitation. The Negro did not respond. Perhaps he was not interested in canes. Or did not care for Mr. Chaplin. You could not tell.

The gatekeeper reappeared. He had several pieces of paper in his paws. He looked at Dolly suspiciously.

"You're already in there," he said, rattling several pieces of paper in Dolly's face. "Go away."

"What do you mean, we're already in there?" said Dolly. "We've just arrived. We're here."

The gatekeeper turned and read from his fistful of documents.

"Dam'rosch," he read. "Six of them, in there."

"But that's us," said Dolly.

"I don't care," said the gatekeeper. "There are six of them and only five of you."

"But they have used our name and they have taken our tour of Paradise! You can't send us away just because somebody else is a liar and a cheat and there are six of them!"

"You'll have to wait your turn," said the gatekeeper and disappeared.

Dolly turned back to the others, who were clustered like mannequins around the purple Franklin.

"This is insane," he remarked. "Stark raving insane."

"He'll let us in," said Ruth. "There's probably only one tourmaster and when the others come back we can get him to take us."

"I want to go now," said Myra.

"Oh, shut up!" said Dolly. He assumed his full height. "I'm going to get to the bottom of this."

He walked over to the Rolls-Royce.

He gave the Negro a tap with his cane.

"Wake up," he insisted.

The Negro came to, stood at attention, flicked at his cap with his long black fingers, and broke the world record for dazzling white smiles.

"Yes suh!" he said.

"Heavens," said Dolly. He couldn't help it. He had to swallow three times before he could speak again.

"What is it, suh? You feelin' faint?" asked the black man.

"No," said Dolly. "No. In fact, I'm really quite angry."

"I ain't did it," said the chauffeur. "I didn't, I swear. I was asleep," he said. His eyes bulged.

"Nothing has been done," said Dolly, feeling a little thrill at the response he had drawn from the man. "I simply want to ask you something. Do you understand?"

"I'm sure gonna try," said the Negro.

"Then answer me this," said Adolphus. The Negro quivered. How thrilling it was for Dolly as he stood there, all in pale-blue, with his cane, asking questions and getting answers from a man so large and black.

"Who is your master?" he posed.

"I don't have none," said the man.

"Nonsense," said Dolly. "Whom do you work for?"

"Miss Virden. I works for Miss Virden."

Ruth was on her way over to them.

"Letitia Virden?" she asked.

"Yes'm."

"Yes," said Ruth. "I thought so. I remember you." She turned to Dolly. "They were on the train, Adolphus. She was behaving very strangely. Wearing veils and everything."

"Yes'm," the Negro asserted. "That's Miss Virden, all right. She wears a veil all the time, now. I ain't seen her without it since we got here."

"And you work for her," said Dolly, furious with Ruth for having interrupted his interrogations, but hiding it because he didn't want to stop the flow of answers.

"Yes suh. That's what I says."

"Is that she in there now?" Dolly asked. "In Alvarez Canyon Paradise?"

"Yes."

Ruth drew Dolly to one side. "Why is she using our name?" she asked.

"I don't know," said Dolly. "I don't know."

He turned back to the Negro. "Who is with her?" he asked.

The chauffeur did a blink dance with his eyes as he tried to recall the names.

"There's one or two mistuhs I don't know," he said slowly. "An' one I do recognize but doesn't know the name of. An' one that I does know the name of, 'cause it's the name I had to give to the gateman."

"And what is that?" said Ruth.

"Mistuh Damarosch. Used to make movies with Miss Virden in them. In th' ol' days."

"That's him," said Dolly, as though they had not even suspected as much.

"Father," said Ruth. "But why here in Alvarez?"

This question went unanswered, because it was just then the apelike custodian returned from the gatehouse.

"I suppose if it comes right down to it," he said, "I could let you people pass."

"There," said Dolly. "Wonderful. I knew you'd see the light."

"Just one small thing," the gateman said.

"What's that?" Dolly asked.

"You'll hafta cross my palm with gold."

"Oh — all right," said Dolly. And gave him a hundred-dollar bill.

Then, they plunged forward into Alvarez Canyon.

12:10 p.m.

Inside the gates something was whistling.

"It's a snake," wailed Myra.

"A whistling snake!" said Dolly derisively. "Don't be ridiculous."

"Well, whatever it is, I don't like it," said Myra. "Anything that whistles gives me the creeps."

"It's just a bird," said Naomi. "There, you see? Up in that tree." She pointed.

"What kind of a bird?" said Myra, holding Dolly's arm with delicate tenacity.

"A mynah bird," said Naomi.

"That's one of those birds that talks and everything," said Dolly.

They advanced. Birds that talked. Miss Bonkers was impressed.

At first there was an undergrowth of fernery, asparagus-like stalks with great fans of lacy tendrils. This reached waist-high and grew in great abundance, but there was a path and it was relatively easy at this stage to make one's way.

Above them giant eucalypti spread their graceful branches like broken umbrellas, and in between, straight as ramrods, green-and-black avocados, thirty and forty feet high, nudged and jostled for a place in the sun.

In the branches birds squalled and squawked, while imported monkeys squeaked and sprang and a million other smaller birds and climbing things spread a wide kaleidoscope of arms and wings and tails over the visitors. At first the noise was almost deafening.

The light faded. It became like evening — a brown velvet haze.

So far, all had been real.

But before them now, in the looming darkness, there were unreal trees with rubber-coated leaves and vines that were only twisted ropes and the sort of giant flowers invented by Rousseau, made here of heavy celluloid and technicolored paints. Reasonably speaking, these man-made charades were out of place in Paradise. But not in Alvarez. There was such a crowd in Alvarez; too many trees to reach the sun, too many plants for all to flower, and so the property departments of the major studios had been culled to replace what could not grow with what need not grow.

The visitors stumbled forward, feeling their way cautiously, trying to open their eyes wide in what was rapidly becoming total darkness.

"Are you sure it's supposed to *be* like this?" asked Myra, looping one of her stoles back over her shoulder.

"And how, may I ask," said Dolly, "is it supposed to be any different? It can only be what it is, after all."

"But it's so dark!"

"It's heavenly," said Naomi.

"Come on!" called Miss Bonkers. "We go this way, now!"

"That's a help," Dolly muttered. "By heaven, *that's* a help. She's completely disappeared and there's an echo."

They trudged on for another yard or two.

"Where are you?" Ruth called to Miss Bonkers.

"Who?" said a voice, quite distant and repeating, "who...who...who..."

"Are there owls in the jungle?" said Myra.

"Shut up," Dolly hissed.

They waited.

"Hallo there!" Ruth called. "Hal — ooo!"

"Who is it you want?" the voice asked. "You-want-you-want-you-want-you?"

"Miss Bonkers," Ruth called back.

There was a slight pause.

"Miss who?"

"...who-who-who-who?"

"Oh, really!" said Ruth. "This is ridiculous."

"Miss who?" said an entire stranger, stepping before them onto the path. She was tall and she wore a knapsack and a pith helmet.

Putting up with it, Ruth said, "Miss Bonkers. Please. We're trying to locate a Miss Bonkers."

The stranger blinked, thought about it, and said, "No. I can't help you. There's a Miss Box in here somewhere, but no Miss Bonkers. I'm sorry."

She stepped away into the foliage and was gone.

"Who was that?" Myra asked.

"I don't know," said Ruth, without pausing to think why she should know in the first place.

They stood there. They had begun to see quite successfully by this time. What had seemed to be darkness was now just a sort of viridescent half-light, entirely pleasant, cool and soothing.

"Well, we've lost Miss Bonkers," said Dolly. "What now?"

"Surely Miss Bonkers wouldn't have left the path."

"That other person did," said Myra.

"Yes. But she seemed to know what she was doing," said Dolly.

Holding hands, they headed on.

12:40 p.m.

"Where are you?" This was Dolly.

"Here I am," said Myra.

"What's that in your hand?"

"Some kind of vine, I think, with flowers."

Myra stood quite near the path. Dolly had stepped into the greenery in order to relieve himself.

"Isn't it beautiful!" said Myra.

She put her face right down into the bell of a giant flower.

"Oh, smell!" she whoooped. "It's gorgeous!"

"Don't you get it near me," said Dolly. "It's probably one of those man-eating things and is just waiting to smell blood."

Myra coiled it around her neck, next to her skin, loosening her scarves and stoles and making it one of them. There was no sunlight here, so she needn't worry about an unwanted burn.

"I've never seen anything so beautiful in my life," she said. "It's like a lovely nest of birds."

"Very poetic," said Dolly. "Just keep it away from me."

"It has such a lovely smell. Like something smoky. Incense."

"Lovely," said Dolly. "Lovely. It will probably set you on fire. Now. Where are the rest of them?"

"Rest of who?"

"Us," said Dolly. "For God's sake, Myra! Mother and Ruth!"

"Oh, well. They went off somewhere. . . ."

"Went *off* somewhere!" snapped Dolly.

"Yes," said Myra, fondling her blossoms.

"When?" Dolly demanded.

"While you were peeing."

"Oh, for Pete's sake!"

"Well, I can't help it. Maybe they had to pee, too. I don't know."

"Why didn't you go with them?"

"Well, Dolly. Then I'd be lost, too!"

A fit of wailing, to which Myra seemed more and more prone these last weeks, appeared to be imminent.

"If you start weeping and whining," said Dolly, "I swear to heaven I'll leave you here in the jungle."

Myra fell silent. She pinched herself for reassurance and pouted.

Adolphus called out, "Mother? Ruth?"

No one answered. Not even an echo.

"You see," he said. "You've let them disappear."

"It could be us," said Myra.

"What does that mean?"

"Well, I mean, it could be us that's disappeared and they're just standing around somewhere waiting for us."

The logic of this burned a hole in Dolly's brain.

"So far as I am concerned," he said, "*they* have disappeared. And *we*," he added with a kind of desperate certainty, "are right here."

"Maybe we shouldn't move," said Myra.

"No. We must keep going," said Dolly. "If only we could see the sun or get a bearing on some recognizable object."

"Should we drop something?"

"That's an excellent idea. Hansel and Gretel. Very clever."

"Oh, this is fun!" said Myra.

"What'll we drop?" said Dolly.

"Well, we could drop my stoles and things.

"You need them."

"Not now." She pointed to the invisible sky.

Dolly nodded. "All right then. Drop your stoles and things and we'll get them back later on."

"Then when we find them at least we'll know where we've been, eh?"

"And where we are," said Dolly.

There wasn't much conviction in that.

They started away, leaving a trail that spelled "Myra" to all the world.

1:30 p.m.

"Now, Mother," said Ruth, "you sit on this log. Here's a good hefty stick. If there's a snake or anything, kill it. I'm going to double back and see if I can find them."

"Very well, Ruth. All right."

"You're sure you're not sick."

"Yes, dear. I'm just tired."

"Are you in pain?"

"No."

"O.K., then. Sit still and rest."

"Thank you, dear. Be careful."

"I will," said Ruth, and set off down the path. Just before she made her turn away into the undergrowth, she looked back over he shoulder at her mother. The brightly colored parasol made a good beacon. However, just in case, Ruth bent a branch on a tree and left it dangling downward to give herself an added sign.

The jungle was pure green here, not too difficult underfoot and filled with areas of space through which, far off above her, Ruth could see the blue fretwork of the sky and an occasional bird sitting on a branch. She took an invigorating breath of damp air. It held the odor of bottled ferns and rotting leaves. It was a lovely smell to Ruth — profound and mysterious.

Birdcalls and a mélange of insect and animal noises cluttered the air. But there was not a single human noise to be heard.

Ruth made for what appeared to be a clearing, but it kept disappearing and not being there. At last she came out on what seemed to be a path. There, lying on the ground, was one of Myra's stoles, which Ruth recognized by its bizarre patterns. She picked it up and wrapped it around her neck.

"Myra!" she called. "Myra! 'Dolphus!"

A reply came but from an unexpected quarter. It was laughter, like a harp being struck, and it seemed to come from behind Ruth, farther down the path. She knew this laughter and now she could give it a name. Letitia Virden.

Intrigued and even alarmed by the thought that perhaps her father was after all accompanying the Little Virgin on her tour of Alvarez Canyon, and equally intrigued and alarmed by the prospect of seeing him again, Ruth fell back into the shadows of the jungle and waited for them to pass.

They came around the distant bend, one at a time — Letitia first, then George, then Cooper Carter, and then three other men in black costumes like uniforms, and finally the warden, who wore green and was extremely thin and small.

The Virgin wore a blue tailored coat, the sort that little girls wear, with a belt at the back, and there were bows all down the front of it. She also wore a sort of toque, from which spread her current trademark, a veil. Her face was not visible, and Ruth again was caught by the fact that she wore long leather gloves — kid leather and soft — but with harsh, bone buttons all the way up under the sleeves of her coat, which came only to below the elbow. She looked very elegant, and the incongruity of her appearance was dead right for the image of the world's most famous woman wandering in the tangle of Paradise.

Having seen this figure and taken it in, Ruth next saw her father, George Damarosch.

His hands were clasped behind his back and he walked splaying his feet like a goose or a duck, with his pelvis and paunch pushed five or six inches ahead of the rest of him. He wore a long coat like a motorist's coat (circa 1910) and he also wore that sort of hat, with goggles appended to it.

"What can he be thinking of?" Ruth thought. "Dressing like that."

Her father. There he was. She had not seen him since before her departure for Germany in May of 1936. They were estranged. Yet they had always been estranged — since that moment of discovery long ago in the hilltop house at Falconridge. That was the day it was announced that her brother Adolphus — George's darling — was a bleeder. It was the day that Naomi had been reviled and cast aside. It was the day when Ruth, for the first time, had heard that she was a carrier. That she carried hemophilia. That long ago. And there he was. She hated him.

The Little Virgin's party strode on. She could see the coats of the men were made of leather. Black leather, white leather — and also that the three anonymous men wore boots.

Her father seemed very serious. Was he arguing with Letitia? Or trying to convince her of something she didn't want to believe? Ruth could not ascertain what it was at this distance. She waited.

Letitia stopped. She turned and said something vehement to George, who seemed to pale — the pallor recognizable even from this far away — and then Letitia could be heard for an instant only, and the words were, "should kill you." And then she walked on.

George hung back a step, letting Cooper Carter and then one of the other men pass him. The two remaining men waited, pausing on purpose, and when George walked on they took up their positions in the rear, as though instructed to do so. The warden wandered along with them, not really privy to the party or their conversation. He was there only to protect them.

As they passed by, Ruth tried desperately to see Letitia's face and to hear the words being spoken by Cooper Carter (whom she recognized at once, because he was notoriously handsome and wealthy). But not a word could she hear, and all she could see of the Virgin's face was the set of its jaw and the metallic glint of its eyes.

Her father walked by, looking very much like a man taking exercise in a prison yard — condemned to death but free to take the air and to contemplate escape. His eyes were fixed on the Virgin's back, and they were filled with desperation.

And then they were gone — the Virgin and the men.

It was at this precise moment that Ruth was first aware of being watched.

2:00 p.m.

To wander in Paradise is all very well if you know your way. But the mapless terrain of Alvarez was utterly frustrating. Even a man with a compass might have had trouble.

Dolly and Myra refused steadfastly to leave the path, which seemed to have no ending. And although Myra had conscientiously been dropping her various tidbits of attire at regular intervals, she and Dolly both had the unnerving sensation they had unquestionably passed this (or that) way before.

Finally, Myra said, "Do you think we should call again?"

"All right," said Dolly. "Stand still."

They stood in the very middle of a crossroads and Dolly took off his hat. He wiped his brow with a handkerchief, cleared his throat, and bellowed.

"*Mother! Mother! Mo... therrr!*"

It was the best he could do but it produced only an extension of the silence.

"*Moth*ER !" he cried.

"The only thing is," said Myra, attempting to be helpful, "that there might be a lot of mothers in here and they won't know which one you want."

Dolly swiveled his toes in the earth, scuffing the blue off his shoes.

"Myra," he managed. "The regulations state that there shall be only six persons allowed in here at one time."

"Well, we've already seen several others," said Myra. She scratched her knees.

"What do you mean by that?" said Dolly.

"Well, that woman in the helmet..."

"Oh, she was just one of the staff."

"Well, then. That blond man in the German pants."

"What blond man in the German pants?"

"The one on the path."

"Myra!"

"Well, there was."

"In German pants?"

"Those shorts they wear."

"*Lederhosen*."

"Yes. Those shorts made of leather."

"What else was he wearing, Myra?"

"Well. A shirt. And a hat with a feather. And sunglasses. And gloves. And socks and shoes."

"And where was this?"

"Well, on the path somewhere."

"Why didn't I see him?"

"You were peeing."

"Why didn't you tell me?"

"I don't know."

She scratched her elbow and adjusted her vine.

"Have you seen anyone else?"

"Yes. Haven't you?"

"I wouldn't ask if I had, Myra. Who and where?"

"I don't know."

"Which?"

"Either."

"All right then. Describe them."

"What? The feet?"

"The whatever," said Dolly. He was practically ready to scream. "Tell me what you saw."

"Well, I saw these feet."

"When?"

"Back there on the path."

"And. . . ?"

"And they were sticking out from the bushes."

"Oh, Myra. In the name of God. Why didn't you say something?"

"Well, I thought you'd seen them. And you didn't say anything, so I thought it wasn't important."

"What position were they in?"

"Sticking out."

"Sticking out lying down or sticking out standing up?"

"Standing up."

"Well. At least they were alive."

"Yes. Only they didn't move."

"Very well. Go on."

"Well. They had on shoes."

"Ladies' shoes or gentlemen's shoes?"

"Ladies'. So it was a woman."

Dolly thought about that for a moment.

"It could have been a transvestite," he said. "But go on."

"These shoes" — she scratched her wrists — "were black leather, I guess, and they had openwork sides. And the feet were wearing stockings, but that was all I could see. What's a transvestite?"

"MOTHER!!" Dolly screamed.

There was no response.

"And so what'll we do?" said Myra.

"We'll go on," said Dolly, replacing his hat on his head. "Have you much else to drop?"

"I've got another hankie and I can take off my stockings if I have to and my bra and that stuff. What've you got?"

"Handkerchiefs. My tie. And that's all. Now listen, Myra. The next time you see anyone... hands, feet, a person, anything human... say so."

"Yes, Dolly."

"This is serious, Myra. It's not a game."

"Yes, Dolly. I know."

"So stay close behind me and keep your eyes and ears open for everything. Understand?"

"Yes, Dolly." Pause. "Are we lost?"

Dolly sighed.

"Yes, Myra. We are lost. O.K.?"

"O.K. Sure. I just wondered, that's all."

"Well, that's something," said Dolly, and they struck out in what, this time, surely had to be a new direction.

2:20 p.m.

It was Miss Bonkers who found Miss Box.

Miss Box had worn a neat green dress, a very pretty slip, some rather old-maidish drawers, lisle stockings, and black leather openwork shoes. She still wore the shoes and stockings. Her expression, as she swung from the tree (her toes neatly obtruding onto the path) was one of gentle surprise mixed with a very mild reproach. As though her lover had refused her some private but ultimately petty gratification. She was dead, of course, and there was a black-handled knife inserted in her vagina.

Miss Bonkers for the first time in a spotless record of professional nursing, fainted dead away.

2:30 p.m.

Naomi, seated on her log at the crossroads of the path, stared off into the treetops and counted at least twenty species of birds. They intrigued and engrossed her until slowly (at first) and then more and more rapidly she began to be in pain. She practiced several stoic patterns of thought, but to no avail. She began to wish ardently for Miss Bonkers and her needle — a longing she had sworn to master, but one which she could not since the pain had begun to intensify.

Dreaming of release, Naomi Damarosch was the first in Paradise to smell the smoke.

She rose.

Where should she go? Which way?

Was it wise to move at all?

Smoke, fire, run, she thought. But where?

Ruth had told her not to move, but then neither she nor Ruth had dreamed that the Canyon — that Alvarez Canyon — would catch fire and burn down around their ears. It was protected — a Government project. There were scores of little men in green, whose only job was to see that the Alvarez Canyon Paradise did not burn down. And so, of course, this could not be fire that Naomi smelled. It must be some fluke, or the remains of some distant smoke carried into the Canyon on the breeze.

She sat down. She was right. She had to be. Some things do not happen, and the immolation of Alvarez Canyon was one of them.

2:35 p.m.

Myra had shed everything but her shoes, her panties, and her vine. Dolly had released his jacket, his tie, and his shirt to the cause.

Standing now in the middle of the path, he was debating the necessity of shedding, also, his trousers.

"If I can go in my panties," said Myra, giving her thigh a scratch, "surely to goodness you can go in your underwear."

"We'll be arrested," said Dolly.

"Who the heck by?" said Myra.

"You have a point there," said Dolly. And he undid his buttons.

Myra giggled.

"Now what?" snapped Dolly, half in and half out of his trousers, revealing knee-length underdrawers and blue garters.

"Oh, nothing," said Myra. Then she began to sing.

"Lovely — never, never change.
Keep that breathless charm.
Won't you please arrange it?
'Cause I love you
Just the way you look tonight!"

Dolly stared at her in disgust.

It had been, until that moment, his favorite song.

2:45 p.m.

Ruth had paused to rest. Her journey, like that of all the others, was leading her nowhere. Occasionally, of course, there were clues. She found another of Myra's stoles and one of Dolly's handkerchiefs. She also found a box of comfits dropped by Miss Bonkers. (As a matter of fact the box was empty of everything but the lingering scent of peppermint, for Miss Bonkers had also seized on the Hansel and Gretel idea and had dropped her comfits, thirty-six of them, on another part of the path.)

It was then that Ruth did something unaccountable. Knowing it was forbidden to smoke in Alvarez, she nevertheless took out a cigarette and lit it.

Perhaps she wanted to see the smoke. Her mind was on the scorched piece of bathing suit and she wanted — perhaps — to conjure fire and complete the burning. If she could complete the burning, perhaps the image of the ragged bit of cloth would cease to haunt her. Perhaps.

Perhaps. Perhaps.

Perhaps, if I shot myself, the world would disappear.

Ruth smiled. She remembered thinking that as a child. Or something very like it. Surely she hadn't really thought of shooting herself when she was ten. But something like it: yes. She closed her eyes and tried to remember.

But that was it. The closing of the eyes.

If I close my eyes, the world will disappear.

She touched the piece of cloth in her pocket: pieces. She was making a collection: the star of Mr. Seuss — the bathing suit of the red-head — Myra's stoles. . . She felt like a rag picker. "*Any old rags! Any old rags!*"

Oh, God. The star of Mr. Seuss; the bathing suit of the red-head; Myra's stoles — they weren't rags. They were emblems. The emblems of violence: of violence being done.

Ruth slitted her eyes and squinted through the smoke from her cigarette. Very slowly, she bent her knees and knelt until she felt her shins touch the earth. Then she hunkered in the center of the path and looked in through the jungle. All the crazy, unnamed birds were calling — alarmed — and there were animals, moving, though she could not tell what they were. Some kind of deer, perhaps. A herd of something moving very swiftly but silently through the trees. . . .

Suddenly, there was a noise behind her — beside her. She dropped the cigarette and stubbed it out with the toe of her shoe, thinking that she had been caught by one of the wardens of the park and already preparing her excuse. . . . *I was frightened. I needed to calm my nerves. I'm lost. . .* And then she would smile and say, "Can you help me?"

She stood up and brushed her knees, the smile already on her lips and the words beginning to tumble from her mouth, "I was frightened. I. . . "

It was him.

Whatever Ruth's next word might have been, it was completely forgotten. The blond man stood before her, staring at her.

"What do you want of me?" she said. "Tell me what you want of me." She could smell the leather of his boots and trousers: his *lederhosen*. But he did not speak.

"If you do not tell me, I cannot help you," Ruth said. "You have followed me all the way from Hamburg and I don't know what you want." Suddenly, she raised her voice and yelled at him, "I DON'T KNOW WHAT YOU WANT!"

Above them, around them, all the birds took flight and animals Ruth had not even been aware of rushed away through the trees. But the man did not move and he did not speak.

"Please," said Ruth. "Don't do this to me. I will. . . "

Go mad.

She shook. Her voice died. She could feel the tears welling up in her eyes. She was angry, not afraid any more.

Now, at last, the blond man seemed to be moved and, for a moment, Ruth thought he was going to speak. But instead of speaking, he lifted his right hand to his left sleeve, tearing the insignia from it and holding it out toward her all in one movement.

She did not take it. Her hands remained at her side.

For the first time ever, she saw an emotion cross the blond man's face. It was not precisely anger; not only anger but also alarm; confusion. She had been meant to take his insignia without an argument. The intention had been that she would receive it with pleasure and, for a moment, he did not know how to deal with this — what to do, when her hand did not rise automatically the way hands should to receive a treasured gift.

At first, it was only his eyes that shifted, but then — all at once — his body was pushing against her and his hands had taken control of her. With one hand, he had both her wrists behind her back and with the other he forced the torn insignia down the front of her blouse. His fingers brushed against the nipple of her left breast and she felt the buttons of the blouse giving way as he moved his hand to cover her breast with his palm. Their eyes met, but Ruth couldn't bear to look at him and she turned her head away.

He stepped back — coldly — apparently now in control of himself. There was just the briefest pause before he raised his right arm, from the elbow only, and gave her the salute she had come to despise: the one that Bruno had given, standing up in the stadium with all the others that day when Ruth and all the young of the world had passed below him in their matchless, perfect bodies.

She felt a chill pass down her spine and she closed her eyes and shivered.

When she opened her eyes again, the blond man was gone: disappeared, and nothing remained of him but the thing against her heart: the insignia.

Rag picker. Rag picker. Any old rags. . .

She reached inside her blouse and withdrew the piece of torn cloth and gazed at it, strangely at peace with it lying in her hand — all her resistance dead of exhaustion. The insignia's black perimeters, its scarlet circle and its broken, mutilated cross no longer disturbed or revolted her. She knew it was a sign — a signal. A message she could no longer refuse to hear. *I want you*, it said. *I want you*.

Ruth took a very deep breath and folded her fingers tightly around the swastika as if she could make its message disappear, the way its messenger had.

If I close my eyes. . . she thought. And she did. She closed them tight as her fingers. But it did no good. It would never do any good again. She had seen — and been seen. She had chosen — and been chosen. She would never be rid of it, ever. Bruno's damned perfection.

3:00 p.m.

Of all the people inside Alvarez Canyon Paradise, only Naomi sat staring at the birds. Only she was at peace.

The pain came and went in what seemed to be a sort of tidal flow, ebbing and rising, always in motion, always there, but mostly bearable and only occasionally not. And at these moments she would clutch her stick and say things to the birds.

She didn't want to leave, not just this Paradise, but life itself.

For a moment it did not matter that she was lost — or that no one came for her — or that Ruth had disappeared. What did it matter if there was not another soul in Paradise? These things that were — the earth, the trees, the creatures and the sky (though she could not see it), they were enough, if only she could stay immobilized in Alvarez forever.

But that would be wrong. That would be unreal.

And so Naomi rose to go.

It is a strangeness that those who take part in others' dreams are always safe. But it is so. Therefore, Naomi returned to the gate and asked that extremely polite, still sleepy Negro to help her up into the rumble seat of the Franklin.

3:00 p.m.

Myra was weeping. She wore nothing now but the vine and a few large welts where she had scratched herself. She also wore her shoes and carried her handbag. She tore a leaf from a tree and blew her nose.

"Oh, this is awful," she wailed. "Oh, why did we come?"

Dolly could not answer her. It had been his mother's idea, or Ruth's. At any rate, he certainly disclaimed it. Standing there, dressed only in his under-drawers, his blue socks and blue garters, his blue shoes and his hat, he felt as unforgiving as he had ever felt in his life. He struck out with his stick and broke some flowers at the edge of the path.

"Of course it's got to be some sort of a plot," he said vehemently to himself. "Look at us, we're two grown people — *lost!* It's impossible. Somehow, they've switched the paths around, or altered the terrain. They've done something. I tell you, it's not natural."

Of course it wasn't. It was a dream. But whose, Dolly wondered.

He bashed down some more flowers and Myra wailed. Dolly gave her a look. For the first time he noticed the large purple welts she had raised on her arms, buttocks, shoulders, the backs of her legs — her stomach and her face as she scratched.

"My God, Myra! What are you covered all over with?"

The expression on Dolly's face made Myra scream with terror, for he seemed to be saying she had been mounted by a troop of giant spiders. She flung her arms in the air, and ran and screamed again, flying amidst a cascade of vine leaves and flowers, right into a dark pool of water that lurked close at hand by the path.

There was a terrible noise of splashing and choking and loud cries of "Quicksand!" and "Alligator!" and "Can't swim!" and "*Dolly!!!*" until, moments later, Dolly felt moved to rush to her assistance.

"Myra, Myra! Be calm!" he called, sliding and falling knee-deep into the waterhole. When he had fully assessed he was neither drowning nor being attacked himself, he regained his composure and asked Myra to pass him his stick, which was floating in the middle of the pool.

She retorted that she was too busy removing leeches from her arms to take time to pass him his damn walking stick, but at the word "leeches" Dolly had already gone berserk.

If ever a more natural enemy had been created for a hemophiliac, surely it had not been heard of.

Literally unable to speak in his terror, Dolly thrashed about like a man possessed. Myra, certain he would harm himself, made for the opposite shore, got out and ran stark naked around the pool and hauled him out onto the bank.

He refused to stop jabbering, so she threatened to hit him on the mouth and, as always, the merest hint of earnest violence persuaded him to faint.

While he was passed out, Myra took the opportunity to check him carefully for leeches. Finding none, she proceeded to divest herself. Or at least she tried.

Of course, without benefit of either salt or a match, it was impossible to make the leeches budge. There were three of them — one on her leg and two on her arms. She yanked at them, pulled at them, scratched at them, and swore at them.

Dolly began to recover. Before he had a chance to panic, Myra told him he had no leeches. But *she* had, and she was frightened.

Dolly said, "Unless we can get you back to the car in half an hour, they will kill you."

"Yes," said Myra, disconsolate. "What a way to end my lovely life."

Then a foot crunched on the path behind them and Dolly whirled.

It was Miss Bonkers, looking very odd.

"Have you got a match?" said Dolly.

Miss Bonkers merely stared at him through her goggles.

"Miss Bonkers? Where have you been?" Dolly demanded. His wrath needed an outlet. He glared at her hotly, but she did not seem to comprehend. He tried another tack — the tack of compassion and pity. "Miss Bonkers," he implored, "have you a match or not? Surely you have a match somewhere on your person. Miss Myra is being eaten alive by leeches — see them? — and we must burn them to save her."

At the word "burn" a strange look came into Miss Bonkers's eye. She lifted up her nose like a dog, tasting the air, and she waggled her head up and down like that, indicating that Dolly should do the same. She clutched at his arm with her gauntleted paw.

"She seems to have been struck dumb," said Dolly over his shoulder to Myra. He looked inquisitively into Miss Bonkers's face. "What is it?" he asked.

Miss Bonkers shook his arm and gazed off into the treetops, bobbing her head and sniffing loudly. Delicately, Dolly did likewise.

"I don't..." he began, but then he did. "Fire," he barked. "Oh, holy God. This canyon is on fire."

Miss Bonkers nodded. She agreed.

Myra rose. The leeches were becoming larger by the minute, and now they seemed to be very, very heavy. Each of them had grown from an inch or so in diameter to the size of a small fist, and they were lengthening constantly, like grotesque balloons. The welts on her body had turned from purple to blue and her hair hung down in muddy blond ringlets to her shoulders. She was a mess.

Dolly searched Miss Bonkers's pockets for a match, but could find nothing save his mother's hypodermic set and the bottle of morphine. There was not time to wonder what effect the morphine might have on the leeches, for by now they could hear the distant roaring of the flames and, far off through the trees, Dolly could see their yellow and orange reflections on the rubber leaves.

"Please — please — oh, please! Haven't you got a match?" he bellowed into Miss Bonkers's goggles. But she shook her head violently. The noise of the fire was beginning to mount and would soon deafen them completely.

"Well, I don't know," said Dolly, turning to Myra, who wavered and felt faint. "I think we'd better get out of here. Don't you?"

"All right," said Myra. "Anything you say." Her voice was flat and bloodless.

Dolly looked around. There was only the one path, the one they had been on for hours, and he did not know where it went, but he was certain, the way things were slanted and fated, that it probably led into the growing holocaust. Still — it was the only path they had and a number of animals seemed to be making use of it, so he concluded they would use it too.

"Are you coming?" he yelled at Miss Bonkers.

She smiled and coughed and nodded and, like a child, she took his hand.

With his other hand, Dolly gingerly clung to Myra's elbow, well away from the bag-like leech that hung nearby at her wrist, and they began very slowly to walk away from the flames.

"We're going to die! We're going to die!" Myra whispered.

"Yes," said Dolly. "You're probably right."

3:30 p.m.

Letitia Virden, of course, refused to run.

She gave the flames a steely glare. It occurred to her that she had been in worse positions before this, albeit most of them in pictures.

She turned to Cooper Carter. "Well, Cooper," she said, "it looks as though we must make a bold decision. Right or wrong, we must choose a direction and follow it up."

Cooper called to the three men in leather coats. He took them a little to one side and counseled them. "It may be necessary for some of us to die," he said. "I want you to devote your last energies entirely to Miss Virden. Whatever happens, she must be saved."

Not a flicker of emotion crossed the faces of the henchmen. Cooper gave them each a pat on the shoulder and turned back to Letitia.

"My men will see you get through, my dear," he said. And then, "Pick her up, gentlemen."

Two of the fellows joined hands to form a chair and knelt before the Virgin. She smoothed her skirts and sat down, supporting herself serenely on their leather shoulders. They raised her up. Her veiling billowed and she looked all at once like the Empress of China riding forth to war on the arms of her servants.

Cooper raised his arm dramatically.

Curse him, George thought, mindful of his own face and figure, and of his own disgrace in Letitia's eyes. Curse him with his profile and his money and his age. He has it all, George thought. He has it all! And now he's going to save her life.

They marched off down the path, Cooper striding first, like a superman, followed by the Virgin-Empress in her leather cradle. George was last, as if forgotten.

3:45 p.m.

The cars and the motorcycle faced the gates of Alvarez Canyon Paradise. Their metal bodies reflected a wall of distant fire.

The people sat upon the ground, disconsolate and lost.

At last, the noise of the animals was heard.

Naomi said, "They will all die."

But Ruth said, "No. Pay attention. Wait."

Gazing at one another, the survivors neither advanced nor withdrew recognition. They were figures in a dreamscape. They were there, but this had no connection with the reality of their names and faces. Naomi would claim later she had had a dream about George. George would swear he had not laid eyes on his wife since the day of their divorce. Letitia, in or out of reality, would not have divulged her identity in any case.

Myra, Dolly, Miss Bonkers, the men in leather, Cooper Carter and the woman in the pith helmet were all blurs. Fading in and out of sight. The Negro chauffeur, the apelike custodian and the wardens in their green jackets were just so many shadows on the grass.

The light dimmed.

It began.

At first, there was a pause. Silence. Whatever had cried did not cry. Whatever had run was still. The fire itself did not roar. The wind changed. It changed down the canyon from the peaks. It harried the wavering flames. It gusted — and blew them up into tree-high torches. It licked and cajoled and persuaded. Sparks flared. Dead embers reared into balloons of fire.

The animals quit all thought of individual flight and joined in mutual panic and terror — fleeing mindlessly in concerted directions, not knowing what death was, but smelling death — not knowing what fire was, but being burned. Some turned back into the furnace. Others crept into flaming trees. Some attempted impossible flight into the sky. Some went into caves where the scorched air burned their lungs. The reptiles devoured their young and were swallowed themselves by fire. Birds fell down like stones and hives of bees and nests of hornets exploded. The living closed ranks.

The wheeling wall of flesh turned round and round. Perhaps it remembered the gate. It seized on that direction. It fled through the corridor of fire toward space. The clearing, with its people, became visible. Green.

"They're coming!" someone shouted.

"Close all the gates!"

"Keep them back! They'll kill us! Back!"

Someone ran and flung himself against the height of the gates and swung them closed.

"Why? Why?" said Naomi.

"Wait," someone said.

"But *why?*"

They all stared.

The wave of beasts appeared. It had one voice.

"Help them!" cried Naomi, and fell back into Miss Bonkers's arms and was engulfed at once in drugs.

Ruth took a step toward the gate.

But she was halted.

The chains of the fence bulged; almost gave — but did not. Paws reached through. Beggars. Dead. Noses, eyes, portions of torn and unrecognizable anatomy dropped before Ruth, melting in the grass at her feet. She turned back. It was over. No more noises. Four thousand creatures had perished against a wall.

But no one saw it. No one heard it. No one was there. Or, so they all claimed. Everyone heard about it, of course, but afterward. In the reports.

Days later Miss Bonkers said to Ruth, "What wall?"

And Ruth said, "The wall they died at."

And Naomi said, "There was no wall, dear."

And Ruth said, "The animals. . ."

But then Miss Bonkers just laughed and shook her white-capped head.

"Oh, no," she stated flatly, opening her copy of *Come and Get It*, "no animals, Mrs. Haddon. There were no animals. Nothing died. Nothing. It was a miracle. The papers said so."

"But we were there," said Ruth. "We saw."

"No, dear," said Naomi. Her patience, in pain, gained an edge. "We read about it. Don't you remember?"

Ruth looked along the beach.

Children played.

"We didn't see it?" she asked. "We weren't there?"

"No, dear," said Naomi. "No."

Miss Bonkers flipped her page.

"It's all in your mind," she announced to Ruth quite comfortably. "It's only in your mind, Mrs. Haddon. You dream too much."

And she read her book.

But Ruth believed. She could feel the swastika in her pocket.

Alvarez Canyon Paradise did burn down. And someone was there. I was.

"Everything isn't a dream or a nightmare," she wanted to say. "Some things happen!"

Instead, she maintained her silence, which was rather like sucking one of Miss Bonkers's comfits. The longer it nested on her tongue, the deeper the flavor became. And the comfort.

Book Two

The Chronicle of the Wish

Tuesday, September 27th, 1938:
Topanga Beach
11:45 p.m.

Ruth could not sleep.

She pulled open the glass doors and stepped out.

Further down the beach someone was giving a party. The sound of gramophone records needled her ears. Youthful laughter mingled with blown words, careless and maddeningly innocent. Several people were dancing tangos à la Bully.

Her mind began to play with the distant sound of the music and the postures of the dance. The wash of the waters — sibilant as whispers — and the stiff-arm of the tango harried her with echoes she could hardly bear.

She closed her eyes.

Slowly, she fled indoors.

11:50 p.m.

"Mother?"

"Yes, dear."

"I'm sorry."

"Sorry for what, Ruth?"

"For waking you up."

"No. No. You didn't. That's all right. I heard you walking and I thought perhaps you might come in."

"Are you in pain?"

"No."

"I wondered. . . ."

"No. I'm not in pain."

"May I sit down?"

"Of course."

"Mother?"

"Yes, Ruth?"

"Alvarez Canyon. . ."

There was a pause.

"Yes, dear?"

"Alvarez Canyon didn't happen?"

"No."

"We weren't there?"

"No, dear. We weren't there."

"Not any of us?"

"No."

Silence.

The curtains fingered the edges of the rug. The breeze was seaweed scented.

"May I ask you something?"

"Yes."

Naomi waited.

"I don't know how to ask. It's so personal, Mother, and I can't think of the right words."

"Ask it just as it occurs to you." Naomi waited again, and when Ruth did not speak, she said, "Is it dying you want to know about?"

"Yes. But dying in your *mind*."

"In my mind. . . ." Naomi paused. "That's impossible to answer, because it isn't in my mind."

"Where is it, then?"

Don't say your heart, Ruth begged, *don't say your heart. I want to know the mind.*

"I guess it's around me somewhere. Still outside of me.

Gathering. I don't know — like a crowd, I was going to say. But gathering like an event — the days and weeks before the event takes place. You know? The way anticipation fills the minds of everyone concerned, and yet they go on doing what they do. The women make cakes and eat meals and scold their children and the men read papers and listen to radios, but the event is always there, waiting to happen. My death. It takes on a personality all of its own, you know. It has a face. And legs and arms and. . . hands. It even has a way of talking. In a sense, that's really true. I talk with my death. I listen to it and I pay attention to it. Because soon it will have me and that is the subject of our conversation and that, I suppose, is the way I look at it — sizing up the size of it — seeing what sort of match it will be."

"You still haven't said you're afraid."

"I am."

"Why don't you show it?"

"I'm surprised to hear I don't."

"Are you brave, then? Is that courage? Is courage silence?"

"I don't think so. I don't know. I haven't the foggiest notion."

"Mother?"

"Yes?"

"I want to have a baby."

So.

Even the sea seemed to stop for a moment.

This is the last thing I expected, Naomi thought, lying propped on her pillow in the wavering dark, watching her daughter, who was far across the room smoking cigarettes, picking at the edges of her nightgown, broken in some mysterious way that Naomi did not fathom. Ruth, who had always been strong, had been weakened — even to the point of wanting the child she knew she must never have. It was impossible.

"Ruth — I have told you a million times — I cannot have this conversation."

"Mother. Please. I must talk about it."

"Talk about it. Go ahead. But I cannot help you. I cannot tell you yes or no. I had to make those answers for myself. . . ."

"And were you sorry? Once you'd made them? Sorry your answers were yes?"

Now. What do you say to the product of the wrong answer?

"I got you. And Adolphus."

"But were you sorry?"

"You are here now. No parent knows any other answer than that."

Ruth closed her eyes. "You love me."

"Yes. I love you. And Adolphus."

"But are you sorry? Do you wish you hadn't? *Please*, Mama! I need answers."

Naomi thought. "May I have one of your cigarettes?"

"Of course." Ruth stood up and crossed the room.

"I don't smoke. But. . . why shouldn't I smoke?" Naomi puffed. And puffed again. "I like it."

She looked up at Ruth, standing near the bed, depositing the match in a cold cup of coffee that sat on the table. There was no ashtray.

"Do you want to sit over here? Sit on the foot of the bed."

Ruth sat.

Naomi held her cigarette like an amateur. Very slowly she began to speak.

"Let me tell you something. The world is round. And you swim. And I was a picture star. Your father is a world-renowned producer. And your brother is a brilliant young director. All these things are facts. Correct?"

"Yes."

"Well. You no longer swim. And I don't star in pictures and your father doesn't make movies. And one day, suddenly, we all know, Adolphus will hurt himself and die. Nothing lasts. But in the meantime, these things form a portion of reality. Right? They are — they were — facts. And vehement facts, at that."

"Yes."

"And what else? What other 'facts'? Well. . . I married your father. He married me. We had two children. You married Bruno, and Dolly is — whatever he is — perhaps afraid of any kind of sex — of love. O.K.?"

"Yes."

"Well. So, my children are unhappy. My daughter married an older man whom she revered. . . ."

"I loved him."

"Yes. But as a schoolgirl loves her teacher. Admit it is true."

Naomi waited, but the admission did not come. So she continued.

"You won prizes. You won them because this man you married was extraordinary and he could make you win them. The way, exactly, that your father made me make pictures. I didn't really want to do it, but that didn't matter. I learned to do it well and I learned, almost, to enjoy it. I had this face and I had enough talent, and above all, the world wanted to take its look at me and it was ready to pay for it. So, there is no difference between us. None. You had a good strong body. Long and lean. Extraordinary. And natural. And you had, too, an inclination not to worry about distance and drowning. You loved the water. You belonged in it. You were born that way. It had nothing to do with choice. And Bruno said, 'You will win,' and you won. And he said, 'You will win again,' and you won again. And he said, 'Now we will go to the Olympics,' and you went, and when you got there you married him. Here I interpret, but let me interpret. . . a little. He wanted you to win for him and that would be good for him. And then he said, 'It is time to have babies. . . you have won. . . you have won everything. . . and now while you are still young, you must stop winning for a while and give birth to other winners — winners of mine. . . you are,' he said, '*perfect*.' And you said, 'I love you... but I cannot have your babies,' and he looked at you amazed and maybe he even laughed at you because, after all, you are six feet tall and strong and beautiful and you have won a million prizes including the Olympics. And so he just sits there and laughs at you and you say, 'No...don't laugh...because I love you but I cannot have your babies.' And he says (let me interpret), he says, 'You are only afraid...so I will *make* you have my babies.' Right?"

Ruth did not speak.

Naomi's eyes were round as marbles, black and hard, seeing nothing in the darkness but the story she told and knew was true. Enough.

"And you," she said, "didn't tell him why you couldn't have his babies. This is what you were really afraid of. Telling him you weren't perfect. That you possessed and were possessed by flaws. And you let him make love to you."

"Yes. I did."

"But you didn't have the baby."

"No. I didn't. There was none to have."

"So. Whose fault was that?"

"Mine," said Ruth automatically, and then, "I don't know." She didn't. She had merely blessed the fact.

"Come into bed with me, Ruth. Come on. Lie here and let me put my arm around you. There."

They lay still. Side by side.

"Do you remember this — the way we used to do this?"

"Yes."

"I'm so glad I had you. Yes, I'm glad I said yes. But that is my gladness. I cannot answer for yours. I wish you could understand. My gladness, my life, my facts have nothing to do with you. Just with life."

Ruth did not answer this. Or try to.

Naomi went on.

"I had an abortion once. Twice, in fact. No. That's a lie. I had so many abortions, I don't remember. I did it all without your father's knowledge. Miscarriages, we called them. I've even wondered if that's why I suffer this cancer. I did so many dreadful things to my body. I don't know. No one knows these things. But it could be. I had the help of a doctor. He told me what to do and he did things and I did things. I aborted my babies for a long time. But, finally, I gave it up and I had you. And then Adolphus. And then, after that, your father discovered about Adolphus. The day of your birthday party. I tried not to tell him. Adolphus was his son and it was unavoidable. I had to let him see the truth. It was there to see. I couldn't avoid it forever."

"Would you have told him if you'd had another daughter, instead of a son?"

"There'd have been no need; you see, I knew that telling him was tantamount to losing him. But I told him."

Naomi butted her cigarette in the coffee saucer.

"Later," she said, "I had to bring the doctor. And the doctor had to bring the lawyer, and the lawyer had to bring us to this — the life George and I have led — the separated life we've led — apart — and the rest you know. But... babies. Will you have babies? Should you have them? That is your life and I can only tell you that I love you."

Ruth lay, childlike, against her mother's breasts. She looked at the curtains blowing across the room.

"Is it right, then," she said, "to say that facts are what you can't help living? Not what you know?"

"No. Facts are what they are and have nothing to do with you."

"Whom do they belong to, then?"

"To themselves."

"And if the facts become militant... what do you do then?"

"Then you watch and wait. You bide your time."

"Until they change?"

"They don't change. The combinations of factual things change. But not the facts themselves."

"Oh, Mother. I'm so afraid."

"The wish for a baby isn't all that's troubling you, is it?"

"No."

"Then tell me."

"Alvarez Canyon is part of it."

"But Ruth, you were *not* there."

"I was there. My mind was there. And something — something happened."

Naomi thought, I'd better listen to this. And see what can be done. And call in a doctor, or one of those psychiatrist people if I need to.

"*What* happened?" she asked.

"They put out their hands," said Ruth, "and asked for our attention. They were *there*. Begging for their lives. But apparently we didn't see them because you say we weren't there. The truth is, we are looking at two different things and calling them both extraordinary. *They put out their hands to us*, Mother, and I was watching. But you turned away to watch something else."

"What else?"

"What you call real life," said Ruth.

"It *is* real."

Ruth stiffened. An angry cry began to swim up inside her, but it did not surface. All her cries, it seemed, fell back before they broke free of her; they drowned, or were drowned, she did not know which. All her life she had tried to bring them out, but her fear reabsorbed them. These cries were about the things she saw and experienced, and when she produced her evidences of them, people just said, "There she goes again. . . Ruthie dreaming." In childhood, Dolly had never believed her, and Naomi had only listened attentively as a kind of precaution against laughter. Ruth's "dreams" had been the cause of much amusement. Ultimately she had fallen silent. She rarely included her opinion in what she said.

Now. She watched the ceiling above her. It wavered. An arm of shadow billowed and beckoned. Her attention focused on something else. Desire.

"I'm being followed," she said.

Naomi shivered. "Are you certain of that, dear?"

"Absolutely," said Ruth. She spoke through barely parted lips. "I have been followed for weeks. All the way from Germany."

Naomi relaxed a little. She apparently considered this story quite plausible. With a touch of almost gauche realism, she produced the fact that "Your father's mother was Jewish. They might follow you for that. Especially since Bruno has remained in Berlin."

"No. That isn't why. I'm sure that isn't why."

"Why then? Or do you know?"

"No. I don't. But I see him everywhere. Even in my dreams and nightmares, Mother." (This was the way to tell it: tell the truth as a Nightmare.) "And in my nightmares, Mother, this man who follows me is. . . Race."

"His *name* is Race?"

"No. No. I mean — he represents Race."

"And have you really seen him?"

"Yes. That's what I'm trying to say."

"And what is this about Race?"

"Well. Just that." The words are now stones and Ruth drops them, careful not to throw.

"Germany, you see. The Olympics."

"Yes."

"My medals. My superiority."

"Yes."

"Bruno."

"Yes."

"And, as you said, I was a winner."

"Yes."

"A breeder of winners."

"Yes."

"In Bruno's *mind*."

"Yes."

"And. . ."

"Yes?"

"I couldn't. Because I didn't want to be a breeder of winners. Not Bruno's winners. But now. . ."

"Yes?"

"Now I need to."

"Oh."

"And must."

"And this man?"

"Wants me."

That is my message.

"So..."

The Nightmare no one understands is more real than this reality.

"I want him, too, Mother."

"I understand."

"No. You don't understand."

"Explain it, then."

"In Germany, I read books. I heard speeches."

"Yes."

"I watched people. I saw things. I listened to things. Unspeakable things."

"And...?"

"And yet, in spite of reading and listening and watching; in spite of overhearing and secretly seeing; in spite of *knowing...*"

"Yes."

"I still want."

"Want?"

"Race."

"Yes. Dear God."

They sighed, both of them. They lay there, sea-blown. The tango down on the beach described the jutting lines of human desire — the arc of male erections — the fall of female contours: the geometric certitudes of nature, driven and Darwinesque. The fittest.

Race.

"I only want a baby."

"But the fact is, that cannot be, Ruth."

"Please! How can you say that cannot be, when it was. In you. You having me. Allowing me life. I should kill you."

"And your child? Wouldn't it kill you?"

"I don't know. Not if he was perfect," said Ruth, desperately. "I don't know. I'm asking you to tell me what I really want."

Naomi closed her eyes and saw the swaying shadow of something unborn.

"You want what you are," she said, watching the shadow diminish and grow, "in your mind."

"And what is that?"

"The myth of perfection, my darling. Which is only what we all want. The cause of all human pain. . ."

"Perfection doesn't have to be a myth, does it?"

Naomi wondered about that. "Perhaps not," she said, "but the truth about *you* is that you are flawed."

The shadow in her brain twisted.

"You say," she said, "that you were there when those animals died at Alvarez. You say this man who follows you is real. Then you say he is only a dream. This is one of your flaws, Ruth. Not to cope with truth. . ."

Ruth wanted to interject, but Naomi said, "You listen to me. Just listen. There *is* a flaw you *will* accept. Your blood. So let that be the flaw I speak of. Each human being is Race. Potentially a whole Race. But each human being is flawed. Great intellects are held prisoner in the bodies of impotents. Physical beauty is trapped in the bodies of lesbians and homosexuals. Poets are consumptive. Artists are bound in by insanity. Saints are clubfooted. Scientific genius is accident prone. Why, God Himself was celibate by nature. And we, like royalty, are overbred. But the greatest flaw of all, the very worst, the most destructive and the seat of all our woes and pain, is this *dream* — this damnable quest for perfection. When I think," she said, the shadow looming larger in her brain, "when I think of the misery and despair caused by people like you who will not accept — and who will not cope with reality as it is, I find it small wonder that humanity is condemned to suffering."

"But I do accept reality," said Ruth. "It's only different from yours."

Ignoring this, Naomi concluded, "You come back here, and we all grant you've come back justifiably depressed over your divorce and so on, but you still come back here and within two days you're telling us you found a body on the beach. You even telephone to the Santa Monica Police Force! Get them out here and what do they find? A piece of torn material in your pocket and nothing more. Then you start telling us we've all been to a great fire in which a lot of animals died. Granted, there was a fire. But we were not — none of us was — there. Now you tell me you want a child, and while that, in itself, is not insane, it certainly is thoughtless when you have *our* blood and you're no longer married. Then you tell me about this racial figure and you say it must be his child. Ruth, Ruth. Put it together. Listen to it with my ears. Watch it with my eyes. What greater reality can there be than my death? And then ask me to accept these dreams of yours. . . ."

Naomi repositioned her neck and shoulders and definitely finished. "There is reality. . . and nothing else."

Ruth, lying in the bed beside her mother, reached out to take a cigarette. She lit it.

Fire.

Her mother was dying. That was real. But there is always death.

"Mama?" said Ruth.

"Yes, dear?" Naomi was drowsy now.

"What is hope?"

Naomi thought very briefly and smiled in the dark.

"That's a very good question," she said.

But Ruth said, "What is it?"

Again the pause, and then, "Hope," said Naomi, "is death in the mind."

Ruth broke at that.

"Then what kept you alive?" she asked. "What kept you alive?"

"You will discover," said Naomi, "if you are able to die as I am — *thoughtfully* — that you die rationale by rationale. All your reasoned frameworks are eventually torn down by reason itself. Finally, there is nothing left but life. And that's what dies. Or will. . ." she had to add, "be what dies in me. Only life and nothing more. The rest is resolved before death happens. Hope is deceptive, Ruth. It blocks reality and therefore it must die first. Hope stands in the path of grace. It's a wall."

There was silence.

Naomi said, really almost totally in sleep, "I often wonder, though, what happens to those who die with a bang. I often wonder if there can be, for them..."

Sleep.

Ruth still lay awake.

Her cigarette broke the dark.

She watched it. It was comforting. What was it like? It was like a...

Ruth did not know.

But Naomi would have said, "It is like...a cigarette."

In the dark.

The Chronicle of Hell's Babies

Wednesday, September 28th, 1938: Culver City 7:00 a.m.

The bushes parted.

A man stepped through. Before him lay a body of water that might have been a pond, that might have been a miniature lake. But it wasn't either. No sailboats, and not a single carp. The man was puzzled.

He wore a blue serge suit with the very whitest of pin stripes. He wore two-tone shoes, black and white, a rose-colored tie, a yellow shirt, and a white carnation (pinned to the wrong lapel). He carried a green suede writing case that had a black handle. He carried it badly. He was clumsy. This man was small of stature, round-faced, and extremely ugly. His nose was like the worst nightmare of noses — large, pock-marked, and hairy. His eyes were small and black and they darted about in their sockets like the swiveleyes of a chameleon. His lips were apparently nonexistent. He seemed to have swallowed them. He was able to fold them both inside his mouth at once. His teeth slanted inward. His cheeks were oily and dark with beard, although he had shaved and powdered not an hour before. His hands, black-haired, were permanently fisted to hide the deplorable length of his fingers, which were so short as to be childlike. The man's name was Cohn, and as he dabbed at the sweat under his chin with the back of one fist, he muttered, "Oi."

He stepped forward into a great deal of light and promptly stubbed his toe. Preparing to scream with pain and rage, he realized that his toe did not hurt him at all. It seemed neither stubbed nor scuffed. He looked around him furtively. Seeing that he was quite alone, he very gently stubbed his toe again. This time, it bounced back at him.

"Rubber rocks!" he said out loud. "As I live to breathe — made of rubber!"

Mr. Cohn found this extremely pleasing and he unfisted long enough to rub his stubby fingers over the lifelike stone.

"I wonder. . ." he said, gazing inquisitively at the trees, bushes, grass, and reeds nearby. But, no. All these were quite real. Yes, Mr. Cohn decided, apart from the fact that each and every one of them was contained in some sort of pot or can, they were quite, quite real.

Suddenly, from far above him, a voice yelled out, "You lost or something?"

"Yes — yes," said Mr. Cohn. "I suppose that is what I am."

He raised his head. A gigantic fellow in rolled sleeves stood to his right.

"Mr. Lost, eh?"

"Mr. Cohn," said Mr. Cohn.

"Well, you'd better get outa here," said the giant, who, from Mr. Cohn's point of view, was haloed in an arc of light.

"I don't know where I'm at," said Mr. Cohn, rising. "And rubber rocks! I don't understand. Some sort of joke?"

He dusted himself with his fist. The giant watched him.

"You'd better not've touched anything, mister," said the giant. "Cause it's all in place, ya know. An' we got a union here can put ya underground if ya mess around with our rocks."

"No, no," said Mr. Cohn quite meekly. "I didn't mess a thing."

The ruffian walked one step nearer, which is to say, he cornered Mr. Cohn between his beloved rock, a potted palm, and himself.

"What are you, anyway?" he asked. "Where are you from, wise guy?"

Mr. Cohn trembled noticeably all the way through his reply.

"Well — I — I — I was over to New York City. Yesterday before yesterday. Flew to Chicago. To Colorado. To Los Angeles. In a plane, you know."

"Yeah."

"Got here..."

"Yeah."

"And I'm — I am — I am..."

"Well?"

"I am...Miss Jacobs..."

"Sure."

"Looking for Miss Jacobs. The movie star. Yes?"

"What do you want with her, fellah?"

"I want — well, I want."

"You weird or somethin'?"

"No, no. No. I want Miss Jacobs."

"You came to see her boobies, eh?" the giant leered.

"Boobies? Boobies? No!" Mr. Cohn protested. Unfortunately, he protested so vehemently that saliva appeared at the corners of his mouth and clouded his words with what appeared to be ravening desire.

"Well, I don't think you're allowed in here, mister," said the giant, and was about to proceed with a forceful eviction when a voice stopped him.

From beyond the bushes came the megaphone announcement that "This set must now be cleared! Everybody off the set, please!"

And the giant disappeared, as though in answer to a wish.

Mr. Cohn immediately seized this circumstance and beat

a hasty retreat into the bushes, where he hid — hoping to see Miss Myra Jacobs, and to present her with the diamonds and sapphires and with his written proposal, all contained, together with a cheque for five hundred thousand dollars, in his green suede bag.

8:00 a.m.

The set was now alive with light.

The palm leaves shone. The rubber rocks were scrubbed. The water had been blued. Mr. Cohn was safely in his hiding place.

Myra, in her dressing room, was being worked over by three ladies and two men. She would not appear for hours. It was ever thus.

Adolphus had to wait. At this hour of every morning, this seemed to be what his job as director amounted to. Waiting. He waited while the lights were set. He waited for the chief grip to become sober. He waited for the cameraman to come out of the washroom. He waited for his assistant director to wake up. He waited, as a matter of fact, for someone — anyone — to say "good morning" to him. And this took some time.

"Good morning, Mr. Damarosch."

"Good morning. Who are you?"

"I'm Walter, Mr. Damarosch. The note carrier."

"Walter the note carrier? What does that mean?"

"Well, I carry notes back and forth. Here. I have a note for you from Miss Jacobs, one from Mr. Feldbruhn, and one from Mr. Niles."

"Oh, well," said Adolphus. "What do they say?"

"Oh! Mr. Damarosch! I never..."

"What do they say, Walter?" said Dolly, inwardly thanking God that at least something was done for him.

Walter screwed up his lengthy face, which jammed all his freckles together like a cloud of lady bugs, and he began to recite — not referring at all to the papers and envelopes in his large red hands.

He first recited Mr. Feldbruhn's communiqué (which was about goldfish) and then he went on to recite Mr. Niles's communiqué (a warning to Dolly not to speak to anyone from New York City) and then, at the last, he came to Myra's.

"And what does she want?"

"She wrote, 'Do I really have to play this scene nude all over?' "

"Ah, yes..." said Dolly. "The old last-minute panic. Typical."

Walter could not avoid blushing with anticipation. One large red hand crept into a pocket and stayed there.

"Mr. Damarosch?"

"Yes, Walter?"

"Well — ah — well..."

"Ah well *what?* Please don't stammer. I can't stand it. It makes my blood gather."

"Then what's your answer."

"I haven't the foggiest notion what you're talking about, Walter."

"Miss Jacobs, sir. Miss Jacobs. Is she going to?"

"Oh, *that*..." Dolly gave the boy a look. "Take your hand out of your pocket, Walter. At once. Please remember where we are."

The hand, reluctant, withdrew.

"Well?"

"The answer is — yes. Of course. It's in the script."

"Nude all over..." said Walter dreamily.

"I'm not the least worried about Myra, my boy. Not in the least. It's Ajax I'm worried about."

"Mr. Apollo?"

"That's right."

Walter gulped. The stray hand fled to its old place, but this time more in shame than in pride.

"Do you mean...?" he said. "Do you mean...?" he

said. "Do you *really* mean. . . ?"

"Yes," said Dolly. "I *mean*."

"And he's embarrassed, of course," said Walter, losing his stammer altogether. "And won't do it. Of course. Will he. No man would!"

Dolly sighed.

"Take your hand out of your pocket, Walter."

Walter blushed.

"I can't," he said. "I can't, Mr. Damarosch."

"Why not?" said Dolly.

"Well —" said Walter. "It's stuck!"

Dolly looked away.

"There," he said cryptically, "you have Mr. Apollo's problem in a nutshell, Walter. Or should I say, in a pocket."

8:15 a.m.

Dolly was still waiting.

Neither Ajax Apollo nor Myra Jacobs had appeared. They were the only two actors in the scene.

The scene itself represented a jungle pool, somewhere in the South Pacific. The hero, Ajax, and the heroine, Myra, were to swim about in the altogether and to "suggest" (the Hays Office) love-making under water. Both would also be seen standing at the water's edge — their privates hidden by carefully plotted foliage. It was a lovely scene, full of sun and trees and tropics.

Hell's Babies took place in Chicago, and it told the story of a floozy's rise to fame.

One day, not long before this particular day, Dolly had described the South Pacific-pool scene for his mother, and Naomi had said, "But, dear. . ."

Dolly, extricating himself from the sensuality of the mood, had looked at her quite blankly.

"What's the matter, Mother?" he asked.

Naomi appeared to be confused.

"Didn't you say that *Hell's Babies* takes place in the city of Chicago?"

"It does," said Adolphus.

"But then why..." She stopped — took a breath and said, "why this pool in the South Pacific?"

"Well — it's a *musical*, Mother," said Dolly — incredulous that she should have to ask. Naomi had just given him a queer look and had wandered away down the beach, accompanied by the yellow dog and carrying her orange parasol.

"Mr. Damarosch?" said Walter meekly, waking Dolly from his reverie. "There are some men here to see you."

From the tone of Walter's voice and from the look in his eye, Dolly was prompted to panic.

"What have I done?" he said, trying to hide in his chair.

"It's not the police, Mr. Damarosch," Walter explained.

"Well, why didn't you say so? You said it was 'some men' to see me. Doesn't that always mean the police?"

"I don't know, Mr. Damarosch," said Walter. "I haven't been in any trouble yet."

"Well you will be. Who are they?"

"Well, that's it," said Walter, faltering.

"Say it, boy. *Say* it."

"The men here to see you are from New York."

"Oh," Dolly understood.

Mr. Niles, head-of-the-studio, had expressly stated in his note that on no account, under no condition, was Dolly to speak to anyone from New York City. The reason was plain. Money talks. New York owned Niles Studios.

Dolly blanched.

"What will I do?" he asked. "They'll want to know why I've spent so much money on this scene. They'll want to know why I've hired Ajax Apollo — who cannot act. They'll want me to tell the story — outline the plot of *Hell's Babies* from start to finish — and I can't. They'll want to know why I'm making this picture and I won't be able to tell them. I'm an artist! I don't answer questions!"

Walter said, "They're coming over, now."

Dolly stared where Walter pointed. Three men, all of whom were the same height, all of whom had the same square, blue-eyed face and the same brown hair, were advancing from the far side of the sound stage. They might have been triplets. They even walked in step; a dancing trio. Vaudeville.

Dolly wanted to fall down.

They all wore blue suits and carried black bags full of either money or sinister weapons — the posture of the bags heavily implying the latter. They were held "at the ready."

Dolly backed away. Surely they would do him some harm and he did not know where to go.

Just at that moment, far off across the sound stage, a dressing-room door opened. Down stepped Ajax Apollo, six feet tall, nineteen years old, the very picture of male sexuality. He wore, over his well-tanned altogetherness, a chartreuse robe.

He was followed by a retinue of tiny men who wore white coats and who carried little blue towels and boxes of tissue. They were like dancers and walked on their heels, with their toes pointed out to either side. They also bore a slight resemblance to penguins. Albino penguins.

Adolphus touched Walter on the arm, turning him in the direction of Ajax Apollo.

"Get him," he hissed.

One of the New York visitors heard this. Dolly smiled in a friendly way.

Mr. Apollo approached. "You want somethin'?" he said.

"Yes," said Dolly, still smiling. "There are three lovely men to see you."

Ajax stood up tall. He smelled of makeup and incense. He rarely smiled. He did not need to. No one ever looked at his face.

Adolphus stepped forward.

He motioned New York to follow him.

They did so. "You must promise not to touch him," he said. "But you may look."

Dolly got to within a cane's length of Ajax.

Ajax was watching him carefully.

Dolly inserted the end of his cane, chest-high, in the front of Mr. Apollo's robe. The robe swung open — at first tentatively, and then, so wide that it fell from the shoulders into the waiting hands of two attendant penguins.

New York trembled. One of them grumbled, "He's wearing a jock-strap..."

"Yes," said another, "but at least it's made of gold."

9:10 a.m.

Walter to Adolphus: "Miss Jacobs will be out in twenty minutes."

"Thank you, Walter. Now we can use the stand-ins."

The stand-ins were called. They wore tights and each had a figure that supposedly corresponded to the figure of the star it represented. In one case, this was true.

9:30 a.m.

No Myra Jacobs.

"Walter! Take a note!"

9:40 a.m.

Ajax Apollo had to be returned to his dressing room. Portions of his body makeup had been spoiled.

New York was seated, gingerly, in chairs and offered drinks. They must recuperate before the appearance of Myra Jacobs. They wiped their brows with borrowed tissues and smiled with anticipation. Nervously. Making movies was more engrossing than they had thought.

9:45 a.m.

Mr. Niles appeared on the set, looking worn and frightened.

"Where are they?" he quavered to Dolly.

"Over there," said Adolphus.

"Ah, good," said Mr. Niles, even permitting himself to smile with relief. "You showed them Myra?"

"No," said Dolly languidly. "The fact is, so far I've only shown them Ajax Apollo."

Mr. Niles, small and gray, brightened.

"So far, eh?"

"Yes."

"Well, well, well," said Mr. Niles. "Well, well, well. Good. Then, if the actors are ready, we should begin. Keep them distracted, Dolly." Mr. Niles referred to New York. "Keep them distracted, my boy! That's what we're here for."

He trotted away, unburdened, for the moment at least, of their oppression.

9:50 a.m.

Walter loped up and said, "Mr. Damarosch to see Mr. Damarosch."

"Father?"

"Yes, sir."

"Let him come on," said Dolly.

The sound stage was now a ship. The passengers had all but assembled. In a moment, George would appear.

9:55 a.m.

George Damarosch made his entrance at some distance from Dolly, at the far side of the stage, and Dolly had a good chance to study him as he made his way across, led by the same bobbing Walter who had announced him.

Dolly really had no idea how old his father was. He tried to calculate it in years, but it was impossible, because George had never celebrated his birthday and Dolly did not know what date it fell on, let alone what year he had been born. He only knew that George had been born in Canada, in a city called Regina, and that, having looked it up on a map once, Dolly found Regina to be in the middle of a rather large expanse of Empire-red plains with no other place names around it. But that did not help in establishing his father's age. What did help was the way he looked, and judging by that, by appearances, one would have to say that George Damarosch was at least sixty. But, Dolly thought, watching him now crossing the shiny, empty spaces of the stage, he must be nearly seventy. To a child a parent is always middle-aged, and Dolly's most recurrent image of his father was when he himself was in his early teens and twenties, when George, visiting or being visited, had looked something between a prosperous and robust forty-eight and a virile but stout fifty-five. Now, he seemed more of a grandparent than a parent.

He got to Dolly's side. Adolphus rose.

There was a silence.

George waited for Walter to leave them, and then he coughed.

Dolly took a step in his father's direction. George immediately sat down in Dolly's chair, leaving the gesture of respect stranded in mid-formation.

Dolly drew another (Myra's) chair from its nearby place, making an irritating squeak on the floor as he did so, and he sat down and stared at his father, and George stared at Dolly and blew his nose in a frayed magenta handkerchief.

"You look in bad condition, 'Dolphus," he said finally. "Have you given up living entirely? You look terrible. You look like a freak."

"I am a freak, Father," said Dolly simply. He was neither angry nor adamant.

"Come to think of it, I suppose you are," said George, looking around over his shoulder for spies. And something else.

"What would you like, Father?" Dolly asked.

"Brandy."

"Brandy," said Dolly. He called Walter. Walter came. A bottle followed.

George almost looked Dolly in the eye.

He gazed around the sound stage and spoke with oblique attention.

"You bled lately?"

"No, Father."

"You look peaked. Who takes care of you?"

"I take care of myself."

"Get a nurse. I always said you should have a nurse. Get yourself a nurse, Doll, and we'll all go free." Here the implication was that George, with a minimum of aid from a few others, had spent his entire life in Dolly's service. Nothing could be further from the truth. "Get yourself a nurse and we'll all go free," said George. "Yes."

"How have you been, Father?" Dolly asked, desperate not to fall into the old pattern of having the conversation revolve for several hours around the question of his affliction.

"How have I been?" said George. "My, my. I find that very touching. Thank you. Nobody has asked me how I've been for fifteen years. I have been down. I have been low. I have been, *and you should know it, Doll, made* insignificant by a bunch of nincompoops. In the parlance of the times, I am old hat." He stared at the set. His voice rose up into the cats. Out to the edges. "I am outré. I am a used shoe. I am a plug nickel. I am forgotten. Abused. Distrusted. Looked at askance. Hated. Dumped. Reviled and thrown out on my backside. In short, I am finished." Then he looked up and said, "Supposedly."

It was quite significant that he had not said he was feared in the course of saying that he was hated. In the old days the two were considered to be synonymous.

"What has happened?" said Dolly, knowing that his father would like nothing better than a chance to explain himself in front of all these people.

"Time has happened," George said. "What they call change and progress. You could say, youth has happened, I suppose. And I am the victim. I was given the boot by the young. I hate the young. They're monsters. No one under forty knows a thing about life and there isn't an important office in this town that doesn't house a bloody (sorry, Doll) but a *bloody* twenty-year-old kissing someone's behind and getting what he wants for it. Well, they'll pay. In time, they all pay. Let me tell you, they do. Someday, they'll be sixty-five. Yessirree." (And therein lay the tale.) "No one," said George, with almost apoplectic emphasis, "no one ever got down on their knees behind *me*, by God, especially no one under twenty-five. And, by God, I never indulged in it either, and I'll be damned if I'll start now."

He was saying he had been asked to, but Dolly did not know by whom.

New York came forward, displaying smiles.

Several technicians watched and listened. Mr. Cohn, in his hiding place, cringed and heard it too.

Perhaps for George the basic problem was that he should have been a dictator — one who must seize and amass power rather than one who assumes he has it. George had never bothered with a purge. He had never called in the firing squad. Never sent messengers in the middle of the night. He merely assumed he would be obeyed, and for a while he had been, until the people he should have been smart enough to get rid of rose against him in their collective wrath and brought him down. Politics is no game for kings. They are too dependent on their blood. And the blood of their sons.

Many more people had arrived on board by now, and George turned his back on them contemptuously. The new Hollywood was nothing to him, compared to the old. It was the old order (his) that had created the picture industry, and these new people, as someone was to remark in a later era, did not even have faces. In the teens and twenties of the century there had been faces and personalities of epic grandeur, suitable to their station as America's pantheon of gods and goddesses. Now, for heaven's sake, there were people like Myra Jacobs, Peggy Gauntlett, Alice Gray, and Ajax Apollo, if you would believe it. Pretty people, nice people, with not a remarkable nose, nor a square chin among them. Without cheekbones, without their own eyelashes, without character and without the majesty of silence. They spoke and when they spoke they spoke with the voices of Potato, Idaho; Rivers, Missouri; Halibut, Massachusetts. Flat, stale, and, for some ungodly reason, profitable. Where was the mystery? Where was the greatness? Where was the allure? There had never been and never would be stars the like of Letitia Virden in this new era. Stars who could incite the passions of the adult, not the louse-brained, sexless passions of a bunch of fourteen-year-olds. (New York blanched and clutched its black bags.) Peggy Gauntlett, indeed! The woman wore pigtails! Or Myra Jacobs, who was all body and no brain, whose fame resided in a pout and a wiggle. A woman who showed what she was, when what was needed was mystery, allure, the promise of virginity hidden beneath the mask of maturity and guile — not the mask of puberty.

George's motto had always been, "Don't give 'em what they want, make 'em want what you've got." For twenty years (between 1908 and 1928) it had paid off. With stars like Letitia Virden, Naomi Nola, and the rest, and with pictures like *Queen of Hearts, Daughters of Desperation, The Belt of Satan*, and so forth, George had had a hand in forging the American Dream. Now his hand was tied. In 1928 he had brought in his six brothers and his seven nephews, and one by one they had eaten away at his empire until even brothers-in-law, third nephews twice removed, and cousins he had never heard of were into his pockets with scissors and into his back with knives. In 1936 (two months after Ruth had departed for Germany) a nephew from Colorado Springs had walked into George's office and said, "Uncle George, I'm here to tell you that they want you in the front office," and when George had replied that "This *is* the front office!" the nephew from Colorado Springs had said, "Not any more, Uncle George. We need this room for storage," and that had been that.

Dolly, on the other hand, had been sensible and lucky. At the age of twenty he had fallen in love with a photograph of J.J. Niles, Jr., and had gone to work for the father, Walter Niles, unaware that "J.J." stood for Jasmyn Jo, who loved horses and dressed like a boy. Thus, at approximately the same time as one Damarosch career was beginning to decline (1929) the other was beginning to ascend — albeit up the wrong ladder, but that did not matter. It could be corrected. . . and was.

The brandy was rapidly disappearing. Myra had not yet appeared. The atmosphere thickened.

George's eyes narrowed.

"Well," he said, "I suppose you wonder why we're here."

"Yes. We do," said Dolly.

"You hold your tongue," said George.

"Yes, sir," said Dolly. "I'm sorry."

"Speak only when you're spoken unto," George snapped. He always had been prone to biblicality, and he always had been rude — part of the trappings of his grandeur.

"You see those tarts and gigs out there?" he said, making libelous jabs with his finger in the exact direction of four or five well-known stars who were visiting the set. "You see 'em?"

"Yes, Father."

"America goes to bed every night with a whore in its arms."

"Yes, Father."

"That's what they want," he said.

"Yes."

"Stop saying yes, you little twirp. When I want a yes-man, I'll get one."

"Yes, sir."

"Look at 'em. Pro to the teeth." He gave the stage a look of disgust, almost launched into a sermon, thought better of it, and turned back to his son. "I won't go into it," he said. "I could, mind you, but I won't. I know the habits of every man and woman in this town. And they revolt me. Perverted. Every last one. A bunch of American wet dreams. Masturbators. Every one of 'em. (New York shifted and stood on one foot.) What we need in this bloody country is a revival of virginity." (Here came the pitch.) "I tell you, every man, woman, and child wants to get back their virginity. They don't know it, but they do. The Virgin Image." (His voice became actorish; it delivered his "speech.") "The Image of the Virgin. This once was known as the Virgin Land. Did you know that?" Dolly nodded. Where was Myra? "Let it return to that. Let it go back from prurience to purity. I tell you, that is the American Dream — not some babe in slacks and a sweater. And the sooner they know it, the better off they'll be." George was red-eyed now, brandy-eyed, and hoarse. But he was delivering his message. His message to his son. And now came the strings.

"Don't you give 'em what they want!" he cried, almost in tears, while Dolly watched amazed and the rest sat incredulous. "You give 'em what you've got! And you've got virginity. You've got it coming out of your ears and that is what this country needs. Is begging for. Is crying for. Is on its knees and praying for."

Ajax Apollo reappeared. Myra's dressing-room door was mysteriously opened, although no one was seen there.

"A long time ago," said George, now aware that his audience had grown in size, "a long time ago I ruled this roost. I told them what to do and what they wanted, here. This little roost called Hollywood. I was the king. Now I am not the king. But that does not matter." (Humility is a great weapon. More faces turned toward him.) "I am here on the sidelines, in the gutter. But I don't care. I was the king and that is enough of that. But when I ruled this roost, I understood this roost. And better still, I understood the roosts beyond this roost. The little roosts all over this great lovely farmyard of a country. America. And I knew what the chicks of America wanted. Wholesomeness. And I knew what the hens of America wanted. Wholesomeness. And I knew what the cocks of America wanted." He breathed in. "Wholesomeness. Virginity. The Virgin Image, personified in the virgin body and the virgin face that could be fit to match the virgin mind of this great wide land. The image of an immaculate hand, worthy of the masculine grasp of American manhood. Worthy of the trusting grasp of American children and the friendly, sisterly grasp of American womanhood. This hand" (he held up his own) "this immaculate hand would lead up, God knows where." His voice shivered with the mystery and promise of his words. "It would lead us to a future worthy of our planning, and a heaven peaceful enough for our dreams. And I tell you that I know," he said, letting his hand fall down into Dolly's lap, "I know unto whom... this hand belongs."

He stopped. The listening stopped. He waited. So did the others. Nothing came of it. Only silence.

George said to Dolly, "Have you got a million dollars?"

"No," said Dolly, whose mouth had dried up. He didn't know how to remove his father's hand from where it lay. "No, sir. I haven't."

"Has anyone?" George turned to the stage in general.

No answer.

"Well," said George, at last reclaiming his hand, "what have you got?"

"Why do you want to know?" said Dolly. His ears were still singing with his father's epic speech, and he could not even begin to fathom the connection. "What has that got to do with things?"

"Never mind that," said George. "Just tell me what you've got."

"Well," said Dolly. Pause. "I have nothing but doctor bills. And that's all."

"You're making a great mistake," said George, his eyes narrowing. "A great mistake." He leaned forward. The secret came out. "Letitia Virden is going to make a comeback."

Dolly gasped.

George smiled.

"The Little Virgin is about to be reborn," he said. "Her image will rise once more to sweep America the way it did before. She has asked me to find investors. I thought you were wise. But I see that you are an idiot."

He gave Adolphus time to reconsider. But Adolphus was staring at Myra's door in silence. Titty Virden. Back.

There was not much time to think about what his father had said, for presently George wept, taking from his pocket the magenta handkerchief, frayed at the corners, with a hole to one side, and blowing his nose and going quite scarlet at the ears, he said, "I'm finished, then. I'm really washed up forever."

"She's asked *you* for money?" said Dolly.

"Yes."

"And you still want her?"

"Yes."

"But a million dollars is ridiculous, Father."

"Is it?" said George. "But, I love her."

"Of course it is," said Dolly, whose disgust spread rapidly from his father to the thought of Letitia Virden. "No one has a million dollars."

"Ah," said George. "Ah, Dolly-Doll. You just don't know where you live. This is America. The land of entrepreneurs and daring. . . ."

He dried his tears and rose.

"Well," he said. "I won't stay." He took two steps away and one back. "Are you sure," he said, "you have nothing?"

"Positive," said Dolly. "But I'm sorry."

George was looking for a line that would not come, and he managed only: "To have a thankless child is like being bitten by a worthless snake!"

And then, as though he had indeed been bitten, just so, on his heel, he turned and limped — stumbling with much drunkenness and some age — out of sight into the washrooms.

Dolly sighed.

Myra appeared.

10:30 a.m.

She wore a blue robe. Her hair, its golden curls curled more tightly to resist the water, looked gorgeously seductive.

Ida, her maid-companion, danced down the steps of the dressing room and over to the stricken Adolphus.

"She's ready, Mr. Dolly," she said.

Adolphus looked.

In blue and gold, with all the promise of what lay beneath the robe, Myra Jacobs was indeed a star of stars.

She smiled her lost smile, her pupils large and black, her eyebrows arched. Her hands were nervous. They had that job to do. The loosening of the robe.

Her slippers were Mexican silver. Her ankles divine. A shell might have served to act as her vehicle. Ida danced back and caught her mistress's hand.

"Oh, Mr. Dolly! This lady is the be-all and end-all."

Dolly rose, using the cane.

Myra Jacobs.

New York frowned.

Mr. Cohn hid higher.

Myra's shoes kissed the floor — one — two — three steps nearer.

Dolly's eyes wet up with tears.

"Hullo," he said.

"Hello," said Myra, the last of the passengers to board the ship.

10:45 a.m.

The stand-ins were removed, Dolly having adjusted lighting, camera set-up, sound, and mood. Ajax disrobed again and housed himself across the pool. Myra stood at the edge. Ida held her hands out.

"Dolly," Myra said.

Dolly toed forward.

"Yes?"

"Kiss me just once before this robe goes off. Please."

Dolly kissed her hand.

Ida sighed. Such a lovely picture...

Walter put his hand (both hands) into pockets.

New York fell upon Myra's image expectantly.

George came out of the washroom.

Mr. Niles, on the sidelines, bit his nails.

Myra...undid the robe.

The ship sank.

The Chronicle of the Three Mothers

Thursday, September 29th, 1938:
The Beach at Topanga
9:30 a.m.

"All right, who's missing?" said B.J. Trelford.

Seated around the twelve-foot plank table, her children were sipping orange juice through colored straws. One glass was unattended. One chair was empty.

"Who is it?" she said. "Come on."

The children regarded their mother with those blank faces that children can muster when they are in the midst of a lie or of a secret game. They did not smile. They did not look serious. They just looked blank.

"All right," said B.J. "Very well then. No beach."

This produced a slight panic, for the children were already dressed for their morning swim. Each wore a swim suit, each carried a pail and shovel, each was loosely tied into green water wings.

"Mama?"

"Yes, Pete."

"We can't tell you, Mama."

"Why not? What is this?"

"Well," Peter gazed with his leadership eyes around the square of faces. He was next to the eldest, the eldest being a girl, Mary Baker Eddy Trelford. Mary Baker was thirteen at this juncture. Peter was twelve. Mary Baker had renounced leadership (she read books) and thus the role of leader had fallen to Peter, a wide-eyed, solemn boy who led more through concern than through desire. Peter, however, had one flaw — the kind that is fatal to leaders of any age. He lacked a good memory. He forgot where he left his water wings; he forgot what time it was; he forgot how old he was; and he forgot the names of his brothers and sisters. What he could remember (and what enabled him to remain concerned about each of their problems) was the set expression of each of the children's faces in repose. Josh, aged six, for instance, had lost his Teddy bear the other day (it had been carried out by the tide) and his expression was now one of brinked tears and no smile. Gloria, aged ten, had stolen a quarter from B.J.'s purse on Saturday, and was now afraid to spend it lest her mother ask how she had achieved her purchase. Consequently, Gloria spent a lot of time hiding, rehiding, and forgetting where she had put her money, and this produced a constant and furtive eye. "Where? Where? Where?" her expression read. That was Gloria.

Michael, the baby, talked to himself, Charity had an invisible friend, Marilyn was a foreign spy, etc., etc. Each private worry or occupation produced its own gaze and it was this that Peter recognized and counted by.

Now, at the table, what bothered him was that he could not recall which gaze was missing. Was it... he looked intently into each face... the lost Teddy bear? No. The broken shoelace? No. The wet bloomers? No.

"Well," said B.J., "we will sit here, *inside*, until someone 'fesses up. It's not me who's gonna miss my swim this morning, and the low-tide sand castles, and the lady with the orange parasol. Nosirree. And it certainly won't be me that's gonna hafta explain this to your father!"

She sat back and lit a cigarette.

In the mother-part of her mind, of course, she was concerned. No child had yet drowned, but the possibility was always present. However, this morning, none of the children had as yet ventured out onto the beach. She knew that. They were not allowed to do so until all were dressed and ready to go.

The faces stared at her.

They stared at Peter.

Then back at B.J.

"Is it Marilyn?"

"No, Mama. I'm here."

"Is it Gloria?"

Gloria went pale under her tan. The very sound of her name on her mother's lips threw her into a panic.

"No, Mama. No. No," she protested.

"What's the matter with you, Gloria?"

"Nothing, Mama. Nothing. Nothing."

"You look pale. You got a temperature?"

"No, Mama."

"Flushes?"

"No, Mama."

"What're you holdin' back from me, Gloria?"

"Nothing. Honest. I don't know *where* it is."

"Where what is?" B.J. said, standing up suspiciously.

"Wha. . . wha. . . wha. . ."

"She means who," said Peter calmly.

"*Who?*"

"Who it is who isn't here," said Peter.

"Oh," B.J. said. Her voice rose. "It beats me all hollow! You kids! Let me tell ya! Don't you people even know who you all are? Each other? What's the matter with you? What is this? Can't you keep *track* of each other?"

Mary Baker dreamily put down her book of verses and spoke.

"Can't you?" she said to her mother, insolently. She was just at that age.

"I'll whomp you one, Mary Baker," said B.J. with equal insolence. She could play all the parts — and had to.

"I was only askin'," said Mary Baker, without losing her infuriating tone of practiced innocence. "You don't need to get all mad, Mama."

"Now you listen to me, you bunch of gamesters! One of your brothers or one of your sisters is missing. And if you do not immediately recall for me which one it is, in exactly and in precisely and in only *one* minute," she paused here and gave the full power of her glare into each of the assembled faces, "you're gonna hafta *pose*. That's what!"

A gasp took in the whole room. And was held.

"Now, *that's* more like it," said B.J., sensing her triumph. "*Children's Crusade!!*" she further announced. "That's what!"

"The Children's Crusade" was the very worst of punishments. It was a gigantic work that sat out back in the shed where, from time to time, Noah added to its dimensions. He was interested in the project, but it was difficult to get the children to pose for it. They had at first been entreated on the basis of filial duty, then on the basis of payment (lollipops, lemonade, and comic books), then on the basis of threats, and finally, when all else failed, on the basis of punishment. Sometimes, when Noah was extra-anxious to work or unavoidably inspired toward the piece, the charges had to be trumped. But this was rare.

Each child had his own pose — some drowning, some bent over with "the agonies," as they called them, some dead (the very worst pose of all), and some dragging reluctant others to the edge of the "sea," which was represented by bales of hay that itched the toes and hurt the elbows. Consequently, each child hated and feared "The Children's Crusade" for his own reasons, and would do anything rather than have to suffer it.

Its threat welded their minds to a renewed effort.

"Y'all got thirty-two seconds," B.J. announced. "Thirty-one. Thirty. Twenty-nine."

"Don't talk, Mama. We can't concentrate."

"Twenty-eight — twenty-seven. Twenty-six," B.J. continued, but in a kindly whisper.

"Twenty-five." She looked around the table.

Mary Baker.

Pete.

Joe.

Gloria.

Marilyn.

Charity.

Josh.

Michael (one year old, in a high chair).

Michael.

Josh.

Charity.

Marilyn.

Charity.

Marilyn.

Charity.

The untouched glass of orange juice sat between them.

Charity.

Glass.

Marilyn.

Marilyn.

Glass.

Charity.

It dawned on both Pete and B.J. at the same moment.

Marilyn.

Glass.

Charity.

The missing child was Charity's invisible friend.

B.J. roared with laughter.

Charity gave her mother a look of reproach and turned to the empty chair.

"I told you there'd be trouble if you didn't drink your orange juice up. Now we've all gotta do 'Children's Crusade'!" she said.

Joe, aged five, burst into tears. He was one of the dead children, lying under a cross.

Michael didn't mind. He got to be carried by Pete.

But Mary Baker Eddy was furious.

"It isn't Christian," she raged, "to make us all Crusade in the morning!"

"Very well," said B.J., who could not much stand the idea of having them all inside at this particular hour, anyway. "You are forgiven. However," she intercepted their stampede by raising her voice again, "however, Charity..."

"Yes, Mama."

"That friend of yours will have to stay behind this morning and wash the orange-juice glasses."

"Yes, Mama."

Charity turned to her friend and made a face at him.

"You ruin everything," she said. "And I think I'm gonna find another friend. You're just a spoilsport!"

And with that she tramped off loudly, after the others, clanking her pail and shovel and banging all the doors.

That noontime, at the table, there was one less chair. And Charity in mourning. Her friend had drowned.

Across the base of "The Children's Crusade" Noah had scratched: OF SUCH IS THE KINGDOM OF HEAVEN — AND OF EARTH.

10:00 a.m.

Naomi was in pain.

Miss Bonkers administered a needle.

Ruth sat down by her mother, on the balcony, to wait for the pain to abate.

"It's going," said Naomi. "It goes very quickly. The only problem is I can't eat anything and I'm hungry."

"What about some soup?" Ruth asked.

"Soup is the worst of all," said Naomi. "So hot. I love soup. More than anything in the world, soup is what I love. And now I can't even look at it. All your best friends turn against you."

She tried to laugh, and picked up her knitting.

"I probably won't ever finish this," she said.

"What is it?" Ruth asked.

"A sweater," said Naomi, holding parts of it up for Ruth's inspection. "For chilly evenings in the grave."

"Oh, Mother. Don't."

Ruth turned away.

"It's my death," said Naomi. "I'll say what I like."

Ruth gazed along the beach.

The needles clicked like bones, Ruth thought. Miss Bonkers turned the pages of her book rapidly.

Naomi said, "What's the matter, Miss B.? Don't you like that book?"

"Oh, yes," said Miss Bonkers, still with the same rapidity, turning pages. "But this is the bedroom scene and I just can't stand it."

"Well, that's funny," said Naomi. "I thought that was why you were reading it. It has the worst reputation I ever heard of."

"Oh, well," said Miss Bonkers, "that may be Mrs. Damarosch, but I read it for the war scenes. And *they're* magnificent."

"Really?" said Naomi. Click. Click. Click.

"War scenes always hold the very depths of my attention," said Miss Bonkers. "Anything with a death is so sad. In a book."

"In a book, eh?"

"Oh, yes. Just breaks the heart. And here, in all these war scenes, there must be twenty deaths on each page. And the most masterful thing is, every one hits you in the same way. Right in the heart."

Ruth got up and walked down onto the sand.

The needles continued to click, and the pages to turn — more slowly. It was a long war.

11:00 a.m.

Mother looked back from the mirror.

This morning she wore her hair bound and lightly powdered with iron gray. This morning her eye shadow was blue, her expertly sunken sockets a dark, unhealthy brown. Her lipstick? Try a little pink — add a little white. Perfect. For this morning.

This morning was an "old" morning. Why not admit it? She felt old. Mother took such very good care of her son that sometimes she felt just a teensy bit tired. Diddums she. Mommums. But only tired sometimes. Only very rarely, hardly ever *really, never* most times — because down deep in her great big heart (so full of love and goodies) nothing, not even the very worst of ill health — her migraines, her stomach cramps, her arthritic hands, her backaches, her agonizing chest pains (brought on by scrubbing all those floors, taking in all that washing from rich folks up on the hill) could ever keep Mummy from the reward of putting herself into an early grave for Baby. Nothing could daunt her desire for his happiness. Nothing. Could it.

No.

Well, one or two things, maybe. She didn't feel quite *that* old this morning.

She removed the dark unhealthy bags from beneath her eyes.

That was better.

One mustn't suffer too much.

2:30 p.m.

By afternoon Mother was feeling very sexy.

She looked in the mirror at her long blond curly hair and brushed and brushed and brushed it.

She adjusted her falsies.

She was seated.

Her cigarette dangled from the corner of her bee-stung lips. She went on brushing. And as she brushed, the bristles lightly touched her naked shoulders.

Oh my, Mommy, didn't that feel nice?

Brush, brush. Harder. Harder.

She took off her hair.

To hell with brushing *that!* She'd brush her shoulders and her arms and her tummy and her thighs instead. My goodness! That was just too wonderful for words.

Now. Where could Mommy go very quickly to get a man?

She set the cigarette aside, took a long drink from her oversized brandy snifter, and thought about it.

As she thought about it, she ate her ruby lipstick avidly, chewed it from her luscious lips, tonguing the lovely strawberry flavors and gulping hotly all the little greasy buds of dye.

And in came Freddy Big Eyes.

Poor Freddy had a thin, dying look. His soulful mind was wasting here in this hellhole of shady business deals that Mother wallowed in. Besides which, she had sold his precious instrument for gain.

Mother saw him in the mirror, or tried to. Her triple-false eyelashes were so heavy with mascara that all save her own image, so close at hand, was a blur.

"What can I do for ya, kid?" she said. "I suppose ya want some more a dem via-lin lessons. Well — I'll hafta see what I can come up with. In the meantime, honey, you come on over here an' give your mother a kiss. Say! You're gettin' kinda grown up, aint'cha, for your age? Well, now. You hobble back over there an' peel me a kumquat, while I pull my nerves together. I'm feelin' kinda blue."

Little Freddy Big Eyes thumped on his crutches across the room.

Mother's boudoir had mirrors in the ceiling. And her bed was a very large swan.

Little Freddy Big Eyes soulfully peeled a kumquat with

his very own precious fingers, but for a violinist he was often very clumsy and juiced things up so that Mother had to hit him with her brush.

"You're gettin' kumquat juice on my one and only bearskin rug," she said. Then she drew her robe up over her shoulders again and tied the cord more tightly around her sixteen-inch waist and put her hair back on.

Sometimes Mother could be hard and cruel. But she loved him. Freddy knew that. Look what she'd done to her reputation to put him through school.

Now Mother picked up her jeweled nail file and drank some more Martini from the oversized brandy snifter. She lit another cigarette and ground the last one out in an alabaster ashtray. She stole a loving mother's look through her lashes at her crippled boy.

"Listen," she said to Freddy Big Eyes, "why don't you stump 'round the block to that Peggy O'Neill's house. She'll play parchesi with you, honey. Ya hear me?"

Distant Freddy Big Eyes nodded.

"Mother's got a little business deal to cook."

So Freddy Big Eyes left the scene. He knew what business was.

Mother sat there thinking. "Well," she thought out loud into the mirror, "I gotta do something for that poor kid. Don't I?"

Her head bobbed and her wide, delicious hips seduced the velvet cushion she was seated on as her mind ground out her thoughts. She knew exactly what she had to do.

"I'm gonna get someone up here t' see me, an' we're gonna get that kid another via-lin."

5:15 p.m.

Now Mother looked like her best set of Cecil Beaton photographs. What lovely hair she had.

What poise. What gracious languor in her wrists.

She sat before the mirror, posed. Mother was like that. Patrician.

Her nose was a little tattletale of breeding. Somewhere in her family tree hid kings of France and also English dukes and duchesses. If Mother shook that tree just hard enough, heaven knows what artistocracy might fall. But Mother's taste declined so rude a gesture. Surely one's lovely self was all one needed. And one's son.

Where was one's son?

Perhaps out of doors in the paddock with Bogart, the groom? Did she not hear the distant neighing of purebred horses? Yes. So comforting.

Ah, la! But was it not contentment itself to know that one's son had all the best advantages?

Mother was very comfy in her knowledge that she had provided to the last detail all that was needed. It had not been easy but Mother had graciously consented to lend her lineage to the marriage bed, and had been tireless in her labors to pull through with a son for Daddy. And for history. Now, there he was in the paddock. Her effort.

Daddy was much too often away in New York City — and Mother usually had to converse with him by long distance telephone. So she was lonely. But Mother was conscientious. She knew that money did not grow on trees, not even family trees. So, Daddy sometimes had to work in order that one did not let down one's side.

And Mother was brave, too. A little loneliness did not harm one, if one endured it for one's son. Which Mother did.

Mother looked out at the swimming pool and at the gardener mowing the lawns and down the long circular drive toward the guards at the gate. Estates were lovely in the spring. She thought of their other place in the Adirondacks and of what that dreadful Mr. Roosevelt was doing to taxes. Dear, dear me!

Oh well, it didn't matter, Mother thought.

Taxes are the burden of the aristocracy, and bear them one must.

She powdered her long lovely nose and pulled her Molyneux cardigan around her gracious shoulders. Was it chilly? Surely not.

There. Was her eyeliner subtle enough?

Mother thought so. She gave her lacquered, lovely cheeks a tiny pat of high-tone rouge. Good. Very good. Just right.

Now, Mother thought, let's see who's coming to dinner.

She consulted the list. Only ten?

My goodness, what were they coming to? She thought of the dinner parties of the past, when twenty-five or thirty appeared like clockwork every evening. And always in evening dress. But these days the men might appear for dinner in mere suits!! It was dreadful what was happening to the world.

Still, Mother had other things to think about. Like one's son.

It was time for his bath.

Mother smiled and rose. Her image in the mirror faded as she crossed the room. She would call him in from outside.

Why, goodness — la! How swift, how prompt, how smartly obedient and quick he was. One's son. It seemed mere seconds before he stood before her, removing his jodhpurs in the bathroom.

She held his boots with a mother's care and gazed at him in the steamy mirror. His breeding glowed.

Bathing him is loveliness itself, Mother thought, bending over the tub. Now that he's sixteen.

8:00 p.m.

The Alhambra Movie House on La Cienega Boulevard was crowded with its Thursday patrons. As was true all over America, there were those who went inevitably on Wednesday, Thursday, or Friday. . . and those who went on Saturdays twice — once with the kids and once without.

Octavius went on Thursdays. Not every Thursday but when he did go, that was the night he went.

He liked the movies. They told him what the world was like.

Besides, he could sit there in the dark and not be bothered by the other people. And not be seen too clearly or too close.

The movie tonight was the 1936 classic, *Camille*, with Greta Garbo and Robert Taylor.

She had a scene where she ate little comfits from a box. She seemed to be so hungry. And this made him nervous. Also, she was dying, which was worse. He'd liked her better as Queen Christina, where she'd dressed as a man. She'd made an even prettier man than Robert Taylor did. But still. . . Robert Taylor was lovelier than Tyrone Power, he reflected, and Tyrone Power was lovelier than Leslie Howard. Leslie Howard was much too cold to be lovely. He was a little like Garbo.

Octavius watched.

Greta Garbo kept coughing all the time. It was quite unnerving, and by the time she'd finally died, Octavius was relieved, even glad. He wondered if it was true that she was a man. They said she was. He'd read that somewhere in a paper. And that was why she had such large feet.

If she was a man, then playing that role in Queen Christina was a cheat. But if she was a man, then all the other roles she'd played were marvelous. Even Camille.

While the cartoon was playing, Octavius thought about it.

Greta Garbo wore his costumes so well. The padding was extremely well done. His hands were extraordinary. (Octavius waved his own gloved hands down in the darkness in blind imitation.) And Greta Garbo knew how a woman held her neck and her shoulders. He must have practiced that for hours in front of the mirror. Necks and shoulders were difficult. And just exactly how to walk. How not to hurry. Anywhere he went across the screen, Greta Garbo never ran.

But best of all was Greta Garbo's makeup and his wigs. They were just absolutely perfection to a tee.

Octavius touched his elaborate hair and thought some more.

He had noticed something else about Greta Garbo.

He never played mothers.

9:50 p.m.

The newsreel came on. It was full of the old stuff. China, Spain, the Duke and Duchess of Windsor.

Dr. Frank Buchman made a speech and told everyone to change. Hitler spoke.

And then came the Hollywood News Vignettes. Little Judy Garland played a tennis game. Norma Shearer was making a movie with Clark Gable called *Idiot's Delight*, and that was worth noting because Octavius had great respect for Norma Shearer. He'd seen her in *Marie Antoinette*, sitting through it three times just to see the ending over. "Oh, Mama! Oh, Mama!" she had cried, sitting in her tumbrel, "I'm going to be the Queen of France!" It was very sad.

Surely Norma Shearer was not a man.

Then on came lovely Myra Jacobs to make a little speech for Jimmy Fiddler in a radio studio and finally there was a garden party given by Mr. Hearst.

Mr. Hearst's garden parties were something to behold. One saw so many movie stars at play. This was of great interest to Octavius, because it meant you saw the stars exactly as they really were, without makeup.

Ajax Apollo, the new nineteen-year-old, did a high dive in a loincloth and Octavius was sorry he did not have a picture of that. Cary Grant and Randolph Scott were undressed, too, and that was quite exciting. Marion Davies fell down a flight of stairs and got up and laughed and said it was all a practical joke, but afterwards she limped and Octavius wondered.

Rochelle Hudson put a rose in her mouth.

And there was Louella.

Then there was a movie star he'd never heard of.

Letitia Virden.

She was walking in the Roman part of the garden, with Mr. Hearst on one arm and Mr. Carter on the other. She was quite a tiny woman and the Voice of the Hollywood News Vignettes said her appearance there was startling. Octavius noted that the audience reacted very strangely when she came on, gasping and saying "good heavens" and finally applauding.

The Voice of the Hollywood News Vignettes went on to say that Letitia Virden just might be back to make another film, and wasn't that exciting, America? And there was more applause and Octavius was very mystified. Who was this star? She was called the Little Virgin. He certainly knew "America's Sweetheart," Mary Pickford, but why had he not heard of Letitia Virden?

Mr. Hearst, from what you could tell, did not perhaps have much to say to Letitia Virden (maybe Miss Davies had something to do with that), but Mr. Carter certainly had lots to say to her and she smiled at him a lot. They seemed like friends.

Octavius made a study of her. What a lovely walk she had. What elegant hands. Her clothes were simply stunning and her head was exquisitely shaped.

He rather liked her. Except for one thing. Her eyes. Something was not quite nice about her eyes. They glistened. Oddly. And then, too, she did a startling thing that seemed quite rude. When the camera got too close to her, she suddenly turned away and placed a veil over her face. Then, when she turned back, you couldn't see her.

Could it be, Octavius wondered.

No. She was much too feminine for that.

Letitia Virden may have been many mysterious things, but she was certainly not a man.

11:45 p.m.

Mother sat once more before the mirror.

She was tired.

It had been an extremely long day.

She took off her little gloves, her jewelry, and slipped off her shoes. She wiggled her toes.

She removed her hair and put it back in its box.

She gave herself a tired stare.

Well.

She removed her earrings. She leaned in closer to the mirror. The shoulders of her lovely green dress made a perfect frame for her face.

She squinted.

If...

She squinted some more.

Yes. If she just...

She sat back, eyeing herself as she might some distant painting.

If she lifted *that* eyebrow — so.

Mother grabbed up an eyebrow pencil.

Touch.

Yes!

Her hands shook.

And if...

And if she...

And if she thinned out... if she just lengthened her upper lip — so. Like that. Like so... just very carefully so. Thus...

(My God.)

And if she...

Yes. A touch by the eyes.

(Great Jesus.)

Mother.

(Jesus' mother.)

The Little Virgin.

Mother stood up and knocked over her chair.

She walked away and looked back at herself and then she walked forward and peered more closely and then she walked away again, staring with her mouth open.

She looked at the whole effect.
It was incredible.
Mother was incredulous. She nearly fainted dead away.
How could it be?
Well, never mind how, it was true. That's all. It was *true.*
Yes!!
A clock struck.
Mother turned.
Twelve.
Midnight.
The witching hour. Yes.
The hour when carriages turn into pumpkins. Yes.
And mothers into sons.

The Chronicle of Evelyn de Foe

Thursday, September 29th, 1938:
The Black Stocking Restaurant, Beverly Hills
12:30 p.m.

When Ruth arrived at the Black Stocking, her father had already been seated and was intoxicated.

He greeted her from a crouching position, neither in nor out of his chair.

Ruth sat down.

The waitress, who wore black stockings on her arms, appeared and disappeared, accepting, in the meantime, an order for drinks.

George glared at Ruth from narrow, blue-red eyes. His lapels were covered with ash and dandruff, one camouflaging the other. He smelled of cocktails mixed over the days and nights inside his stomach. His rust complexion could be only barely seen through the gray patina of ill-health. He rumbled.

"Well," he said, "you're not as smart as all that after all. Eh?"

"What do you mean, Father?"

Ruth's approach was distaste mingled with distrust.

"You couldn't... stick. Stick it out with Br... uno."

"It wouldn't have taken brains to've done that, Father."

"Pizzlesticks! Bah and poop! Don't you wool-pull on me, daughter. That Bruno is the very *rage* of Europe. But you didn't have the sense to stick it out. Only a fool would leave the rage of Europe in his hour of glory!"

"The rage of Germany, perhaps. For now. But not the rage of Europe, Father. Bruno's mystique, or whatever it is, won't last."

"It will last. It will last. He has stamina, that Bruno. Stamina and guts."

George glared at Ruth, the implication of her lack in these departments quite clear. He smiled his yellow smile.

"So you ran, eh?"

Ruth sighed. Boredom mingled with fear.

"If you want to put it that way, Father, all right — I ran. Now what do you want with me?"

George sidled into the corner of his chair like a giant, molting bird. His little red claws clutched the arms of his nest and he sniffled. Then he wiped his beak with the magenta handkerchief and took a drink. From the way he was drinking, Ruth realized that she was going to pay the bill.

"You're pretty Jeedy certain I *want* something, aren't you?"

"Of course I am, Father. Otherwise you wouldn't want to see me. So, what is it? A message for Mother?"

This was a mistake.

George immediately bellowed his vulgar laugh and rocked in the chair, nearly falling over backward in the process.

"Ha! That's a good one!" he roared. "Oh, that's just peachy precious!"

At once he sobered.

"No! No, I don't want to send messages to your mother.

I don't want you to mention your mother. I don't want to know how your mother is, or what she is. I don't want to *know!* Dead! Alive! Anything about your Jeedy mother!"

"Very well, Father. But please be quiet. You're making a spectacle of yourself."

"Well, it's about damn well time I did! Eh? Make a spectacle — or make *some*thing."

He roared an accusatory look around the room.

"They know who I am," he said. "I don't need to tell them who I am."

He stood up.

"All right, Father. Sit down." (He sat down.) "That's fine," said Ruth. "Now please. What do you want?"

"What's the matter with your hair?" said George, taking another gulp of drink. "You look like a bloody effing lesbian."

"It was cut off," said Ruth, as simply as she could. She was attempting to avoid the stare of what felt like the entire world.

"Are you a Jeedy lesbian?" said George.

"No, Father."

"Hunh. That would be a dandy," said George. "My son's a hemo-homo and now my daughter's a lesbian."

"No, Father. I'm not."

The red eyes poked and pried.

"Well, you should be. What else are you any good for? You can't have babies."

The last sentence was uttered, word by word, like the separate volleys of a firing squad.

"No."

"You aren't going to have any babies, are you? I hope. By God."

"No, Father."

"You have tainted blood, you know."

"Yes, Father."

"Tainted blood. All my children have tainted blood."

"Yes. I'm quite aware of it."

"Tainted blood. Any baby of yours'd bleed to death. In five minutes."

"Yes."

"Like my son."

"Yes, Father. Like Dolly."

"Don't call — him — Doll-y."

"Adolphus."

"He's going to die."

"Adolphus who's going to die. Yes, Father."

"A terrible, horrible, ghastly, bloody, awful death. Bleeding. To death."

"Yes."

"Aaah! You don't care. You don't care. You don't give a Jeedy damn. You don't give. . ."

"*Father!*"

"What?"

"Stop it. Stop. Be quiet. *Please*."

George pulled his head back and stared, or tried to, at his daughter.

"You telling me to shut up?"

"Yes."

Silence. The room waited.

The quiet was circular. It surrounded them and held them prisoner until the waitress, bearing more alcoholic ammunition, broke through and set some freshly filled glasses on the table.

"Now," said Ruth, once the waitress had gone, "what-is-it-you-want-of-me?"

"I won't tell you," said George with genuine petulance.

"Oh, really!"

"Don't you 'oh, really' me girl. I'm your father."

Ruth bit her lip.

"You always were an impudent no-good. A nothing. Cipher. That's what you are. An impudent cipher. Everything you wanted you had — and all you could do was — talk back."

This was all so patently untrue that it silenced even George.

Ruth drank for dear life from her own glass. This was unbearable — to have to sit here with this drunken man who everyone knew was her father, and to have to listen to him rant and roar about her private life in public, and not to be able to escape. Unless she could, somehow, contrive to leave him. Perhaps if she went to the ladies' room. Perhaps...

But escape, at least temporary, was provided for her. The attention of the room was withdrawn from their table by the entrance of someone at first not visible, far away across the restaurant.

It was a movie star, Evelyn de Foe, but she was new and had not got around to being used very much. She did not generally "hit the hot spots" in the daytime. She was a night person, young and still unscathed in appearance. She was very much the new style of girl, the style just coming in, with square instead of round shoulders, and bosoms and bottoms instead of hands, feet, and face.

The new girls, too — like Evelyn — were mostly tarnished looking. Blonde, but not blonde; tanned, but it was makeup. They did not know how to dress and consequently wore too much Technicolor. They were "tough."

Evelyn de Foe strode in, a painted collage — overlipped and overlashed, with her brassy hair yanked back so that her profile seemed enormous. She wore large gypsy earrings and her ensemble included red trousers with fly buttons, a man's yellow shirt, and (looped down seductively over ample buttocks), a double length of white angora stole. Her wrists made cymbalic noises, for they were sheathed in bangles and a jangle of other bracelets and beads.

Men walked in front of her, clearing a path for her progress, and behind her there followed a retinue of oddly dressed women with male hair and no makeup.

While George busied himself lighting, misplacing, finding, and relighting a cigarette, Ruth took advantage of his preoccupation to watch the progress of this astonishing creature.

Evelyn de Foe seated herself and arranged her assorted favorites around her. Everyone at her table seemed to be very bad tempered. The reason was quickly obvious. Evelyn de Foe had been pinched beneath her angora by someone standing near the door. Use might have been made of this gesture if the pincher had been someone well known, but since he was of the class *non grata*, nothing could be done with it. Thus, the gesture and Evelyn's consequent reaction had wrecked the arrangement of her triumphal entry into the room. She had lost her place in the line-up (carefully prearranged in the parking lot) and so it had seemed that one of the male women in the retinue (the masseuse, in fact) was the center of attention.

As Ruth watched and listened, a tide of vicious language rose about Evelyn's table. Ruth had just endured a fairly normal tirade of her father's favorite words, but she had never witnessed an oral display to equal this. The words were archaic, almost lost to civilization, but had been retained with a kind of determined and sadistic wrenching of animal memory.

Evelyn's words could hardly be contained in her mouth but, like bile, were spat with the appropriate facial gestures onto the tablecloth, where they lay in the physical incarnation of salival excrement. The words hurt the mind. And the phrasing had the cadence of Neanderthalic orgies. Perhaps, exactly as there should have been in the given circumstances, there was also a great deal of table-pounding, handbag-thumping, and chair-banging. This language was foreign and unknown.

Finally, a waitress crept over and served Evelyn's table as graciously as was possible. But then, Ruth remembered, the waitress was paid to remember where she was.

At this point George mastered his recalcitrant weed and, puffing away on it like a Lazarus returning from the dead, he spoke. His manner was that of someone who had interrupted himself to die.

"Excuse me," he said. "Where are we?"

Ruth looked away from Evelyn de Foe, but could perceive nothing where George sat except a smoke screen.

"What do you mean, Father?"

"Where are we in our Jeedy conversation?"

Ruth approached her glass with tentative fingers.

"I wasn't aware that we were having a conversation," she said.

"Well, we are. We are. Who's that?"

"I don't know, Father. She just came in."

George looked, or rather squinted, at the Devil. There she was.

"Well," he said. "She sure beats Titty for tits."

"What?"

"She wins, that's all," said George. "Now listen, Ruth, and listen to me very carefully."

"All right."

George averted his gaze. His fingers played nervously and undecidedly with glass, cigarette, table silver, and the magenta handkerchief.

"I need," he said, "your help."

Ruth could not tell what was coming next. His voice was not demanding and it was not pleading. It was thoughtful, which was extremely rare.

"Do you know the name Cooper Carter?"

"Yes. The industrialist. He produces steel or something."

"That's right. Steel. And weapons."

"Weapons?"

"Weapons."

"What sort of weapons?"

"Any sort you want. Guns, tanks, bombs. Anything. Sometimes," he gave a long, significant pause, and then: "Sometimes. . . movies."

"Movies?"

"*Mo-tion pic-tures.*"

George raised his eyes and there was a terrible fanaticism in them. It was sad.

Ruth watched.

"A motion picture is not a weapon, Father," Ruth said.

"But it can be," said George. "It *can* be."

"Yes. I suppose. . ."

George reverted to his introspective tone. His fingers busied away with ashes and alcohol, smoke and handkerchief.

"Titty Virden has come back."

Ruth shuddered. Yes. Ruth knew that. It had been

Letitia on the train. At Alvarez, too. And hadn't George been at Alvarez?

"Father?"

"Shut up. Listen to me."

Ruth suddenly realized that tears were wandering slowly down his cheeks.

"What is it?"

"I've always — I have always..."

The tears wandered faster, finding their mark on the backs of his fat little hands.

Again, Ruth waited, and at last George continued.

"She wants to make a film, you see. An immensely important film."

"Yes."

"And she needs a great deal of money. She doesn't want studio bosses hanging over her head telling her what she can and cannot do. This film is too important for that. You know what I mean?"

"Yes."

"Well, Cooper Carter..."

The tears welled up in another threat, but abated before the fall.

"Cooper Carter is already interested. He's building her a studio...."

George blew his nose at this point, startling Evelyn de Foe, who dropped her embossed menu with a clank and a loud *God damn!*

"They're going to make a picture, you see. You see? Oh, don't you understand? They're going to make the most important motion picture ever made. And they're going to make it without *me*."

This did not amaze Ruth and she wondered why it should amaze her father. His inability to work, his condition — he was notorious.

Now he blubbered like a little boy into his handkerchief.

"I'd walk through South America for Titty Virden," he said, knowing full well he would never be asked to do any such thing. "South-effing-America! On foot!"

Ruth thought she might feel sorry for George if he were

not her father. Or perhaps for her father — if he were not George Damarosch.

"Yes," he said. "South-effing-America."

There was a pause.

Possibly George was watching himself float out over the Andes and down the Amazon.

Ruth had a headache. She tightened into silence. She drank.

Suddenly, there was a crash at the de Foe table. A waitress had dropped a tray of food.

Evelyn, invective flying, rose. Two of her men and one of her women rose with her, but she barked at them and they fell back into their places.

The poor waitress got up apologetically, but seeing Evelyn, impulsively backed away.

Evelyn rang her bangles busily. She had a hungry, fangy pout like a petulant lioness. There was seafood sauce on her stole. The waitress had put it there.

Evelyn barged two and a half steps forward through the empty space between herself and the hapless girl. (Evelyn, it should be said, barged everywhere. She even barged where no one and nothing barred the way. Touring abroad, Evelyn de Foe would barge into St. Peter's Square. She would barge into the Sahara Desert. But for now she merely barged those two and a half steps across the floor of the Black Stocking Restaurant fixing the waitress with her bawling gaze.)

She raised her glistening, false-nailed hands.

"Someone should do something," said Ruth. But no one did.

Like a helpless martyr standing on the sands of the Roman Colosseum, the waitress stared with horror at what had been released from its cage before her.

Evelyn spoke to her — zoologically.

The waitress went a Christian shade of pale.

Evelyn's words fell between them, or were flung onto the floor as though someone should bend down and pick them up — perhaps even dust them off and hand them back to her. But instead they just lay there until, like worms, they wriggled a little, oozed a few liquids. . . and dried up.

Slowly the waitress joined them as in supplication. She fell to her knees.

The maître d' approached as close as he dared, looked down at the humiliation on the floor, and said, "You're fired."

"Well," said Evelyn de Foe, bumping each word with a hip, "I would for fuck's sake, think so!"

And that was the end of it. Or nearly.

Waving her red-and-white smile and doing forbidden things with her angora, Evelyn made it all the way across the room, untouched by human hand. A triumph.

Her retinue followed. More triumph. Plus applause.

Intoxicated by this reaction, Evelyn turned to blow a few red kisses at the crowd. But instead of offering more applause and accolades, as might have been expected, the diners and drinkers burst into instant laughter.

Laughter? Evelyn was furious.

But even the swiftest perusal of her person would have given her the answer.

Her fly was undone.

1:45 p.m.

Only Ruth ate. George just went on drinking and arranging things on the table top.

Finally, when her coffee came, Ruth said, "You were about to tell me about Letitia and her comeback, Father."

"Oh, yes," said George, as though there had been no interruption at all.

"Well?"

His red eyes slid toward her.

"You a rich woman?" he asked.

It was gentle.

"Moderately," said Ruth, who had her answer all prepared. She feigned ignorance of his true intent.

"Well," said George. "If I could have a little money — if I could have a little money — you know," he said, the tears welling up again for the last time, "you know — I have always. . ."

"If you had a little money — what?" said Ruth. She got out Hermann Goering's compact.

"If I had a little money, I could buy in. Take an interest. And with my interest they would have to let me — they would simply have to let me be the one. . ."

Ruth powdered her nose industriously.

"Be the one to what?"

She licked her lips.

"Be the one to direct Titty's great comeback film."

The simplicity of it was appalling.

"How much is a little?" Ruth asked, by now at the lipstick touch-up stage.

"A million dollars," said George.

There.

Ruth snapped the lid shut, carefully dusted her suit front and put the compact away, and the lipstick, and lit a cigarette and inhaled and exhaled and said, "Father, I have lied to you."

George's eyes lit up. Visions of millions danced brightly in the red-banked fires of his little eyes. His daughter had lied to him. It was charming. She was not just moderately rich after all. She was a multi-millionaire. Millionairess.

"Yes? Yes? What lie?" he said, the saliva mounting.

Ruth stared straight into his face.

"I cannot let you have any money, Father," she said.

"Can't? Can't? What do you mean *can't?*"

"Just that. I can't."

"Why?"

Ruth paused and then said, "I can't because I'm going to have a baby."

The Chronicle of Myra Jacobs

Monday, October 10th, 1938:
Beverly Hills
11:00 a.m.

Adolphus picked up the telephone and carried it across the white expanse of his living room, so that while he was talking he could look out of his window at the shaded tennis courts and the sunny swimming pool beyond. It was not his pool and not his tennis court, but he liked to look anyway — at the beach hats, the bathing suits, the tennis rackets, the tennis balls, and the net. He also liked to look at the water.

He sat down, placing the white telephone on a large glass table beside him. He was wearing slacks, sandals, and a sport shirt and he dialed CRestwood 5329. The table offered support to, besides the telephone, a bottle of rye whiskey, an ice bucket, a tumbler, an ashtray, a cigarette lighter, a cigarette box, and a copy, in plaster, of a Grecian frieze depicting a one-legged white man on a horse. Everything excluding the rye bottle was white.

Far away in Brentwood the telephone bell was jingling in response to its dialed message. It stopped ringing and a Negro voice said, "Elbow?"

"Hullo, Ida. It's 'Dolphus Damarosch speaking. Is Miss Myra there?"

He lit a cigarette.

"Toozabed. Shizabad." (Too bad, she's in bed.)

"Is she asleep?"

"Zzzz. Fotodin." (Yes. Folded in.)

"Listen, for heaven's sake, surely she'll talk to me, Ida. I'm not Studio."

"Zizint mother. Shintin nomaddtax." (That doesn't matter. She ain't in no mood to talk.)

"Well at least for gawd's sake ask her. Tell her I'm on the line."

"Ho kaymizindamenpsst. Isst casaway." (O.K., Mr. Damarosch. Just 'cause it's you.)

Clank. Ida laid the phone down distantly. Adolphus could hear her walk away across the tiled floor of Myra's house. He heard her perform moving-all-over-the-house-looking-for-Myra noises, plus a questionable imitation of Myra's dainty sibilance, and as he listened he made a picture for himself of the scene.

Ida had large, white-shoe-encased feet. She also had large hands, tall legs, a long, flat body, and a small head. She looked as a giant must look to a baby lying on the floor — the top parts of her receding into diminishing perspective. She clothed herself entirely in white, and since there was no mixture of blood in her veins, she was that uncommon North American phenomenon, a truly black Negro. To look at her you might imagine she had been born on the outskirts of Nairobi, instead of on the outskirts of Philadelphia.

Drawn to Hollywood on a general principle of racial ambition (engendered by the successful rise of Ethel Waters and Bojangles), Ida had failed as a singer and dancer, but she had succeeded mightily as a servant to the rich and famous. Before working for Myra Jacobs she had been employed briefly by Alice Gottschalk and then by the Bronson Baileys, and when Myra first used her, it had been when the Bronson Baileys were away on their much-publicized European vacation, without servants. When Mr. Bailey died (a famous tragedy) Ida became Myra's permanent property. Then Myra left Huge Company and went over to the Manning Brothers Studios. That was in 1934. Then she went over to Tremendous, '34 – '35. Then she went over to Marvel, August '35. Then she went over to Civic. Then she went over to Gaylord, '36. Then she went back over to Huge Company, '37. And now she was at Niles, '38, which is where she was about to go phhhht!

Ida had been with Myra ever since her rise to the top, '34, and she always talked about "us killing Mr. Danton" (a perfectly ordinary scandal) in 1936 (hushed up) and "us being counteracted to the new studios" (whichever, whenever) and now "our trembles" (presumably troubles) in October 1938.

Ida bumped around in the tiled hallway, giving her performance.

"Miss Myra! Miss Myra!"

(Change of voice.)

"Yes, Miss Ida. Yes, Miss Ida."

(Nobody, least of all Myra Jacobs, knew the origin of the "Miss" in front of the "Ida.")

"Mr. Dolly's on the telephone. Mr. Dolly's on the telephone."

"Yes, Miss Ida. Yes, Miss Ida."

Clump, clump, clump. Ida did a little large-footed imitation of Eleanor Powell.

"He wants to talk to you Miss Myra. Mr. Dolly wants to talk."

(Adolphus listened to all of this impatiently. He had heard variations of it every day for over a week. He poured himself another drink and watched the bathing suits and the tennis balls, thinking that he had the answer to Ida's failure in show business.)

"Tell Mr. Dolly no. Tell Mr. Dolly no."

(Dolly whispered involuntarily, "Tell Mr. Dolly no.")

"Yes, Miss Myra. Yes, Miss Myra."

Dance.

(Bill Robinson.)

Clump. Clump, clump, clump. Clank.

Adolphus winced aurally.

"Yes, Ida. What'd she say?"

There was a short moment of hard breathing on the other end of the telephone.

"She's out," said Ida.

And hung up, still tapping her white-boxed toes.

October 11th, 1938:
Brentwood

Myra Jacobs owned a sparrow and the sparrow lived in a large cage which sat in the window beyond the curtains of Myra's mezzanine sitting room.

Every day began with Myra drinking coffee on the mezzanine and listening to the sparrow sing. Every single day: workdays, Sundays and days you got fired by the Studio.

The sparrow loved to sing, especially in the mornings and evenings. So, daily, when it was bright and sunspangled and again when it was shadowy and cool, the sparrow sang its song.

Two years ago Myra had fallen in love with the sparrow at a time when they were both singing in a picture together. "Two little chippies," everyone had said, except that it was not a chipping sparrow but a song one, as Myra herself told the jokers who threw that kind of dirt around, and, "Don't think I don't know what a chippie is," she said, "either. Which I am not, nor is my sparrow."

But this morning the sparrow did not sing.

"What is it, sparrow? Are you sick?" asked Myra.

The sparrow just sat there looking through the bars, out the window, and did not reply.

"But I can't," said Myra, thinking that she knew what was in the sparrow's heart. "If I did let you out the sparrow hawks would get you. And we don't even like the thought of that."

She looked out the window herself.

There it was, her property: the long driveway and the lawn, the gate and the police car. The policeman was asleep. Day and night the police car was parked there for Myra's protection. When she had gone to the studio in her own chauffeur-driven Rolls, the police car had followed all the way until she was safely inside the studio walls. Then it had followed her home again at night and parked down by the gate.

Myra thought about *Hell's Babies* and Adolphus Damarosch. So far it had been fun in itself, and all the grips and electricians and studio personnel and everyone all said it was sensational and lovely. Except some of the executives. Those people from New York. They wore blue suits and had dirty minds.

"She's fat," said one.

"She's old," said another.

Fat and old. Fat and old.

"Nonsense."

The next day she had been late.

"Now she's late and fat and old. See? What'd we tell you."

And the next day she had quarreled with the hairdresser.

"*Bitchy*, late, fat, and old. See? We told you. We told you what would happen."

The next day she developed a rash.

"Bitchy, old, and fat, Myra got a rash and now that's that!" The New York executives had chanted it. But the front-office Hollywood executives, especially Mr. Niles, were worried. Myra was precious to them. They had their picture to finish.

"Give her time to get well," they said.

"We'll give her two days."

"Give her time," said Hollywood.

"She's had three weeks," said New York.

"Just a few days more," said Hollywood.

"No. No damn whore is gonna hold up our schedule," said the man from New York. "Cancel that contract. Get Mitzi Tomahawk."

"Mitzi Tomahawk can go to hell," thought Myra when she read about it.

So, old-fat-bitchy Myra wandered for a few days around her house. The rash was gone. The itch remained. The fat had come. She watched Ida baking a cake and listened to the sparrow singing. And she was lonely. There was no one in the house to look at her.

She wasn't really so fat. Not really. Men liked her like that. That she knew. Didn't they like her in *Kiss Me Hullo* when she was like that, and didn't they like that lovely transparent net-and-rhinestone dress she wore? Sure they did. And she wasn't even old, either. Thirty-two isn't old. Is it, sparrow? No. Thirty-two is just not old. And that's all there is to it. Besides, the Studio always said she was twenty-six and everyone believed it. Everyone.

She wandered around the house for a couple of days more. Maybe she'd renegotiate her contract. Maybe she'd go back over to Huge Company or over to Mega, where she had never been. Wouldn't that Mr. Mugging just love it if she came over there and knocked on his door. Wouldn't that make everyone jump? You bet your boots it would.

Dolly phoned every day. She was sorry for Dolly. It was his picture, too, after all, and they'd been such good friends. They'd almost had an affair. But she didn't want to talk to him. She didn't want his pleas or his sympathy. She was sick of driving his car, anyway. She wanted the phone to ring and it would be Mr. Niles and Mr. Niles would say, "Come back, Little Myra. Please come back." Maybe he would say, "We're sorry."

But Mr. Niles didn't phone and neither did Arnold Niles, his brother, and now there was something wrong with the sparrow and Ida was uppity and Adolphus was beginning to dislike her, too, and he probably thought she was a bitch after all. Which she wasn't. How could she be?

She just wanted them to let her look like herself, that was all — and be like herself and give up running around the studios all the time. If only they'd make *Hell's Babies* the way she was, then they'd see that the public did like her that way, with her body plump like that. And they'd see that if they'd only leave her alone she could still make it at the box office, too. After all, she'd had a nervous disease and was entitled to a little consideration. (The nervous disease was eczema.)

But they wouldn't have her. Not like that. Not fat. No. It was final.

"What is it, sparrow? What is the matter with you?" said Old Fat, standing there by the cage. Old Itchy Fat.

The sparrow stared out of the window. It got down on the floor of its cage and ruffled its feathers and sat there, staring and molting and not eating its seeds. It would not drink its water, either, even when Old Fat herself put it in as a drop on the end of her finger. The sparrow just hunched there like a little, thin, unopened package on the floor of its cage, and finally Old Fat Myra fitted her finger through the bars and touched it good-bye on the head and touched it again on each wing. Good-bye.

Then Old Fat sat down in a chair and drew the curtain and they both stared out the window, Old Fat and the sparrow, and later that evening the sparrow died without having sung another song. Not even a note. And Old Fat cried.

October 15th, 1938: Brentwood

Adolphus finally decided that he would simply show up at "Myra-treat" without telephoning, a tactic arrived at through his acute awareness of Ida's past mastership of the telephone as an instrument of war.

So he took a taxi over on a Saturday afternoon. It was still quite hot and dry. Myra's garden smelled of lemons and flowers and cut grass.

There was no policeman at the gate. The Studio had removed his negligible, sleepy protection, and consequently, the front of the estate seemed naked. The policeman and his car had been like a set decoration. The loss was comparable to the loss of a shady and protective tree.

Having got out of the taxi two houses up the road, where he would not be seen arriving, Adolphus strolled up to the iron gates of "Myra-treat" and, pushing them open with his cane, walked up to the house on the brick walk.

He saw Ida, dressed in her whites, sitting on a large padded wicker chair on the colonial porch. She had a palmetto fan in one hand and a gin in the other and she was fast asleep. He could hear her snoring almost as soon as he came through the gate. This was a blessing. He could walk straight through to Myra.

3:00 p.m.

The lower hallway was filled with roses — all in baskets — all from the desperate Mr. Cohn, who was in love with Myra.

Adolphus tiptoed up to the mezzanine and stopped. He looked at the cage emptied of its movement and its song. Now it, too, was filled with roses. Dead and rotten. From Mr. Cohn.

He went on.

At the top of the stairs he turned left toward a partly open door. Beyond it he could hear someone rustling little bits of paper in a box.

For a moment he closed his eyes and tried to forgive himself for ever having thought Myra was obstructive or had bad taste or was stupid or ought never to drive a car or any of the bad things he had thought about her.

He took a step nearer to the door.

He wavered. He must go in and bring her back alive. Onto the screen. For her own sake. And for the sake of seeing New York, squirming with hats in hands, watching the money roll in past them down those long executive corridors in Manhattan.

He pushed open the door.

"Myra?"

"*Oh!*"

Old Fat sat in her bed.

She was wearing a high-collared, open-necked Chinese robe, and she was eating candies. She had one box open on her lap and another, empty, lying beside her on the covers. The rest of the bed was strewn with little brown papers that had once been wrapped around the candies already eaten. A Victrola played softly in the background.

"What the hell are you doing here?" Myra asked.

Her mouth was full of caramel, marshmallow, and nuts.

"Just passing..." said Adolphus, working so hard to control his stare that he could not finish the sentence.

"Oh."

Old Fat swept off a portion of the coverlet and spread the brown-paper stars helter-skelter over the floor.

"Sit down," she said. "I'll be with you in a minute."

She shut off the Victrola.

He sat facing her at the foot of the bed.

She closed the chocolate box, tossed aside the empty one, drew the Chinese robe tight around her expanded body, and hunched down under the covers. Her hair was stringy and uncared for. Without makeup she looked yellow and the shadows under her puffed-out eyes were deep green. There were one or two raw spots where she'd scratched the itch.

"How've you been?" she asked him. Her eyes wavered. "Pardon my appearance." She waved a chubby hand, saw that her nails were dirty with chocolate and marzipan and folded both hands into the double disability of fists. She sat there, heavily, with her wrists curving over the immense roundness of her raised and swollen knees.

Adolphus gave a real smile. "Do you mind if a friend wants to say hello once in a while?"

The accusing bravery left her eyes. She smiled back. "Not a real friend, Dolly. No."

"Good. How've you been keeping?"

"Fat."

They both laughed at that and when they were through she giggled a light cadenza that ended suddenly in a pout.

"I came to ask you to come back," Adolphus said abruptly.

She looked right at him. Then away.

"Back where?" she said, watching the room mess up around her. Chocolate wrappers had suddenly appeared everywhere.

"Back to work."

She seemed to consider it. "Work, eh?"

"Unh-hunh."

"It's too late," she said. She lifted a fat arm and let it fall. "The damage is done."

"No," said Dolly. "It isn't. No damage. No damage, my dear."

She sat up. She let the robe fall open. Her breasts broke forward like cellophane bags full of water. Her chiffon nightgown held them back from total collapse. Her weight had tripled.

"Look at me, Dolly."

He looked. And looked away.

She sneered. This was the extremity of ugliness and sadness combined.

"Old Fat!" she exploded over the bed. "OLD-ITCHY-MIDDLE-AGED-*FAT!*"

She closed her eyes and her gown and huddled.

"You can diet, Myra. Anyone can diet. In a week..."

"I can't diet my age. I can't diet my damn eyes. I can't diet my mind. Diet — hah! Don't eat that, Charlie! Not eating won't do anything. I'm finished. You bleed. I got old and fat. It's over."

Delicately horrified, he listened to her, looked at her — and knew that she was right. Something *was* suddenly over. Nothing could change what had happened to her will. And he knew that it was her person, not her body, that everyone really loved. Himself included. And he saw that it was her person that had taken on so much weight, had so voraciously and heftily bulked. It had grown so far out of proportion that she could never hone it down. The fineness of her vulgarity was gone. Her spirit was gone. She had lost the love of the challenge and now she was merely passive. Which is what age is, he thought. Wrinkles and fat. Passive acceptance makes all of these. It gives you fat hands.

"Well," he said. "Well."

"So. Well."

They sat in silence.

She was only thirty-two. It didn't matter. She thought it was sixty.

Finally, Adolphus sighed and rose and walked around the room. His toes kept butting up against chocolate boxes and paper wrappers and every time they did he gave a little kick of frustration. He forgot his own fear.

"You'll make yourself bleed," said Myra. She tried to smile.

Her face mooned out at him from pillows and sheets and blankets.

He looked at her expectantly. Perhaps if he promised her something. . . .

"We'll go to the Black Stocking every night," he said. "We'll drink gin and cocktails and brandy Alexanders and get tight as ticks. We'll dance around to the rhumba band. Eh? Wouldn't you like that? Artie Shaw playing solo while you entertain the Duke and Duchess of Windsor, Elsa Maxwell, and the Count of Monte Cristo? Louis B. Mayer sending you mash notes from a table across the room and everyone saying, 'Look, there she goes, that's Myra Jacobs, the girl with all the friends. There goes. . .' "

". . . Old Fat, ex-queen of the movies," said Myra with a slump in her voice that brought them both down so hard that the dream could only wither and die.

"It will happen," said Adolphus, out of breath from dancing.

"You bet my itch it will," said Myra. "It'll happen when hell freezes over and the North Pole has palm trees."

"Well then. What will you do?"

"Sit."

"Just sit?"

"Yes!"

Her vehemence was slightly hysterical.

He watched her carefully. Then he tried to lighten the blows by saying, "Who's gonna pay for all the candies?"

"Me."

"You're broke."

"No. I've got some money."

"Where from?"

She fidgeted. "Never mind where from. I'm not broke, that's all. Fat ladies have *some* friends."

"O.K., O.K. Well, I guess I'd better be on my way, then."

"Where to?"

She looked up, afraid at last of his absence.

"Back to the Studio."

"It's Saturday."

"That doesn't matter. I've got to tell them. Start tearing down the sets."

"What sets?"

"Your sets."

"My sets?"

"Your sets."

"Tearin' 'em down, eh?"

"Yes."

"Oh."

He stood by the door.

"Good-bye."

She was looking at her fists, laid out flatly on the blankets, either side of her legs. She seemed to be only partly with him and only partly with herself. The rest of her had swelled and burst and lay about the room like discarded clothing that was out of style.

She looked up at him and made a fumbling motion with her eyes.

"Really tearing 'em down, eh, Dolly?"

"Yes. I'm sorry, but they must."

"Oh, that's all right. That's all right."

He moved a few more steps out into the hall. He could no longer bear to look at her.

"Dolly?"

"Yes?" He put his head back around the door and saw her reflected mercifully in the soft distance of a mirror.

She smiled. "You want one for the road?" She held out the full box of chocolates. He looked at them.

"No thanks, Myra."

"No? Come on. Just one. Please."

She seemed genuinely disappointed.

"No," he said. "I might choke and bleed."

He smiled.

She laughed.

"Good-bye," she said, "I'll see you, won't I?"

"Not if I see you first," he said, and by the time he'd finished saying it he was halfway down the stairs.

Even there he heard her sigh and lay the chocolates down and smooth the covers. Then he went on to the bottom, slowly and quietly. He knew his heart was broken and he wondered if anything could ever mend it.

October 16th, 1938:
Beverly Hills
3:00 a.m.

In the middle of the night, Adolphus was awakened by the telephone.

He did not like using the telephone for anything more than business calls, so the only one he had installed was far away in the living room. For a moment he lay in his bed, listening, knowing that if he got up and went into the other room he would probably stub his toe on the big table, start internal bleeding, and find it was a wrong number. This had happened to him once before in the middle of the night and he had sworn never to let it happen again. Except that the white phone kept ringing.

He thought that it might be Ruth. Perhaps Naomi had reached the crisis. Maybe she was dead.

He pushed aside the covers with a tired gesture of martyred resignation. The phone kept ringing. He switched on the bedside lamp and stumbled carefully through the door into the darkened living room. He found the light switch on the wall and turned it on. The phone kept ringing. He pigeon-toed across the room without incident or accident. He was naked. The phone kept ringing. With one hand he reached for the receiver and with the other he reached for, caught at, but dropped a large glass box of cigarettes. The phone stopped ringing. Dead.

"In the name of gawd," he said, "for heaven's sake, couldn't you just wait one more ring?" He yelled this into the dead receiver against its buzz.

He slammed the phone down and picked up the spilled cigarettes. Now he was thoroughly awake. Damn it all. Now he would start thinking and not be able to sleep.

Wouldn't that kill you! It must have rung a dozen times and it still had to go dead just when he picked it up. Just in that one second. Well, the bloody thing! Never again. He swore it. Never, never would he answer or try to answer a phone again in the middle of the night.

He rose wearily and was about to leave the room when he was caught by the sight of his own image in the window glass. The delicate glow of his nakedness seemed to swim across its surface away from him. His own elusiveness challenged his imagination and he paused, waiting. It really wasn't a bad image, he thought. Slim, good lines. He advanced on himself, holding himself up, pelvis forward, erect. He might not carry much weight, but for twenty-seven years he still had a damn good figure. Ahem. Damn good.

He swallowed. He also toyed with the cigarette.

With a final glance at himself he turned and strode away across the room. Now that he was wide awake after all he might as well do something. Get out the books — or something.

His hands flew over the shelves, selecting material. Tomorrow was Sunday. Today was Sunday. No obligations. He could spend as much time as he liked. It didn't matter how late he stayed up. *Moby Dick, Madame Bovary*. He went on selecting for about five minutes. *The Autobiography of Alice B. Toklas. The Selected Poems of Edith Sitwell*. Finally he walked, burdened with his books, into the bedroom. Naked, he closed the door.

October 17th, 1938

> On Sunday, October 16th, Myra Jacobs, the film star, was discovered dead in her bed by her personal maid and long-time companion, Miss Ida Forsythe. The actress's bedside table contained a box of candy, a copy of *Photoplay* magazine, an empty glass, a carafe of water, and a bottle of sleeping pills, also empty.
>
> When discovered by Miss Forsythe in the early hours of the morning, the body was sprawled across the bed with the arms and head in the direction of the telephone. Apparently Miss Jacobs had been overcome while attempting to call for help. One hand held the receiver of the telephone and the other had fallen across the cradle in such a way as to disengage the line. Her personal telephone directory was lying open beside her, but it did not disclose whom she

might have been calling, beyond the fact that the book was open at the letter "D." It can therefore be surmised that Miss Jacobs was probably trying to reach her doctor, whose name was Durbin — as in Deanna.

Miss Jacobs, who was recovering from a rare disease, was to have recommenced work Monday morning on her film *Hell's Babies* at the Niles Studios.

The actress was thirty-two years old. No funeral plans have been announced.

ITEM

There is conjecture in some circles close to Miss Jacobs that she was depressed over recent developments in her romantic life. A mysterious Mr. Cohn is said to have been sending daily bouquets of roses which Miss Jacobs accepted without reply. This information has been verified by Mr. Arnold Stern, the florist who supplied the flowers.

A picture of the carrier boy, Jesus Martinez, appears below. When questioned about Miss Jacobs, whom he saw only once during his calls to her house, he said, "She was fat."

Jesus is sixteen and wants to be in movies.

Book Three

The Chronicle of Race

Friday, October 14th, 1938

ITEM: From the *Bozo Bulletin*, Venice, California

The College of Botanical and Zoological Sciences at Venice, California, announces the following excursion dates for the month of November.*

November 1st:	To Del Mar to observe suspected Phylloxera in the vineyards.
November 10th:	To the home of Mrs. John Porter-Temple, which is being devoured by a recently introduced species of termite (*Cryptotermes*). Mrs. Porter-Temple will serve a barbecue.
November 21st:	To Catalina Island to observe the pelican cemetery. (Wear rain apparel.)
November 23rd:	To Salinas to pray for rain. (All Christian denominations welcome.)
November 28th:	To Fringes Bay to observe the butterfly trees (roosts of migratory phase of *Danaüs plexippus*).

*For the October Calendar, see *Bozo Bulletin* of September 16th.

All those wishing to take part in these field trips are requested to register with the Excursions Registrar (E.C.D.F. Smith, B.A., M.Sc., Ph.D., F.B.S., F.A.Z.S.) at the Biological Sciences Building, 215 West 14th Street (at 3rd) between the hours of 9:12 a.m. and 4:55 p.m., Mondays to Fridays, at least two weeks prior to the excursion date.

Note: Equipment will be limited to specimen bottles, killing jars, binoculars (where appropriate), and notebooks no larger than 6" x 8". No microscopes, cages, or picnic baskets may be taken into the field. Lunches will be provided at a nominal cost by the College.

Further note: PLEASE! No alcoholic beverages of any description. Our recent trip to Tijuana to observe body lice was badly marred by intemperance. Further occurrences will not be tolerated!

Furthest note: For the excursion of November 28th, it is hoped that we shall have enough interested trippers to fill our three buses. In previous years we have observed the *Danaüs plexippus* phenomenon at more commercial points. This year's choice of the little-known trees at Fringes Bay should afford a better opportunity for observation.

ANNOUNCEMENT!

Will the gentleman who collected carrion beetles with the lady in the purple hat on our excursion of October 2nd please contact Miss Eva Allen, c/o Doctors' Hospital, Santa Monica. She has important news for you.

Saturday, October 15th, 1938

On the radio news broadcast of 9:00 a.m., there was an item about a Santa Monica woman who had been attacked by a rapist wearing an arm band with a strange device on it. This occurred in the small hours of the morning and the woman had managed to escape with a description of her attacker.

He was something over six feet tall. The woman, Mrs. Ingmar Nielsen, had suggested he was six foot seven or eight, but it was felt that this could be an exaggeration. He had blond hair, blue eyes, and the victim admitted with some chagrin that he was "handsome." Aside from the fact that he wore the arm band, the police were particularly interested in his shoes: he didn't wear any. Apparently the attack had taken place in a back alleyway strewn with broken glass and several sheets of tin roofing, yet, according to the victim, the man had pursued her and caught her with great agility — even in his bare feet. She described him as "a guy who could have been Superman — except he didn't wear no cape. . . ." His description was widely circulated, and citizens were requested to keep an eye out for him and to report anything pertinent to the police.

The victim took the opportunity of her momentary notoriety to speak out on what she called the "inalienable right of female American rape victims to be provided with legal abortions."

The State should be made to pay.

Sunday, October 16th, 1938

Fire was discovered in the garage of Mr. and Mrs. Morris Reinglass of Santa Monica. The fire, spreading by way of a high board fence, ran quickly along the whole row of garages behind the houses on St. Finian's Street and destroyed them all, together with many automobiles. It was a well-known fact that the residents of the district, of which St. Finian's is the main thoroughfare, were retired people, mostly from the East.

Tuesday, October 18th, 1938

The late film beauty, lovely Myra Jacobs, was laid to rest in the cemetery at Forest Lawn. Many dignitaries and well-known personalities of the film world were present. Miss Jacobs had no family. The principal mourners were Mr. Adolphus Damarosch, the director of her last (unfinished) film, his sister, the famous Olympic star, Ruth Haddon, and Mr. Ogden Cohn, of New York City.

Tuesday, October 18th, 1938

The body of Gracie Hinxman, onetime usherette, was found in a mutilated condition, sitting upright in a 1936 Ford, license plate 4289-B8. The car was parked on Gate Avenue, district of Watts, Los Angeles. Harvey Tepperman made the discovery while delivering papers. Mr. Tepperman is nineteen and wants to be in movies. On the side of the motorcar a strange device had been drawn in mud.

In the evening, only moments after sundown, there was a fire in a warehouse on Cort Street, district of Watts. The warehouse, property of Washington Jefferson Adams, was burned to the ground. It contained ten thousand Midway kewpie dolls. Mr. Adams, a member of the colored community in Watts, was arrested.

Later that night, Mipsy Peterson of Jones Avenue, Westwood Village district of Los Angeles, saw a tall blond man in his bare feet. She declined to go into details.

In the Soviet Union, two writers, one a novelist (Gregori Grigorin) and the other a poet (Mikhail Shalansky) were purged for having written TROTSKY LIVES! on the

Kremlin walls.

All told, an eventful day.

Tuesday, October 18th, 1938

Ten thousand Jews were deported from the Third Reich to Poland. They traveled in boxcars. Among them was one Theodore Grynzspan.

Wednesday, October 19th, 1938

Fire in Burbank, California. A small factory, manufacturing nurses' uniforms. All was lost. Mr. Daniel Seidman.

Mavis Seaton reported that she had been raped the previous day in Westwood Village.

Thursday, October 20th, 1938

Alice McKnee, a visitor from Idaho, was attacked while walking in the park at Pacific Palisades, California. Miss McKnee is blind and did not see "whoever it was did this to me." But she said she was strongly aware of the "smell of leather."

There were no fires on this day.

In the city of Chungking, Republic of China, nine hundred and fifty-two scholars were blown up or suffocated when a bomb, dropped from the sky, landed near their cave.

Friday, October 21st, 1938

In Los Angeles, police officials, alerted by the rash of rape and arson, have renewed their interest in the reported death of Miss Jean Pollux (real name: Henzie Fine), whose body was said to have been washed ashore on Topanga Beach in September. They requested another interview with Mrs. Ruth Haddon, who had informed them of the body's presence on the beach. (The police never saw Miss Pollux's corpse. It is believed to have drifted out to sea.) Had there been a fire? Mrs. Haddon replied that yes, there had been — a small one. It should be noted that Mrs. Haddon (an Olympic swimmer) is also the only witness in the matter of Clara Box, whose mutilated body was discovered by Mrs. Haddon while walking in Alvarez Canyon. Miss Box's body is thought to have been destroyed in the great fire at Alvarez, September 15th of this year.

The police began to draw a map. They listed locations of the various crimes: Topanga Beach, Alvarez Canyon, Santa Monica, Watts, Westwood Village, Burbank, Pacific Palisades. A circle began to take shape.

What are the connections among the events? The police asked one another about similarities in the cases. All the murder victims had been women. All the victims of rape were women. To help formulate a pattern, the following list has been drawn up:

Jean Pollux — murdered (?)
Clara Box — murdered (?)
Mrs. Neilsen — raped.
Gracie Hinxman — murdered.
Mipsy Peterson — (dubious witness).
Mavis Seaton — raped.
Alice McKnee — raped.

If they eliminated Mipsy Peterson (characterized by some as "a liar"), there was indeed a pattern: a pair of murders, a rape, a murder. A pair of rapes. Now, they wondered, would there be a murder and a rape? If that occurred, in that order, the pattern would be firmly established.

They waited.

Nothing happened.

Six days passed.

In the English Parliament, the Prime Minister, Mr. Neville Chamberlain, wearied by the ordeal of the Czechoslovakian situation, developed a cold and stayed home.

In China, more bombs fell.

In the Soviet Union there was a state banquet at the Kremlin for Herr von Ribbentrop. Joseph Stalin prepared a toast to Adolf Hitler.

Leslie Howard and Olivia de Havilland were contracted to play featured roles in *Gone With the Wind*.

Meanwhile, in Los Angeles, there was not even a fire. Bets were laid. The police (and indeed, the citizenry) became impatient. The reputations of those who put forward the pattern theory rested on what would happen next. Jobs were at stake. Would it be rape? Or murder.

It was murder.

The theorists sighed in relief. For the time being, their positions were secure.

Thursday, October 27th, 1938

The victim was Nellie Bergdorf, of Hollywood. A wardrobe mistress at one of the major studios, she was murdered with a pair of pinking shears. On the floor near her body an unknown insignia had been drawn with tailor's soap.

The next fire was at 111138½ La Conga Boulevard. A taxidermist's shop. Burned to the ground. Mr. Gaylord Cohen.

Sunday, October 30th, 1938

Silent screen star Naomi Nola celebrated her fifty-eighth birthday today. She began her career on the stage and entered films after the turn of the century, appearing first in *The Thin Red Line*, for her husband, director George Damarosch. She is currently in retirement. Best wishes, Naomi.

Monday, November 7th, 1938

Herschel Grynzspan, a seventeen-year-old German Jew who had managed to find refuge in Paris, France, mortally wounded Ernst von Rath, Third Secretary of Hitler's Embassy in that lovely city. This murder of an innocent man, for no apparent reason, drew shocked response from Washington, London, and Paris.

Wednesday, November 9th, 1938

To celebrate the anniversary of Hitler's Beer Hall Putsch in Munich, an array of German dignitaries gathered, including Herr Hitler himself, Reichsmaster Goering, Dr. Goebbels, Julius Streicher, and the notorious American Nazi, Dr. Bruno Haddon (honorary doctorate in biology, University of Bonn).

There were thirty-six deaths.

Twenty thousand arrests.

The celebrations were held by torchlight.

Friday, October 28th to Tuesday, November 8th, 1938

In Los Angeles during this period (twice the length of the previous hiatus in crime) there were no significant events — no fires, no rapes, no murders.

The populace seethed with curiosity. Something was bound to happen.

Friday, November 11th, 1938

In the evening two events occurred in rapid succession. A woman was brutally raped, and five synagogues, eleven delicatessens, and one old-persons' home were burned to the ground.

The news of the rape and the fires created mayhem. Congratulations and promotions were spread far and wide. Lotteries were won. Fortunes on a minor scale were solidified. The pattern theorists had been proven incontrovertibly correct in their assumptions.

The next crime to be committed in the calendar of rampage (apparently being drawn up by a single protagonist) would undoubtedly be a murder.

The authorities (some of them in their new offices) awaited history with interest. The events of November 11th, however, proved to be conclusive. The pogrom was over.

Its final victim had been Ruth Damarosch.

Friday, November 11th, 1938:
8:30 p.m.

"Where are you going, dear?" said Naomi. She reclined in her bed. Her eyes were clouded; she could barely see.

"Out," said Ruth.

"Come, come, dear. Be kinder than that."

"Just driving, Mother. Really. Nothing else than that."

"You seem upset, Ruth. Nervous. Please tell me what's wrong."

"It's nothing, Mama. Please don't fret."

"It's me, isn't it," said Naomi. The shadows cast by the light from golden lamps seemed to menace the edges of her pillows. "It's because I'm sick and you can't stand being near me."

"No, Mama. No."

"You hate me. You want to get away from me because I don't believe the things you say. I know you hate me, Ruth, and I know you'll be glad when I'm dead."

Ruth beckoned to Miss Bonkers, who stood behind her in the living room.

"Shouldn't Mother have a sedative, Miss Bonkers? Perhaps even another shot? She's terribly upset."

Miss Bonkers low-voiced it back that "She can't have more right now, Mrs. Haddon. I've got to adhere strictly to this schedule" (she held up her clipboard with the morphine timetable appended to it) "and if I get away from this, then there's nothing I can do for her when the pain becomes unbearable."

"She's so unhappy," said Ruth. "And so suspicious. It's unlike her."

"Yes, but it's typical," said Miss Bonkers, popping a gumdrop into her mouth and dusting the sugar from her hands onto her uniform. "This is always the worst stage of cancer. Paranoia sets in, and there's nothing a person can do."

Ruth glanced, attempting nonchalance, back into Naomi's room. The figure in the bed was tense and twisted. But its eyes were closed.

"Tell her not to worry about me," said Ruth. "I'm only going for a drive."

"Very well, Mrs. Haddon."

Ruth got to the front door.

"Oh, by the way, Miss Bonkers," she said, turning back to speak. "I think it's time you stopped calling me that. Mrs. Haddon."

"But. . ."

"No buts, Miss Bonkers, please. I'm asking you to obey me. From now on, call me Miss Ruth. And if you must refer to me on the telephone, or elsewhere, please refer to me as Mrs. Damarosch."

"Mrs. Damarosch!"

"Yes, it's perfectly legal. Don't look so shocked, Miss Bonkers. Lots of divorced women do it, revert to their maiden name. I shall henceforth be Mrs. Damarosch. It's quite simple."

Miss Bonkers performed a few vulgar expressions, but said nothing.

Ruth opened, went beyond, and closed the door.

"Mrs. Damarosch," muttered Miss Bonkers into the pages on her clipboard, "is the mother's name." Did this mean she must now call Naomi Nola "the Dowager Mrs. Damarosch"?

9:00 p.m.

The Franklin climbed.

Since Myra's death, Dolly had been making life difficult for taxi drivers, while Ruth fell occasional heir to the purple-painted motorcar that her brother never drove himself.

The car responded cautiously to the unprecedented demands which Ruth now pressed upon it. It seemed never to have known a speed above thirty miles an hour.

In the hills above the city it was hot and dry. A fog of road dust and heat waves lay between the winding road and the view below. Through this veil, the lights came on street by street — avenue by avenue — until all at once the whole of La Cienega Boulevard was lit up by a thrusting arrow of white electricity, and there was fire, or so it appeared, all over Los Angeles.

Now Ruth drove higher, moving farther away from this vision, closer to the darkness.

He would be up here somewhere. That much she had surmised. He had to have somewhere to hide, and since the city afforded no such place, the hills, with their tall, sunburnt grasses and copses of low shrub, were the only sensible and safe place from which to direct his operations. She was determined to find him.

9:30 p.m.

She parked the car.

She sat very still. In the last of the cityglow and the first of the moonlight she had seen what must have been a figure striding along the ridge of the hill that now rose above her.

She had parked the Franklin off the road in the lee of this hill, and looking up, she could see the clear black heat of the sky with its starspots and pale cast of moonlight. The rim of the hill was unmistakable and clear.

She rolled down all the windows and lit a cigarette.

She listened. Surely he was there.

Would there be the whisper of bare feet in the dust and dry grass? Or would he shake the earth with his approach?

She wanted to get out of the car, but something was still afraid inside of her.

Was this rape, since she was willing? And since she was willing, would he have to kill her? What were the terms? How did you survive him?

The grass crackled.

Ruth closed her eyes. She prayed for moisture in her mouth, for motion in her tongue. For words. There were none.

Some birds flew up and away from the hillside. Ruth opened her eyes just in time to guess at their silhouette as they beat away into the moon.

Then silence.

He was there. Somewhere. She'd seen him. She couldn't doubt that. She'd seen him, striding across...

A stone was turned and lifted. It began to roll.

Only a human foot could turn and move a stone so violently. No animal would be that clumsy. Not in its own terrain.

She peered out into the darkness.

She wanted to call, but was afraid of who might answer. It could be some tramp, or a pair of lovers, or a troop of boy scouts. ... She smiled at the thought. Boy scouts.

She lit another cigarette. Part of her mind was still calm, even practical enough to have the thought that once the baby had begun to grow inside her she would have to give up smoking. But the rest of her mind was listening and watching out into the night, waiting with neither patience nor impatience, but only with the insistent and unshakable certainty that he would come.

Somehow, too, she had known all day long that this was the day, that this would be the place, and that she would be the one.

The golden head would hover over hers...

She thought of Dolly. Dolly would be pleased. A child was being born. A Damarosch.

Ruth gasped.

He was standing just beyond the motorcar.

His uniform was soiled. His bare feet were darkened with blood and dust. A faint aroma — leather — smoke — filtered through the air and made Ruth ache with nostalgia and longing. Her cigarette fell to the ground.

Where was his face? What did he look like now? She could not quite make it out, so perfect was the dimness of the light. But something glimmered there and she guessed it was his eyes.

"Are you there?" she asked. "Is it you?"

Nothing responded. Neither voice nor movement.

But he was there. She could see his shoulders. His hands. His feet. His uniform. His hair.

Staring at him, trying with all her might to see his face, Ruth unlocked the door of the motorcar, opened it, and waited.

Would he come over? Must she go to him? What?

He stood stock still.

For a moment she thought, He's a tree...and then his fingers moved.

She got out.

The odors of leather and smoke grew stronger, almost overpowering. Ruth advanced.

"I'm here," she said. "See me? Here I am."

She fumbled in her pocketbook and withdrew the torn insignia. She held it out toward him as a signal of her submission.

"Speak to me, please. You've come so far. It's taken me so long to understand. Now, surely, you can tell me that I'm right and that you want me."

Closer.

"Weren't you in Alvarez?" she asked. "In Alvarez with me...?"

The figure moved.

It trembled.

"I was there," said Ruth, "with you."

From a long distance — so far away that Ruth's ears could not encompass the distance — a siren wailed a tale of fire.

Unafraid, Ruth walked up to him and grasped his hand.

With her other hand, she showed the insignia.

There at last was his face. It was sad. His lips would not part. His cheeks had hollowed but he was beautiful still — more beautiful than she had remembered. He seemed no longer pure and young, but troubled and mature. He eyed the insignia. His fingers moved to touch where it had been on his arm. Its twin was still in place below his other shoulder.

"You're growing more like us," Ruth said. "You're growing more like everyone. Oh, hurry — hurry before it's too late!"

She dragged him, running, to the dried-up hillside, to the crackling golden grass.

She lay down, drawing him with her.

"Undo me," she said. "Undo yourself. Be quick."

He would not. Or could not. She did not know which.

Her mind twitched. This was impossible. All this time. All this way. The intention; the intention must be fulfilled.

She undid her blouse.

"I will, then," she said. "I will do it."

Quickly she spread the blouse beneath her, rising in the same motion to unbutton her skirt. This she removed, and her slip, and spread them widely where her buttocks and legs must lie.

Sideways would be easiest, she decided.

He's tired.

How practical the desperate are, she thought, bending over him now, her knees spread for support, undoing the buttons of his shirt.

At last she was able to roll him out of his sleeves and as she knelt farther in toward him, reaching for the buckle of his belt, she caught sight of his eyes watching her. Those eyes will be the eyes of my child, she thought. Placid and unafraid, neither curious nor repulsed. The expression was unforgettable.

The buckle momentarily jammed and she was about to cry out with frustration when she felt him move beneath her fingers. He lifted his hips and instantly the buckle opened. He was moving with her now, still letting her command his actions, but obeying more swiftly.

She had to alter her position in order to remove his trousers. She knelt down between his feet. In her hands, his feet were dry and covered with healed sores. She pitied him. She pitied him his commission and the conditions under which he had to commit it. Then, staring down at the golden lengths of his body, she pitied him more — pitied his perfection and the curse it had laid on him. He had to be the messenger of Race: chosen — not choosing.

She crawled around to his side and faced him.

She lay down with him, breast to breast.

She stared into his eyes, and he, unblinking, stared dispassionately back.

"Begin," she commanded, but her voice was as low and gentle as a mother asking her infant to feed. And just as obedient as a hungry child, the blond head arched inward to her rising breast.

Ruth wanted to breathe him like air into her lungs. She wanted to bleed him instantly into her veins. To absorb him.

His hand fell lightly on her tilted buttock. His knees insinuated themselves between her. Ruth's pelvis burned forward; she grasped him, held him warmly for a moment in the sheath of her hand, and then she thrust him into the wound prepared for him, impelling her body onto his blade so suddenly their union was completed in a single spasm of alarm.

There was no thought in Ruth's mind. There could be none. Everything but fulfillment had been driven away. She knew there was life inside her. She knew it as surely as the sky was there and the stars and the moon and the silhouettes of hills and scrub.

She lay there fully an hour, unaware of both sound and silence, unaware of the ghostly holocaust that was whispering around her.

Suddenly waking from whatever it was that had possessed her, Ruth sat up, fully aware. Each sense was alert with panic.

The darkness was awash with orange waves. Fire.

She touched herself. Naked.

She lurched sideways to waken — to save him...

But he was not there. Gone. But when?

There was no time. She rose to her feet, staggering into her clothes, lurching toward the parked, endangered motorcar.

"Where are you?" she started to cry, but the flames would not let her. She breathed in smoke and heat and her throat constricted. She gasped for air.

Ashes and cinders rose up with every step. Embers and sparks set fire to her sleeves, her hair and her eyebrows.

She struggled into the car and rolled up all the windows. Somehow she remembered how to turn the key, how to make the car function, how to accelerate and how to steer. The road was barely visible through smoke and flame. She did not know yet that she, herself, was on fire.

"Alvarez," she kept saying, but as a question. "Alvarez? Alvarez?"

At last she broke free of the flames and brought the Franklin to a halt just in time to avoid smashing head on into a fire truck that had pulled to a stop on its way up the road to the inferno in the hills.

Hands battered at the windows all around her, but Ruth could not move, for now she knew that she was burning. She began to scream, but was immobilized. At last, one of the firemen broke his way into the car with an ax and lifted her out onto the road and into a blanket — safe and unharmed.

"Are you all right, lady? Are you all right?" he yelled. Everywhere the noise was ear-splitting.

Ruth tried to nod.

"There's someone," she gasped, "up there. A man."

"We'll find him, don't you worry," said the fireman. "You rest here and then we'll try and get you home. You're all right now. Only your clothes were on fire. You're all right."

He dashed away then, with some others, to haul an ineffectual hose toward the burning hillside. All around them the grass smoke blasted the air with its message of fire and ruin, but Ruth just sat in the middle of the road, covered with dust and ash and told herself over and over again that fire and smoke could never frighten her again. The smell of them was the smell of imperfection burning — of imperfection being burned away forever.

She rested.

There was life inside her. She had put it there.

Or claimed it. She did not know which. Or care.

It was done.

Saturday, November 12th, 1938

> Fire broke out in the Hollywood Hills late last evening. Several homes were endangered, including the house of screen star Corinne Castle and her husband, gambler Stoney Blake. Miss Castle and Mr. Blake fled their mansion in night attire (see picture, page 9) but were able to return later when Los Angeles, Hollywood, and Beverly Hills fire brigades brought the blaze under control.

It is thought that the fire was started by a cigarette thrown or dropped from a motorcar. Hollywood's Fire Chief, Herman Anders, issued a statement in which he warned of the consequences of such carelessness. "Smokers who do not use their ashtrays cause an awful lot of trouble," he said, and went on to praise the good job of fire fighting done by his men. Miss Castle later entertained the firemen at an impromptu dancing party, which was held until the early hours of the morning, on the lawn of her home. Dressed in a handsome hostess gown, she informed reporters that she hadn't "had so much fun since playing the role of Lulu Lightbright" in her latest film, *Lulu Lightbright*. Mr. Blake concurred, admitting with a sly grin that Hollywood firemen were excellent poker players and honorable gentlemen when it came to paying up their losses. Music was supplied by Tam Morgason and his Alhambrans. A good time was had by all.

The Chronicle of Naomi Nola

Sunday, November 13th, 1938:
Topanga Beach
6:30 a.m.

Though the ocean was attempting silence, Naomi heard it. She awoke now, automatically, half an hour prior to every shot.

Morphine.

Miss Bonkers.

7:00 a.m.

It was only 6:30. Naomi wondered how she felt. If she lay still enough, she remained numb, but if she moved so much as a finger, body-consciousness was restored. She had developed a theory that pain had to do with the flow of blood. If you lay quiet, nothing happened, but if you even thought profoundly the blood flowed and caused pain.

There was some light now, beyond the curtains. Not true light, but the beginning of it. She was practiced at watching the sun set at sea. But she had never seen it rise. To see that, she would have to move three thousand miles to the other coast. Too late for that.

This thought made her laugh.

Pain.

Damn. I'm alive.

6:35.

Wouldn't Miss Bonkers get up soon?

Didn't she make coffee around now? And sterilize the needles? And get out the phials? Little packages of sleep in white paper. Rolled in gauze, slipped into envelopes, locked in cabinets.

Naomi never asked about the keys. Suicide had not occurred to her. It wouldn't.

A dreadful hunger persisted, but she was unable to eat. Nothing would stay down. Even tea and coffee, even milk, twisted back up to her mouth as though they were afraid to venture farther than her throat.

They had offered her a room at the hospital, but she was adamant. She was going to die here. In this place.

Miss Bonkers was rattling in the kitchen.

"Miss Bonkers," Naomi called. "I need my needle."

"Coming soon," Miss Bonkers answered sleepily (but pleasantly). Naomi could hear the slap of her book as she placed it on the counter and opened it to read. Every waking moment, it seemed, that woman was reading. She'd gone through every book in the house and was buying more every week. This pleased Naomi. Somehow, silently as the words themselves, restive but quiet on their pages, the thoughts and ideas in Miss Bonkers's head were altering and changing page by page, volume by volume, as she read. The grim-eyed caretaker who had come on duty all those months ago was slowly but surely turning into a gray-eyed Nanny with alerted sympathies and more considerate fingers.

Nanny.

Yes. It was quite true, Naomi thought. She herself had become childishly dependent and felt at all times as though this room she lay in was, indeed, more nursery than boudoir. And Miss Bonkers did things, more and more, as though they were being done for a child — a child who became progressively younger until, at last (and Naomi knew this) she would be little more than a babe-in-arms, lifted, petted, soothed, and changed. Sleep was everything, the great safety, the purger of fear, the keeper of the gates to death, the slayer of pain. Miss Bonkers was its guardian, purveying sleep like pills and potions. Naomi welcomed it, resented it, feared its permanence and then, slowly, came out the other side, begging her nurse for more. They formed a strange triumvirate: Miss Bonkers, Naomi, and Sleep.

At last she came.

"Good morning, Mrs. Damarosch. What can I offer you?"

"A shot," said Naomi.

"Almost time," said Bonkers. "Don't you want the pot?"

"I'm afraid to move," said Naomi. "Maybe I'd better wait until I've had morphine."

Miss Bonkers slipper-slappered over to the curtains and drew them open.

She wore a mauve-colored robe over a voluminous nightdress, the collar of which was so high it made her hold her head out like a turtle. She smoothed the drapery with her square little hands, the color and texture of inferior mother-of-pearl. Her fingers seemed to have been chopped off, they were so short, and it was always a shock to Naomi to perceive that there were nails there, beautifully formed and manicured.

"Going to be another scorcher," Miss Bonkers said, looking out at the sky. "And here it is November."

They looked at the day, the one from the bed, the other from beside the curtains. Miss Bonkers's round pudge face was decorated with glasses. She began to be awake and to look like herself.

"Anyone out on the sand yet?" Naomi asked, each word pinched by her teeth.

Miss Bonkers looked along the beach. "No one but that dog, Mrs. D. My, what a pretty dog that is."

"The yellow one?"

"Yes. Miss Ruth's friend."

"Is she awake yet?"

"No, ma'am."

Miss Bonkers came over and rearranged the things at Naomi's bedside.

"What do you make of her behavior yesterday?"

"Oh. Normal. Normal. I mean, for someone who got caught in a fire — normal. Sort of stunned is what I'd call it. But she's all right."

"Yes. That's what I thought. But I thought something else, too. And I wondered if you'd noticed it."

Miss Bonkers considered for a moment and then spoke reflectively. "You mean happier? She's happier and more relaxed."

Naomi sighed. It hadn't been her imagination. Miss Bonkers had thought so, too.

"Yes. That's it exactly. Happier. Relaxed...and..."

"And what?"

"And something else. I don't know what."

Miss Bonkers smiled. "You're sure it doesn't begin with an 'M,'" she said.

"An 'M.'"

"A man," Miss Bonkers said.

Naomi thought about this. She hadn't previously. It hadn't even crossed her mind. Ruth was having an affair.

"She was married, you know," said Miss Bonkers, pottering farther into the room. "And she's young, yet."

"All this driving around in the motorcar," said Naomi, imagining things. "Oh, dear! I hope not."

Miss Bonkers sighed and nodded and sighed again, not noticing that Naomi was beginning to knead the bedclothes with her hands.

"We live in different times, Mrs. Damarosch. Different times, indeed. You don't know what to think in times like these. Except," she reflected, beginning to make her way out of the room, "except it seems a shame that all those young men died in that Great War of theirs, for a world that doesn't exist any more, and a bunch of moral behavior people just laugh at now. It's like I always say, though. Nothing beats a lost cause. I mean, there isn't anything the whole world over that'll beat your lost cause for frustration."

"Isn't it seven o'clock yet?" said Naomi suddenly.

"Yes. Just. Are you ready?"

"Of course I'm ready. Get it quickly."

The pain made a leap high up into Naomi's womb. It seemed to be clawing at her with hot knives.

"Oh, hurry, Miss Bonkers. *Hurry!!*"

Miss Bonkers called out, "Yes. Yes. Coming. Coming."

"At once. At once. Oh, please, at once!"

Ruth heard this last cry and came sharply awake.

"Now! Now! Now!" Naomi began to chant, battering the headboard behind her with her fists.

Ruth came running from her room. "What? What?" she said.

"It's worse," said Miss Bonkers. "Every time now, it's worse. And always so suddenly."

"Help me," Naomi cried.

"Stand aside, Miss Ruth. Keep out of my way. I wouldn't want to drop this now."

Ruth stood away and then followed Miss Bonkers to the door of her mother's room.

Both Miss Bonkers and Naomi had to struggle to loosen Naomi's grip from the headboard, and finally Ruth had to go to their assistance.

"There. There now. There," said Miss Bonkers, withdrawing the needle from its place. "Let's all count together," she said. "Everybody count."

"One," said Ruth.

"Two," said Miss Bonkers.

"Three," struggled Naomi.

"Four," said Ruth.

"Five," said Miss Bonkers.

"Oh," said Naomi.

"Seven," said Ruth.

"Eight."

"Niii. . . ne."

"Ten." They all spoke together.

"There. There. There," said Ruth.

"There," said Naomi. "Much, much better."

They all smiled and patted each other's hands with pleasure and relief.

"So. So. So. So. So."

In the kitchen, four minutes later, Miss Bonkers handed Ruth a cup of coffee, turned her back on her, and said distinctly, indistinctly, "Four or five more days, Miss Ruth. Only four or five more days."

Then, not knowing why she did it, not anywhere, at any time prior to the moment it happened knowing or sensing it was going to happen, Miss Bonkers put her face into her hands and wept.

Monday, November 14th, 1938:
2:30 p.m.

"What is your friend's name?" Ruth asked.

And Charity said, "Eugene."

"That's a very grown-up name for a friend, isn't it?" Ruth asked.

"He is a grownup," said Charity.

"Oh."

They were sitting on the sand in front of the Trelfords' house — Charity, the dog, and Ruth.

Charity's bathing trunks kept falling down, so Ruth had been elected to fix them. The older children were still at school and B.J. was inside squeezing oranges in anticipation of their return.

"What does he do?" said Ruth, sewing busily away. Charity, naked but for sand, sat beside her petting the yellow dog.

"He's an orchestra conductor," she said.

"Fascinating," said Ruth, knotting the thread and biting it off. "Where?"

"Up at Salinas."

"Oh, really?" Ruth shook the bathing suit out. "I didn't know they had an orchestra up there."

"The Salinas Mickey-Minnie Orchestra," said Charity.

She stood up and stuck one chubby, bronzed leg out at Ruth. Ruth helped her into her trunks and drew the newly mended string into a bow at her waist.

"There."

Ruth gave the child a pat and then put away the thread and needle into a round wicker basket at her side.

"A Mickey-Minnie orchestra, eh?"

"Yes."

"How many instruments are there?"

"A hundred."

"Heavens. That's a big band."

"They don't march, though. They sit down."

"I see."

"They sit in a giant circle and Eugene stands in the middle and plays."

"Don't they play, too? Doesn't Eugene conduct?"

"No. They watch and he shows how to do everything."

"I see."

"They play in the middle of the night."

"Yes."

"At nine o'clock."

"My goodness! That's certainly late enough."

"I can hear them, though, anyhow. I listen out the window."

"Oh. I see."

"It's too dark to see. But I can hear them."

Ruth stood up and dusted the sand from her legs. Charity walked around in a circle, holding onto the dog's tail.

"Do you like music, Charity?"

Charity thought about it and then said, "No."

"How come you like Eugene, then, if you don't like music?"

This required no thought at all. "He's hairy."

She gave the dog's tail a yank, but the dog did not respond.

"Hairy!" said Ruth. She wasn't sure whether she should laugh or worry. "How exactly do you mean that?" she asked affecting a degree of nonchalance.

"You can't see his face," said Charity, finally and mercifully letting go of the dog's tail. "Fact, you can't see any of him but his hair."

"And you like that."

"Oh, yes. It's long and pretty like Rapa. . . unzz. . . "

"Rapunzel."

"And you can play hide-and-go-seek inside him."

"I see. Well. That must be fun. Where did you meet him, Charity?"

"Under there," said the child, pointing under the house.

"You should be careful, going under there. There might be scorpions. . . ."

"Not with Eugene there. He's a murderer."

"I thought you said he was an orchestra leader."

"He is. But he kills people, too."

"And scorpions."

"Everything. Fish. Crabs. Gully birds. Insecks. Children. And then he eats them and wipes his mouth up with his hair."

"Dear!"

"But *we're* friends."

"Well, I'm glad to hear it."

"He has a green dress he wears sometimes, too."

"Unh-hunh." Ruth peered into the darkness beneath the house. "Is he there now?" she asked.

"Oh, no," said Charity. "He's upstairs with Mommy."

"Oh."

"They lie in bed all afternoon sometimes and Eugene hangs some of his hair on the wall where I can see it."

"Goodness."

"And the rest of it he keeps on."

"Well, that's good."

"And then he makes Mama sit in a circle and he conducts her with music."

"That's nice."

"And then Mama conducts him."

"I see."

Charity caught her breath and went on. "One night I woke up and there was light from the moonlight and Eugene was walking on the beach in his dress."

"Are you sure it was Eugene?"

"Yes."

"How were you sure?"

Charity thought this over and then said, "'Cause he took his hair off."

"Oh."

"After that he sat on the sand and cried."

"How sad."

"I wanted to go down but Mommy caught me and said we should leave Eugene alone."

"Quite right," said Ruth. "If he was sad, then he'd want to be alone."

"That isn't what Mama said."

"Oh? What did she say?"

"She said Eugene was waiting for somebody and we mustn't. . . interrup' him. She said someone was coming for him and he didn't know when and he didn't know who but he was waiting."

"Goodness."

"An' Mama said Eugene was a good person and only wore his dress when he was sad."

"Poor Eugene."

"But I think Eugene must always be sad."

"Why is that?"

"'Cause every night, now, I see him, every night. In his dress."

"Really!"

"Yes. An' I see you, too, some nights, Auntie Ruth."

"Oh, dear," said Ruth. "If you see me then you're up very late. . . *much* too late for little girls."

It was true. Ruth did, on some nights, walk the beach.
"Are you sad, too, Auntie Ruth?"
"No, dear."
"Are you waiting for someone, then?"
"No, dear." (Not anymore.)
"Then why do you walk on the beach and cry?"
"Well, maybe I cried because — a while ago I was sad."
"An' you're not sad any more?"
"No."
Suddenly Charity said, "Where did your hair go, Auntie Ruth? Where did all your hair go?"
Ruth thought for a moment and then smiled and turned to Charity and said, "Why, I gave it to Eugene, of course. It's my hair that he's wearing."
This didn't faze Charity at all.
"I thought so," she said. " 'Cause that's ezzactly what Eugene says himself. An' I believe him — every word he says."

Tuesday, November 15th, 1938

There is a sea drift in morphine, and Naomi gradually began to float upon it.

Her mind hung back in the past where the waves of old events licked at it — gently one moment, violently the next; but through it all, through memory and fear, amusement and regret, she did not alter course. It could not be altered now, either by turning back or by turning aside. There was only following, forward.

Thus, on the drift, she perceived her wavering dream; on the sea drift of morphine and memory:

George's loved ones. His women. They were a subject of amusement to Naomi. They always had been. She would see him walking, hands at war behind his back, making love-circles down in the gardens at Falconridge. The current mistress (or the woman currently being wooed, as the case might be) would always look her best in these garden walks. She would have worn her best dress. Been to her hairdresser and received the best treatment. She would be at her best silence. Silence was important in a woman, so that George could make noises.

In the gardens, which were cunningly laid out in circles (a circle mesmerizes, lulls) George would walk his ladies with passionate steps. He led; they followed gracefully after.

Lying in her woolen bed-coat, Naomi saw them all as of old, name by name, face by face, and she drifted.

She moved through a selection of times, never pausing where she did not care to pause, remembering — reliving swiftly what had taken years to endure and years to survive. Other events, short in themselves, required hours of circling — a wide and long approach — a certain charming wariness.

The building and organization of Falconridge was ignored. It had taken four years of dust, carpenters, stonemasons, and yelling. Now, she only saw it as it was — or had been — finished and resplendent. Twenty servants. All those Chinamen. In hats.

Her birth was ignored. Her distant parents wavered on the brink of memory where both had been killed in a railroad accident in the year when Naomi was ten. She and her sisters had grown up in the home of her grandparents — more vividly remembered. Her grandfather had manufactured pianos. The house seemed endlessly filled with visiting celebrities — pianists — conductors — touring opera stars — even, from time to time, actors and actresses. Thus, the bug had bitten when she was sitting, in fact, upon the knee of Edwin Booth in 1892, the year before his death. She was twelve. She had provided a small drama in her grandma's parlor that day, by asking Mr. Booth to recount for her his memories of the shooting of Mr. Lincoln. No one had thought to forewarn her that the subject of assassination was taboo and, in fact, no one had thought to inform her that Mr. Booth was not *the* Mr. Booth, but only his brother. However, Naomi forgave him for not being the assassin she imagined him to be, because he recited so beautifully for her Caesar's speech from Shakespeare: "Cowards die many times before their deaths; the valiant never taste of death but once." Naomi never could nor ever did forget the flavor of that voice, nor the lack of reproach in his eyes, nor the somber, bony grandeur of his knees.

But George. She always, by whatever channel, returned to George — and Falconridge.

He was already entertaining mistresses. She knew there was no real difference between their experience and her own. Naomi had insisted on marriage, that was all. And being in a position of responsibility (the whole country was looking at his films), it was easy for George to be convinced that he needed the image of a father and a husband.

This is not to say that George did not love Naomi. He did. But he was like a man with worms. His appetite was appalling. It could not be satisfied.

His mistresses had a few things in common. "George's List," Naomi called them. They were all wealthy. Each had fine ankles. Each had large eyes and each had an unending sense of the possibilities of her own femininity. They did not at all (but for the size of eye and the shape of ankle) resemble one another physically. Some were tall, some tiny. Some had busty bosoms, some had none. Some smoked and swore, some were dainty. They all were women of rare beauty. Most of them were film stars, stage actresses, singers, and this, of course, was all taking place in the Dream of 1905 to 1922.

Seventeen years.

They were married in New York in 1904. She was twenty-four years old. It took Naomi three years to decide that she would brook fate and have a baby. Ruth was born. That was good. Ruth being a girl, she need not and did not remark on her blood to George.

In 1910 they began making movies in earnest. (Before that it had been almost a pastime, between stage plays.) In 1910 George went back to having his mistresses.

Naomi became popular.

She appeared not only for George but for Griffith and Mendes. She made eleven films in one year.

They moved to Hollywood in 1914. They were the first. The others followed.

Meanwhile, Adolphus had been born.

This was the beginning of Naomi's nightmare. She kept the secret for eleven years. Until 1922.

Then George found out.

It wasn't that Dolly didn't bleed in that first year. He did. But Naomi rushed him in a blinding parlay of speed and secrecy to the right people at the right times, and many tragedies were successfully aborted.

In Russia, the Tsarina was going through much the same thing. Naomi read of it all with great interest. The figure of Rasputin loomed large in her dreams. She sought religious cures herself, in secret, from priests and charlatans. Many hands were raised above Dolly. Many prayers were said. But there was only one Rasputin. And his days were numbered. Ultimately, he died, very much against his divine will, and soon afterward the Tsarina and the stricken Tsarevitch, her son, were murdered, too. Shot with guns. They bled to death. After all that staunching and praying.

There was nothing left to read in the papers. Hope dwindled. So Naomi sought out and read the histories of the European royal houses. What had *they* done? Suffered. That was all. Endured and died. Many died in accidents. Carriage deaths and motorcar deaths. Assassinations. Plots. Europe was cruel to its kings and princes. They were cruel to themselves.

Whatever she read, it was collectively a history of scratches and disasters. A hemophilic child cannot, like every other child, be stung by bees, pick up nails, cut out paper dolls, fall down, have boisterous friends, or stand by windows.

Invention is the enemy of such a child.

To be a parent to this child is to know, never, any peace. Any sleep that is not afraid. Any pause in searching.

There is no medicine. There are no doctors.

There are only Rasputins. And they die.

Naomi, however, was able to have a career, and this provided her sanity. You are aware of this career. More's the pity if you aren't. Those eyes! That nose. The laughter — always silent. She was retired before sound. Small-waisted, dressed in ankle-length chiffons and silks, she stormed the hearts and imaginations of America. Naomi Nola. Sprung from the forehead of Jove and the knee of Edwin Booth.

Oddly enough, she had no public abroad. She was totally American. She exuded (in silence) sweetness of breath and softness of touch. Her allure was circular. Round-eyed, round-minded. She maintained the promise of virginity without its pallor. She was marvelously alive. She bespoke, before the fact, wholesome American motherhood. (Irony.) She excelled in three basic emotions which were much cherished by her public: laughter (an emotional state all its own), sadness (undefined, just "sadness" — a sort of tranquil melancholy), and gaiety. Gaiety is not laughter. Having watched her, you know that. It is a state of mind. But Naomi was gay. She was beginning to understand.

She was perhaps not a great star. But she was wonderfully popular. She founded George's reputation, and when the time came to retire (twelve years is a long time for one face and one smile) she retired with absolute composure. She always knew when something was over. It did not disturb her.

Her contemporaries (Mary Pickford, Theda Bara, Pola Negri, the Gishes, Letitia Virden) came back and back and back. They wanted more. Naomi smiled. In 1923, Theda Bara made a comeback. It was tragic. But funny. A comeback in 1923! Movies were ten years older, but it seemed, sometimes, they were only ten years old.

Now it was 1938.

And there was still the dream, and the drift, as she remembered.

Her screen lovers — her husband — her children — her home.

She had loved retirement.

Perhaps it was the fact of her great beauty that made her retirement professionally easier. She did not have to fret about what she had been. She had been perfect. And knew it. Simply.

It was a chapter. She closed it finally, with love.

Now she was a mother. And a wife.

It is hard to know which comes first, or should be placed first. You chose to love your husband. You love your children without choice. One involves privilege. The other — wonder.

George tampered with the mechanics of their marriage. He was off on a journey of his own that more and more rarely involved either his wife or his children. One of his objectives was a bigger — a better — a more astounding film than he had ever made before. The other objective was a mystical bed, filled with made-up, imaginary women.

George's greatest gift as a film maker had been his devotion to self-improvement. Unlike so many others in that "industry" (Naomi hated the word; George hated it, but it was becoming increasingly a fact of life), unlike so many others, George never set out to better or to beat another man's product. Only his own. There were many screenings on the specially whitewashed wall in the Falconridge library. (George liked the granular texture of a wall more than the new and always-being-improved textures of professional screens. He said walls were an ingredient of his ideal film. A wall gave substance. It had those wonderful lumps and dots. It added depth to the projection.)

Naomi sewed and knitted, did petit point, and even painted pictures (water colors, flowers, birds, beasts, and insects). She was beginning to celebrate life. She watched her husband's creations. They grew in stature, but she sensed that there was something missing — something that George had not thought of. She did not know for a long while what it was. Ultimately (he made *Tarnish and Rust*, his lyric masterpiece, in 1921), the films no longer reached the public he had made them for. *Tarnish and Rust* had left both critics and audiences speechless and spellbound. The decline began immediately after this work. It was slow and at first unnoticed. He invited his elder brother to join him. Then his younger brothers, one by one (they "offered" to come; discreetly). George was beginning to look under stones for his ideas. He panicked. But that was later. By the time the cousins were arriving in what seemed to be droves, George had forgotten what he was looking for. He was looking for "something" — and that was all.

What had happened to his films and to him and what Naomi puzzled over and wondered at and could not define (and afterward, could) was that following *Tarnish and Rust*, the films ceased to imitate life and to celebrate life. They began to imitate and to celebrate film. He ceased to be an artist. He commenced the life of an industrialist. He might as well have made furniture. Pianos.

Then there was the party.

1922.

Ruth's birthday. She was fifteen.

It is not known why this birthday party was to have been so special. No one was going anywhere. Nothing had happened. Perhaps George was simply showing off to his daughter. It was too bad that he had not chosen to show her off, instead.

Ruth wore a blue dress. How well Naomi remembered all of this. Each single detail. Her own dress was rose and gray. Dolly's suit, specially tailored, was white and had satin facings. He wore long white stockings, the way children had before the war. Naomi maintained always a sense of her own period. It had been right for her. Fashionably, she never grew out of it, until these recent weeks, the weeks of her death, when she had broken her own traditions to celebrate such colors as orange and green and turquoise and yellow.

And this is her dream of celebrations.

Ruth's fifteenth birthday.

It was an exemplary day for nature. All that was best, existed. The flowers were more spectacular than they had ever been; there were more of them and they shone with brighter colors and scented the air with deeper mysteries. The lawns were like emerald rugs made in China or Turkey. The trees filled up with birds (so many of them, in fact, and so brilliantly colored that someone remarked to George that he must have hired a wandering company of opera singers and induced them to stand among the trees in their costumes for *The Magic Flute*. This same someone credited George with the wrong imagination; Naomi might have done this, but not George).

The air was crystal clear and cool. The temperature hovered just over seventy-two degrees. Not a single cloud appeared.

The coolies wore their blue uniforms and their hats. Some were in silks. They threaded the crowded lawns with large straw trays of sandwiches and hors d'oeuvres. They passed drinks on inverted brass gongs. The glasses were tall and each was encased in woven raffia of bright colors.

The guests themselves had nothing whatever to do with a fifteen-year-old child or with her birthday, and Ruth remained alone. (She was an early romantic; she believed in undiscovered princesses. It was the following winter she began to swim. Disillusionment? Naomi never knew.)

Everyone was in love with Bully Moxon that year. He was everywhere.

A vaudevillian, he told visual jokes and danced. His art was movement. Mimic art. He rarely, even in theatres, needed words. His films were noted for their lack of printed titles. He was not handsome. He was downright ugly. He drank too much. He was afraid of women. He worshipped them. He had an exemplary cleanliness, a sense of neatness and correctness of dress common among alcoholics. His shoes were like stars, always shining brightly. His cravats were exquisite. He changed his collars four times a day. He ate peppermint drops to keep his breath from startling the effect of his appearance. He parted his hair in the middle. He gave such pleasure and like a child was capable of so much adoration and wonder that you could not revile him. He wore flowers and Naomi remembered him with tears.

He came across the lawns of memory. He always came in silence.

In this dream in the heart of Naomi Nola, Bully dances toward her with gloves on his hands. He is mock serious. He presses her fingers to his lips. He exudes peppermint and bourbon, a delightful aroma of mixed sweetness and acid, the aroma of a comically wicked child.

He lisps kisses onto her fingers and they play the game. There is no laughter. Not even a smile. Naomi blinks with mischievous alarm, retrieves her hand, and assumes one of her more famous poses. "*I am not to be had for a kiss and a smile!*"

Bully bowed. Naomi grinned.

"Dear Bully..."

"Madame!"

"No. Now, be serious, Bull. No more games. Tell me how you are."

(Every word. She could remember every word.)

He slackened his hold. For a moment she could see an honest feeling struggling to hide itself in the comedy of his eyes.

"I am in love," he said.

"You always are," said Naomi. "Dear, dear Bully." She took and held his white-gloved hands. Both of them. (She recalled the little padded fingers, the fact that the gloves were made of cotton. Waiter's gloves. An old routine.)

"No," he said. And this was absolutely true. "No. I have never been in love before."

"Is it me, Bully?" (She wanted to help him. She knew it wasn't.)

"No, my dear. You I simply adore. That is all."

"Thank you."

He looked off over the lawn.

He struggled for a line — a joke — a dance — anything for relief.

It was Letitia. There she was.

The Virgin.

He stared down at his feet. Once more he kissed Naomi's fingers. Silent, he drifted away.

Later he danced for them.

On the nasturtium bed.

And stole a white carnation from the garden.

And went into some kind of private history.

And would never be forgotten.

Until now, when Naomi must wake.

Wednesday, November 16th, 1938:
8:45 p.m.

Naomi stirred. The dream always became unhappy. She wished that she could master that. Then she went back again, searching.

There were two incidents.

The first was a death.

One of the Chinamen fell over the cliff into the canyon, and died. This was one of those scandals of silence, in the same vein as Myra Jacobs's shooting Mr. Danton. It happened at the party. Ruth's birthday party. The circumstances were clouded. Very little was said. The police came, were paid, and went away. It had something to do with George. Naomi never knew what. She did not glean the connection with her husband for many years.

At any rate, it was on this day, at the birthday party, that George discovered her secret.

It was on this day that he dismissed her from his presence.

The discovery was made in the following manner:

Adolphus was sitting under a table. . . .

(Miss Bonkers entered the room on the toes of her white shoes, and approached the deathbed.)

"Hello, my dear. Hello, my dear. Hello," she said, very softly, very carefully enunciating every syllable of every word. But there was no response. Her patient's eyes were open, and they gave her a look that was distant, but alive. Still, there was no real response — no indication that Naomi wanted to have or to say anything.

Miss Bonkers gave the folded hands a gentle pat and wandered over to the window.

The pelicans were flying. . . .

Miss Bonkers sat down in her chair. She did not care to read. She had her book there, but she held it almost as though it were offensive — carefully, to one side. She would watch now, instead, and see what really happened.)

Adolphus was sitting under a table. . . .

He often did this if there were large numbers of people. He did it because his mother and his doctors had made him aware that he was safe under tables and chairs. He was afraid of feet. And of falling.

The only place you could not fall from was the ground. The only place people did not walk was under tables. *Ergo*, he sat on the ground under tables.

George took his son's eccentricities at face value. He adored Dolly and was proud of his strangeness. "My son sits under tables!" he would announce, proudly introducing Dolly to his friends. "My son, Adolphus, lies for many hours on the ground," he said. And, "This is my son, who sleeps under his bed," and, strangest and proudest of all, "Say hello to Adolphus..." and then, leaning in, confiding, perhaps, the laurels of genius, he would whisper with eyes significantly narrowed, "My son is very strange, you know." With a wave of the hand he would indicate Dolly's clothes. "His mother dresses him in white. She won't tell me this, but she takes him to visit priests. Could be a saint. Maybe even the Pope, some day. My son, Adolphus. Very strange."

So, Adolphus was sitting under a table.

It happened that a woman dropped a brooch.

Adolphus reached for it. A foot appeared. He withdrew

his hand with overviolent self-protection. He was stabbed.

The brooch stuck into his palm.

He screamed.

The sight of blood was rare to Dolly (so much care had been taken) and he rose, spilling the table and its contents onto the grass.

Under ordinary circumstances, nothing need have gone wrong. A doctor would have been summoned (George was never there; today he was). The flow of blood was minimal, but to Dolly it looked like a flood. He screamed and screamed and screamed. He screamed about bleeding to death. His father (closer than his mother) rushed across the lawn to his side. In his fear and in the urgency to get help for himself (Naomi had said, always let me know at once if you bleed), Dolly told all. He said it to his father. The well-guarded, the perfectly hidden facts and eleven years of lying fell by the wayside, victims of panic.

Now George knew.

The party continued around them.

Bully danced with Letitia.

Three hundred guests applauded. Dolly was removed to his room and a doctor was called for, came, and mended the damage. But it was the end of a marriage.

George summoned Naomi to the library.

He closed the doors.

He was white with fury. Livid.

She bowed to fate.

("Mrs. Damarosch! Mrs. Damarosch! Please, Mrs. Damarosch, let me take your arm. I'm going to help you, Mrs. Damarosch. I'm trying to help you. Let me help you!")

All the time George yelled at her she stood there (in rose and gray) staring at the sky outside through the windows. She could remember that particular shade of blue for a long time.

As the tirade continued, she began to make plans. She would take the children to Topanga Beach. They would build a house. They had always wanted to live by the sea. Later, Ruth could be finished in Italy. She had always dreamed of that. Dolly would need doctors. More and more care as he grew older and more and more vulnerable. She had a great deal of money. That was all right. Falconridge had been lovely (she went right on thinking these things as the voice rose and the eyes blazed and little flecks of foam appeared at the sides of the mouth. He was screaming about purity of line, something to do with *his* children. He kept screaming "my children" this, and "my children" that, and things like "you are a blot on motherhood!" and "you have infamous blood!" or "for eleven years that boy has lived in the terror of your lies!" It was senseless to listen).

Falconridge had been the first home she had created from the ground up. But it had always seemed unreal. A fairy-tale castle. A monument to tenuous fame, tenuous happiness.

The very steps leading down from the gardens to the driveways and garages were built of people's names. Wally Reid — Letitia Virden — Marie Dressler — and away down at the bottom was Naomi Nola. The first and last step. It depended on which direction you were going.

So that was Naomi's dream.

Or parts of it. There was much more. But these things can be guessed at. We know she loved her husband. We know that she left him obediently. We know he was a fool. But Naomi knew that he was, like her, a dreamer. That she had buried his dream forever. She forgave him his foolishness and his selfishness, as perhaps readers of this chronicle may not.

When the tirade was over (and all else with it) George made his way blindly from the library. (Later that day he committed a murder.)

Naomi stood in silence for a while.

Then she remembered her guests and went outside.

At nightfall, she began to pack.

(At last having called Ruth to help her, Miss Bonkers was able to release the hand from its twisted grip on the bedpost and, taking the arm, she smoothed its tension and applied the needle to its place.)

12:00 midnight

Ruth made the telephone call, but Adolphus, afraid of both darkness and of how the taxi driver might react to the darkness, did not come till morning.

Thursday, November 17th, 1938:
8:45 a.m.

It was a long night — a vigil shared by both Miss Bonkers and Ruth, and it so happened that when Dolly arrived by taxi, Ruth was asleep.

Miss Bonkers admitted him, and once he had looked in and seen that both Ruth and Naomi were *non compos mentis*, he returned to the living room, where the nurse gave him a cup of black coffee.

"What do you do now, Mr. Dolly? Are you making another film, or what?"

"No. I'm hard at work trying to salvage *Hell's Babies,*" said Adolphus. "Every day I go down and we edit and edit and edit, but I don't know what we're going to do. I've come to a kind of strange conclusion, Miss B., and that is that every movie should be made as though it were going to be your last. Miss Jacobs's memorial film, alas, is not appropriately somber."

"Oh, well, now. You mustn't fret about a thing like that. Myra Jacobs was always a gay little girl; at least, that's what I thought. It wouldn't be right to remember her sadly."

"I just hope they'll let us use that footage of her swimming. Enchanting — enchanting — just enchanting."

"Was there much left to film when she died?"

"Well, not much, no, but what there was, was vital. The last scene of all, in fact."

Dolly sipped his coffee loudly. He could not drink anything too hot right down.

"What do you think you'll do then?"

"I don't know," said Dolly. "This is what I'm working out now. I had thought that I might find some other actress — the way they did for Harlow's last film — and try to get some way of telling the end with her off in the distance, or even with her back to us. But I don't know. Who could play Myra Jacobs's back?"

"No one, I guess. Still... always leave them laughing, Mr. Dolly. Isn't that what someone said? Seems like a good motto to me for Myra Jacobs. Always leave them laughing. Eh? How about that?"

"I'll think about it, Miss Bonkers. But it's getting pretty difficult to laugh these days."

"Oh, pshaw! Go on with you! I can laugh right here and now. I can laugh any time I want to. Listen..."

Here Miss Bonkers commenced, indeed, to laugh. It began as a low, husky chuckle and it rose, by grades, to a thigh-slapping, almost masculine locker-room roar. It ended, abruptly — and without a smile.

"I learned how to do that at nursing school," Miss Bonkers confided. "That, and how to cry."

"Yes," said Dolly, impressed against his will. "I imagine it comes in handy from time to time." He looked into the death room.

"Well, it certainly does," said Miss Bonkers. "We medical people are human, too, you know. I mean, we get tired and sick of it all just like you movie people do, and we have to fall back on *our* techniques." She thought about it for a moment.

"Do you want some more of that coffee?" she said.

"No, thank you."

"Well, I'll go and see what I can do about those two in there. Your sister's had an awful night. She just won't leave your mother's side."

Miss Bonkers strode into the death room, on her heels.

"Extraordinary," said Dolly, out loud. "Just extraordinary. Should have been an actress."

11:00 a.m.

Ruth was persuaded to retire to her own room and bed. Adolphus went walking on the beach.

Miss Bonkers sat in the watching chair, and, again, she truly watched. Book reading was behind her, it seemed.

9:30 p.m.

The doctor came. He approached all that Miss Bonkers had done with approval. He expressed the opinion that Naomi would now probably slip away without regaining consciousness, and suggested that as long as one of the vigilants remained awake and in the room with her, the others might as well retire and rest.

He provided Miss Bonkers with what he judged to be enough morphine to see his patient to the end and, telling them that he would be happy to stay but for the fact that he had children to deliver and an appendix to remove, he bade them all farewell.

Adolphus, sitting ramrod still, essayed the first watch; Miss Bonkers the second; and Ruth the third.

It was during the third watch that Naomi disappeared.

Friday, November 18th, 1938

Ruth, dreaming her own dream, had slept. It was not a conscious drifting into sleep, but that sleep which possesses the sleeper while she's still awake.

Later, she swore that she was not aware of sleeping at all, but the fact is, she did sleep, and apparently soundly enough for Naomi to wake, rise, dress herself, and leave the room.

By what miraculous power Naomi was able to do these things — against not only pain and drugs but against the incredible weakness of her own body, as well — no one was able to discover.

Something, however, of sheer determination must have done it, for, on waking, she sensed that death was very close beside her, and, seeing that Ruth slept, and knowing that anyone awake would prevent her, she had risen to take her last moments on the beach.

The dressing was hard enough. She chose the green dress and the tennis shoes and the orange parasol and out she went. The descent to the beach was worse.

Every step seemed like total collapse.

She was hardly aware of pain, although there was pain. And hardly aware of weakness, although there was this, also. She was aware only of not being in proper command of her body. It would not go the way that she directed it, which had been some distance up along the beach. Instead, it kept leading her down to the water's edge, and from her drug-clouded eyes she kept perceiving the froth of little waves and the dancing of sandpipers, certain that this water and these birds had miscalculated their place, and should be driven back down to the shore. Thus, she made driving motions with her hands and mumbled objection at them until, finally, forced to agree with the fact that they did not seem to be aware of her, she stumbled away and found herself seated on a sandy knoll created by the late high tide.

Somehow, she was able to raise the parasol. Even to spread her skirts, with her innate sense of decorum, about her legs. The lotus position was beyond her now, so she had to be content with a straight-legged support, her feet at what seemed to be a great distance before her, toes up, like two little tombstones in shoes.

She smiled.

She took a deep breath.

George and Naomi. Rest in peace.

Some part of her came awake — alive.

It was past dawn, but still cool, still quiet. No one else had ventured onto the sands as yet.

She thought, Where am I?

Then she knew.

Clarity came and went.

Part of it was dream.

Part of it was life.

"Good-bye, seals," she whispered, thinking she waved. In reality she only barely lifted her free hand, seal-like, in the direction of the rocks.

"Good-bye, birds, good-bye," she called.

The sandpipers ran and cajoled, jabbered and ran, and did not hear her.

No matter.

"Their legs are as thin as mine," Naomi thought.

Where was she? Oh, yes. At Falconridge, packing.

And then the long night.

How long?

All these years.

All.

These.

Years.

Good-bye. Good-bye. Good-bye. Good-bye.

All. These.

Was it not profoundly moving that Bully had loved Letitia?

Yes, it was.

Dancing.

Was it not amazing that her own children had survived?

Yes. It was. Amazing.

Was it not incredible that George...

Now.

The drift was lifting her forward into the light.

Now.

Why was she weeping? Why? This was the end of her pain. Then why the weeping?

Her dream would tell her. She tried to open-close her eyes. There seemed to be a sound somewhere... of rustling and of voices hushing.

It was a theater.

For the first time in her life Naomi believed in the magical and absurd words of her films. The dialogue cards flashed on and off in her wondering, almost dancing mind.

"I shall abduct you sharp at midnight, madam."

(*Ladies Please Remove Large Hats.*)

"I am promised to another."

(*Will the Tsarina of all the Russias please report to the box office.*)

"Does this mean there is hope?"

(*Patrons Will Kindly Refrain From Whispering.*)

"I shall wave my favorite tear-stained handkerchief. Adieu."

(*Next Week:* EAST LYNNE.)

"As dawn slowly broke in the East..." (Three thousand miles away.)

(*Little Naomi Nola go home.*)

(INTERMISSION)

"...Good-bye."

7:30 a.m.

They found her, with her hand full of sand, at 7:29 a.m.

The yellow dog was at her feet and would not move until Ruth came.

It was B.J. who said it best.

"It was wrong, somehow, to close her eyes."

The Chronicle of the Butterfly Trees

Scientific note: It has already been stated see: The Chronicle of the First Butterfly that *Danaüs plexippus*, the monarch butterfly, overwinters in California, and that it begins to arrive as early as the first weeks of September.

All up and down the coast and in some inland areas, colonies of these migrated monarchs cluster in willow groves and stands of cypress. They roost by the hundreds and thousands on orange trees and Monterey pines. When they cluster in these numbers, the trees they have chosen become known as "The Butterfly Trees."

They settle in Bodego Bay, on the Tiburon Peninsula. They settle at Stinson Beach. They settle at Pacific Grove.

They extend, in their colonies, from one end of California to the other: Monterey, San Luis Obispo, Santa Barbara, Cayucos, Morro Bay, Pismo Beach, Santa Monica, Redondo, San Pedro, Laguna Beach, San Mateo Point, Oceanside, Merle, Del Mar, La Jolla, False Bay, and San Diego.

In the autumn of 1938 a dual phenomenon occurred. Although it is quite normal for the butterflies to overwinter in California, it is not at all normal for them to be active at this time. Usually, they do little more than rest in the sun, and occasionally feed. But in 1938, the butterflies were remarkably restless. As though agitated; as though unsure.

It was a season unlikely ever to be forgotten, for in that year the coastal regions were overwhelmed with monarchs, and this constituted the second phenomenon.

Many people who have survived these strange events speak of fields, trees, and even houses smothered in blankets of butterflies. They remember babies who suffocated, and helpless elderly persons who choked to death on butterflies. Crops were utterly destroyed — not eaten, but weighted down by monarchs. Tormented sheep and cattle leaped to their deaths into the ocean and into canyons, and in many instances, citizens awoke at night to find their bedroom walls and their blankets seething with rusty bodies. Incidents, too, are remembered of window screens and panes of glass blackened with crawling butterfly bodies — bodies in such stupefying numbers that for the first time within memory in California there were autumn bonfires to equal those of New England; not bonfires of fallen leaves, but of fallen wings.

However, these things did not happen all at once, or in any one place. As events, they accumulated and grew between the months of November and March. They began with the normal demarcation of the Butterfly Trees and they ended with the horror of the Butterfly Plague.

In between there were dreadful times and normal times, but the butterflies were never far from anyone's mind.

Sunday, November 27th, 1938:
Topanga Beach
10:00 a.m.

In the morning, Adolphus proposed that he, Ruth, and Miss Bonkers should journey to Fringes Bay, thirty miles to the south of Santa Monica, to see the Butterfly Trees.

At first Ruth did not want to go. She had not left the house since Naomi's death, except to attend the cremation of her mother's body, and the longer she had remained indoors, the more difficult the decision became to venture out. But at last, Dolly and Miss Bonkers convinced her that Naomi would have found no fault in this journey, and Ruth relented.

"Very well," she said. "I'll go."

Without telling Miss Bonkers of her suspected pregnancy, Ruth had retained her to care for her on the pretext that she could not bear to be alone and that she would suffer from depression if the nurse were to leave her. Miss Bonkers, for her part, was only too glad to remain, since she had become attached to the Damarosch clan and could not quite picture herself working for anyone else. She still had hopes of learning how to fly, and even, perhaps, of buying an airplane one day, and there were certainly no better wages nor circumstances to be had in any other situation. So she stayed. Secretly, this pleased Dolly, too, who liked the security of having "a nurse in the family."

Ruth wore black — a black suit that had slightly padded shoulders, and black stockings and a black hat, with a small, spotted face veil. Adolphus, feeling the need to make some concession in the direction of mourning, switched from pale-blue clothing to a suit of creamy-white silk with a black arm band. He also went out and bought a black walking stick with an ivory handle in the shape of a ram's head. A black handkerchief at his wrist completed the ensemble. Miss Bonkers, of course, wore her white uniform and her aviator's leather helmet and jacket, the gauntleted gloves and the jack boots. As a trio, they were befittingly subdued in garb to appear in public so soon after the death of a loved one.

They set out at 11:00 a.m. Luncheon, with wine, went with them in a wicker basket.

In one of those unlikely coincidences that plague the chronicler of history (the writer of fiction usually doesn't dare employ them), it so happened that, besides the

Damarosch group on that Sunday, not only the whole Trelford family, but Octavius Rivi, as well, decided to travel to Fringes Bay to see the Trees.

Ruth and Adolphus, Ruth driving and Adolphus riding in the rumble seat amongst his pillows and pads, went down in the purple Franklin.

The Trelfords went down in the Ford.

Octavius went down in a hired limousine.

And Miss Bonkers went down, of course, by motorbike.

They made a large party.

It was ominous.

12:00 noon

"Shall we have lunch in the car or shall we wait till we get there?" said Ruth. She could not bear the speed at which she was being forced to drive. The boredom was appalling.

"Oh, do let's stop by the side of the road," shouted Dolly. "Picnic on the grass. It would be so lovely. Besides, we have to feed Miss Bonkers, too."

"Very well," said Ruth.

Miss Bonkers, who was cruising lazily along behind them, drew over to the shoulder at Ruth's signal.

"What's happening?" she yelled above the din of her motorcycle.

"We're going to *eat!*" Ruth screamed back.

Miss Bonkers nodded.

They parked under a tree and spread their tablecloth on the wild flowers, the moss, and the creepers that flourished there.

As they ate, they watched the cars go by, and the bicycles, and even, on one occasion, a troup of hikers who strode by on foot, chanting numbers.

"Do you think they're all going to Fringes Bay?" Ruth asked.

"It's very likely," said Dolly. "Last year everyone went to Monterey. Once the public makes a decision. . ."

"... It's very hard to decide against the public," Ruth finished, with a hard smile.

This had been one of George's mottoes.

"Still no word?" said Dolly, referring to their father's lack of response to Naomi's death.

"Still no word," said Ruth.

"How strange..." said Adolphus.

"Downright queer, if you ask me," said Miss Bonkers, biting into a ham-on-rye. "Married all those years and not a word when she dies. I call it thoughtless and cruel. Thoughtless and cruel."

"Oh, I don't know," said Ruth, picking a small blue flower and twirling it between her fingers, under her nose. "Wild flowers rarely have a smell. Have you noticed that?"

"Skunkweed smells," said Dolly.

"Yes, but flowers. Flowers. Wild flowers."

Dolly leaned over, prepared to sniff.

"There isn't a bee in there, is there?" he asked. "By any chance?"

"No," said Ruth. "No bees."

Dolly drew a deep breath through his nostrils.

"Not a touch," he said. "You try, Miss B."

Miss Bonkers took her turn smelling the flower.

"Isn't that peculiar," she said. "Not the faintest whiff."

"Almost as though it was dead."

"Or artificial."

"Or deodorized," Ruth smiled.

"Deodorized flowers! Isn't that lovely?" said Dolly, chuckling at the thought. "Deodorized flowers — like a white sunset."

"Yes," said Ruth. "Or like us."

"What do you mean by that?" said Adolphus, knowing exactly what she meant.

"Oh, nothing," said Ruth. "Just a joke that didn't work."

"I should think so," said Dolly with a soft edge of petulance. "Indeed, I'd damn well say so."

"All right," said Ruth. "Forget it."

Miss Bonkers had watched this exchange and had listened to it with that excessive nonchalance that enforced eavesdropping on family matters demands of outsiders.

"I always say..." she said.

"That you can't beat a lost cause?" said Dolly with a sigh, picking up a sandwich.

"No."

"That a motorcycle isn't an airplane?" said Ruth.

"Oh, no," said Miss Bonkers. "Never."

"Then what?" said Ruth.

"Yes, what?" said Dolly. "What do you always say?"

"I always say," said Miss Bonkers, "what I always say is — that an apple a day keeps disease at bay." And so saying, she picked up the object of her maxim and gave it a very large crunch.

Ruth and Adolphus laughed in spite of themselves, and Miss Bonkers smiled. She felt she had eased a difficult situation and was proud of herself.

The Trelfords drove past at this point, some of the children leaning, or being pushed, far out of the windows, and all of them singing a song at the top of their voices.

"Oh, my darling,
Oh, my darling
Oh, my dar——ling Clementine,
You are lost and gone forever,
Dreadful sorry, Clementine."

A cheer went up.

"Damarosch — Damarosch
Rah! Rah! Rah!
Damarosch — Damarosch
Siss boom bah!"

And finally, as they sped away into the dusty distance, one forlorn, evaporating voice was heard to call out, "Hi...Auntie Ruthie...bye, Auntie Ruth...ie...."

"That was Charity," said Ruth.

"Oh," said Adolphus, who had not met Charity. "I would have called it gross indecency, yelling at people on a highway. Really!"

"They're very dear friends," said Ruth. "Very, very dear to me."

She sat back down and started to pack away the picnic things.

"Do you know," said Miss Bonkers, staring after the Trelford car, which had now quite disappeared, "I think they even had that dog in there with them."

"I should hope so," said Ruth. "He's my *best* friend."

1:00 p.m.

They were on their way again.

"You mustn't associate with people beneath you, Ruth," Adolphus was saying. "These Trelfords look like a scruffy lot, to me."

"He's a very fine artist," said Ruth. "And they're not scruffy at all. In fact, you'll like them enormously, once you get to know them."

"That sounds like a threat," said Adolphus.

"Oh, don't be silly," said Ruth. "They're perfectly marvelous people."

"They've obviously bred like rabbits," said Adolphus. "That's clear enough. Anyone who has children by the gross is obviously from the lower classes, and possessed of the worst bad taste."

"I mean to have children by the gross," said Ruth.

"Hah!" Dolly roared. "That'll be the day."

"I'm carrying one right now," said Ruth.

There.

Dolly very nearly fell backward out of the rumble seat.

"Stop the car!" he shrieked. "Stop the car! Stop the car!"

Ruth slowed to a stop and turned to look at her brother. He was livid — as white as his clothes.

"What's the matter?" she asked. "Do you need to go to the toilet? Or are you bleeding?"

"Don't tease me, Ruthie. Please don't tease me like that."

She perceived that he was almost in tears.

"I'm not teasing you," said Ruth. "I'm telling you the truth."

"You're going to have a baby?"

"Yes."

"Oh. I don't believe you."

"It's true."

"But you don't look — and Bruno is. . . and you can't!"

"It isn't Bruno's child. As for 'can't,' I *can* and I'm going to."

"But you — you — you mustn't. Think what will happen. Think what will happen."

"Nothing will happen."

"It will *die!*" Dolly wailed. "Die!"

Ruth just looked at him.

"Everyone dies," she said.

Dolly raged.

"Platitudes!" he roared. "How dare you say a thing like that to me?"

"Well, don't they?" said Ruth.

"Yes. But not like that. Think what you're doing, Ruth. Think what sort of life this child will live — and it's bound to be a boy and it will suffer like me and live an eternal life of. . .! Who the hell's the father?"

"I thought you'd never ask," said Ruth.

She started the car and made her way back onto the road.

"Well, aren't you going to tell me?" Dolly roared, bouncing about dangerously amongst his pillows.

"Not yet," said Ruth. "Sometime I will. But not yet. I want you to see the child first. Then you won't care who the father is."

Suddenly she pushed her foot down hard on the accelerator and, Dolly be damned, the Franklin shot forward like a bolt of purple lightning. Fifty, sixty miles an hour.

"She's gone crazy," Dolly muttered. "She's gone stark raving mad."

"What did you say?" Ruth yelled back at him.

And he yelled back at her, "Mad! Mad! Maddened! That's what I said! You have gone completely, absolutely *mad!*"

But Ruth did not hear, and only drove faster, and smiled.

1:30 p.m.

They passed the hikers, who were still counting off their steps, and they passed the Trelfords, who were parked at a gasoline station.

Ruth and Dolly themselves were passed by Miss Bonkers on her motorbike, and by the enormous rented limousine of Octavius Rivi.

"Who was that?" Dolly asked, as the dust settled.

"Now, how would I know!" said Ruth.

"Well, whoever it was," said Adolphus, sitting bolt upright in the rumble seat, and lightly rubbing the side of his nose with the ram's head handle of his brand new cane, "it was the most beautiful face I have ever seen."

2:00 p.m.

Fringes Bay was a small town. Little more than a village. It no longer exists.

It depended at that time for its livelihood on the migratory habits of four species of creature: smelts, swallows, butterflies, and people.

The populace of Fringes Bay declined to speak of the migratory people as tourists. Instead, they called them visitors. Tourists were foreigners, and the people who flocked to Fringes Bay three times a year (smelt catchers, swallow watchers, and butterfly collectors) came from nearby places. There were other beaches where the smelts threw themselves in suicidal fervor into the shallows, and there were other missions to which the swallows returned each year, and there were other groves of willow trees sheltering droves of monarch butterflies. To these others, "tourists" journeyed — those who did not know of Fringes Bay. But the pilgrims of Fringes Bay returned there from year to year. They brought news of friends and relatives. Their children, hand-held at first, returned in the accumulating years with hand-holders of their own. They were visitors, not tourists.

Ruth and Dolly had been brought as children. They had been many times. This was only the second time B.J., Noah, and the children had been. For Miss Bonkers and the dog, it was the first visit, and as it turned out, probably the last.

The butterflies excited Ruth and Dolly with visions. They founded dynasties of dreams that lasted through time. They blazed with colors, hardly stirring in their trees, sleepers and dreamers themselves, providing sleep and dreams of peace. Golden. Red. White and black. Some called them rusties. Some, monarchs. Some, dotties, and the rest, just butterflies.

They were, however, dreams.

The word occurs and recurs in their history. Dreams of color. Dreams of gentleness. Dreams of flight.

Or, the virgin's dream.

Now there was a plague of dreams. A plague of butterflies.

They stood in the insect presence like priests and populace before a shrine.

The trees were three in number — a mystical figure. There was silence, the sort of silence that includes sound — a sea breeze, a child's sudden question and a parent's whispered reply.

To one side stood Octavius Rivi, dressed all in black. (To

the other side stood Dolly, all in white.) Octavius had much to dream about. He was not yet certain who his mother was, nor who his father had been. He knew nothing except that he was alive. People stared at him. He was most impressive in his silence. He wasn't large. He wasn't loud. He was not well known. He did not exude wealth (in spite of the limousine). But people stared. It was his stillness. His concentration.

Picture the three trees, covered with butterflies instead of leaves. Even the largest leaves were hidden by wings and bodies. All the wings were closed. Like prayers. This added to the sense of silence and mystery.

A semicircle of watchers extended from right to left. Beyond the trees a cliff gave way to sea views and the long curve of Fringes Bay with its beach and its gentle breakers below. The village was hung like seried steps upon the hill. Behind, was the mission with its silenced bells. The waiters and the watchers, waiting and watching. If silence could be seen, they saw it.

Even B.J. and Noah stood silent. Noah's thumbs worked in mute frustration in the air, aching with their inability to sculpt a butterfly. The children stared. The dog sniffed uncertainly at the breeze, and the hair along his spine bristled with menace.

Ruth stirred.

"They're moving," she said.

"Be quiet," said an old woman. "Be quiet. Listen."

There was nothing to listen to, except the faraway surf and a few cries from some distant, floating gulls.

Ruth watched the gentle fluster of brown-and-red butterfly bodies. Perhaps the temperature was rising and that was why they moved. No one else seemed to notice. The wings did not open. They remained closed.

Adolphus, who had seen the butterflies so many times before, was concentrating more on the view he had of Octavius. (They had never met; it seemed as if Octavius had never met anyone.) But there was something disturbing about the figure in black. Dolly did not link it with the naked form at the end of the beach. That figure had no face, no complete form. It was never seen except in pieces — an arm, a leg, a hand, a buttock. No. He did not make the connection. The connection lay elsewhere. But Dolly could not tell where or in whom. It was just a way of standing. The way the head was held. The stillness. (Serenity?) The brevity of gesture.

Dolly was standing up in the rumble seat. Miss Bonkers sat up on the leather back in front of him. Ruth stood on the grass beside the car.

A breeze rose. The willow ropes swayed. The butterflies held fast.

Their wings were closed. Still.

And Ruth thought, Hold on.

The breeze died. The silence deepened.

Five hundred people held it, like a single breath in one lung. And then it broke.

All the wings had spread. In the sun. It was very sudden.

Every eye, even Dolly's, strained to witness the cause of this change. Some movement in the sky, perhaps. Danger. But there was nothing to be seen.

And then, gradually, there was.

Clouds.

From beyond the houses, from under the cliffs, from behind them over the milkweed meadows, from above them out of the sun itself. . . Butterflies. One by one, hundred by hundred, thousand by thousand; it seemed there must be millions of them. Some were the size of little birds.

The visual signal of the trees seemed to cause a panic amongst the new arrivals and before anyone could believe what they were seeing — their eyes and ears filled up with butterflies.

Children tried to scream.

People ran.

Some clambered into their cars, calling names: Bertha! Hilary! Leroy! Run! Engines started. An old man was knocked down. A woman by the name of Francine Quigley was struck by a backing truck and instantly killed. Priests from the mission and police from the town arrived and fought for order and calm. But the air was filled with dazzling wings and any call to order was stifled by them. People began to choke on inhaled butterfly scales. The air was full of dust. Later, twenty-two victims were operated on. Parts of butterfly wings and masses of powdery scales were removed from their lungs. Three died, all children.

Dolly crouched low, now, in the rumble seat, and threw a blanket over his head. Miss Bonkers sat down on the floor and drew the aviator helmet over her face. Ruth struggled to make the top rise. Dolly scrambled up beside the nurse, and at last they were all safely inside, with Miss Bonkers squashed in the middle and the windows raised.

"What is it?" said Ruth, pulling wings out of her veil. "It's terrifying — terrifying! What is it?"

"I'm sure it's a nightmare," said Dolly. "Or I pray to God it is!"

To her relief, Ruth had seen Noah wrestling B.J., the children, and the dog into their car. From time to time, as the insect tide fluctuated, Ruth caught glimpses of the excited faces of Charity, Peter, and Joe mouthing exclamations behind the windows, while the dog mimed a frenzy of barking.

A child, unknown to anyone inside, came and banged on the Franklin's side window. Dolly rattled his cane against the glass and the child fled across the field, choking and terror-stricken, where it was lost in the stampede of its panicked elders.

On the far side of the field, Octavius sat, erect and quiet, in the back seat of his limousine, while a thousand wings beat in soft adoration against the dusty glass of the car's windows. It seemed as if he had expected this to happen, that they should so mutely clamor to reach him, to catch a glimpse of him. To be with him in the car. His expression was a mixture of terror and aloofness. As though he might have been their long-lost sovereign, returning from exile uncertain of their mood, and finding them jubilant.

Elsewhere in the field, motorcars would not start or could not start, or be made to move. Engines were clogged with butterflies. The ground was inches thick with a sodden mass of dead and dying insects. There was no traction to be had; people could no longer run, but fell as though shot on a battlefield. Butterflies pelted themselves at the windscreens of cars and the spectacles of the old. Still, but for the sounds of spinning wheels and desperate engines, and but for the sounds of moving wings and slipping feet, there was silence. Human silence, now. Whatever mystical silence there had been had fled.

No one dared breathe. No one dared cry.

At last the clouds of wings settled, merciful and benign, upon the trees. The terror was over. The people withdrew.

In years to come it was known as Fringes Field. A cross was erected. The butterflies returned yearly. But the people had left forever.

And yet the Butterfly Plague affected different towns in different ways. Perhaps it should be said it affected different people in different ways — different spirits.

Remember Edwina Shackleton in the city of Pacific Grove?

She was instrumental in putting forward the petition that brought about the creation of the following ordinance:

City of Pacific Grove *Ordinance No. 352*

PROTECTION OF BUTTERFLIES

Adopted Nov. 16, 1938

Ordinance No. 352

An Ordinance providing for the protection of the Monarch Butterflies during their annual visit to the City of Pacific Grove:

THE COUNCIL

OF THE CITY OF PACIFIC GROVE

DO ORDAIN AS FOLLOWS:

Section 1. It shall be unlawful and it is hereby declared to be unlawful for any person to molest or interfere with in any way the peaceful occupancy of the Monarch Butterflies on their annual visit to the City of Pacific Grove, and during the entire time they remain within the corporate limits of said City, in whatever spot they may choose to stop in; provided, however, that if said butterflies should at any time swarm in upon or near the private dwelling house or other buildings of a citizen or the City of Pacific Grove in such a way as to interfere with the occupancy and use of said dwelling and/or other buildings, that said Butterflies may be removed, if possible, to another location upon the application of said citizen to the Chief of Police of this City.

Section 2. Any violation of this Ordinance shall be deemed a misdemeanor and shall be punishable by a fine of not more than Five Hundred Dollars ($500.00), or by imprisonment in the County Jail of Monterey County for not more than six (6) months or by both such fine and imprisonment.

Section 3. This Ordinance is hereby declared to be urgent, and shall be in effect from and after its final passage. The following is a statement of such urgency: Inasmuch as the Monarch Butterflies are a distinct asset to the City of Pacific Grove, and cause innumerable people to visit said City each year to see the said Butterflies, it is the duty of the citizens of said City to protect the Butterflies in every way possible, from serious harm and possible extinction by brutal and heartless people.

PASSED AND ADOPTED BY THE COUNCIL OF THE CITY OF PACIFIC GROVE, this 16th day of November, 1938, by the following vote:

AYES: COUNCILMEN: (Mayor) Fiddes, Norton,
Galbraith, Burton.
NOES: COUNCILMEN: Lee Matthews.

ABSENT: COUNCILMEN: Solomon.
APPROVED: Nov. 16, 1938.

William Fiddes,
Mayor of said City.
ATTEST: ELGIN C. HURLBERT, City Clerk.

Thus it was, the Butterfly Plague came to California in November 1938.

The Chronicle of Dolly D.

Wednesday, December 14th, 1938

Any act of courage requires a little anger — a little or a lot, as the case may be. With Dolly, it was a lot.

After all these years in his smart white bungalow, with the pool and the tennis courts next door, someone had offended him. They'd thrown a ball (and it had seemed quite deliberate) which broke his plate-glass window.

He'd been sitting there staring out — but not, he was certain, offensively — when one of the players, a guest, Dolly assumed, had turned and seen him watching. With excruciatingly accurate aim, this person had thrown the ball right at Dolly's face. Naturally, it hit the window — and naturally, the window broke.

The pitcher had roared with laughter and disappeared, but moments later an apologetic neighbor had appeared at Dolly's front door.

Still trembling from the frightful experience, Adolphus had gone to answer the beckoning bell.

"Oh, Adolphus, I am so terribly sorry. What *can* I say?"

"You can say that you'll pay for my window, that's what you can say, Dorabella."

"Very well, I will pay for your window."

"I accept."

"You weren't hurt, honey, I hope."

"No. Oh, no. If I'd been hurt, Dorabella, I'd already've bled to death. I'd be lying there dead and you'd be standing here ringing this doorbell till kingdom come!"

"Goodness, Adolphus. I just tremble at the thought. Is the damage ex*ten*—sive?"

"One totally broken window. That's how extensive."

"Well, I blush with shame."

"I couldn't believe my eyes, Dorabella. Why, he took aim before he threw. And he leered at me. I tell you, he leered. He just loved breaking that window. Loved it. Who the hell is he, anyway?"

"Why, that's Jackie Manta Stupa, the famous baseball pitcher. Didn't you recognize him?"

"Well, I recognized him for an ape, my dear. But that's all."

"I must confess, he's had an eye on your window for a whole two days now."

"I believe you."

"But it's understandable."

"I beg your pardon? Understandable!"

"Well, it is. I mean, it's terrible, but understandable. He pitches *ball*, honey. Think how seldom a really great pitcher like that gets to break a window that size."

"Or to kill someone . . ." said Dolly.

"Now, now, Adolphus. Don't be silly."

"You didn't see the look on his face, Dorabella, and I did. He's a killer."

"Well, I'm sorry. And I'll pay for the damages."

Dorabella swung around, hip first, to take her leave.

"It's really the fault of all these dreadful butterflies, anyway. I mean, if it hadn't've been for them, why, we wouldn't have had to drain the pool. And if we hadn't've had to drain the pool, well, we wouldn't have been pitching ball. And if we hadn't've been pitching ball, well . . ."

She gave her shoulders a lofty shrug.

"He's just so full of energy, and now, I don't know *what* we'll do."

"Why don't you go and fly a kite," said Dolly.

"Oh, 'Dolphus! There isn't a lick of wind, not a lick!" Then she got it.

"Why, you're joshing me! You mean thing!" She laughed. "Imagine Jackie Manta Stupa flying a kite! Oh, that's just precious!"

She ambled seductively away, still laughing, until a circle of butterflies rose up and fluttered around her head, at which point she began to scream and curse.

"Get away from me, you crazy monsters!" she screamed. "Fucking *maniacs!!!*" Then she commenced, as best she could, to kill them. "Bloodsuckers!"

Dolly watched, amused and horrified.

At last Dorabella had repulsed the attack and stood fuming and raging on Dolly's side lawn, brushing corpses from her blouse and hair. Then, as one might retrieve a broken egg, she reached down between her breasts and eased a few more bodies out onto the lawn. She wept at this, in disgust.

"Oh, Dolly! They was right down in*side* me! *Haagh!*"

"They're only butterflies, Dorabella. Quite harmless. There's no need to kill them."

"They're sons-of-bloody-bitches," was all Dorabella would say. "Sons-of-bloody-bitches!"

"At any rate," said Dolly, "you owe me a hundred dollars."

"Oh, go fly a kite!" screamed Dorabella, frustrated and maddened by the butterflies.

"You forget," said Adolphus, calmly. "There's no wind."

He shut the door in the face of further protests.

How dare she, he fumed. She'd started away quite content to pay the bill and then those butterflies...

Why, wasn't it terrible! She was blaming him for those butterflies in her bosom, just because those butterflies had been on his property.

He looked out through the broken window.

There was Jackie Manta Stupa.

What on earth was he doing?

He was murdering butterflies with a baseball bat. And Dorabella was egging him on. She just stood there screaming, "Sons-of-fucking-bitches!" while Manta Stupa yelled something else.

At first Dolly couldn't make it out.

Then he could.

"Kill! Kill! Kill!" the baseball pitcher was yelling. "Kill! Kill!! Kill! You orange faggots!"

Dolly went quite pale and it was soon after this that he decided that he would go out and drive his car.

Himself.

Alone.

After all, it wouldn't be safe to stay there. Not with that man killing things. With a baseball bat.

9:50 a.m.

The Franklin was parked in a tidy stucco garage at the side of Dolly's house.

Every time he saw it sitting there he thought of Myra and was sad.

Some evenings he would just go out, around sunset time, and stand there in the shady driveway and stare at the purple rump, morosely.

Other days Ruth would come and take the car away, and as it drove off into the distance (if Dolly was there to watch its departure) he would stand on the sidewalk watching it dust off the road, and he'd mutter to himself, "Some day...Some day..."

He often half-heartedly gave sighs, thinking about it, and envisioned himself ensconced up front, alone, driving into some orange sky somewhere.

But Dolly did not know how to drive.

However, on that Wednesday, after Manta Stupa's attack on the butterflies, Dolly flung caution to the winds and came, actually running, out of the house and nearly fell to his knees on the rolling ball-bearing sea of gravel, and practically ruptured himself yanking open the garage doors.

"Orange faggots, indeed!" he said aloud, as fifty or sixty monarchs flew into the sunlight from what had been their prison. "I've got to get out of here!"

Dolly gave the Franklin the once-over. He was so used to sitting in the rumble seat that he barely knew, in his panic, how to get into the front. In fact, he did not get into the front at all, but piled in amongst his pillows in the back and stared from there at the mysterious dashboard, the pedals, and the steering wheel.

How did they work?

He tried to envision all the drivers he had watched from over their shoulders: Myra, Ruth, cabmen, chauffeurs, and friends. Men with Negro hands. Women in leather gloves. Boy drivers with golden, flicking wrists. Bus drivers with hirsute knuckles. . . .

He closed his eyes and watched all these fingers working in his mind at once.

They yanked at things, pushed things, pulled things, and slid things. They wiggled one thing and wobbled another. Then there was a long passage of jerking something knobby back and forth, back and forth back and forth back and . . .

Oh, dear.

Oh, my . . .

Low down, out of sight, they slid in and withdrew darkly oiled contrivances. They battered momentarily at something which shook and quivered, gurgled and slipper-slappered. But what?

Now, all the many drivers together settled their buttocks with firm resolve. They stretched their legs — massively thighed — bulgingly calved. They pushed and paddled and finally jammed hard down with their feet. Then with their heads hunched forward, shoulders lunging, they grabbed at the whole shaking, slipping, farting contraption, nearly ready now to explode in giant petroleum spurts and giving off heaving sighs of breathless satisfaction, they roared off into endless rhythmic journeys.

Oh, dear.

Oh, my. . .

But how to drive a car?

Dolly got out of the rumble seat into the front.

He turned the key.

That much he knew.

Miraculously, the Franklin at once slid into action.

Backward.

Backward — *backward* down the drive.

"Help!" Dolly screamed. "God help me! I'm moving!"

At once, the car jiggered to a stop.

Dolly blushed.

Although God had apparently heard him, he sincerely hoped the neighbors had not.

So there he was, immobile in the center of the road, broadside to oncoming traffic.

Luckily, however, there was no traffic coming on.

Looking both ways to ensure at least temporary safety, Dolly pulled a few knobs, and after one or two backfires that nearly cost him his life in heart attacks, he heard a faint rumble, felt a promising jolt, tingled with delight at the first jiggling and juicings of the engine, and realized that indeed he had somehow mastered the mysteries of internal combustion.

Now, all he needed was a destination.

There was no orange sky, unfortunately. It was the wrong time of day for that.

Still, it hardly mattered. There was Dolly, sitting in the front seat — all by himself — driving.

It was lovely. Not a single other car was in sight. Only people walking their dogs on distant sidewalks.

Dolly wanted to wave at them, but he didn't dare. That would mean taking his hands from the wheel. And if you took your hands from the wheel, the car stopped. Everyone knew that.

Didn't they?

10:15 a.m.

The journey extended as far as Topanga Canyon Beach.

When he arrived with a crash, Ruth and Miss Bonkers could not believe their eyes, and kept going back outside to make sure Dolly did not have someone else in the car with him. They did not notice that he had been forced to bring it to a stop by crashing into a convenient sand dune.

"You've got a woman hidden out there," Ruth teased. "You must have."

"No. No. Not at all. Quite honestly. I really did, Ruth. I drove it all the way myself."

"Well, I think that's marvelous," said Ruth. "I think that is simply marvelous. Don't you, Miss Bonkers?"

"Oh, yes. Yes. Marvelous," said Miss Bonkers, and left the room. She had beds to make.

Adolphus beamed from ear to ear. He did a sort of knock-kneed march from one end of the living room to the other. He gave his goatee several patronizing pats with the flat of his hand. His clothes (pink trousers, blue blazer) seemed to shout "Success!" and even "Bravo! Bravo!"

"It was nothing," said Dolly. "Nothing."

"Well, I think it calls for a good stiff drink," said Ruth.

"I feel," said Adolphus, leaning elegantly and delicately against the stones of the fireplace, "like the whole of emancipated slavery! I shall drive everywhere from here on in — slowly, I admit. I still have no wish or penchant for speed, but I shall do all the driving myself!" He smiled. "I simply adored it."

"Oh, Dolly! I'm so proud of you," said Ruth. "Driving your own car! Why, it's marvelous!"

She had made some highballs in the interim and now she passed him his. He snuck a look at her figure.

"How do you feel?" he asked with as little commitment to interest as he could muster.

"Fine," said Ruth. "Fine."

"Ha—hum!" Dolly said.

"What's the matter?"

"Well, I mean to say — I mean, well. Do you know yet?"

"Oh, yes," Ruth laughed. "I'm certain."

"Certain, eh? Well. Well."

"I hope you approve."

"How can I approve when I don't know who the father is?"

"Don't fish, Dolly. All in good time. I'll tell you, all in good time."

"Can you tell me if it's somebody I know? I should, at least, think you could tell me that."

"No. You don't know him."

"Do you think. . . ? I mean, one day. . . ? What I mean to say is, whoever this is, do you think. . . ? Well?"

"Marriage?"

"Yes."

"No."

Dolly found his way to a chair and sat down.

"What am I expected to say when this child appears? That you've had some sort of unhappy affair?"

"We can decide that when the child comes. For now, it's sufficient that the child *is* coming."

"Sufficient for what?" said Dolly, miserable with ignorance.

"Sufficient for my peace of mind."

Ruth, too, sat down.

"How can you do this, Ruth?" Dolly pondered. "Inflict life on this child. Don't you know how awful it is for me to be alive. . ."

"But you stay alive," said Ruth.

"Only because death is too repugnant to contemplate."

"Come on, now. You don't believe that for one minute."

"I do. I do."

"But just now, just now, driving the car it was triumphant for you and wonderful to be alive. . . ."

"In that moment, Ruth. Only in that minute."

"But that's all life is," said Ruth. "Moments and minutes — one by one."

Adolphus stared at her. She was his sister, but he did not know her. Certainly, she did not know him. As children, yes. As adults, no.

"You're very positive," he said, "all of a sudden."

"I have another life inside me," said Ruth. "It's easy to be positive when you carry the future around with you." She smiled. But this only angered Adolphus.

"You never did grasp philosophy," he said. "Never. You have the mind of a child. Up and down. Up and down. Here today and gone tomorrow. Pessimist. Optimist. Stoic and pleasurist. The shy gregarian. That's what I ought to call you, the shy gregarian. You won't talk to anyone, and then, when you will talk, finally, who do you choose? A bunch of gypsies on the beach. You marry a perfectly extraordinary man who, from all appearances, certainly loved you, but you won't have children by him. Oh, no! So what do you do? You come back here and meet some total stranger..." Dolly paused and then said, "Some slavering sex maniac, for all I know, and you give yourself to *him* without a thought. One minute you're devastated by depression and everyone's sick with worry that you've gone mad, and the next minute you're bouncing around like a schoolgirl who's discovered boys, telling us you're going to have a baby. I think you *are* crazy, that's what I think. Crazy as the March Hare — or just plain simple-minded. And for my money, there's very little difference."

There was a silence and then Ruth said, very quietly, "When Myra died, didn't your life change?"

Dolly couldn't follow that. He said, "No," and stared at his sister, who was sitting near a window, her face invisible in light.

"We are the living dead," said Ruth. "Walking around dead, until..."

"Until what?"

"Until we are forced by circumstances to live."

"No 'circumstance' could possibly make *me* live."

"Yes, it could," said Ruth. "Yes, it could. The threat of extermination could."

"I have lived my whole life with the threat of extermination! Really, Ruth!"

"It hasn't been sufficient, then," said Ruth. "It can't have been, or else, when Myra died, your whole life *would* have changed."

"Why, why, *why*, do you keep saying that?"

"Because she died wanting to live. That should mean something to you."

They stared at each other.

"And Mother?" Dolly asked. "Don't tell me she didn't want to live."

"She didn't," said Ruth, very simply.

"She hated dying. She hated it as much as I do. Or will."

Ruth shook her head. "No," she said. "She was prepared and ready. She was eager."

"And what are you saying about Myra? What are you saying? It's just a stupid paradox. Myra wanted to live and killed herself? Mother wanted to die but let a mere disease kill her when all she had to do was take poison? What are you saying?"

"I am saying..."

"Well?"

"Wait a minute."

"Haven't got it thought out, eh? Hah! I thought so."

"No, I have it thought out," said Ruth. "I have it all thought out. Only..."

"Only what?"

"Is it wise to tell you?"

She jiggled the ice in her glass.

"Myra was murdered," she said at last.

"Murdered! Nonsense. She did it herself with sleeping pills."

"She was murdered," said Ruth, "and that's the difference between the effect death has on me and the effect it has on you. The difference, now too, between the effect life has. No one loved Myra enough to make her. . .*force* her to live for *their* sake.''

''And Mother? Are you saying no one loved Mama enough for that?''

''No. I'm not saying that, at all. It's just that Mama wasn't a victim. And Myra was. And so are you. And so could I be. In fact, for a long while, I was.''

''Fiddlesticks.''

''Victims are victims, by choice. Other people's choice at first, and then their own.''

''Drivel.''

''But they still die — the victims of killers.''

''Name one.''

''I have already. Myra.''

''Myra was loved. I loved her.''

Ruth slowly shook her head. ''No,'' she said. ''No. You don't understand me. There is only one love that can save life. And that love is the love that has killed, buried and replaced the love of self.'' Now she looked directly at Adolphus and he could see the expression of her face, at last.

Ruth appeared to have been possessed. It was not a pleasant expression. It contained no element of contemplation and too little confusion to be a recognizable human expression. She was not, he suspected, speaking to him at all, but to herself, and, from the way she looked at him, he also guessed that she was not for a moment even aware that he was there. She was speaking, not at all about Myra, or their mother, or himself, but about some other thing — some other time — some vision she had had or some experience that had returned to haunt her. She was speaking not of persons, one by one, but of people, hundreds by thousands.

''I don't,'' he said, but quietly, as though afraid to interrupt her or even to allude, by his voice, to his presence, ''I don't — and I am sorry — understand.''

Ruth stared at the floor and then back out of the window.

"Victims," she muttered. And then, Dolly swore, she added, "Butterflies," but so gently and with such private wonder that he rose and left her there, knowing, inside himself, that the private wonder was at some private message and that, indeed, his sister had not changed. She did not vary, but only rose up, like a fish to dragonflies, from the depths of a dark and desperate lake, to the challenging surface of its element wherein there was safety, but beyond which for more than mere seconds, the fish could not hope to trespass and live.

"Imagine," Dolly thought, rising to leave her there, "that we must strangle on the very air we breathe."

The air of hope.

Hope, Naomi had said, is death in the mind.

But Dolly did not know that. He only knew that there was hope inside of *him*. The hope of eluding death — the subject of all conversation.

He wavered on the brink of the doorway to his mother's room. He looked inside. The empty bed seemed deprived of more than Naomi's presence. It was sadder than a mere deathbed. The echo of something alive had rumpled the edges of its coverlet. Just a breeze, probably, for the windows were open. But someone undoubtedly was there.

Adolphus had the very strange and almost sinister experience of thinking, with what he thought was rationality, that he must go in and check between the mattress and the spring, to see if his mother had left her integrity there, or some message about death that could assuage his fears of it — or the name of some place where one could go for safety.

What had Ruth meant about no one loving Myra enough to force her to live for their sake? And "victims" and "butterflies"?

Butterflies?

Ruth cut his thought in half by speaking suddenly, aloud, from the living room.

"I'm going to go and have a swim," she said.

Dolly stared at her.

"Is that wise?" he asked.

Ruth smiled.

"Of course it's wise," she said. "Exercise is always wise."

"Well, you know best," said Dolly.

"Oh, by the way," said Ruth, lowering her voice. "I think you should know I haven't told Miss Bonkers. In fact, I haven't told anyone but you. And, judging by the way you're reacting, I think it's a damn good thing I haven't. So, I'd appreciate your silence."

"I'm not going to say a word," said Dolly, appalled by the mere idea. "Not a word."

"Thank you."

"Ruth?"

"What?"

"Did you, by any chance, tell Mother?"

Ruth thought this over for a moment.

"Yes," she said. "I did."

Of course she hadn't.

But she thought it might help Dolly to think she had.

He needed lies to keep him going.

11:30 a.m.

Ruth changed into her bathing costume, an old one-piece Olympic suit that needed mending at one blue shoulder, and passed, carrying her towel and sandals, through the living room.

She paused to look into her mother's room.

What she saw silenced her.

Adolphus had gone to the bedside table where he'd picked up the last book read by Naomi. It was at this very moment that Ruth stopped to watch him.

He looked askance at the bed.

So did she.

It was easy to imagine it occupied. Easy and sad, for both of them, for different reasons.

With the pages of the book still dripping down, suspended in their own hoarse whisper of movement,

Adolphus stood staring at the pillows, staring at something there that moved. He tiptoed quietly over.

Closer, sidling up, he extended the backs of the fingers of his free hand, five little whisks of bone and vein, and he passed them gently across the pillow faces so that a fly, having settled there, rose up in a slow but definite retreat.

Then Dolly turned away and sat down in the watching chair, still holding the book in his hand, and he began to read.

The Bridge of San Luis Rey.

Ruth quietly closed the door between them. He did not even notice.

Dolly in the watching chair.

Ruth, already swimming in her mind, went down to join her body to the legendary waters of peace.

Something was about to happen. She knew it and was trying to escape. But action would not stop it from happening. Whatever it was. Neither action, nor stillness.

So she swam.

One.

2:45 p.m.

Adolphus had read all through the remainder of the morning. He had read through lunch (without eating) and now, at midafternoon, he was finished.

He sat exhausted and elated in the watching chair, with *The Bridge of San Luis Rey* still clasped in his lap.

He stared at his mother's bed.

Naomi was gone forever. So was Myra. And what was the pattern? There was none. None that was discernible. Like the butterflies — they came and went, lived and died. Migrated. Counter-migrated. Stood still and fled.

He dangled the book and tried to see through the curtains to the sea.

He saw light; perhaps he saw motion, but nothing was clear — there were no definitions, no demarcations — only a sense of presence, of weight and movement — light and dark — all mingling and marking like a star where Myra was, and Naomi. Or what had taken them, whether by urging or demand he could not tell. Tides. The pull of death.

He wanted to sit on the book and brood over it like a hen, so that in this room, sitting on this nest, he might hatch an unshakable answer.

But he laid the book aside.

It was a book about people on a bridge — vulnerable people, vulnerable bridge, obeying together a vulnerable god. They had fallen in another time, to death.

He looked at his booted feet. There they were. Vulnerable. He looked at his careful knees, encased in the pink impeccable ducks. Vulnerable. He stared into his crotch. There was life itself, denied. And vulnerable. He glanced across his stomach. Vulnerable. His thin, indented chest, his hands. All vulnerable. He touched his bearded, neat sharp chin — a point for impact and entry. Vulnerable. He gazed into mirrors, and there he was, all twenty of him, thirty of him. Forty. Vulnerable. Ad infinitum. Vulnerable. Frail.

Could he not select one? Could he not choose one from the images and make it safe? Could he not escape, as his image had, into a mirrored existence somewhere safe? Could he not live forever? Safe?

No.

The bridge, all bridges, everywhere, must fall. And the bridge was love. Or did it mean that? No, it did not mean that. It meant the bridge that wasn't there was love. The invisible, unseen bridge.

All those people. Falling.

All those people. Falling down.

Falling down forever. Into love.

3:00 p.m.

When he emerged from the bedroom into the living room, Miss Bonkers was asleep over her knitting. (Why do people knit in California? Dolly wondered.) Ruth was nowhere to be seen.

He would not disturb them. Ruth was probably asleep herself, in her room or on the beach or somewhere.

Dolly watched Miss Bonkers.

Miss Bonkers's profession was death. Without it, she could not live. The list of her clients was long, and it culminated, altered, in the demise of Naomi.

It seemed that there would be no more deaths for Miss Bonkers until her own. Now she would minister to life. She didn't know this, of course. But she might have sensed it. She had changed. There was no doubt about that. The glint was gone from her eye — the purse from her lips — the twitch from her fingers. Her laughter had gentled down and her voice had softened around the edges of consonants, broadened through the centers of vowels. What had done all this? Not just her books and her knitting and the presence of the sea and her dreams of airplanes.

It was Naomi's doing, Dolly thought. For such is the power of how we die. And live.

Adolphus tiptoed onto the balcony and looked along the sand.

The gypsies were out. But only the very youngest, and their father. The rest must be in school, still, and perhaps B.J. had gone off in the little Ford to pick them up.

Noah was not wearing his shirt. He was a very handsome man with a well-defined, rather than a muscular, body.

Adolphus watched him. He wore dark trousers, and his feet were bare. All at once he hoisted a little girl onto his shoulders, and Adolphus could see that she brandished a butterfly net. The other children, who were all boys, carried tin pails with sailboats, rubber balls, and choo-choo trains painted on them. They all began to run.

Noah's run was like a horse's canter. He joggled Charity up and down, holding onto her fat little legs. Now, all of them were laughing, Charity crying out in her high-pitched, strident sing-song, "Take me to a butterfly, take me to a butterfly!" And Noah, running, would spot one and veer in its direction, trying to point it out to her with little ducks and jabs of his head.

How beautiful they were, Dolly dreamed: Noah with his coltish gaiety, the little boys with their ragged flags of uncut hair, the wild Boadicea-child with her net, and the barking, joyous yellow dog who circled and fell and circled and rolled and circled and jumped among them.

They moved in Dolly's direction. The running became leaping. The leaping became a dance — the dance became a celebration.

Charity caught a butterfly. It was given into an upraised pail. The little boys pounced on the corpses that littered the beach. It did not seem cruel; it did not seem callous. It seemed — *useful*, somehow, what they were doing.

Noah began to fly. Charity held onto his hair with one hand and flapped the net with the other. Noah whirled and whirred and flew with his arms. They were all laughing, all playing, all — unbearably — alive.

And Dolly watched.

The celebration fell in a circle.

Adolphus heard one of the boys (it was Josh) say, "Papa, all the dead butterflies: I think it's sad." And Noah said, "Nothing is sad that's as it ought to be."

Then Adolphus thought, Yes, the butterflies are dying — but they've lived.

Now the children began to sing, and Adolphus had to sit down in a chair to listen, because a bleakness was rising in him — the bleakness of loss. That he had not taken what existed to be taken — which was life — and had never drifted, as these real people did, on the current of his existence, freely floating, waving at the sky, certain of the shore, dabbling with complacent fingers at the bright stones, the little pebbles, the colored, sparkling sands of the shallows.

All his life had been a picture of life. Something through a lens, far away at the end of a camera, beyond telescopes, caught in binoculars, laid out under glass. He'd thrived on pictures. On scripted situations, on the careful, brilliant assemblage of pretended beauty. On prearranged trees, modified mountains, altered architecture, Max-Factored faces, flattened or padded bosoms, dyed hair and wigs, well-modulated vowels, coached consonants, and perfume from Paris.

Down there on the sand there was something that he had never known. It was something he could never have arranged, or set, or directed. He could not have coaxed it from a thousand writers or described it to a million cameramen. It could not be done because it was.

That was why Myra had died. She hadn't believed. She hadn't believed in what she was — in the fat lady — in Old Fat. She had only believed in what she thought she was — in what she thought she ought to be — in what was expected of her — and, finally, demanded.

You die when you can't be real, Dolly thought. When you can't see who you are and when you cannot see what is.

You die when you forget the Milky Way. What is there. What *is — there.*

The butterflies.

The gypsies on the beach.

Naomi's seals. Naomi herself.

Just as he had fallen in love with Jasmyn Jo, who wasn't there. Who didn't exist. Who wasn't a boy. Who was a girl. Who masqueraded.

Stop the masquerade. Take off the dominoes and cross the bridge.

It all fell together, and Dolly closed his eyes and felt faint with the pleasure of it, sick with anticipation. He was going to meet reality.

The sea sounded its afternoon hush and the circle of gypsies, the Trelfords — Noah, his dog and his children — sang. They all seemed to sing together — children, man, dog, and sea — even the birds were singing.

Myra won't die, Adolphus thought. I'll make her live. It will only be in my mind, but it will be real because she'll be walking around alive in me — in everything I do so long as I try, so long as I believe in what she really was.

A cloud of butterflies drifted overhead, close enough to touch. They didn't make a sound.

At Fringes Field the dead had died. That was real. He'd been there. He'd seen it. But it wasn't the butterflies' fault. It was the fault of people. People who didn't believe. Who hadn't believed what they saw with their own eyes. If only they had stood and stared, had laughed at them, joyously, as Noah and his children did.

Adolphus stood up. He could feel his knees gently touching one another.

He looked over the rail.

Noah was staring at the sky. The boys were digging pits in the sand.

Charity had laid aside her net and had stretched out one arm, and a platoon of monarchs sat there now, examined and spoken to by the little girl.

"Don't fly away," she said. "Don't fly away from me. Rest for a while. Stay here. And rest. Please."

Adolphus smiled.

The dog slept.

The butterflies waited.

Adolphus understood.

3:30 p.m.

He drove away, dangerously and quickly, down the highway winding toward Santa Monica.

The Franklin behaved with noisy surprise at the speed.

The past fell back from his departing shoulders like the sea from a swimmer.

He curved out, racing, into the oncoming lane, but there was no traffic there. It was all right for him now. He felt so elated that even the enormous threat of speed did not seem to frighten him. He had not known he could drive like this. Or that anyone could.

As a matter of course, the old nightmare came up at his mind from the grayness of the highway, but it did not disturb him any more. He watched instead with gradual fascination, all the while abandoning his ancient fear of danger, stooping across the wheel, gazing at the road with a kind of analytical candor that, in itself, caught at his interest as he drove.

"Yes," he recognized, "the nails, the glass, the windshield breaking. Me crushed by the steering wheel, face gone, ears, nose, and eyes torn free. My hands thrown up to stop the impossibilities. What rubbish. Why, it's never going to happen."

And so he drove faster. Faster still. And on.

The free danger of his driving caught at him with joyous anticipation. It was a kinship, newly found. Anticipation without fear. The fist that had formed down in the heat and liquid of his stomach was gone. The saliva leapt to his mouth, flavored with forbidden acids. He wanted to close his eyes. One by one, they came. The signalings of new pulses, floods of perspiration, cold showers of sweat against the inner parts of thigh and biceps. Excitement. Speed which is faster and faster without limit — shedding its bright fears like leaves across the highway. Unbearable speed. But borne. Wet and wetting. This was a race of time against his heart. Against reality. The slashing glitter of a piece of glass. The lust of nails on the road. Pictures of death. And speed. And finally, the recklessness of knowing who you are, and giving room to danger. And the possibility of something real.

All this Adolphus felt and saw in seconds — images — until, terrified at last, knowing who he was and what real danger was, he slowed and stopped the car. A strange heat, unknown to those who do not race, touched his nostrils. He wanted to breathe.

But what had he done? What was the matter with him? Why should he suffocate from courage?

He closed his eyes against the staring accusation of the road where he had nearly died.

"On Friday, noon, July the 20th, 1714, the finest bridge in all Peru..."

He heard his blood admonishing him, astounded. He sighed. The light of the great sun knocked warnings against the pale opaqueness of his leaf-shaped eyelids. But he lay there, unresponding, head thrown back, afraid to move.

So much, he thought, for the end of the world.

"Hullo."

Adolphus sat bolt upright in the car.

"What?"

"I said hullo," said a voice coming from outside the window on the passenger side of the car.

"Where are you?" said Adolphus.

"Here. Right here."

Adolphus snapped his head to the right, staring, and he saw a face so young that it looked unborn. The sort of face the gods must have, he thought. Pan-eyed and -eared, with a child's brow and the lips of some deft relative of Eros, with the whole face formed of curiosity and wonder, slandered by a monstrous nose, inept of nature, which was more a gesture of strident nobility than it was of flesh and blood and cartilage — a nose — it was really a tirade on design — across the bridge of which the rest of the face was stretched out tight and flat. A high collar, a cravat, a pair of slender shoulders in a suit, all white, giving the indication of someone sadistically immaculate, immune, through cruelty, to dust and sand. Like Dolly himself.

"I want to go to the city," this person said.

"Oh."

"I don't drive, you see."

(The image of a figure, ramrod straight in a limousine, intensely oblivious of the papery battering of wings, toyed with the idea of entering Dolly's conscious mind.)

"Well, I'll drive you there," said Adolphus, "if you're not in a hurry, that is. I want to sit here for a moment longer."

"That's all right," said the person, speaking with the extreme formality of someone rehearsing an unknown language. "I can wait as long as you like. Are you ill?"

"In a way, yes."

"What's wrong? You're an incredible color, if I may say so."

"Say anything you like," said Adolphus. He was hurt at the statement. He had hoped to look his best at such a moment as this, obviously one of the few moments-of-meeting that his dreams would ever in his whole life give up to reality. The boy was too beautiful for words. "What do you mean by incredible? Have I gone blue by any chance?"

The other person laughed as only other people can laugh — never as we laugh, ourselves. It was a laugh so free of premeditation that it seemed hard to believe it had ever been thought of before. It signified nothing. No privacy of meaning, no contemplated private insult. No meaning but itself. To laugh.

"I'm quite serious," said Adolphus.

(This was not going well at all. For some reason, physical beauty aside, he found himself disliking his encountered dream.)

"Once, I did turn blue and I was very ill and had to be put in an oxygen tent and treated by many, many doctors. I nearly died and was in hospital for three solid months."

"I'm sorry."

"What color am I, then?"

"Just white. Sort of yellow, maybe. But it's going now. Now, you look much better."

"I see. Well. Do you want to get into the car?"

"Yes. Thank you."

He did.

They did not start. They sat, instead, quite still. Side by side. Alone.

"Haven't I seen you before?" said Adolphus. (The figure in the limousine decided against appearing, and gave place to the face of Jasmyn Jo. Boy-girl. Girl-boy.)

"I don't believe so. I very rarely do this. Go into town or anything. Just sometimes. To the movies."

"Ah. A fellow dreamer, I suppose." Adolphus smiled.

"I don't understand you."

"It's nothing. Just a private thing. People who live alone. I live alone, you know."

"Completely alone?"

"Unh-hunh."

"But you travel. You go about on the road. I've seen you."

Adolphus looked at his guest in surprise. "Seen me?"

"Yes. I live on the beach, you see. I've seen you there and I've seen you on the road. Being driven by different women."

"But I thought you said..."

"Oh, I did. And it's true. I hardly ever go out. But I watch from the roof of my house, sometimes, and there's a sort of cliff behind it...."

"Oh!" said Adolphus, with the lights coming on. "Oh-ho! Then it's you. You live in that house with the fence at the end of the beach!"

For some reason this made Octavius blush. He felt like someone who has told his real name to the police without intending to.

"Yes," he said. "It's me."

"Then you really do live alone, like me. I've heard about you."

"I'm not famous."

"Well, put it this way. You're famous with my mother and my sister."

"Oh, why?"

"Because they live at the other end of the beach. At least, my sister does. My mother died."

"The orange parasol and the swimmer?"

"Precisely."

They both smiled. It was like meeting lifelong friends in the remotest Congolese village.

"But, tell me why you don't live there yourself," said Octavius.

"Well," said Adolphus, "that's a very long story. The story of my life, you might say." He laughed. "Single, I came into this world, to borrow a phrase, etc.," he said, "but to answer your question, I don't live there because I would not be happy there." Nevertheless, he continued to smile. His sense of intrigue and his sense of dislike fluctuated as alternating tides. He looked again, more closely and less guardedly at the face beside him — boy and man, girl and woman.

"But you must have met me somewhere," Dolly said in the inverted way he had of saying things ("you" must have met "me"), "you really are so familiar."

He frowned. A thought came. No.

He looked again. Perhaps. Why not?

The pictures. Was it that? His secret pictures of "goings-on."

But how to say so?

"You aren't by any chance any kind of model, or anything? Are you?"

"I'm not sure I know what you mean?"

Adolphus's heart leaped up. The perfect answer. An invitation delicately flavored with a coy smile.

"A photographic model, perhaps?"

"No. . ." (but still, uncertainly).

"Uhmmmm. . .pictures. You know. I have some. Of gentlemen. . .doing things."

An utterly blank expression was the only reply.

And then, "I think I may have relatives in pictures, but, you see, I don't know. I am not acquainted with my parents."

Adolphus scrutinized the features one last time. The ultimate realization must have taken all of thirty seconds, the way one might count out the seconds before an explosive noise, and as each second passed, it left its scar of recognition and amazement on the listener's face.

"Letitia. . ." Adolphus barely breathed the name.

Octavius said it too. "Letitia?"

Dolly knew enough to turn the subject aside.

"But, it's incredible. No. Not Letitia."

"Why?"

"She doesn't have a child."

This still seemed to make sense, even with the child quite palpable and real beside him.

Octavius waited, wanting coyly to say, "Yes she has," but holding his secret tight.

Adolphus almost reached out and touched him, as he might a copy of a famous statue, just to see if its texture was as true as its lines made it seem. "But it's amazing," he could not help saying. And so his impulse that he knew this person had been right. "What's your name?"

"Octavius."

Adolphus blinked.

Octavius said, "You know my mother?"

"Oh, no," said Dolly. "Please believe me. That was a mistake." A mistake. "Just someone you vaguely resemble. In films."

Soooo. . . thought Octavius. Then it's absolutely certain. The Virgin is my mother.

"Are you a movie star?" he asked, out loud.

Adolphus did a kind of gentle double take. How enchanting it was to meet someone who did not know who he was. . . .

"No," he paused.

Pause.

Octavius stared, waiting.

"Please go on," he said. "Tell me who you are."

"I am Adolphus Damarosch."

Dolly was filled with amazement. His name sounded like a bell to him.

The child (for he had seemed up to then no more than a child) smiled. But it was not Dolly's name that made him smile. It was his own elation. Certainly it is marvelous. Both of them thought so.

A flight of gulls took off from some nearby rocks, flinging as they flew away a lot of noise back over their shoulders at the pair in the parked car.

There were butterflies, too. Just a few. In the warmth.

Adolphus decided that it was time for a cigarette. Something to make his poise at least appear less self-centered than it was. He was a new man. "Do you smoke?" he said.

"No," said Octavius. "But I will if you want me to."

"Oh, heavens!" Dolly laughed. "There's no necessity to do anything that isn't natural to you, my dear!"

"It's natural," said Octavius. "But not to me." (Mother had smoked, from time to time.)

Dolly lit his own, going through the whole process of the ritual with great elegance. Then he settled back and said, "You say you've never met your mother."

"That's right, yes."

"May I be so inquisitive — please don't think me rude — but, why?"

A flick of ash. A noncommital gaze across the sea. Idly looking at the haphazard flight of a butterfly. What an unholy conversation. How do you play a scene like this? Well, play it by ear. Just say the lines. In the end it will all make sense.

Octavius stammered for a moment, mentally, and it affected the appearance of his face. Adolphus, withdrawing his eyes from the silently snapping wings outside, observed the change.

"Take your time," he said.

"No. It isn't that. It's just that the answer is so point-blank."

"Well, then. What is it?"

"Well. I don't want to meet her. Yet."

Don't reach. Stop making faces. Ask questions.

"But why? I mean, can't you find out exactly who she is, walk up to her and say, 'Hello, aren't you my mother?' "

Octavius shook his head.

"You really have no idea at all who she is?"

Another shake, less forcible, but still a "no."

"It seems so crazy," said Adolphus.

"Well, I do have an idea," said Octavius, who was not clever about absolute lies. "I'm just not sure."

He had waited so long for the answer that now, knowing it, he did not want to share it with anyone. He wanted to hoard it for a while.

"So you still haven't met?"

"No. And I'm not sure we ever will."

"Why?"

"I rather hate her, at this stage."

Ah. Yes.

Silence. Broken by the distant — very distant — mutter of an approaching car.

"I like you very much," said Adolphus. "I have never met anyone quite so honest before. Imagine, not wanting to know your mother. . . ."

He smiled. This, too then, was part of his revelation. An honest sense of hate.

("There is a land of the living and a land of the dead and the bridge is love.")

And hate.

Octavius lay open another blank page. He said, "In a way, I'm afraid of losing my hate. You see, I've lived with this so long."

Yes, Dolly thought, and tossed his cigarette away.

"You'll start a fire!" said Octavius.

"Oh, goodness," said Adolphus. "Surely not. We're right beside the water."

"That doesn't matter," said Octavius. "The grass is dry. Everything is. The least spark on the wind could burn us all out."

"Oh, very well. . ." said Adolphus, whose hand had been on the starter. "I was just going to drive you into town."

"Good," said Octavius. "But it can wait another minute or so."

They both got out of the car.

"Where did you throw it?"

"I don't know. I just flicked it over my shoulder."

The distant motorcar, no longer distant, appeared around the corner, but was not at once observed. It whirred like a biplane and Octavius did at least give a slight glance at the sky. But fire is all important and in drought, such as the drought now, it could mean death.

"On the road? On the verge?"

"I tell you I don't know."

Whirrrrrr. . . whirrrrrrrr.

And, stooping blindly to retrieve the blazing canyons from the grass, they searched. Above them, the sun blazed on butterflies that seemed to be on fire.

"Must have gone. . ." (whirrrrr) ". . . out on the. . ." (whirring. . . whirring. . .) ". . . road." And thinking. Someone new. So honest. Revelations. Funny. Fires and trips to town and the mysteries of mothers. Never met. Oh, goodness, the way the world is set ablaze is strange. With. . . (whirring). . . strangers. . . bringing revelations, innocence, and (whirrrr) death. The (whirring. . . whirrrrrrrr) innocence of death. That bridge. . .

Adolphus cried, "I have it. Here!" And instantly upon the spot was struck and hurtled upward by a small red roadster driven by a traveling salesman who had come all the way that day from San Francisco on an errand of the utmost urgency.

The salesman, whose name it is important not to mention (it is such an ordinary name and would not look appropriate at this moment), sat in his roadster, whimpering. He said first of all something about being in a hurry, and then he sobbed, and then he just shook and made noises, like a dog whose chain has become wound around a tree in the panic of a thunderstorm, and who is forced to sit out the thunder and lightning and to contemplate their violence from a seated position.

For a brief moment, too, it seemed that Octavius was not going to move. Never going to advance on the prostrate form which lay, glazed with agony and stillness, on the road.

Having seen so many films in his life, Octavius was only aware of the semblance of death. He did not know that, in real life, blood was a signal for absolute panic and concern.

"We should do something," he finally whispered, "I suppose."

The salesman from San Francisco whimpered as bravely as he could, still sitting in his place. He managed to convert part of his shaking fit into a nod of approval.

Octavius had been searching for the cigarette on the far, sea-side of the car. He rose and ran the tips of his ten fingers, one by one, over the cottony sheen of his thighs. "Will you — or will I?" he seemed to say, giving a few jabby, unrhythmic parts of his black-and-brown stare to the salesman. Like a choice of gifts. But he received no reply. The salesman merely sat and abhorred his deed.

Guiding himself through the tender aid of his fingers, Octavius found his way around the hood of the Franklin. He brushed against the full dusty length of its silvered bumpers, and thus the properly soiled appearance of an accident began.

He got as far as the very edge of the road, and stopped.

It seemed a physical impossibility to trespass further. Out there in the middle of the river of cement lay a man in pink trousers, drowning in blood.

Octavius could not recall the man's name. Idiotically, he was only aware of what his mind was doing, up against the brick wall of this terrible event; it was relieving itself in a stream of yellow nerve ends, and there seemed to be a panic-stricken signaling from various other parts of him which called out for information. And thus he felt that the first imperative thing to do was to remember the man's name.

He crouched, contracted, over the dry grass at the edge of the cement and let his hands dangle almost obscenely between his knees.

The salesman, by now, was apparently having to eat his fists in order to contain himself. He gave this strange figure (which to him looked like an elegant Neanderthal squatting at the mouth of its cave) an even wider stare than he had thought himself physically capable of. His eyes ached with the urgency of messages, all of which tried to form the word "do." "Do something," he finally managed with his mouth. But it came out flat against his knuckles, which were inserted so far that they bled at the application of the letter "d".

Octavius called, just as though darkness surrounded them, just as though his whereabouts was a precious secret to his safety, and he was a sentry, crying in the dark for the gentle reply of a familiar name. "What is your name?" he whispered. But the prostrate figure did not reply.

The salesman now stood up in his car, about to step out over the door like a trembling conqueror.

Octavius signaled him to wait.

"But. . . but. . ." the salesman stammered.

"No," said Octavius. "Wait."

And then again he said, "What is your name?" to the senseless sprawl of limbs upon the road.

From the beach, about twenty feet below them, came the faraway cry of voices. Children in a game. Chasing butterflies.

"I'll go and get help," said the salesman, looking off at the sand and its people.

"No. Not there," said Octavius. "Drive back down the road until you come to a turnoff on the left. Topanga Beach." He thought. "It's about three miles."

The man sat down.

"When you come to the turnoff, drive to the first house you'll see. Ring bells. Knock. Whatever. I've never been. I don't know. But get them to come. It should be this man's sister."

"His sister."

"Yes. His sister."

"What's her name?"

"I don't know. I don't know. I don't know anybody's name. But hurry and go."

"I don't want to. Why don't you go? You're his friend. You know him. I'm nervous. I've killed a man."

"No," said Octavius. "I don't know anyone and I can't drive."

The salesman sat still.

"Why can't we get those children? Why do we have to go away back there?" he said.

"Because at the house they'll know what to do. Go on. Now. Go."

The salesman put his hand out toward the dashboard of his car. He shot a look at Octavius and another look of wearied horror at the figure on the road.

"All right," he said. "I'll go because you're stupid."

He started fiddling with the paraphernalia arranged on the dashboard.

Octavius stared at the widening blood bath, some of which was beginning to trickle in his own direction. Three large butterflies had settled by the scarlet patch, attracted by its wetness.

The salesman was madly running his many fingers (too many) all over the face and latches of the machine before him.

Octavius waited for the motor to start. "What's the matter?" he said.

"I've forgotten what to do," the salesman replied in his whimper. "I don't know how to start the car."

(Dolly could have told him.)

Octavius thought for a moment, concentrated very hard on the apparent logic of machines.

"Turn the key," he said. "Don't think. Turn the key. Maybe the next thing will come to you."

The salesman turned the key.

He closed his eyes. His hands paused in the air, desperate for information. He attempted a severe expression, which slowly failed and became concentration. At last his fingers reached for the choke and then for the gearshift and then his feet did a precise little dance — perhaps a tango — over the pedals and at last the engine roared and the car shot away, scudding up sand and dust, which settled as he turned the car and drove off.

The butterflies were blasted up into the air, and they settled with the dust over the map of staling blood and over the crouched white Buddha by the road.

Down on the beach the children had been joined by adults. Vaguely, in an inner ear, Octavius was aware of their music. Someone had brought a gramophone and records to form a background for butterfly-chasing. Octavius heard the familiar strains of Artie Shaw's record, "Begin the Beguine." (Mother in ruffles, dancing with Fred Astaire. But not any more.) The music arched up, borne on waves of heat, mingled with orange-and-brown wings, against and then over the edge of the runted, stunted short-legged cliff behind him. The sea sang also, sibilant and sandy-throated. While he waited, watching by the fallen friend he would never know, the fingers on the road moved and stirred in Morse-like spasms of life.

Within ten minutes it became so hot that Octavius was forced to remove his jacket and place it, cowl-like, over his head. He peered out now, unblinking, from between the white lapels, while down the beach they began the beguine, for the seventh time in a row. He wanted to go to the man on the road, but, catatonically, his will was locked in waiting.

And then the people came.

There were two cars. One belonged to B.J. and Noah, and was driven by Ruth Damarosch. The other was the salesman's. There was also a motorcycle driven by a figure in white. Miss Bonkers on call. Octavius shaded his eyes and stared. Ruth got down and went immediately to the prostrate Adolphus, whose eyes were open.

His voice said, "I've been watching a butterfly up there.

I'm afraid to close my eyes."

Ruth said, "Miss Bonkers is here. She'll help you. You're going to be all right."

Adolphus said, "I met him, Ruth. I finally met him. My dream."

Ruth said, "Yes. You'll be all right. We're here."

Then there was silence; a great deal of stooping near the body; much waiting.

From far away (perhaps at first it was only another instrument in the band, caught in that vicious circle down on the beach) they heard the approaching identification of an ambulance.

"Good," said Ruth. "They're coming with the blood."

They waited as the wail got nearer.

4:10 p.m.

When Ruth had explained Adolphus to the doctors (there were two of them) she stood back, folding her arms into a neat package of flesh, and watched their expressions.

One said, whitely, "Impossible. He cannot be moved yet." His eyes were just two balls of wooden color removed from some Chinese abacus.

The other one, suited, and carrying a black bag, said, "We must at least remove him to the side of the road, Charles."

"Very well," said the abacus-eyed Charles. "Put him on the stretcher and we'll bring him over here."

Ruth turned away. Frozen.

Somehow, however long you are prepared for such a mischance — somehow, even knowing (as they always had) that violence could not forever be avoided — it was still so modified by aversion that she could not cope at all with the event as a piece of realism. She decided instead to go and look at the sea.

Standing at the cliff edge (if you could call it that; the drop was so shallow and such a stint on grandeur), she tried to take one last look at the scene by the road. It must serve as indelible strength against giving up the birth of any child who must die this way.

The greatest impact, like a bruise on her brain, was the presence of strangers. That so many people who cluster (like the butterflies around wet ground) over the dead and dying are unknown people. People who crop up for deaths and dyings.

Hearing Adolphus cry out as he was lifted onto the stretcher, Ruth ran, in her mind, to go back. Thinking that she had moved, she was shocked to find that she hadn't.

A police car at last approached, and one or two people, drawn by the familiar whine, had drifted, hand over hand, up the cliff from the sand. They wore bathing costumes, ludicrously nude-appearing, and Ruth thought how Adolphus would have loved to gaze at them and dream.

Then she saw Octavius, who still sat helplessly by the side of the road.

He had folded his jacket now, and it lay like a worn-out flag across his knee.

The policemen were questioning the San Francisco salesman. In his attempt to be coherent, he was making it seem, somehow, that he had struck Adolphus on purpose.

Ruth thought, Why can't I think about Dolly? He's going to die.

This was so different from the death of their mother. That seemed like death. This was more like a crisis that would pass.

Octavius was assisted to his feet by a youth in a black bathing suit. He found his way to the stretcher.

"What is happening?" he said.

Miss Bonkers said, "He is going to die. Go away."

Octavius stared. He looked down into the face of his friend (his almost-friend; his nearly) and their eyes caught for the briefest of seconds.

"Hullo," said Octavius. And then he remembered. "Adolphus Damarosch."

Their eyes parted company and Octavius could not retrieve the contact he had made. He fiddled with his jacket, trying to put it on, and just as he got it halfway up his arms, with his shoulders thrown back and his head forward, he heard Adolphus die.

Something wet happened and he was covered with blood.

The two doctors, Miss Bonkers, and the ambulance drivers all fell back, bespattered.

"Cover him up," someone said.

A sheet fluttered, glided, and sighed itself down over the gentle breakers of Dolly's blood that tided up over the walls of his life and seeped away into the grass, looking for a place to hide.

There was a long, deep hissing silence.

Ruth tightened her arms upon themselves, and around what was inside her, and tried with every ounce of her years of training to reduce the size of her mind so that it would hold only that one taut precious (to an athlete) admonition.

Pull.

Pull, pull, pull. Pull, and pull, and pull, and... Pull, pull, pull, one two three.

One-and-two-and. One-and-two-and. One-and-two-and. One.

Two.

And.

But wasn't it wonderful?

The very last thing the dying man had heard had been his own name.

On the lips of his dream.

"Adolphus Damarosch."

Saturday, December 17th, 1938:
Bel Air
7:30 a.m.

Ruth sat in the Franklin, which was parked in front of Dolly's house. She had to go in. They wanted something to dress him in, and Ruth had said that she would find it. The last time she had been here, Myra had been here, too, and the three of them had sat up late at night, laughing at jokes and drinking and making fun of one another — of how serious they all were.

Now the house stood empty.

Ruth turned the motor off. Like an unwilling messenger, she got out of the car and stood before the house, mutely communicating the absence of its owner. The house was condemned now, probably to the ownership of someone who would say, "That Dolly Damarosch lived here. The strange one, you know? Who got killed by a car."

Ruth went to the door.

The last time I was here...

She unlocked it and pushed it open.

There was Dolly's house. All white. With its smashed-up window.

Dolly had not told her about that. It was a shock. The violence of the act was still present in the jagged edge of the broken glass. Ruth gave a cry, just like someone who had been struck.

Instinctively she listened and then looked for an intruder, but there was none. Nor were there any signs of robbery or violence beyond the shattered window itself.

Well. It had been done. It was senseless now to conjecture why or by whom. All of these things could be discovered in time.

She went into the bedroom.

His suits, pale-blue or white, hung in faultless rows in a cupboard. She selected one of the blue ones and, from a drawer, a blue shirt, some underwear, a pair of socks, and a handkerchief. Then she found a tie and a pair of shoes and turned out of the bedroom to go.

The sun rose into sight.

The whole white room was filled with light.

Ruth sighed.

She stood there, central, holding her brother's clothes, engulfed in a sun-flood, dazzled and dazed.

He was gone.

From all around her the photograph eyes of film stars stared. From the walls, from shelves, from table tops, from the piano. Glossy eyes, pretending to smile, pretending to brood, pretending to hypnotize, pretending to live.

Adolphus was gone.

Ruth had never before been in these rooms alone. She had never gone to the bookcase or listened to the swimmers next door, or fallen asleep in one of the big white chairs. The place was antiseptic — arranged and bloodless. A borrowed place. Nervous. Brooding. Empty.

Why had he lived like this? Did fear, as Dolly knew fear, predetermine absolutely such an apprehensive arrangement of ornaments and furniture? There were pathways everywhere — routes of escape. Nothing sat freely in its place, but had been set there, probably according to a diagram. It was faultless and cold.

Ruth set the clothes down and gazed more widely about her.

It was a lonely place, but not by Dolly's absence. Ruth sensed the planned loneliness of a recluse. Whether he had given parties, whether he had been much visited by friends, she did not know. She suspected not. People who are permanently ill tend to be solitary. Their homes become dens and caves, like the dens and caves of wounded or stricken animals. They themselves are seen only from a distance, the way, essentially, Ruth had seen Dolly. Remote. Aloof, with an aura of loneliness that, in the mind, was unbearable to contemplate.

He was gone, now.

Ruth poured herself a drink. She had not slept all night. The continuity of drinks was not surprising. It did not shock her to find herself with gin in her mouth at 7:30 a.m.

She walked around the room.

The one-legged Greek stared at her from his little carved horse. The whiteness of everything exaggerated every shadow and every patch of sunlight. The milky room was sterile. Pasteurized. Weird. There was the white telephone and, beside it, the whitely covered telephone directory.

Everything was astonishingly neat; even the placing of pens and pencils seemed exact. It was a room so completely without clutter that it seemed that the ashes in the ashtrays were ordered and sparse, like a prized collection. "This is my ash collection, and over here, my Renoir on the wall."

Ruth had to smile.

But he was gone.

There was blood on the road.

The books provided the only color there was in the room, with the exception of the view through the broken window, and the green of some rose leaves in a bowl on the piano. The roses themselves were white. But the books, the books were vibrant — even gaudy.

The selection was classical. There was *Moby Dick*, there was *Anna Karenina*, there was the poetry of T.S. Eliot. *The Autobiography of Alice B. Toklas* (only recently published and already a classic) and *Don Quixote* sat side by side. A book of French fairy tales, illustrated by Edmond Dulac, leaned affectionately up against the Bible, and the plays of Oscar Wilde played wife to a large, masculine volume of the poems of Catullus. *The Brothers Karamazov* sat in lonely splendor, extremely red and stamped with gold, up on a shelf with a satyr's head.

This satyr's head was made of plaster and bore an expression of evil so repulsive that Ruth shuddered. Some unforgotten, unremembered image reached out from it — handless — and touched the back of her neck.

She brought her face slowly around to regard the grinning visage once more. The light was strange. Ruth wanted to take the head down, in order to see it more plainly, but she could not contrive to overcome her revulsion. Instead, she drew a wooden chair from its place and stood up on that, face to face, eye to eye with the old demigod.

Alvarez.

The satyr's tongue was laid lasciviously against his lower lip.

"Dear God," Ruth nearly fell right off the chair, and she stood there for at least a minute, gripping the edge of the shelf with her fingers, spilling her gin, unavoidably, relentlessly down the front of her suit. She heard it touch the floor, drop by drop.

"Is everything only in my mind?"

At last, shutting her eyes, she was able to climb down blind and turn her back on what she had seen. But she could not turn her mind away from it.

She placed her free hand on her stomach and pressed her fingers against the new life.

"It *is* there," she said out loud. "It's there. It's there. It *is* there."

She was praying, but she did not know she was praying.

She slow-marched her way back to the gin bottle, and this time poured herself a good four ounces. Dolly's clothes lay placidly, like a straw figure emptied of straw, on their chair.

Ruth fumbled in her bag for her cigarettes and, lighting up, she heard herself moan — heard it so distinctly and was so divorced from the sound that she turned, thinking momentarily that someone else had entered the room.

She sat down.

There, beyond the shattered window, there was sunshine and a garden. Flowers. Trees. Birds. The curiously large influx of butterflies — so large that some called it a plague. There were the bees. The dragonflies. Avocado leaves. Pale grass and blue sky. A row of boxed Chinese elm.

It was nothing, this madness. Nothing but madness.

She was a notorious liar. A gross exaggerator. People said so. It must be true. She lied even to herself. They said that, too.

But her fingers pressed against her womb, and it had to be true.

It was.

It had to be.

She rose.

She went back, Alvarezing, to the bookcase and looked deliberately right up into the satyr's face.

"Are you real?" she said.

For a brief moment she dwelt all the way back to the ancient mysteries: the dancing satyrs in the groves of Arcady; the lonely seduction of Panpipes in the moonlight; the shadows of deities beckoning from the trees; flowers that were heroes; stones that had souls. Ruth might have been a priestess then, since she could conjure so much from a plaster head, and such a potent lover from a stranger glimpsed beyond her shoulder.

"I don't think about it," she said to the satyr, and drew out the Dulac fairy tales, determined to alter the course of her thoughts before she left this place to go back to where they waited with Adolphus cleansed and mended, waited for her to clothe the dead.

She turned to the story of Cinderella.

"Once upon a time, etc., etc.," Ruth read.

She turned the page.

". . . There was a blond man whose eyes were perfectly blue."

Ruth covered the words with her hand.

They weren't there.

Rapidly, she turned more and more pages until, suddenly, something glossy and loose — a page that did not belong in the book — moved beneath her fingers.

She drew it out.

It was a photograph.

The fairy tales fell from her lap to the floor.

Two men . . .

Two men.

Two.

Men.

Ruth knelt down and tried to open the book, but the pages behaved like spiteful enemies. They refused her fingers entry. She grabbed it up in both hands and fought it open. At last the covers spread and, in beside the portrait of Rapunzel, Ruth jammed and crammed and threw the photograph. She pressed the covers tight. It wasn't there. It was gone. It didn't exist.

What was it?
What were they doing?
Who were they?
Why was it there?
Why must it exist? This terrible photograph. What did it mean?

She rose and carried the book, devoid forever, now, of loveliness and innocence, back to its place. Sadly, she lifted it up and slid it onto the shelf.

She stared with apprehension at the other titles there.

Alice's Adventures in Wonderland.

The Adventures of Huckleberry Finn.

The Tale of Peter Rabbit.

The Wizard of Oz.

Horrible. Horrible. Forever horrible.

So many children's books, for Dolly had always loved his bedtime stories, and had loved (Ruth shuddered) particularly the illustrations, the simple make-believe. He'd kept them in good condition.

Slowly, determined to know what the pictures portended, Ruth reached the other books down.

One by one.

The photographs fell from every page. Like rain. They were not in envelopes, not pasted, and not protected in any way from the chance inspection of a guest.

The faces of the models were odd. Neither handsome nor ugly, they seemed like the faces of automatons. Their eyes held no expression whatsoever. Occasionally, one appeared to be smiling, but, studied more closely, it could be seen that the smile was superimposed, not conjured the way an actor might conjure an expression contrary to his own emotion, but literally laid on, as though, just before the photo was taken, the photographer had rearranged the facial features with his fingers.

They were tragic.

Ruth wept for them.

Life was a posture, forever.

8:30 a.m.

At length, Ruth replaced the paper people gently, one by one, pair by pair, and, closing the books, she replaced these, too, one by one, pair by pair, back up on the shelves.

She turned the satyr's face to the wall.

Dolly had lived here.

He was gone.

There was blood on the road.

He had dreamed here and looked at pictures.

Nothing, anywhere, was real.

She reached into her purse for the car keys. She wanted to go.

She looked around her, standing in the center of the room.

Myra stared at her from the top of the piano.

Naomi stared from the wall.

Adolphus himself, his arm around an actress's shoulder, smiled raucously, as though a joke had been told.

George glared.

Ruth, dripping wet, looked down, twenty-two years old, from the beach at Catalina. Victorious.

There, too, was Bruno. Smiling.

She couldn't leave it like this. All these faces, the faces, too, inside the books. It was horrible.

No. She could not leave it.

She removed her matches. She strode to the sofa. She emptied the gin onto a pillow.

She struck a match, applied it, nearly scorched her hands, stepped back, looked for forgiveness into Dolly's face, picked up his clothes, went to the door, looked back at the rapidly spreading holocaust, opened the door, stepped out, murmured, "He is gone," and shut the door behind her.

She got to the car.

She threw in the clothes and shoes, ran back to the house, ran in, found Dolly's canes (there were five of them), grabbed them up, saw the flames, and finally departed.

Driving along, she began to weep.

He was all gone, now.

All gone. Forever.

With Naomi and Myra.

And his blood was on the road.

And his flames were everywhere.

Ruth knew that.

She could hear the sirens, and prayed they would be late.

The Chronicle of the Little Virgin

Monday, December 26th, 1938:
Somewhere in Culver City
10:00 a.m.

Her chin tied in place with black chiffon, her forehead swathed in Spanish lace, her cheeks taut with egg white, her eyes blazing with ambition, and her fingers drumming, Letitia Virden sat in the mottled dark of the theater watching herself "up there."

Cooper Carter sat beside her — not right beside her, but beside her, one seat removed. For the past few weeks, Letitia had not tolerated the presence of anyone within three feet of her person. No one was allowed to touch her. Not even Cooper. She applied her own makeup, adjusted her own clothing, brushed her own hair, and the kisses of allegiance touched only the very tips of her extended and gloved fingers. In her handbag she carried a revolver which ensured adherence to the rules laid down by herself and enforced by Cooper Carter.

"We will have to reshoot that," said the Virgin. "My mole is showing."

"Hold it," Cooper Carter roared. "Roll it back!"

The film shuddered to a stop, blinked at them, faded, and went out. It jabbered its sound track in a reasonable facsimile of Swedish as it sped backward, spewing numbers on the footage counter below the screen.

"What mole?" said Cooper Carter. "Where?"

This was tactful. He knew, of course, the mole was on her neck.

"My neck mole," Letitia said. The words were pushed through her all but frozen lips, like letters through a mail slot. Her face had recently been lifted and the effects were strenuous. However, they would pass. They always did.

"Roll forward," Cooper called.

The screen shimmered with lights. The color was magnificent. Photographed through tinted gauze, Letitia seemed all of twenty — and at the worst moments, twenty-five. She was dressed, in this sequence, as a Western woman of the 1870s.

"There," said Letitia.

"Freeze it!" Cooper yelled.

The frame froze before them. The Virgin's features were in profile, looking up. The hero's chin obtruded three feet into the frame, screen left, but it was Letitia's neck that loomed largest.

"You see it," said Letitia. "Just there, about a foot below my ear. The edge is visible at scarfline."

A tiny black or brown mark, like a half-moon — a mark that might only have been a shadow, were it not for the Virgin's keen, professional eye — lurked for exactly five frames (they were counted over) as she tilted her head upward. On the screen, it could not have been more than six or seven square inches in acreage, but it might as well have been Texas, according to Letitia.

"You're sure it matters, my dear," said Cooper.

Letitia mangled a few syllables of protest, and Cooper then said, "Very well, we will add it to our list."

Madonna ha sempre ragione.

Mussolini is always right.

The reshoot would require a half-day's work, full lighting crew, one actor at minimum wage, camera crews, producer, director, etc., etc. The total cost would be twelve hundred dollars. But Letitia must and would be satisfied.

"Let's go on," she said. "We're nearly to the end."

They were viewing what is known as a rough-cut, a loosely edited but complete version of the film, prior to the addition of sound effects and music. It was a critical stage, because the performances and direction stood alone, without the benefit of editorial taste and censorship.

Letitia's performance, of course, was impeccable — the supporting performances suitably less effective, but adequately professional. The direction, credited to one Leslie R. Whitegown, was actually Letitia's own, and it sparkled with invention and daring.

The script, written under the tutelage of the Virgin, had been dictated to Paul Tarrogon, Mercy Harper, and someone cryptically known (and credited) as Madame Rivi. This latter name could easily be traced to the Virgin, if you wanted to apply a little memory and much desire to know such things. For exactly one week, in 1923, Letitia had been secretly married to Prince Ottavio de Luca-Rivi. The Prince had died. He had been found at the bottom of a ravine in the Pyrenees, two weeks after the annulment of the marriage had been granted to the Little Virgin by the Vatican.

Now Letitia watched with mounting anticipation as her film drew to its close.

The composer, sitting three rows back, was in tears. The projectionist had similarly lost control of his emotions, and Cooper Carter was fighting back with intellectual vigor.

Letitia was beginning to hum over the tunes she would later dictate to the composer. They were sad tunes, noble and resigned, with religious overtones drawn from the works of Wagner.

However, one did not acknowledge debts. One simply spent one's plagiarisms with a firm gesture of ownership. "These properties come out of *my* purse," Letitia seemed to say, "and there you are." It simply did not matter who filled the purse in the first place.

She tightened her grip on the padded arms of her leather chair. Here was the last scene of all.

"Up there," the Virgin stood in the light of a wide orange sunset. The setting was Texas, with California's mountains unaccountably visible in the distance.

There had been a terrible battle. Dirty little Mexicans littered the field with a wide variety of postures. Dead.

This was not the Alamo. ("The Alamo be damned," Letitia had said. "I want something where we win and I want it *big*." The Alamo was merely a sort of mote in her eye.) No. This battle had seemed forever a victory over the dirty little Mexicans and now there were only the Indians left to conquer.

Letitia portrayed Virginia Mary Washington, defiled by Mexicans and consequently unfit for marriage to her lifelong hero (played by Peter St. Paul). Unable to become a bride, Virginia Mary had nobly devoted her life to the founding of a convent, which even now was being raised on the field of battle. And all this before the last Mexican had twitched into eternity.

In this final scene, Peter St. Paul was being sent away by Letitia to kill the Indians and found America.

It was heart-rending, their saying good-bye, because, of course, the Virgin would turn back into her convent and close its doors forever on her love and on the world.

But: "Go in peace," the Virgin said, "as I shall."

There was a shot of waiting, nunlike figures, their gaze averted from the sexual implications of this man who was talking to their mistress.

Bells began to chime (and here the music would swell, pregnant with heaven's promises) and the sunset altered its orange to red.

"May I not even kiss your hand?" said Peter St. Paul.

"No," said Letitia. "No. It would be wrong. It would be wrong." There were tears in her eyes.

Peter St. Paul leapt athletically and gracefully onto the back of his blue-tinted pony.

"Good-bye, Virginia Mary," he said.

"Good-bye, my darling," said Letitia.

"Good-bye."

The hero raised his hat, the heroine her shining face.

(Letitia's mole shone forth once more at this point, but no one noticed this time, least of all the Virgin. The tears were flowing in universal concord.)

The hero kicked his pony with his spurs and fled away into history.

Virginia Mary and the sisters filed decorously into the nearly complete chapel.

Nothing remained but the rotting Mexicans in the field.

America was safe.

THE END

12:30 p.m.

Everyone had gone to lunch. Letitia and Cooper were eating in her dressing room, which was located on one of the five mammoth sound stages so far erected by Cooper Carter at his new studios, Vir-Car Productions.

It was a gift to Letitia.

Cooper's leather coat, full-length, hung from the back of the partly open door.

He poured champagne and ate another triangle of chicken sandwich.

There was a noise, a sort of clicking sound, which came, echoing itself, from the far side of the stage.

"What's that?" said Letitia. "What is it?"

"I don't know."

"Is Harold there, guarding the door?"

Cooper looked out.

"Yes. Although he appears to be asleep."

"Botheration. If he wasn't such a good driver, I'd fire him."

"Harold!" Cooper Carter called.

The Negro body jerked and twisted. It came awake.

"Yessuh, Mr. Carter?"

"There's a noise out there, Harold. See what it is."

"I don't hear nothin'. Where 'bouts, Mr. Carter?"

"On the sound stage. Someone is there. Go and look."

"Yessuh, but it's awful dark out there."

"I don't care. Go and look."

"Yessuh. I's goin' now."

Carter stepped back into the dressing room.

"He's gone to look now. I'm sure it isn't anything."

Letitia laid out a hand of solitaire.

"I don't like spies," she said. "And I'll bet you it *is* a spy."

"Come, come, now. We're perfectly safe."

"I don't like it," she said. "Have you got your revolver?"

"Yes. Have you got yours?"

"Yes."

"Then nothing can happen."

"Pour me some more champagne, Cooper."

"Of course."

Harold stumbled and bumbled around in the dark. The stage was enormous, and it was quite empty, except for lights and camera dollies and cables, placed in strategic positions.

"Is you there, anyone?" he called. "Who is it?"

There was no reply. Only a contained clicking, as of...what?

Harold wandered to the far end.

As of revolved chambers.

"Oh, my," said Harold. "Oh my! Feet, get me outa here!"

He fled into the light.

Cooper reached for his revolver.

"It wasn't no one," Harold lied.

"Well, keep your eyes open."

"Yessuh."

Letitia went on laying out cards.

Some leaders are calm, while others keep watch.

It was Cooper who ate his sandwich, revolver in hand.

"Do you think it was anyone?" Letitia asked.

"No," said Cooper. "Probably not."

"I do," said Letitia. "I think it was George."

"George?"

"Of course." Letitia smiled. "Haven't you guessed?"

"Guessed what, my dear?"

"George wants to kill us," said Letitia.

And they laughed.

"Just think," Letitia said, "for the rest of our lives, champagne and chicken sandwiches, bullet-proof glass and armored limousines."

"Will you mind?" said Cooper Carter. "Always having to live behind a wall?"

"Not a bit," said Letitia. "That's our privilege. It's what we've worked for. And, besides. . . I've been living that way an awfully long while. The difference will be that I don't have to live that way alone any more. I've never cherished being alone. It's just been the price, up to now. But, once we launch this picture — all that will be over forever." She looked across at Cooper and gave him a rare smile. "We've done all the right things, haven't we; made all the right moves; taken all the right steps. We've brought in all the right people. There isn't anything we can't accomplish, after this."

Cooper was watching himself in the mirror — mindful of the open door behind him. Letitia couldn't take her eyes off him. His wonderful profile — the strength of his bearing — the fervor of his vision: the *way* he looked at his own image.

"One day," she said, "that glorious head of yours will adorn the coin of the realm. Do you realize that? The Presidency."

Cooper Carter laughed and waved the idea aside.

"No," said Letitia. "You mustn't make light of it. That's what we're working for."

"I'm not making light of it," said Cooper. "I was only thinking: *first things first*. This is, after all, the beginning — and nothing more."

"Yes," said Letitia. "I know. This is just the beginning.

But *what* a beginning! Do you know — I'm just beginning, myself, to realize what it is we're doing. This film is our personal declaration of freedom. This is what we've wanted — always: the money and the power to be free."

"No, no, my love — it's more than that," said Cooper Carter. "A great deal more than that. What we have now is the money and the power to define our freedom — any way we like. With your image and my empire, what we have now is the freedom to *seize* power."

"Oh," said Letitia, "all our dreams..."

"Yes," said Cooper. And he stood up behind her so they made one image in the mirror. He even dared to lay his hand upon her shoulder. And she let him.

"There," said Cooper. "The two of us."

Letitia narrowed her gaze. Her grip, on Cooper's hand, tightened.

"What is it?" he said.

There were tears in her eyes.

"What is it?"

"It's just — it's just that I've suddenly realized exactly how the movie ends. I mean the music, Cooper — the music. . . ."

"What, then? Tell me."

"Why, 'America the Beautiful,' of course."

"Of course," said Cooper Carter. " 'America the Beautiful'... How else could it end?"

Reflected in the mirror, the Virgin seated — Cooper Carter standing behind her, they began to hum the anthem — very slightly out of tune. But that hardly mattered. The point was — they were singing it together.

9:30 p.m.

George Damarosch had wandered the streets all afternoon, seeking out bars where he would not be known, bartenders who would not take one look at him and say, "Get out!"

This part of the city was rarely visited by celebrities. Their haunts were in Beverly Hills, Santa Monica, and Hollywood. Los Angeles itself was a city of bums and businessmen, clerks and secretaries, salesladies and hardware salesmen, religious fanatics and writers.

The bars were for truck drivers and garbage men, resting prostitutes and people going to and fro from perfectly ordinary, everyday jobs. Their faces were plain and uncomplicated. Their minds were engaged in college football, the news from China, and how to pay back the bank. They paid no attention to George. George was only one of them.

He came out into the evening and found himself near Sherman Square. He went in.

He sat on a bench.

Nearby, a pervert was trying to attract the attention of a student who was reading a book under a lamp. Yesterday's Santa Claus, now out of work, rested peacefully on another bench, feeding an occasional pigeon with stolen peanuts. A man and a woman, whose home was breaking up, argued about their possessions in low, unemotional monotones. A young girl was weeping. Two children climbed a palm tree. Or tried to.

George closed his eyes.

He knew that it was over. The long dream that had pushed and prodded him and kept him from total collapse — was over. Letitia was re-entering history without him and he didn't know what to do.

He had vowed he would destroy her. But wasn't it true already that she had destroyed him? And how could the destroyed destroy his destroyer?

How?

How could Letitia Virden *be* destroyed? The Little Virgin. The years had not destroyed her. Scandal had not. Age never would, so long as film could attest to her youthful presence. Society wouldn't. History couldn't. He could not.

How could he?

He'd loved her so. It seemed to George that he had always loved her, but of course he hadn't. In his heart of hearts he knew that if he'd had her, had her when he first wanted her, she would now be long forgotten. But he hadn't had her, and now he could never forget her.

He thought about death.

Naomi was dead. And now Adolphus. Would *he* die? George?

No. He was indestructible. There was no place for death in George's life. He would drift, but not toward death.

He'd killed once.

He remembered it.

Again it was that fateful day.

The day of Ruth's birthday party, 1922.

George, when he was George — *the* George Damarosch — had had a fearful temper. He spoke in tirades and he dreamed in broadsides.

"Motion pictures will die with the advent of sound. They will cease to be an art and become a mere industry, fulfilling the needs of the public, and never again the needs of the artists."

"The history of ancient Rome, the history of Europe, the history of the British Empire — these all belong in books. The history of America will be told on film."

And perhaps his most famous epithet: "Beware of a future that does not mirror the past."

Attention. He had had a great deal of attention when, all those years ago, he had been the famous George D. Damarosch.

Now he was a derelict sitting in a park, regretting his memories.

His mind was full of shouts — his own voice raised against himself.

Why did I miss it? Why?

He sat on the steps with Letitia. He wooed her and he lost her to Bully Moxon.

How long ago it was he could not calculate — not in his heart. In his heart it seemed like yesterday. In his mind he knew that it was sixteen years ago, at least, but his mind was full of anger. The love was in his heart. George's heart and mind had never met. They argued from a great distance. They were never reconciled. He was split — not down the middle, but in half.

He had been just so, that faraway afternoon. Letitia had rejected him in the heart — and when he fled from that scene, he was confronted by his wife and son — rejected in the mind.

He tore his life apart with words that afternoon, for it should not be forgotten that tantrums and tirades change the lives of their instigators as well as the lives of those they scream and yell at. Naomi was not the only loser. George also lost. Her. His children lost their father — but he also lost them. They were willfully misplaced, but still lost to him. His tantrum cost them all their futures. He broke them into individuals.

The park darkened.

The pervert left without the student.

The girl stopped crying and the children sat beneath, instead of high in, the tree.

George remembered that when he had left Naomi standing in the library at Falconridge, he had rushed out into the midst of his guests. He'd run (an unusual sight, George Damarosch running), tipping over friends and tables all the way to a private arbor at the rear of the house.

Three people were there already.

Letitia Virden. Bullford Moxon. And a Chinese-American gardener by the name of Ping Sam.

Ping Sam was unusually conscientious. Even on the day of the giant party, when he might have had every excuse not to work in the gardens, there he was, in his coolie hat and blue-denim uniform, weeding the flower beds and trimming the roses.

Letitia, a mere girl, it seemed (as George cast his eye back on the scene), dressed in blue, was seated on a wooden bench. Bully was standing. Ping Sam, about ten feet away, unaware of either film star, was fingering and hoeing out weeds in a bed of red and white carnations.

George, in the white heat of his brainstorm, arrived in the arbor gasping for breath. There was something desperately silent about him. He wanted to cry out in his anguish, but language rejected him. Voiceless, he remained undetected.

Bully had just said, "I love you," to Letitia, and she, the nominal guardian of a nation's virginity, had cast down her eyes in the secret admission that she, by some girlish miracle, loved him.

Bully, sensing his victory, rejoicing in it, and ecstatic with anticipation, danced out of the arbor over to the carnation bed. He clapped Ping Sam on the back and he said, "To-day, my good fellow, I am loved. Give me one of those flowers."

Ping Sam leaned against his hoe, pushed back his coolie hat and laughed. He often went to the pictures and, like all Americans, he knew and adored this odd little man before him, and the tiny sainted woman in the arbor. He watched approvingly as Bully plucked the fatal flower.

The dancing man returned to the Virgin.

He did a strange thing.

He did not present her with the flower.

Instead, he adorned his own lapel with it, and took her by the hands and danced away with her onto the lawns and among the guests and over the nasturtium beds and along the terrace past Ruth and under the windows from which Adolphus watched while the doctors stemmed the flow of his blood and down the Star Steps and into the parking lot and through the assembled motorcars and out among the trees and onto a bank of hybrid grass and into Letitia's astounded arms and into the future of her unmasking — generating, flooding her with child and with his own re-joicing. And all of this was seen or known (in his rage, he mentally saw what he did not actually see) by George

Damarosch, who turned, now, white and furious, to the Chinese-American gardener, Ping Sam.

"Why?" he said, his voice shaking with his sense of incalculable loss, "why did you let him do that?"

Ping Sam blinked and reached for the hoe and returned to his weeding. Mr. George was often angry. Work and silence were the answers.

But not this time.

George advanced over the flowers, marched like an army over the carnations and roses and lilies.

"Why did you allow it?" he screamed. "What have you done?" he roared. "Why did you stand there, hoeing your Jeedy weeds? Ping Sam? Why have you done this to me?"

In his mind, George had leaped far ahead of Bully. He saw the child, he saw the son he would not have of Letitia, saw it rising in the world of the healthy and the whole, running away from him. A son that was not Adolphus, who must die. An object, not a being.

Ping Sam began to retreat, with his wide black eyes on George's face. He tripped over his hoe. He made his way, backward, to death.

And George pursued him with all the vehemence and hatred at his command. A strangely malevolent torrent of words descended on Ping Sam. Scalding rain. He was castigated for disloyalty. Roared at for his virility (Ping Sam was the father of eight sons) and lashed for the providence of his bright and beautiful offspring and his handsome, silent wife. He was even decried for the rape of America's Little Virgin. And murdered for his part in the destruction of George's hopes and plans — his exploded future — his exploded dream.

George reached out with both his hands.

Ping Sam reached out with his.

The canyon beyond Falconridge is deep. Now, it was haunted.

George returned to the birthday party his hands behind his back. This was to become a characteristic stance for the remainder of his life.

He looked at his daughter, Ruth.

Her hair had not yet turned to its shade of premature white. It was long and brown, done up with ribbons.

George thought, "The perfect image of a girl. A murderess."

Like her mother, she carried the blood.

The infamous, killing blood.

Damn her.

Ruth blushed, as though she had known what was in his mind.

George turned and walked away.

All his dreams had faded and gone out in one blinding afternoon.

Now, in the park, he opened his eyes and stared hopelessly into the dark sky and the faraway stars.

"Oh, God," he prayed, "if there is one, kill me now."

He waited.

Nothing happened.

"Kill me now," he pleaded. "Now."

Still nothing happened.

"This is a sign," George thought. "A sign that there is something still to do."

He wondered what it was.

"Kill me now," he had prayed. "Kill me now."

Then he knew what it was — the thing he had to do. The meaning of the sign.

He had killed before.

The second time is nothing.

And as he bided, he wondered.

When?

It was the day after Christmas, and the lights were still ablaze as George rose, and with a jaunty air, hands neatly, firmly and calmly folded behind his back, walked out of Sherman Square and down along the boulevard toward the nearest shining bar which beckoned him with electric messages of hope. And cunning.

To kill is to destroy. He hadn't thought of that.

Till now.

Sunday, January 1st, 1939:
Topanga Beach

New Year's Day 1939 fell on a Sunday. There was nothing extraordinary about it. Those who had had too much to drink woke up with headaches. Those who went to bed with problems still had them in the morning. Those who had rashly proposed marriage under the midnight mistletoe awoke to the question of how to tactfully break the vow. The happy were still happy, the sad still sad. The doers did and the nondoers didn't. It would be a year like any other.

Ruth had spent the night on the beach.

First of all she had sat on the balcony, watching Noah and B.J.'s bonfire, and later, when everyone had gone to bed, she had walked along the sand and paused beside its embers.

This fire was going out. But others still burned. For Ruth, it had been a year of fires. Real fires, imaginary fires, symbolic fires. All burning — all eating — most of them conjuring death.

She slipped her hand under the loose blouse of her beach pajamas. There it was — whatever it was — whatever it would be. It should be born in June 1939. That sounded grand.

A blue-eyed baby, with blond hair and fine, long limbs, a straight mind and a health-infested system. She would will it. She was convinced of this.

What would Bruno think — if Bruno should ever find out? Had it been done at his instigation? Certainly the blond man had followed her all the way from Germany, as though by plan, as though obeying orders, proceeding by rote.

In that case, Bruno would know. He would doubtless rejoice. Well. Let him. This was her child. Not his. Not Germany's. Hers.

It was a butterfly child, she thought. Conceived and born in the butterfly year — an era of plagues and ruin. But that didn't matter. What he grew toward — the years in which he would flourish and mature — they would be different years, not years of anguish, as these were.

She thought of what he would miss. He would never know his father. But she would tell him, somehow, some persuasive story. She would make him believe in her belief, in the children of determined hope.

He would never know Dolly, and that was a greater loss than the loss of his father. Not to have known Adolphus — that was a desperate thing. But then, it could not be so desperate to those who only heard his name or read about him, or were told how odd and strange he was.

And Naomi.

Probably George.

They would all be gone then.

Certainly this world he was being born into would be gone.

It would all change. Be changed. Would vanish.

Ruth did not know how sick her heart really was in the midst of this world, until she thought of that word — the word "vanish."

It will be over, she thought, before he grows to be a man. When I am old and he is my age, what a wonderful thing it will be to look back and to say, it never happened. The dreamers did not die; Bruno did not exist; the butterflies were beautiful — whole treefuls of them — loved and applauded by everyone who saw them; Hitler is dead. No more wars. No more threat of wars. No torment. No apprehension. And a cure for every disease. . . .

She smiled. She even laughed out loud.

She was dreaming everyone's dream.

A strange, unnerving thought crept into her mind, taking her by complete surprise while she was laughing, throwing out the romance of her generalized Eldorado. It crept in and sat, hugging its knees, waiting for her attention.

It was a picture. At least, it seemed to be. There were no words connected with it. The thought did not speak to her. It just sat there, watchful and cruel.

The picture was of her womb.

Empty.

She didn't know what this might mean.

It could mean the child had been born.

It could mean she was remembering herself as she was before its conception.

It could mean it was never there.

The thought blinked a little and smiled and waggled its fingers and shifted on its haunches.

Not there. The child. Not there.

How could it not be there? Everything was happening, progressing, functioning exactly as it should.

But she hadn't been to a doctor. She had no verification beyond her own instinctive sense of pregnancy, her own knowledgeable (but hardly professional) appraisal of the facts.

Not there.

It *was* there.

She walked around the embers, making a nervous, uncertain circle.

It was there.

It had happened.

Why, in a matter of months, just a few short months, the baby would be kicking her and then it would be born.

What baby?

This baby inside of me.

1939. The year of the Butterfly Plague.

It's there.

It isn't there.

The thought began to rise and, having risen, to walk around her mind, exploring the crowded rooms, calculating where it would rearrange things, reschedule tables of habit, refashion beliefs, relieve reason.

Ruth watched it, literally felt as though she could watch it, as it studied the situation inside her and laid the ground-work for takeover.

It wore boots. It was beginning to wear a long leather coat. It put on a helmet. It crashed about on studded heels. It carried a baton, a neat little baton, and it was counting, but not out loud.

I'm pregnant.

The thought paused, shook its head and beat a few messages into the palm of its hand with the stick.

Ruth closed her eyes.

She placed her fingers against her left temple, then her right. She massaged very gently.

The thought assumed a stance. It stuck its chin out.

Ruth fought to reclaim the image of the blond man. Of the moment in the hills. Of the incident at Alvarez.

She would say, "You were born in the year of the Butterfly Plague. What better designation could there be?"

Not there.

She placed her hands on her stomach.

Her panic increased.

She looked around her, as if someone might help her. But there was no one there.

And then there was.

A woman was walking down by the sea. A woman in a long dress, with elaborate hair and with what appeared to be a veil.

The moon was out. The sea reflected light. There was even phosphorous at the water's edge. Not enough light to see color by, but ample to see features — to judge expression.

The woman was about fifty yards distant, walking very slowly.

She was becomingly small, with the same stature that had made Naomi a successful image for her times. The sort of stature known as petite, which is not the stature of a midget, but a normal stature, finely modeled and proportioned.

This was no woman that Ruth had ever seen. At least, sitting by the embers of Noah's fire, she thought not. She was more elegant than anyone Ruth could think of, offhand. This elegance was studied and exact. Almost performed, certainly not inherent. But nevertheless, beautifully done. The carriage was astounding. The figure floated. The head was erect and could not have been more perfect, for every nuance of the profile could be studied at a precise and unwavering angle. The arms moved, just so. The legs stepped with just enough assurance not to be accused of mincing, but with such exact precision that the knees did not disturb the fall of the dress. There was not a single awkward angle in the whole appearance. It was perfect.

The veils were drawn back and floated becomingly behind. The arabesque of hair was as gorgeous as something drafted by Botticelli. The whole effect was breathtaking.

Not there.

Ruth had all but dismissed the presence of the thought.

As much there, she thought, as that woman walking by the water.

The iron footsteps echoed painfully inside her head.

Not there.

Yes. It *was* there.

She was going to have a son.

In the year of the Butterfly Plague — portending gentleness and peace.

The woman was gone.

The beach was empty.

As empty as Ruth.

Who cried aloud.

Wednesday, February 1st, 1939

Ruth was the size of a house.

She hardly dared venture from her bed.

Miss Bonkers kept looking around the doorway and shaking her head and muttering, "I don't know why you didn't tell me. I don't know why you didn't say."

She threatened several times a day to get a doctor, and Ruth, more terrified that a doctor would tell her she was not pregnant than that he would say there were complications, forbade it with threats of murder, suicide and abortion.

She kept saying to Miss Bonkers, "The pygmies in Africa go out in the jungle and have their babies amongst lions. They don't ask for medical opinions. They don't ask for help. I'm going to have this baby by myself, without consultation."

"May I ask the origin, Miss Ruth?"

"You may not."

"May I ask just when you expect it to arrive? 'Cause looking at you now, I wouldn't be surprised to see it drop on the floor in the next minute!"

"It isn't due till June."

"Till *June!* You must be daft. Or unmathematical, or really to god you must have a terrible memory or *something!* That baby'll be born within the month or else I haven't been in my profession five minutes!"

"June."

"You're crazy. At the very latest, March."

"It cannot be till June."

"Very well, Miss Ruth. Have it your own way, but I'll have the crib ready for it tomorrow. And in the meantime, I'll be thinking of a doctor I know who can get here at a moment's notice. When the time comes, you'll want him — lions or no lions — whatever the pygmies do!"

With that she went away.

Desperately prodding her swollen, mammoth front, Ruth fought against the horrible thought that there was nothing there but gas.

Thursday, February 2nd, to Wednesday February 15th, 1939

She developed a fever.

She could not sleep.

Her heart (or someone's heart) began to make noises as soon as she lay back exhausted in the dark. Then she'd have to turn the light on and smoke a package of cigarettes.

Miss Bonkers brought her cold towels and cups of tea and took her pulse and took her temperature and shook her head and began to sleep in the chair at the foot of Ruth's bed.

"You Damarosches," Miss Bonkers said one night, "are having quite a year of it. I'm beginning to believe in curses."

Ruth was read aloud to, again by the nurse, but every page that was read seemed to contain veiled threats and certain innuendos that Ruth could not bear. None of the books was finished. She never did find out what happened to Emma Bovary or to Anna Karenina or to Cathy. Probably just as well.

The swelling increased, and so did the temperature, and so did a certain delirium that Ruth was not aware of. And so did Miss Bonkers's concern.

On the night of February 17th, the bag burst.

It was water — nothing more. There wasn't even the hint of a fetus.

Ruth tried to disfigure herself with some scissors, but Miss Bonkers was there and only the sheets were damaged.

When at last she was almost asleep, and the fever had abated, Ruth was aware of an absence in her mind. The thought, wearing its Prussian boots, was gone. And there was only the hollow moan of a wind that blew with melancholy persistence through the hallways and passageways, the parlors and the studies of an empty house.

In her dreams that night, for a reason she would never know, Ruth followed down the endless beaches of her loneliness, a figure in a long dress, with arabesques of hair, with floating veils and impeccable gait, with a studied grace and a careful air. And a face she could not decipher.

For it was...

...Not there.

Monday, March 20th, 1939: Morning

Octavius was raking butterflies in the garden.

Ruth came and stood beyond the boards.

She looked in at him. They had become close the day of Dolly's death. They sometimes (really very seldom) swam together. They often talked together like this, through the fence.

Ruth wanted to talk to someone but everyone else was busy. B.J. had organized the children into work gangs and they went about doing odd jobs along the beach, and at the houses nearby, or back in the fields. Even as far away as the canyon. They taped up people's windows with adhesive, they cleaned butterflies out of eaves troughs, they filtered them with long-handled nets from swimming pools. They burned them in carefully supervised fires. Marilyn cut the wings from four thousand carcasses. This was for Noah. He wanted to experiment with butterfly-mâché. All day, every day for weeks, he boiled his mixture at the back of the house, in various little pots, adding the wings to these glues in varying quantities and making up different textures. He developed some very interesting pastes which he applied to various bits and pieces of plastics and woods. He also made several butterfly "skeletons" out of wire and applied the mâché to these. He felt that the Butterfly Plague should be interpreted and preserved. He made them in copy; he drew them on different shapes and size of paper; he sculpted them. (It is impossible to sculpt a butterfly, he had thought. He fought with this statement and found that like most things, it did not remain true if you persevered.)

B.J. herself was newly pregnant (end of January) and this meant redecorating the nursery (butterfly motif) and reorganizing the children's wardrobes. When each new child arrived (or was prepared for) the wardrobes shifted along by one. The one-year-old got the two-year-old's clothes. The two-year-old got the three-year-old's. Etc. Mary Baker Eddy (the eldest) was reclothed from the underwear out. She was seen everywhere (a gay and lovely child of fourteen) resplendent in bright new polka dots or stripes. She wore shoes with bows on them and had her first grown-up skirt and blouse. (Four years later, in January of 1943, she died in this same blouse when a car she rode in fell from a cliff in Mexico.)

At any rate, all of this activity, revolving around babies and butterflies, meant that there was no one for Ruth to talk to. She was in a state of constant somnambulism. Miss Bonkers hovered over her (rather like a grotesque butterfly herself) with a pill in one hand and a swatter in the other. Sometimes, when Ruth sat absolutely still, the butterflies would collect on her figure until she looked like one of those Buddhas, overgrown with vines and insects in the jungles of Siam. She had miscarried. She believed that. Nothing could shake her faith in dreams.

She hung about at the far end of the beach, childlike and bereaved.

"Octavius?"

"What?"

"What are you doing?"

"Raking."

"Are you going to have a fire?"

"Yes. Later."

A long look at the seals. A long listen to the silence. "Octavius?"

"Yes."

"Do you want to go swimming?"

"No. Not now, Ruth."

Ruth quietly killed some butterflies which had been sitting quietly on the board fence. They fell with little thuds to the ground.

"Octavius?"

"Yes, Ruth?"

"Let's go up to the Maine and have a drink."

"Oh, no. It will just be full of people."

"No it won't. Not now."

"What time is it?"

"I don't know. I only know it's morning."

"You shouldn't drink before noon, Ruth."

The sound of raking, of the rake passing over stones.

"Octavius?"

"What?"

"Come out and talk to me."

"No. I can't."

"Then let me come in."

"No, Ruth. I'm thinking."

A massed screen of monarchs, flying quite high, passed between Ruth and the sun. It wheeled like a slow-moving flock of birds and headed inland. They were everywhere now. Soon they would all be gone.

"Octavius?"

"For God's sake, what?"

"What are you thinking about?"

"Adolphus."

"Don't think about Adolphus. You musn't."

"I can't help it. I didn't know him."

Ruth thought of her son.

"Nobody knew him," she said.

Octavius raked.

Ruth said, "I met a dead man once. Walking around dead."

"What do you mean?"

"Like Adolphus. His name was Mr. Seuss. This was in Paris in 1936. He will be dead now. But he might as well have been dead — even before I met him."

"What was wrong with him?"

"I can't explain. But he carried his death with him in his pocket. He called it his star."

"Hunh."

"The condemned, you see? Born that way."

She killed another butterfly. Her method was direct and swift. She pressed down on their heads with her thumb.

"Like Adolphus."

"Yes. Like Dolly. Only a different death. Do you see that Mother was different? Mother wasn't condemned. . . ."

"Yes."

"Yes."

"Adolphus . . . Mr. Seuss . . . the butterflies . . . these other people — it's in their pocket. It's in their blood. It's with them all the time. Whereas. . ."

"Yes?"

"Whereas we. . ."

"What?"

"Whereas we are killers."

"You and me?"

"Yes. And everyone else. Like my blood — that's my weapon. Like your lack of interest in women — that's your weapon. Like father's selfishness and Bruno's Master Race. Weapons."

"What about Noah and B.J.?"

"I don't know. They'll probably survive all this."

They were both silent.

"Did anyone ever love you, Octavius?"

"No."

"Does it matter?"

"I don't know."

"Do you care?"

"I don't know."

"Have you ever loved anyone?"

"I've never known anyone."

More silence.

"Do you know something?" said Ruth.

"What?"

"There isn't anyone I know who loves. . . ."

They thought about it.

"It depends on what you think love is," said Octavius, finally.

Ruth gauged his tone of voice.

She recognized the hidden meaning.

She went home and opened a long unopened drawer in her bureau.

Underneath the clothes she found a little paper packet. She drew it out and looked at it. Then she opened it.

Then she kissed the contents and pinned them to her shirt.

Mr. Seuss's Star of David.

She knew, now, how it felt to be a dreamer.

Afternoon

It had been announced first in the trade papers. Then it had been announced in the public press:

FRIDAY, MARCH 31ST, 1939,
THE PREMIERE SHOWING OF LETITIA VIRDEN'S
RETURN TO THE SCREEN!

SEE THE LITTLE VIRGIN'S TRIUMPHANT
PORTRAYAL OF
VIRGINIA MARY WASHINGTON
IN
AMERICA — I LOVE YOU!

ALSO STARRING PETER ST. PAUL
:::: A VIR-CAR PRODUCTION
8:00 P.M. :::: GRAUMAN'S CHINESE THEATER
HOLLYWOOD BOULEVARD
###PLUS A PERSONAL APPEARANCE OF THE STAR###

It was the event of the season.

Everyone would be there.

Tomorrow.

Ruth glanced at the photographs. There were pictures of Letitia and Cooper, of Peter St. Paul and the supporting players. The photos of Letitia had been outrageously retouched. She looked like something carved in marble.

There were also photographs of her in her old films and in one of these she was paired with "the late Naomi Nola."

Ruth threw the paper down on the floor.

The juxtaposition had never occurred to her. She did not like it.

Evening

Ruth stood looking at the water.

It was a gray evening; it might even rain.

She tried to immerse her mind in the thought of the sea. How vast it was.

She counted off the strokes.

One. Two. Three. Four.

The sun splashed down, knifing open a wound in the clouds, spilling its blood onto the distant waters — vital and tremendously red.

Ruth clenched and unclenched her hands.

A string of butterflies flew north.

They were going now. The antimigration had begun in earnest.

No more butterflies to kick.

They had fallen like leaves from desiccated trees.

They were leaving, tens of millions of dead remaining behind them. Little corpses, easily brushed aside with brooms. They had left dusty red stains on the sidewalks, which people washed down with hose water.

Far away in her mind, as she watched the departing strings and tails, the dreamers shifted to and fro, lined up in silence against their walls, swaying in unison as though there must be music.

Ruth touched her star.

She began to rock, as a mother rocks with her child.

The ocean fell — swelled up and fell — swelled up and fell — touching her toes with its tongue.

The whole world was in motion, rising and falling — a gentle motion. Compassionate.

Yes. Then there must be music.

Or was it counting.

The butterfly strings — the dreamers in a row — the ocean in its shell of earth — the birds drifting on homeward wings — the cadence of the first stars — and Ruth...

Counting.

Rising.

Falling.

Being one.

Forming one.

With the music and the flowering of numbers in their beautiful sequence. The easy sequence man had devised for his passage through time.

Nightfall.

Monday, March 27th, 1939:
Topanga Beach Canyon
2:30 p.m.

Octavius read all the papers, too, and in one it mentioned that Letitia Virden would attend her *première* in blue, white, and silver — the colors of her tradition.

He made a phone call.

Blue, white, and silver. Good. In the form of a sari. Thank you.

Mother looked in the mirror and was happy.

She played around with her wig and makeup and they were good, too.

Octavius made another phone call.

One Negro. Thank you.

Good.

Mother was now extremely happy.

She had everything she needed.

She took off all her clothes.

She stood there looking at herself.

"This," she said, "is the best of all possible worlds."

Octavius wondered if the Negro, like Harold Herald, would have a hungry look.

He hoped so.

Mother hoped so, too.

They went and took a bath.

They were both so happy.

Soon they would separate. Soon they would be free. In fact, freedom would come at about 8:00 p.m. the following Friday.

Wouldn't it be wonderful?

They sang.

Friday, March 31st, 1939:
Grauman's Chinese Theater, Hollywood
7:30 p.m.

In deference to the Virgin's popularity and the likelihood of riots, three times the normal contingent of police had been dispatched to the area of the *première*.

They stretched, leather arm linked in leather arm, five blocks either side of the theater, on both the north and south curbs of Hollywood Boulevard.

Traffic was rerouted. No motorcars were allowed to enter the area save those transporting celebrities — and these must enter singly, deposit their royalty, and be gone at two minute intervals.

A marquee of silver and blue silks had been erected at the theater entrance. It sheltered a gold carpet.

Police on horseback trotted officiously one way and then the other up and down the cleared pavement of the road.

Above the theater, prodded and poked at by twelve varicolored searchlights, the Virgin, thirty feet high from twinkle toes to tinsel veil, raised her galvanized, gaudy arms in a blessing that seemed to extend across the whole of Los Angeles.

A band was playing, "Hail, Columbia," "America," "Columbia, the Gem of the Ocean," and the "Battle Hymn of the Republic," in close order, repeating the first when the last was concluded.

Across the road from the theater, a choir, stationed in surpliced ranks on the roof of a hardware store, bellowed other hymns and anthems — and once even sang a Christmas carol (thought to be appropriate), "*Adeste Fideles.*"

By 7:45 most of the celebrities were already inside the theater. An order had been issued from a mysterious (no one would claim it) source, stating that absolutely no one — not even Clark Gable — was to arrive following the entrance of the Virgin. This order was meticulously obeyed. At 7:57 Clark Gable arrived.

There was then a three-minute hiatus.

7:58 p.m.

George Damarosch, in faded serge, unshaven, smelling of gin and body odor, muttering obscenities to himself, so tense that he might have been on the verge of a heart attack, made his way eight difficult, forceful paces forward through the crowd. He achieved a position diagonally opposed to the edge of the gold carpet. He was exactly three hundred feet from the marquee.

He roughly gauged the distance between the raised, extended arms of the two nearest policemen, touched with great care the ribbed handle of his .38 automatic Webster, and blew his nose.

7:59 p.m.

Six blocks from the theater, a custom-built, heavily armored Rolls-Royce motorcar, driven by a massive black man, made its way at a snail's pace to the stop light.

On the far side of the intersection began a police cordon.

A hush fell upon the crowd.

A motorcycle police escort, red lights blinking and flashing, rode beside and fore and aft of the automobile.

Inside, illuminated from a mysterious source, Letitia Virden sat frozen with poise on two extra cushions and a board — in order to be seen by the crowd.

Cooper Carter sat diagonally opposite, on a jump seat.

As had been advertised, the Virgin was dressed in blue and white, with silver veiling. She was tense but regal. There was no outward hint of her inner fear and distrust of mobs. Neither she nor Cooper Carter spoke.

As the light changed and the motorcycle sirens were thrown into high pitch, and only seconds before they were to proceed forward, an identical motorcar, carrying an identical passenger — identically lit and regal — pulled around the corner, cutting them off.

Those near enough to catch glimpses of both interiors had ample cause to think they were losing track of their reason.

Both cars contained the person — the very incarnation of the Little Virgin — Letitia Virden.

8:00 p.m.

The first car jolted to a stop.

The second car — the intervening one — picked up speed to assure itself of the lead place and proceeded to the position marked by white paint at which each arriving limousine was to stop. This white mark brought the rear passenger door exactly opposite the gold carpet beneath the marquee.

A Negro personage of immense height descended rapidly from the Rolls and ran around to the lady-door of the car. He opened it, expressionless and huge.

The Virgin stepped down.

She was younger than anyone remembered her to be. Surely no more than sixteen or seventeen years old. She was beautifully clothed from head to toe in sapphires and a blue sari. On her feet were silver slippers. She carried a small silver bag and her fingers were ablaze with emeralds and lapis lazuli.

She advanced on careful toes — one — five — seven paces. Then she turned and faced the lights.

Her black man got back into the driver's seat and drove exactly one and one-half car lengths forward and parked. If it had been any other than the Virgin's Rolls-Royce, it would have been moved on — forcibly, if necessary.

A shout went up.

The crowd raised its arms in salutation.

The band brazened the air with fanfare.

The choir sang "Hail to Thee, Sheba, Solomon's Wife" by Handel-Wagner, and the Virgin, waving with one bejeweled hand, made semicircular turns in slow motion so that all might see and honor her.

Her stance was practiced. Perfect. Poised. Her expression was studied and her carriage aloof. From a distance you could not see the short shaved stubble on the crests of her wrists.

8:03 p.m.

The anthem ("Hail to Thee," etc.) was over.

The band began to play.

George Damarosch blinked. There were tears in his eyes. Her image was so dear to him that he could not force his hand into his pocket. Yet, he must act — and now — if he was to accomplish his deed. The Virgin might, instanter, turn and leave him victimless.

He prepared to stoop, crouch, and run.

His hand flushed the gun like a startled bird from his pocket.

8:04 p.m.

At that very moment, two things commenced to happen.

The first was the arrival of the first Virgin (or the second — no one, later, could remember which was which, a fact which laid the grounds for legend).

Her car, containing, also, Cooper Carter, and accompanied by its horde of motorcycle policemen, drew up with screeching brakes to the curb side.

Harold raced around and opened the rear door. Cooper Carter descended. He then reached in for Letitia's hand.

It appeared. Her arm appeared. Her bowing head — her shoulder — her back — her entire being materialized from within the motorcar.

She stood upon the golden carpet.

The silence that followed was profound and upset. Not a word was spoken.

Letitia, stunned by the reception she was receiving, turned to seek its cause and saw, as though in a mirror, her own person standing there, eight paces distant, smiling at her, and holding out its hand.

"Mother," it said, in a voice unmistakably masculine.

Then it was that the second thing happened.

Letitia stepped back, as though struck.

Her hands flew to her mouth, stifling what might have been a scream, had it been allowed to escape.

Cooper Carter, intervening, stepped into the outstretched angle of hand and arm and gestured, as though to strike out at the advancing face with its intolerable grin.

His hand, however, had been raised too high, and it struck, instead of the cheek, the top of the coiffure.

There was a scream — two hundred women, hystericking in chorus — for it appeared that the head of the Sari-Virgin toppled from its place and fell to the ground.

But no such thing happened.

It was a wig that fell.

Letitia turned away, ill, reaching for the sanctuary of her car.

Harold had already returned to the driver's seat and was unable to let her in.

Cooper made a half-circle and now stood directly behind the masquerading figure.

He reached out to pull it by the shoulders and thus prevent it from harming (for that seemed the intent) the true Virgin.

But his hands grasped only sari.

The figure spun — and, spinning, half-spun itself out of its dress.

Two cups made of rubber, with tiny rubber nipples, fell upon the golden carpet.

A naked male torso, heavily tanned, appeared from beneath the blue silk.

Octavius, wheeling back now, grasped the sari and yanked it back around him, covering so instantly what had been exposed that no one could tell for sure that he had seen what he had seen.

His action threw Cooper off his feet and the industrialist fell onto his back, helpless.

No one, save Octavius, moved.

"What do you want of me?" Letitia screamed.

"But, Mother," said Octavius, "don't you recognize me? Mother?"

He backed her up against the car, inside which Harold was struggling to open doors.

Octavius placed his hands on Letitia's shoulders, which he pressed back with unintentional force, hurting her terribly and jamming her hard into the metal body of the automobile.

At this moment, George made his play.

He ran out of the confusion, straight across the road, around the tail of the car and up, point-blank, against Letitia's side.

She turned her face and saw him.

Octavius clawed at her veils and tore them loose.

"Mother! Mother! Mother!" he screamed. "Please! You wanted to see me and here, Mother, I am!"

George looked from face to face in utter confusion, made his choice, stepped back, leveled the gun and fired.

"Oh, Mother!" Octavius cried out. "It's *me* — Octavius!"

Immediately, George ran forward, stepping into the space between the autos of the two Virgins.

Harold, meanwhile, in a panic, had turned on the engine. Hearing the shot, he raced the motor and gunned forward.

George's lower limbs were eradicated.

He screamed but no one heard him.

8:04:55 p.m.

The second Virgin reached for her wig.

8:04:56 p.m.

The second black man turned on his motor, reached back and flipped open the rear door of his Rolls.

8:04:57 p.m.

Letitia made a sliding motion into the gutter, falling on her back. Cooper Carter rose.

8:04:58 p.m.

George Damarosch twisted in agony and took second aim.

8:04:59 p.m.

He fired.

Cooper Carter was thrown by the bullet and landed, dead, on his side, with his brains blown out onto the pavement.

8:05 p.m.

George Damarosch vomited and died, leaving his body sprawled on the hood of Letitia's car.

8:05:01 p.m.

Octavius Rivi Moxon, rewigged — a tailor-made Virgin — walked with impeccable grace to the open, waiting door and climbed in.

It was over. Whatever it was, it was over.

Some said, in later years, that the Virgin herself had been seen speeding away from the scene of her mortal death. She had ascended into heaven. Triumphant.

This is the genesis of legend.

The believers say that when the police rushed forward to investigate these happenings, a figure in blue was seen being whisked into a large black car by a large black hand. They say that this car then drove away at such a high speed that it was gone in the winking of an eye, away into the night. They say that no one saw a boy step out of the sari at all. They say it was all a hoax. For proof of this hoax, they say that a dead *man* was found, half in the gutter, half on the hood of the parked Rolls-Royce, and that this was the person who had been seen discarding the masquerade.

They say, too, that the woman lying dead amidst paint and blood and lacquer — lying dead on the pavement — could not have been Letitia Virden. She was much too old to have been the Virgin. At least fifty. (An uncharitable few said sixty-five to seventy.)

At any rate, these facts are certain:

A woman and two men were dead. They were lying there. That was indisputable. One of the dead men was world famous. Cooper Carter.

Someone was seen fleeing in a large black motorcar driven by a Negro. But this was in all likelihood merely a frightened celebrity.

A magenta handkerchief was found.

A woman's .38 automatic (three bullets fired) was found (explaining the battered "A" in the word "Letitia" on the marquee).

A Negro by the name of Harold Herald was arrested in a chauffeur's uniform and imprisoned for impersonating the driver of Miss Virden's motorcar.

Aside from that, only one other fact might be added. This concerns a silver pin attached to the neckline of the dress worn by the anonymous dead woman dressed in blue. Taken to the County of Los Angeles morgue, this woman was stripped of her clothes and of her few valuables and placed in a plain wooden box. The blue dress was burned. The valuables reposed for many years after in a brown manilla envelope. On the obverse side of the silver pin (a carnation design) the following words had been engraved: *I hope it's a boy. With all my love, from Bullford.*

Meaningless.

This woman remained unclaimed.

She was cremated after the appropriate period during which identification might have been made.

One man was discovered to be George Damarosch, who was once married to Naomi Nola, the film star. He died in the final moments of the Butterfly Plague, at 8:05 or thereabouts on the evening of March 31st, 1939.

His daughter claimed his body.

She escorted it to a small chapel in Santa Monica, driving a 1934 Franklin coupé. Painted purple. She was the only one who mourned him. He, too, was cremated.

Note: On the 1st of May, 1939, a beach house at Topanga Canyon Beach, long the subject of intrigue and controversy, was sold by the firm of Chadd and Gold. It brought forty thousand dollars. Its former occupant departed for parts unknown, leaving behind the following missive:

> Dear Ruth,
>
> I don't know where I'm going or how long I shall be away. I'll miss you, but you should know that, at long last, I have a friend. He's black and will protect me. I have a feeling that I need protection. I don't know why, I just feel that, inside.
>
> The strange thing is, I love him.
>
> Is that wrong?
>
> Will you think of me? Thank you.
>
> I will think of you.
>
> Good-bye, with affection,
> from
> O.

> P.S.: I wish my mother had recognized me. Do you think she did, before that man shot her? If so, do you think it would make her happy or sad? Let me know. I'm interested, and you know so much more about Mother than I do. Have to rush now. There's a building on fire down the street, and we are both very fond of flames. Are you? They seem to make one feel well.
>
> O.R.

There was no address. But Ruth was almost glad of that. She would not have been able to answer without telling Octavius that it had been her father who had killed his mother. And, too — in answer to the final question — she would have had to say that she was not fond of flames. She only wished that she could say one final thing to Octavius Rivi, and it was that flames make you feel well, friend, because they burn with their own intensity, not yours. When your intensity is finally involved, the flames are then called fire. . . and don't ever fall in love with fire.

But he already had.

Book Four

The Chronicle of the Exodus

Saturday, April 1st, 1939:
Falconridge
4:00 p.m.

Ruth came to the bottom of the steps.

This was the only way up from the parking lot — up the Star Steps to the top.

She wore her mother's black-fox coat, Dolly's Panama, and had placed George's magenta handkerchief in her pocket.

She carried their ashes, mingled, in an urn. She had consigned George's broken body to ashes that morning, at 7:30.

She paused. There was the first step.

NAOMI NOLA.

Whether it came first or last depended on which direction you were walking. The family joke.

It was a long climb. Three hundred and forty-two steps.

The sky was ominous — gold and green.

She sweltered in the coat, but her determination to wear it cooled her. Her mother had left it to her in her will. "My beautiful black-fox coat, which I have cherished. Gift of my husband, George, on the birth of our son."

Its style was outrageously dated, but it was Naomi's — it suited her period — and, thus, it had always suited her.

Ruth clambered up the stairs — names babbling at her feet. What a crowd of memories was there — NAOMI NOLA — MARIE DRESSLER — LETITIA VIRDEN.

Ruth paused and smiled. She could not help it. The thought had just occurred to her that — given her relation to Octavius — the Little Virgin could only be called: *The Immaculate Deception*.

But, oh — death. What a dreadful way to die.

"I won't think about that," thought Ruth. "I won't think about it now."

There have been other deaths. The mode was relative.

The letters were in faded paint. Chipped and screwy and sad.

GEORGE D. DAMAROSCH.

The top.

Before turning to the house she turned back out and looked down on the spreading cities far below and beyond her. Westbury, Hollywood, Brentwood, Beverly Hills, Culver and far, far — far away, Santa Monica and the sea. Of course, she could not really see that far. But it was all there for her mind to conjure. To form and to grasp by implication. Elucidations from a known distance.

The premonition of excitement shook her. There is death, of course, she thought. Our hated-loved ones and the dear ones whom we argue with, must die. The dialogue ends, sometimes abruptly, but the sense of dialogue persists. Dolly would go on talking. Naomi, too, would continue her silent, marvelous thoughts. And George, with clasped hands, would stand forever, rigid with tantrums on his tongue. It didn't matter. Ruth only had to be there. What, she wondered, looking at the cities, is this strange exhilaration in someone else's birth, in someone else's death?

She wanted the dead and the unborn to talk to each other. And to the living.

She turned.

There it was.

Falconridge.

She had been a girl here. Her room had five windows, each with its own vine and its own leaded panes. The vines were not real. They were made of rope and wire and paint. Her father had no patience with growing things that might not reach the zenith of their perfection until after he had walked away from them. The trees were all boxed and movable, and in the twenties there had been coolies whose only job it had been to rearrange the trees twice daily, even four times (if there was a lawn party). If their employer had been in a truly Macbethean mood, he would yell at them through his megaphone (which he kept at home), upbraiding them for their lack of artistry. "Garden hacks!" he would scream. "Landscape forgers!" Or, "Willy-nilly bush-puller!" and (Ruth's favorite) "Ham-fisted bush-league tree surgeons!"

The trees had been moved so often that even the most frequent guests never had seen the landscape in the same order on two consecutive visits. Douglas Fairbanks called the house Dunsinane. He swore to Ruthie (aged ten) that one day there would be a gardeners' revolt, and that George would regret it.

Ruth continued down the long stone walls. The boxed trees, dry and lichen-encrusted, had all died from lack of the coolies' loving care. They stood, bone-branched and ghostly, in their unpainted wooden graves.

The grass abounded on the lawns, tall, uncut, and bleached. A few plaster casts of Valentino and Bushman reached out with their pseudoancient salutes in the direction of the house.

In some of the windows glass was broken.

"He's gone," she said. "They have all gone. Forever."

At the sound of her voice, several birds flew up out of the grass.

She stood, waist-high amid the alien roses, delphiniums, poppies, and ferns, and she felt like Eve deserted in a whispering Eden. Unmanned, Paradise had not been long to press in close around the house, and the sun, smelting a golden afternoon, poured it out hotly now over gables, roofs, chimneys, windowpanes, and gardens. All alike were turning dry and brittle.

Ruth wheeled back like a lone survivor to the doors of the castle. They were not locked.

"Halloo!" she called into the long darkness of the hall. But there was no reply.

She left the door open, forcing a crowd of shadows to huddle in the twin corners of the central staircase.

"Father? Dolly? Mother?"

Mice.

They scurried away from their meals of carpet, wood, and damask curtains, belting hell-bent-for-safety into long-deserted cuboards and crevices. Holes. Cracks. Missing floorboards.

"Daddy?"

No answer.

"Mama?"

She wandered. The living room was on the left. Probably only two or three living rooms in the whole world were large enough to hold fifteen wing-back chairs and ten sofas. This was one of them. At the far end there was a walk-in fireplace large enough to contain three men, side by side, with their arms outstretched.

"Where are you?" said Ruth.

She turned back. She crossed the hall to the dining room and library, the study and the kitchens. No one. Not a sign.

She went upstairs. In the upper hallway the twelve gilded cages that had once held her father's parrots were empty, their little gilded doors flung wide, the water bowls so dry that dust had formed a quarter-inch thick on the bottoms.

Certain at last that there was no one there, Ruth did not even bother to look in the Louis Quatorze bathrooms, or into the Carolinian boudoirs, or the marble-vaulted lavatories, or the sitting rooms modeled after Victorian antechambers. She did, however, walk out along the balcony at the rear of the house, and there at last she sat down on the great stone steps that led in a wide Renaissance gesture to the terrace below.

She lit a cigarette.

She was sweating. The black-fox coat fell back from her shoulders, and what little breeze there was cooled her briefly. She stared out through dark glasses, unwilling to remove them, unwilling to admit the impediment of reality, how harsh it all might be. Dolly's hat was pulled down close over her brow.

Everyone dies and is gone.

Who will remember Valentino and Virden and Arly Robinson ten, twenty years from now? Or my father or my mother or my brother. Or me.

Like the flowers, she thought, in her youthful garden. They grow huge and gorgeous and then one day a gardener comes to cut them down. Or a bulldozer. Probably a bulldozer would come here now and push through this mountain of improbability, and the house standing on the precipice, filled with its ghosts, would topple down into the dreamy sleep of all those tormented and forgotten-to-be dolls who wallowed in their present fame below her in the valleys.

Ruth felt the sun leaving her and she knew at last that the promised rain would come. She sat there, very still in her mother's furs, and her brother's hat, on the steps of her father's terraced mansion. All had left her. All had waved good-bye, and gone. She felt like a hostess whose most popular guests have departed, and who is left alone with a handful of dull and difficult strangers. She sighed into the moratorium between sun and rain.

Even her own vocation and her own fame had left her. She felt no sense of place or position, felt as though someone — perhaps a policeman — might challenge her presence the next time she walked or wanted to walk down the street.

Like the Nightmare of Germany.

Like America, she thought. I have come home. She laughed, very lightly.

Slowly, in the early twilight, still waiting for the rain, Ruth became aware that the gardens below her were coming wanly alive with the pleasant voices of insects and birds.

A lone old butterfly, staggering through the dense atmosphere, laden with the burden of its age, crept upon the air with scarred, exhausted wings. Ruth watched.

Were they really going? Was it really over?

The butterfly flew in a crazy zigzag daze, searching desperately for one last other butterfly to dazzle with his colors. But the air was empty of his kind. Under the trees the cicadas horded themselves in the sweet groves of grass. The grasshoppers waited with crooked energy for the aphids to be driven from the roses. Golden-backed spiders, scorpions, phosphorescent beetles — all hid among flowers in anticipation of rain. The birds had gathered in the branches of the avocado trees, so thickly that they could see each other's fleas. There was a crowd of everything but butterflies.

This was that sudden season of change — constant in nature and in history. The season when things go.

Far away, the pleasant thunder corroded the silence with a thin, metallic hum. The air was filled with the smell of electrical activity. The clouds turned green and bronze and brass. Toledo. El Greco. Los Angeles. California.

The butterfly knelt on the outstretched tongue of a fern. Ruth watched with a careful silence as it rested.

And then the rain came.

She did not move and neither did the butterfly.

Ruth stared while the first deluge of relief beat out the little remaining brightness in the butterfly's wings, and at last she saw them crumple and melt. She watched as the slim, black battered boat of its tiny body slid, still clinging at first, this way and that — until the flood upon the fern became so torrential and overpowering that it swept the beaten remnants, finally, far down into the mold and mud below.

And then the rain fell in such a crowd of drops that there was nothing left in sight but the vaguest outline of the thing it could not hope to wash away.

And Ruth thought, Now there will be no more fires... And a moment later she thought,...And no more butterflies. This rain has extinguished them. Forever. Or a while.

And she spread the ashes.

And they were mud.

And there was nothing to do but turn around and go.

WINNER OF THE TRILLIUM BOOK AWARD • PRIX TRILLIUM

TIMOTHY FINDLEY

STONES

Against a vivid terrain of images, Findley continues his exploration of the many diverse and destructive acts played out on the personal battlegrounds on which we live our daily lives.

From the realities of contemporary relationships to a fantastic vision of urban life; from social comment to the deeply personal — *Stones* is a powerful collection of stories from one of Canada's best-loved writers.

O

"*Stones* is a masterful performance by Timothy Findley and sheds bright, perfect light on a part of that strange, strange thing called the human condition."
— *Montreal Gazette*

A PENGUIN BOOK

"Findley is one of the world's greatest storytellers, and in *The Telling of Lies* he has a marvellous tale to tell."
— *The Globe and Mail*

TIMOTHY FINDLEY

the telling of lies

THE BODY
is that of Calder Maddox, who owned half the world and rented the other half.

THE SLEUTH
is Nessa Van Horne, whose photos of the beach on the day of the murder may obscure more than they reveal.

THE SUSPECTS
are the many people who spend their summers at the beautiful Aurora Sands Hotel. Could it be Lily, Calder's diaphanous mistress? Or Nigel, the perfect civil servant? Or the disappearing chauffeur? Or the mysterious doctor who appears from nowhere?

A PENGUIN BOOK

TIMOTHY FINDLEY

Not Wanted on the Voyage

"It is one of those rare books that provide delight and surprise and sometimes a shock on every page."
— *The Montreal Gazette*

Not Wanted on the Voyage is the story of the great flood and the first time the world ended. It is a brilliant, unforgettable drama filled with an extraordinary cast of characters: the tyrannical Noah and his indomitable wife, Mrs. Noyes; the aging and irritable Yaweh; Lucy (the enigmatic, disturbing woman who is not what she seems); Mottyl (Mrs. Noyes's endearing talking cat); a chorus of singing sheep and a unicorn destined for a horrible death. With pathos and pageantry, desperation and hope, magic and mythology, *Not Wanted on the Voyage* weaves its unforgettable spell.

A PENGUIN BOOK

TIMOTHY FINDLEY

WHAT HE DID WAS TERRIBLE AND BRAVE...

Robert Ross, a sensitive nineteen year old Canadian officer went to war — The War to End All Wars. He found himself in the nightmare world of trench warfare; of mud and smoke; of chlorine gas and rotting corpses. In this world gone mad, Robert Ross performed a last desperate act to declare his commitment to life in the midst of death.

"He did the thing that no one else would even dare to think of doing."

WAS IT AN ACT OF COMPASSION OR AN ACT OF MADNESS?

"*The Wars* is quite simply one of the best novels of the Great War... A magnificent book."
— *Vancouver Province*

A PENGUIN BOOK

TIMOTHY FINDLEY

the last of the crazy people

One brilliant summer morning, Hooker Winslow commits a shocking and unpredictable crime. What drove him to this act of insanity?

The Last of the Crazy People is Timothy Findley's first novel, the compelling story of an eleven-year-old boy's private world of bewilderment and conflict. Hooker doesn't understand — why doesn't anyone talk to him? His mother won't leave her room, his adored older brother is drinking heavily, and his father is obsessed with the family's disintegration. Left to himself, Hooker becomes more and more separated from reality. As he broods on the events of the summer, he builds a child's confused understanding of family crisis — and takes terrifying steps to end the confusion.

"Not a word out of place... the writing, clear and clean, is close to the bone." — *Kirkus*

A PENGUIN BOOK

TIMOTHY FINDLEY

"It is one of those rare books that provide delight and surprise and sometimes a shock on every page."
— *The Montreal Gazette*

In the final days of the Second World War, Hugh Selwyn Mauberley scrawls his desperate account on the walls and ceilings of his ice-cold prison high in the Austrian Alps. Officers of the liberating army discover his frozen, disfigured corpse and his astonishing testament — the sordid truth that he alone possessed. Fascinated but horrified, they learn of a dazzling array of characters caught up in scandal and political corruption. The exiled Duke and Duchess of Windsor, von Ribbentrop, Hitler, Charles Lindbergh, Sir Harry Oakes — all play sinister parts in an elaborate scheme to secure world domination.

In a brilliant blending of fiction and historical fact, *Famous Last Words* in another highly acclaimed novel by the award-winning author of *The Wars*, *Not Wanted On the Voyage* and *The Telling of Lies*.

A PENGUIN BOOK